The Urbana Free Library

To renew materials call
217-367-4057

	DATE DUE	
JUN 2 7 2009		
JUL 2 0 2009		
AUG 2 1 2009		
JUL 07 2012		

The

ANNUNCIATIONS

of

HANK MEYERSON

Mama's Boy and Scholar

A N O V E L

SCOTT MUSKIN

Hooded Friar Press
Nashville

Publisher's Cataloging-in-Publication Data

Muskin, Scott.
    The Annuciations of Hank Meyerson, Mama's Boy and Scholar: A Novel / Scott Muskin.
    p. cm.
    ISBN 978-0-9817609-2-6
1. Meyerson, Hank (Fictitious character—Fiction). 2. Love—Fiction. 3. Family—Fiction.
4. Friendship—Fiction. 5. Relationships—Fiction. 6. Art-Fiction. 7. Psychological fiction. I. Title.

PS3563.U8358 A8 2009
813.54-dc22   2008936456

Published by Hooded Friar Press, Nashville, Tennessee

For information regarding permission, write to:
Hooded Friar Press, 214 Overlook Court, Suite 253, Brentwood, Tennessee 37027.
Web site: www.hoodedfriarpress.com

Library of Congress Number: 2008936456

Printed in Canada

First Edition: March 2009
10 9 8 7 6 5 4 3 2 1

Cover Photo (Glass):
©iStockphoto.com/Steve Dibblee

ISBN-13: 978-0-9817609-2-6
ISBN-10: 0-9817609-2-9

for Andrea

The Annunciations of Hank Meyerson,
Mama's Boy and Scholar

In any true life you must go and be exposed outside the small circle that encompasses two or three heads in the same history of love. Try and stay, though, inside. See how long you can.
—Saul Bellow, *The Adventures of Augie March*

A single thrill can end a life or open it forever.
—Emily Dickinson,
from a scrap poem found with her Otis Lord letters

PART ONE

A Beautiful Thingy

Chapter One

In the spring of that eventful year I took up hammer and crowbar to tear apart the sole bathroom in the bungalow I owned with my wife, Carol Ann. I ripped and scraped and pried out everything except the toilet: pickled pine paneling, speckled four-inch shower tiles, rusty recessed lighting, tinny cavity of medicine cabinet, petrified linoleum flooring glued over infuriatingly thick plywood. This was new work for me—I was just out of graduate school and hardly versed in demo, let alone the plumbing, tiling, and drywalling to come. I was bumbling and porky with bemusement, my hands as slick and pale as the spring issue of *American Literature,* to which I still subscribed, on the student rate. A tool belt did not become me.

But I liked it. The dust and wholesome aroma of age-dried lumber, the clattering tile and snapping lath, the bullying it took to move the cast-iron tub into its indefinite internment in the backyard—it left me a pure, voided, swept-clean space that was as foreign and marvelous to me as the ham salad sandwiches Carol Ann would make me as reward. I'd go in there and sit, cross-legged with my sandwich and a bottle of beer, impressed with myself and careful with the crumbs.

I had no idea what I was doing, and by April the whole thing took on the shorthand term "The Project." The Project was noble. The Project required a small truckload of tools. The Project was good for my self-esteem, but The Project might have to be scaled back some, since cutting a window into stucco was apparently kind of complicated, and involved diamond-tipped blades. And with all the tools and tile and drywall and new fixtures, I was afraid I would spend too much money on The Project, but then again it was still the boom boom real estate years and The Project would return 110 percent of its investment when The Project was finished. When The Project would be finished was anyone's guess—it felt Herculean just getting the insulation stapled in under 2-mil plastic sheeting. Not to mention the Minneapolis building code, which read like Borges.

I have to say that Carol Ann's acquiescence was impressive. Without plumbing or a tub, we were forced to bathe in the basement, standing over the thoroughly bleached mainline sewer drain with a washcloth and stainless steel bowls of hot water. At the tail end of winter, both of us pale and traumatized and still reliant on at-the-ready fleece blankets collecting dog hair—well, disrobing in the basement wasn't exactly a pool party. But the previous owners had insulated well down there, and, all in all, Carol Ann gritted it out—she never complained, never called me an idiot. No, one thing about Carol Ann, in times of hardship, she found her mettle. Early in our marriage she had worked in the nonprofit world, helping poor neighborhoods retain businesses and market themselves for development dollars, which required a certain brute optimism, not to mention courage. Both of which served her well when, just after the Y2K scare came and went, she sat me down and told me she'd had an affair, a serious one, and wouldn't it be better if I went and stayed at my goddamn brother's place since I was always over there anyway?

On the first Friday in April I tackled the plumbing. I was using plastic pipe, sealing the connections with a thick, noxious glue the color of an orange pushup from the ice cream man. Connecting it, despite the fumes and the toxic orange dollops on my scaly skin, was disturbingly simple. You cut the pipe, you cleaned the cut with a swabbed-on thinner, then swabbed on the glue and joined the two ends and held them together for thirty seconds with your face turned the other way on account of the carcinogens that were already seeping through your skin anyway. Busywork was what it amounted to: going to the store for a sixty-degree angle joint, and then again for another ninety, then again for a box of every kind of joint piece they had, followed by endless calculating, measuring, cutting, drilling pass-through holes in the studs, then glue-glue-gluing and holding the connections together long enough for them to set—all while wondering who was going to pay for my chemo.

But connecting the new plastic pipes to the rest of the house's copper ones down in the basement was a different matter. Thanks to Stu at Riverside Hardware, I had found plastic-to-copper adapters. I would orange-glue one side of the adapter to the plastic pipe coming down from the bathroom, but the other had to be soldered to the copper line in the basement. Then, if your soldering was good, the two sides screwed together and held pressurized water like a champ.

It was a Friday morning when I turned off the water at the main valve and tried the soldering—heating the copper end with a butane torch, slipping the solder stick into the connection so it melted silkily and got heat-sucked inside just the way it was supposed to, then waiting for everything to cool. With the water back on, the hot-water line held just fine, but the cold-water line sprayed like a nicked garden hose, and when that happens, you can't just resolder, or at least I couldn't—you have to cut the failed connection off and redo it from scratch at the new cut with a new adapter. Three times I did this. By the fourth attempt, Carol Ann was home from work, and I was a bramble of cords plugged into one outlet.

"Son of an ass-licker better fucking hold!" This was how I greeted her. My ragged hair, my arthritic knuckle of nose, my jowly maw of mouth. Poor Carol Ann. What a pain in the ass I must have been.

She kept her calm, laid her bag and blazer on the sofa's rotund arm. She still wore suits even though she'd been in her new job a year and a half now and could probably get away with twinsets. She was a project manager in the marketing department of a division of a corporation that was responsible for packaging the snacks made by another division of the same corporation. Somehow, in logic that was never explained to me, her experience in community development made her ideal for getting snacks properly packaged. She was home early, in fact, because she'd been chosen to attend a weekend series of snack-oriented focus groups in Los Angeles. She'd sit in a dark room with some marketing bigwigs and watch through a one-way mirror as a table of average women had their snacking histories and package preferences groped by an overeager moderator—all in hopes of boosting brand loyalty in the tricky, snack-crowded West Coast market.

She toed off her flats and left them where they lay. "The plumbing?"

"It's my fourth fucking try. I'll be under the goddamn street before I'm done. There's no water, by the way. Not until I get it right."

The Project was rife with such self-doubt—sheer, terrifying impotence. She eyed me, soured by the water thing. Carol Ann was a tall woman with a broad face and small, sharp teeth. With her short hair she looked every bit the sallow-mouthed progeny of her Slavo-Croatian forebears, except for her nose, which was muscular and magnificent, with a proud, show-horse profile. A common joke between us was that we wished her boobs had gotten some of what her nose got. Her eyes were guarded but bright and often outright warm. Except sometimes, when the world wronged her, she could get this look of dispossessed sadness, like a captive chimp—and everyone outside the cage was culpable.

"I have to get on a plane in three hours," she said.

"We'll get you there," I said. "You want a beer?"

She frowned full-out now. Her nose flared a little, then paled. In my presence, she skewed prudish. One time she missed a flight and called me in a rage. "Why does this happen to me? Why don't I just die. This is my life all the time." I'd gone to the airport to wait with her to get a standby flight.

"We can take Steve on a shorty," I said, "while we wait."

Steve clicked in via the kitchen. She was a petite, foolish, submissive black Lab-ish mutt with perky triangular ears, brilliant white teeth over mottled gums, and an Elizabethan collar of fur above her husky torso. She was no longer a puppy, but her exuberance for her mommy still involved plenty of jumping and barking and face licking. Over the past couple years, Carol Ann would come home while I was in the middle of some academic busywork and say, loudly, into Steve's tongue, "Well, at least *someone's* glad to see me. Yes she is! Yes she is!"

I went and found Steve's leash and waggled it at her; she went and found her rawhide chewy and waggled it back at me.

"I want to go by myself," Carol Ann said.

"Okay."

"I just don't want to talk. I'm exhausted."

"You're exhausted."

"For a deep discussion, yes."

Dog walks that winter and spring were when we dove in. It was a routine of self-flagellation, more like jujitsu than actual conversation. Part honest communication, part self-preserving restraint, they hadn't gotten us very far. Just always back to "it."

Do I have to go into detail? It had happened that fall and was as pedestrian, I suppose, as all these things probably are: No tripped-over cache of love letters or e-mails. No cologne not my own. No walking in *coitus interruptus* and falling to my knees like a fatty version of *The Scream*.

There'd been late nights, sure, Carol Ann out partying with her corporate crew, that coworker-bonding protocol I'd never really experienced. It had been the same a few years earlier with the do-gooders on the East Side. She'd be out till three or four in the morning—someone knew a bar owner, and so they got to hang out after close. Some of the snack-packaging finance guys were so young they got nicknamed "the bed wetters"—I think one of them, drunk, actually had wet the bed recently. Anyway, she'd told me stories of dancing with them and them getting weirded out by it and not talking to her the next week at the office. This had made her angry.

Why couldn't *she* be flirty? *They* got to. They were just boys, double-standard weasels. Letting loose was all it was. If they couldn't handle it, it was their problem, not hers.

I had agreed emphatically.

But it was her problem, and it became mine when she finally just blurted it out, after a cold, joyless New Year's Eve. She was so so so so so so so so so so so so so so so so so so so so so so so sorry, Hank. So so so so so so so so so sorry. But then again, as to her being sorry, she said, she wasn't *so* so sorry. She couldn't really apologize for something she'd been caught off-guard and helpless by, something so wholly unintentional it hadn't even seemed like her doing it at all. She'd felt a power and a lack, was what had happened, and when you combine a power and a lack, Hank, the lack loses.

This is what all the books on the subject say as well—or at least what their introductions say, which was as far as I had ever gotten reading them. Which meant I was forced to ask Carol Ann questions: How did this happen? Power and lack. Oh, right, sorry. Was it someone I knew? Kind of. Was he a work attachment infatuation (another term from the books' introductions). Yes, one of the bed wetters. They'd had coffee a few times, the picture of innocence, and his father had died, and since Carol Ann's had died a year before that, they talked it out, mutual consolation, and she'd even told me about said mutual consolation at the time it was happening, though I have no recollection of it, which was her point. She'd told me, I'd ignored her, then "it" happened—one of those "intentional accidents" the books talk about—and her heart told her: What would I care? I'd been ignoring her for years, first during my grad school stint, getting my MA, dreaming of guest lectureships at Yale, and then suffering the aftermath as a lowly proofreader. Neither made me happy, she said, and neither made me love her more. So "it" happened a few more times, then a few more, then "it" got its own day planner and credit card and, I can only assume, its own lingerie—she wasn't forthcoming as to details.

I listened as best I could. There were scenes. Her: This marriage is held together by a dog and a dental plan. Me: I found us the dental plan while you were out fucking your bed-wetting boyfriend. Her: We can divorce, Hank, to-fucking-day! Ad infinitum.

A divorce I didn't need. Like an aneurysm, I needed divorce. Not that I was immune to the "it"—I'd play the scenes over and over in my head, the porno of her stolen hours at the corner of Power and Lack. But I convinced myself that my actions had left her little alternative, much like real-life porno actors, as I'd learned as an impressionable undergrad at Grinnell College in Women's Studies 215: Feminist Perspectives of Pornography. So I begged as much as she ranted, made concessions when she demanded them, accentuated the positive. Think of all the many things we shared, I told her: our twenties, good old Grinnell College, Steve, arguments over what to name Steve, love of fresh tomatoes…snacks! No, we needed to stay calm here—that was my take on the whole thing. Stay focused, get into a project. I'm a load-bearing husband—you can't just knock me down.

So here we were, this April afternoon with the plumbing. It made sense. We were not ones, Carol Ann and I, to up and start new lives from scratch. We'd been a couple since freshman year at Grinnell, and even before marrying we'd had an oddly cemented concept of Togetherness. That is, everything felt better Together. It wasn't that she couldn't leave my side, although there was a time when that had been true—a letter from her during a college winter break expressed such abject misery at being apart that "I'll just keep buying you presents until the semester starts"—but it was more about *feeling* like we were side by side. Carol Ann needed us to meet eye to eye on everything, especially things emotional. We both worked at the same coffee shop after college, and it would truly bother her if she'd had a lousy day but I'd had a good one. It was a betrayal of her affection, like I was supposed to sulk with her—not just *understand* how bitchy our bitch of an assistant manager had been, but actually *feel* it. If I didn't, I was on the assistant manager's side. She was often a zero sum game that way. And forget about any suggestion that working at the same coffee shop might not be such a hot idea in the first place—might as well scream it in Russian.

Because why wouldn't I want to be Together with her? If I didn't want to be Together with her then I should just say so and go ahead and find someone else to be Together with, maybe the fucking assistant manager I love so much. No? Okay then; it's Together, and don't forget it.

This wasn't just her nose talking; it was her whole being. Her parents had raised her on Montessori values—only to throw her to the wolves at a public high school—and *Masterpiece Theatre* and idealistic Mississippi River Valley artists like Edgar Lee Masters and Thomas Hart Benton. After dinner they would read aloud from Sandburg's *The People, Yes* over gooseberry pie. They bought corn and seed by the fifty-pound bag to feed the backyard birds and migrating geese. I of course loved them to death, but it all gave Carol Ann an unrealistic sense of Togetherness. In college if I wanted to go to a party and she didn't, and I went ahead and went—I'd return to find my stuff neatly packed in a corner, Carol Ann in tears and dry heaves.

Facing such fierce Togetherness, you either bail, or abdicate.

I chose the latter. I fit the part, too. I was that guy who was happy as a birthday party to accompany my wife to the suburban mall's eye clinic while she got fitted for contacts, poking into nearby stores like I did when I was young and my father would bring me to his store with him. Aimless, not really wanting anything, half-frightened of the sales people, then returning to find a blinking Carol Ann insulted by my suggestion we get some Karmel Korn at the Karmel Korn store. "No, ick. It'll make me sick." There, that's it, the sad fact of it: I was a man who needed his wife's permission to buy Karmel Korn.

"I was thinking," Carol Ann said. She was standing in the little foyer area, her REI jacket zipped to her chin. Outside, it was that April chill that's worse than winter itself. "Do you think we've ever had a shared vision?"

Steve lowered her head, nosed at the screen door. Carol Ann and I had installed it ourselves, one long Saturday of bickery torture, and we'd had to replace the screen three times on account of Steve's personal issues with the postal carrier.

The dog looked up at me now, then at Carol Ann. She nosed the door again, clicking her claws on the hardwood for good measure.

I held my tongue. Shared vision? We were going to use the matte-white six-inch tiles she wanted in the new shower. And then there was the shared vision of her "it" playing over and over in my head, with the lunging and acrobatics and sweaty chins—all the ways she and I had never done "it."

I'd waited too long. Carol Ann opened the screen door and let Steve pull her out, leaving me to hold some more of my tongue.

Of course that stupid copper joint held, too. When I turned the water back on, it all stayed put, the basement dry and quiet as shame.

I blame my family. Neither my brother nor I were raised to play emotional hardball. With us it was much talking, little meaning. If there was a cliché or quip to be made, we would make it. If there was someone who'd let their figure go, if there were prices that were outrageous, if there was a purchasing rationale or encounter with a salesperson, a complaint about someone's kids or lawn, a rebuke about elbows on the table, a moral landscape crisply unfolded like plastic placemats—this was where we shined. Weather, clothing, funny TV ads.

Mom was a grade-school teacher and came from hardworking Scottish Presbyterian stock not known for emotional purging. Before Dad, she had been married to a door-to-door drapes salesman—our biological father—who moved her down to St. Louis, then one day called from the road and said he wouldn't be coming home. My brother and I were in diapers still; we never knew his real name. So she hauled us back upriver to Omaha where she met our old man and somehow fell in love with him, giving him the perfect excuse to drop out of law school. His wasn't a head for law anyway. To support us he bought into his father's business, a trio of children's stores called Kidsville, and as soon as the drapes salesman had been declared sufficiently AWOL, Mom, Carlton, and I converted to Judaism in a ceremony that involved nudity and bathing and through which I apparently screamed bloody murder while my brother toughed it out, which was how he was made.

Dark-haired and olive-skinned, Mom could pass for Jewish no problem, replete with the chops for mindless chatting. Kibitzing, it's called—and it's amazing the leverage it will get you with the Finkelsteins and Scholnicks of the world—or maybe said Finkelsteins and Scholnicks are a charitable, accepting lot. Either way, Mom just slipped into it, natural as sunshine, and the past went poof. It's not like we were expressly forbidden to ask about, say, our drapes salesman, or even how Mom and Dad met—it just never occurred to us in that organic etiquette families create. It would be like looking at a patch of plowed earth, then closing your eyes and expecting a gardenia to be there when you opened them again. Too much to ask. And I guess when you look at it from Mom's point of view, anything more was pretty iffy—no way was she going to risk rocking the Meyerson boat, opening her trap and blowing this second chance she'd been given.

But what of it? Really, would an open-book family life have prepared me for Carol Ann's corporate travel needs? Or, specifically, bathing her over our basement's mainline sewer drain?

She was naked, my wife, slick and streaming. I was pouring, and also naked. I was involved because of the general Togetherness tenets, and also because Carol Ann used a potent prescription dandruff shampoo, and rinsing it was a two-handed job. Which meant another two hands had to pour.

I had six more bowls of water ready to go. I knew the temperature she liked. I knew the rate at which to flow the water. I knew her breathing breaks and what her flaring nostrils meant ("stop pouring idiot"). Togetherness.

This was not as awful as it sounds. We'd made the basement drain fairly cheery, all things considered, with a plain pink shower curtain hung from the exposed floor joists overhead, a small greenish lampshade affixed over the 60-watt bulb, stacks of purple towels on a clean piece of plywood over the utility sink, and a white plastic deck chair so Carol Ann could shave her legs. There was little we could do about the cold cement floor, though. We had taken a large pink tub mat, of the kind meant to help old people avoid slipping their way to a new hip, and cut a hole in its center so we could stand over the drain but not on the drain. Carol Ann's square feet flexed on either side of the rusty metal hole, the brown shampoo sudsing down between her wide-spaced breasts, over her knoll of stomach, between her hips too wide for ballet (as she'd been told in tenth grade), through a tangled filter of pubes, and straight into the drain.

In the greenish tint from the lampshade, I got a hard-on, and the hard-on made me cry.

If I'd been a little more extraordinary, this might never have happened. My hard-on, Carol Ann's bed-wetting boyfriend, everything. I'd be too intelligent for it, too orbital with gravitas—something of the Malcolm Gladwell type, groomed for luminous, if quirky, insight. I'd still be in grad school, printing off ream after ream of a meaninglessly big-brained dissertation, rather than folding after my MA was approved. Or I'd have taken my MA and said "the hell with you all!" and joined the staff at Minneapolis's version of *The New Yorker*, whatever that was, instead of folding and going back to proofreading. Or I'd have slimmed down and taken Kama Sutra classes instead of folding into eremitic masturbation. Well, enough said. The point is, extraordinary people never fold. Except maybe extraordinary poker players, but it's a metaphor, for Christ's sake.

And see, extraordinary people don't have thoughts like these. For extraordinary people to contemplate their un-extraordinariness, metaphorically or no, would be foreign to their very nature. *They* don't worry about risks or consequences. They're simply driven to be extraordinary, and they do it; they inhabit it. Carl Sagan and Paul Robeson come to mind. And my brother the businessman, the fuckwad baseball player who never finished college but managed to make hundreds of thousands of dollars in the toy industry. It's fate I guess, or genetics, or maybe reaping the fruits of a successful past life—whichever bullshit you want to believe. Whatever. Fatty, it ain't.

Why all this made me ripe for adulterous betrayal, I had no idea. But rarely does not knowing stop the tears.

I kept pouring Carol Ann's water, she kept rinsing, and the hard-on went nowhere. Rush Limbaugh, Rush Limbaugh, Katie Couric—didn't help, even with my cold feet and tears, my face now squished like an apple in a vice, wet pulpy lips and wrinkled skin.

My bowl ran out of water, and I set it behind me on the table with the others and the towels. Carol Ann pushed the bangs from her face and wiped water from her squinched eyes. The first thing she saw was my hard-on. She rock-stepped backward. "Where'd that come from?" she said.

Then she saw me crying, and put a hand to my elbow.

"I'm sorry," I said.

She offered a thin, sad smile—the chimp loosed from the cage, free to rampage.

I wiped my eyes and face. "I don't want to fold," I said. "I wanna have a shared vision."

"You have a stiffy."

"Well," I said, "I wanna have both."

She inspected me. Was I being honest? Was I using pain as a ploy? I had no idea, so I started to turn from her, but she dropped her hand and held me. I thought about objecting on principle, or pride, but that just wasn't going to happen. Her hand was still slightly soapy. She tugged just a little, putting pressure up near the top. I thought how stupid a word "stiffy" is, and she put her second hand on me. I closed my eyes, and that was all it took.

"Oop," she said.

There was an emptiness for a moment, then that queasy aftermath filling it back in.

But since she now had a stupid half-smile on her lips, I tried to mime it back. It wasn't the wrong thing to do. Carol Ann smiled for real this time, nose and all.

"You don't want your water to get cold," she said.

I nodded. I moved so she could reach a towel and go.

Chapter Two

"The b-day partay is underway," June said over the phone. "A-hay," she added. "Carlton's doing steaks for me and Angie and Bob but thank God not their kids. Omaha steaks. He just picked them up. Not from Omaha."

This was my brother's wife with an invitation that over the course of The Project had become standing. I'd go over there to shower, at least once every several days, and also just to…I don't know what. To get away from the tension. To remind myself what it was like to be family. To wallow, too, in my brother's success, like Steve rolling in squirrel carcass.

June was turning thirty that Sunday, and was disgruntled by it. Not that her age showed. She was small and lovely, wheat-blonde and pale but for freckles and a pink line of lips beneath a small arrowhead of a nose. She came from Kansas and clearly had more compassion in her stubby pinky finger than I did in my whole body, because 1) she put up with my brother, which for many reasons was no small feat, and 2) when they met, she had been working at a group home for developmentally disabled adults, whom she privately called retards, as I suppose loving them the way she did gave her the right to do. But she wasn't choked by compassion, all mournful enthusiasm and self-satisfied sighs, like some of the do-gooders Carol Ann used to run with during her days on the teetering East Side. June kept conversation intimate and worthwhile, she cursed as casually as you'd leave pennies in a penny dish, she tried to shoot the moon too often when playing Hearts, and she had a way of walking into a room and simplifying things. Her gray eyes were as calm as milk, and she could drink. My brother had fallen for her the minute he met her, in a goddamn coffee shop, of all places. It remained unclear why she had responded in kind—I joked that it was God's revenge on her for going atheist, as she herself had described herself doing, in college. Such a God would truly be an awesome God.

Before I could comment on the Omaha-ness of the steaks, she said, "How are you doing? Your brother bought this 'Jewish artisan bread,' it says right on the label. You'll love it. You'll have some comment to make, I'm sure. So I want to hear it when you show."

"I just got back from taking Carol Ann to the airport for her snacks trip, so I'm out."

"Wuh? That's not the right answer."

Something was off in her. I was used to her imprecisions like "wuh." This was something else.

"Are you drunk?" I said.

"Shhh," she said. After a second she whispered, "How are *you* doing?" she said now. "Carol Ann called and said she was worried about you. She called from the effing airport. Hank, she never calls me. We aren't misbroken. Is that the word for family?"

"Mish...boke...ha," I said. Though really I didn't know for sure—it's just how my grandfather had always said it.

"So now I'm worried about you. I guess that's how it is. We women worry. It's like genetic, like you and your slow metabolism. Mine's slow too. Wuh?" This she said to Carlton. "He's telling me to tell you that the steaks will be better than the old man's. Wuh?" she said to him again. "A rare occurrence, he says. He says it's a joke."

"It's an old joke," I said.

"Fuck Carol Ann," she whispered then—she was trying to clean up her language, on account of the fact that they were trying to have a baby, but this whispering had more to do with respect for my suffering. "She can eff off. Who would do that to you? You are the sweetest. I know, you told me not to say anything or whatever, so I don't, but I have my advice for you. It's the same as your dad's."

I'd told my father, who still lived in Omaha, a sanitized version of how things were with me and Carol Ann—that, like Ireland, we were merely having "the troubles." His advice amounted to the fact that if it didn't work out with Carol Ann, God forbid, there were lots of fish in the sea. "Charlie Tuna, Hank, Charlie Tuna." He knew it was hard, he said—boy did he know, "With how your mother was taken from me, bam, like that." I'd told him I didn't think the comparison apt, and he said oh it was apt all right, apt as apt.

June ground gears. "Carlton says get your nancy ass over here right now."

My brother's house was within a bike ride of my own, but I took my Jetta anyway. I parked at the curb in front, as I'd been asked not to do. He'd begun to call their neighborhood "Hutch"—in honor of Hutchinson, the rather stagnant Kansas town where he played college baseball—and wanted to move to the suburbs, or even Linden Hills, especially when and if a baby came into the picture. June disagreed and asked me not to make matters worse by getting my car into the act.

The car shuddered to a stop, shedding me like a wet dog shaking dry. I crossed the driveway behind the bumper of June's Subaru wagon—Carlton's Volvo sedan, white and pristine and boxy-beautiful, would be in the detached garage that faced the rear alley. The house was boxy too, a bungalow, stucco with sage green trim, with a screened-in porch that didn't see much sun except in the morning. They'd bought it with a 20 percent down payment provided by the first big checks from Roller Rings—this was his invention, a grade-schooler accessory made of colored ball bearings strung on circles of slightly stretchy but super-sturdy nylon. Sold in a multicolored ten-pack and hawked by our father, who by then had closed down the store and become a specialty toy rep with Kansas, Oklahoma, and Nebraska as his territory; Roller Rings stole a sliver of the tween pie. They felt good to roll on; they could be traded to other kids and stacked up on many fingers for a deviant look that made school principals bristle. They even caught on for a while with some adults as fetish toys, and after two years they had had a life of their own.

So my brother was looking to upgrade wherever he could. What he found "Hutch" about his neighborhood had originally attracted him as un-Omaha and unpretentious: carefree yards choked with creeping Charlie, landscaping that ran the gamut from full-out multi-tiered vision quests to a couple of hostas skulking in cedar mulch as if out for a smoke break. My brother had leaned lately toward the former, as best he could, edifying the house in bright flora whose genera escaped me, all of it edged with an edger, trimmed with a trimmer, and leaf-blown with a leaf blower. Can't say he was lazy, my brother. Between the yard work and the Volvo waxing and the logistics of sending off trinkets to kiddy purveyors everywhere—he'd created a few other toys ideas, in addition to the obvious Roller Rists and Roller Toze, to only so-so success—he hardly had a social life.

As I let myself in, he greeted me from the kitchen: "Can't you park your Nazi mobile down the block?"

Some people, life streams to them; they have only to cup their hands and drink. My brother was like that. Went right from being a freeloading, washed-up ballplayer in Omaha to a job up here in Minneapolis at a toy store, which he then quit to make Roller Rings happen. Maybe it was the great first impression he made: tall, tight, and strong, with blunt, knobby elbows hard as hammers. He had a good tough chin, but not too tough, and his eyes were blue and clear and his lips were still thin and his cheeks cherubic. Even his front two incisors—which folded inward and twisted the other two outward like fangs and caused him terrible cold sores—even they didn't take away from his easy allure. In high school, girls couldn't get enough of him.

Someone once told me my brother looked like Brad Pitt. Well, maybe, if Brad Pitt were a little soft in the cheeks and had bad teeth and thought about toys all the time. No, here it is: if you had lived with Brad Pitt as a kid and had once seen Brad Pitt's poop-stained underwear in the dirty clothes hamper and had laughed so hard at it that Brad Pitt then held you down and shoved his poop-stained underwear into your mouth—then yeah, my brother'd look a little bit like Brad Pitt to you.

And here he was prepping his steaks.

"Drink," he said to me. It was not a question. I sat down at the kitchen table, a built-in tucked into the far wall, where he had a big sweaty glass full of gin and tonic all ready to go.

"Where's June?"

"Upstairs napping."

"Was she drinking this afternoon?"

He shrugged.

How he'd blossomed, my brother. Hundred-dollar slacks certainly helped—June's doing. But he wore them well, too: the success of Roller Rings had re-sculpted him. This was not the same guy who had been an ex-athlete loser before Mom's death and then a basket case afterward. No, now he was the epitome of benevolent, invasive paternalism. A regular Daddy-Do-What-I-Say, just waiting for a kid of his own to bestow it on. In the meantime, none were spared.

I watched him monkey with his platter of steaks. They were bloody and limp. He was going to season them while we talked and drank. Rather, while he talked and I drank—he'd been on the wagon a few years now.

"She might have been. It's her birthday weekend, she says. Leave her alone, she says. It's like she caught a case of Carol Ann."

He stopped short, looking down at the steaks. "Sorry," he said.

"Hey," I said, "it happens."

"Speaking of that," he said, his voice a little hushed, "I think it's time."

I sighed and rubbed my face with my palms. "Time for what, chief?"

"For spring cleaning, with your life. You've got to make some decisions here."

"I'm working on it."

"You're working on the bathroom and a case of diabetes," he said. "That's what I see. You bitch and moan, but nothing happens. It's like Elian Gonzalez with you guys. Do you have any kind of plan whatsoever? What if I told you she has a lawyer? I've always liked Carol Ann, but she's the kind of woman who will kick your ass in this type of thing."

"A lawyer. You know this? How?"

"Does that make a difference? Would it make you get your head out of your ass?"

My first instinct, as always with my brother, was to tell him to mind his own fucking business, but he got to me first. "Just quit being a pussy and do *something,* anything. Go out and get laid, get even with her. Or counseling. Have you done counseling?"

"Carol Ann doesn't believe in counseling."

"*Make* her go. What, you think being a pussy's going to work?"

My brother was picking up slabs of cow, drizzling them with a handful of oily, herby seasoning from a nearby bowl, and dropping them onto a platter the size and shape of North Dakota. My drink suddenly looked excruciatingly delicious. I pulled it close to me and squeezed the lime. I dried my fingertips on the shelf of my own gut.

"I mean, if you're going to be part of this family and come over here and sister up to my wife and some day be a role model for my kid—which don't get me wrong, I'd like to see because I'm for *mishbucha* as much as the next guy—but if you're going to do that, then you're going to have to be value-added. The Germans could gas-van a whole town faster than you can even decide what to do about your slutty wife."

I finished off my first drink, pushed the glass aside.

My brother's macabre taste for Holocaust trivia had by then become like normal. He said it started in college when he toured the Cosmosphere, a museum of rocket and space technology located on campus at Hutchinson—in all the many didactics in the World War

II section about how the Nazis developed the first long-range ballistic missiles and paved the way for the space race, there was plenty of mention of the Hitlerian evil this technology had been created to serve, but in a war that claimed twenty million lives, not one mention of Jews. Not one. He had found this troubling—it was a genocide of Jewish specificity—and he took a course or two down there and back in Omaha after his blown knee, and it'd been a thing with him ever since. I probably shouldn't have encouraged it as much as I did—but it had gotten him reading, everything from Primo Levi to Levi-Strauss, and I supposed that made it okay. Besides, maybe he'd come up with a toy idea out of it. A plush called the Zyklon Bee, or a gag light switch that shocks you called the "Ouch Switch."

He was slathering meat still; good lord, we had enough food to feed ten. The sound was starting to ick me out, like footsteps in shallow mud. "The point is," he said, "you're not getting anywhere— you're not getting a PhD, you're not getting laid, you're not getting divorced, you're not getting nothing."

All this was too true. "Yeah, like you're in the sack all the time, aren't ya?" I knew he wasn't because June had told me. "And just for the record—"

"Yeah? Tell me for the record, little brother." He kept slathering the steaks.

"I," indicating myself with my hands, "got a hand job this afternoon. Did you?"

He frowned and snapped, "I don't care for hand jobs."

In half a second this had us both doubled up with laughter, me over the bench, him over the steaks. For all I knew, he was telling the truth, which made it funnier. I mean, though my basement hand job had been awkward and charitable at best, you'd still have to say I'd "cared for" it.

My brother wiped his eyes with the back of his hand and sighed. "Ah," he said, "nope, don't care for 'em one bit."

We were still laughing when June came down, looking sleepy. Her jeans, two sizes too big, were topped by a gray hooded sweatshirt that had twisted during her nap. She looked like a little kid.

"The fun's already started," she said.

My brother recovered himself. He looked her up and down, then went back to his steaks.

"I have a Master theory," June said to me.

She was talking about one of the biggest mysteries in Dickinson studies: the intended recipient of three letters, discovered after Emily's death in draft form (the final drafts possibly never even sent), in which she lays herself prostrate at a lover's feet, a lover whom she speaks intimately to, declares her undying love to, references past physical encounters with, and addresses only as "Master."

It bored me. Dickinson had been the subject of my MA thesis, "'I Could Not See to See': Dickinsonian Aesthetics and the Art of Ed Ruscha." It wasn't bad work, just nothing special. The title's about as interesting as it got; the rest was filler for my advisor's sabbatical application.

I had loaned June my copy of Richard Sewall's biography and told her where the soap opera parts were—the Master letters, the infatuation Emily had with her sister-in-law Sue, Emily's brother's adulterous affair with a married woman over the course of fourteen years or so, and all that. For a bunch of Massachusetts Puritans, I guess it was juicy stuff, but what had June addicted was the realization that an actual woman with an actual family and actual drama wrote those weird poems we read in high school.

"Let me get the book," June said, but Carlton stopped her.

"Not that crap right now—I'm trying to talk sense into him."

June's jaw tightened. She pushed her lips together and left us to our giggling.

My brother went to the sink and washed his hands, an elaborate process for him, like a surgeon's. I shook my head in his direction, and felt it bounce off him. In grade school he was the kind of kid to boast that he was the best basketball player in the school, and no one really challenged him on it. He was the one our father felt comfortable knocking to his ass to teach him a lineman's three-point stance—because he always got back up. Infield grounders hopping into his face, too. For a while there, it made him leader. One time a neighbor kid was hitting golf balls over the four lanes of Pacific Street traffic, and Carlton made him stop by taking the club away and whacking the kid's thighs with it. I know because he brought me along to watch him in action. He made blintzes for Mom on her birthday, too. Little shit.

His hands were clean now, wet. He held them aloft, looking off toward the living room.

He turned to me. I threw him a dishtowel, which he had to snag by scooping almost to the kitchen floor.

"Ball four," he said.

This wasn't always the garage sale waiting for me at my brother's place. I usually got a warm shower, for one thing, in the main-floor bathroom with a shower curtain sporting bright yellow duckies splattered with mold—I took a moldy schadenfreude from their cheerfully feathered pates.

I also got genuine solace.

One Tuesday night in February, June and I had been sitting on her porch, rehashing my marriage with that endless speculative scrutiny people tend to indulge after a spouse informs them of an affair. It was an enjoyable moment of reprieve, with the added benefit of keeping me out of the bar.

We were under blankets with a couple portable heaters firing away at our ankles, watching a light snow falling in the conical areole of streetlight outside. June was prodding me for my own good, and feeding me beers, and I was bitching about how it had been Carol Ann who'd been in the rush to get married in the first place—she'd gone on and on about it, and about how her aunt Jeanne had waited for a succession of three guys to marry her, and each had declined, taking years of her youth with her as they went, and Carol Ann's thing was: no way was that going to happen to her.

"If there's a reason you want to wait," she said, "we need to have it out now. Because there's nothing wrong with me that I should have to wait."

It was a bizarrely conservative thing for a Grinnell College student to say, given the fact that I could look out our apartment window at any random time and see students, many we considered friends, staging a sit-in for Tibet, or swinging from rock-climbing gear in the Burling Library oak trees, or having a "masturbate for the wetlands" marathon on the Smith Hall loggia balcony. But that was Carol Ann. Eager to say black to your white. At Dartmouth, she'd have been head of the Green Party. But at Grinnell, she wanted to get married. She'd been Daddy's girl, his partner in crime. This was a guy who wore Spandex bike shorts with suspenders and Tevas with socks, just heading out to the store. He crammed fifteen tomato plants into their tiny backyard, and he roasted a turkey every other Sunday. Carol Ann's mother was the one to rein him in, insist on some reverence, but Carol Ann learned how to play him for what she wanted, to fantastic rewards. That's the psychoanalysis. Does it account for her desire to get married as a college senior? Meh, probably not. Life doesn't go for straightaways, but prefers the scenic route. Carol Ann in spades.

June hadn't bought it either. College seniors don't normally obsess on major life decisions, she'd said—they trip into them. The marriage-obsessed woman was a pre-existing bucket, a stereotype, something for me to dump my bullshit into.

"Truth is," she said, "people tend to put themselves in positions they think they deserve, bad or good. You were probably ready to play the put-upon husband way before Carol Ann even came into the picture."

"Right," I said. "Blame the victim."

I scowled into my blanket. It's not exactly enjoyable to hear you are complicit in your own cuckoldry, but June had a way of administering the sharpest of suppositories with only a little discomfort.

"Not blaming the victim," June said. "It's just that you have the power to change it. I mean, when you realize you're like a co-conspirator, you see it for what it is. Every situation is literally what you make of it. So now, you know—you can do anything. It's a power thing."

"Well I'd like to make this particular situation," I said, bringing my pale slab of hand out from under my blanket to motion to the both of us, "a little more beer-y."

"Beer the victim!" she said.

When she'd gone inside, after a furry splash of warmth from the front door's opening and closing, I promised myself I wouldn't be in tears when she came back with my beer. There's a certain kind of happiness to being in pain, a comfort in wallowing. Emotional pain, at least. It's a tonic, your pure, convalescent sadness. Is that why June and I we were sitting on the porch, freezing our tits off? Despair is an addictive niggler. It's a part of you that hangs there, some extra skin or a scab or a goiter that you can't stop fingering. The gross, the abscessed, the pus-filled, the peeling, the enlarged— our despair gone ripe for the picking.

When June came back, I asked her if we could not talk about it anymore.

"Sure," she said.

"It's like a loose tooth I'm fiddling with."

"One time I had this thing behind my tonsils," June said. "The ear, nose, and throat guy called it a 'cryptic cyst.'"

"All cysts are a little cryptic, I'd say. I mean, *I've* never gotten a straight answer from one."

She shook her head. "It was a little white hole in the lining, way at the back. Stuff got caught in it, and it would wax and wane. And I'd check it every night, with a flashlight in the bathroom mirror."

"Could you reach it, to like pick at it?"

"I bought a water pick to hose it out."

"Ugh, gross."

"Yup. Carlton says it was a huge turn-off."

"That's too bad," I said.

Outside, the snow froze—in place, I mean. It just stopped, hung there in the air, and switched directions, and suddenly we were watching it snow up. This is not unusual during blizzards or generally windy days, but on a still, soft night—and it had to be still for us to have lasted on the drafty porch so long—it was remarkable, like a sudden exhaling of something too large to be seen out a porch window.

I shuddered underneath my blanket.

I wondered aloud if the snow would keep Carlton from getting home. His plane from New York City was supposed to arrive at midnight or something outrageous. The way my brother did things was a mystery to me. He'd been at Toy Fair, the number one industry expo, hawking Roller Rings and Roller Toze and the whole line of addenda. It was thousands of vendors selling millions of units of kiddy crap to everyone and anyone who wanted in on the action. June and I had gone with him the first year he attended, and it had been memorable.

"I'm glad it's not us," I said.

"Remember the Starbies?"

June let out a little grunt of agreement, which made her crow's feet tighten. She had a new fleshiness, everywhere except the face, which was still sharp. She'd wear a size P balaclava, probably a ten everywhere else.

My brother had ridiculed the guy who sold Starbies. "Some of these people," he said, "they're just pathetic. Who gave them the money to pitch this crap? Starbies?" They were essentially Barbies, but more glamorous, the guy said, because they all lived in Hollywood. He had ten pages, single-spaced, of back story for each Starbie. Starbie Tina was on a soap opera, and Starbie Diane was a hang glider. My brother told him Starbie Patricia had better be a lawyer, cuz his ass is gonna get sued.

"Starbies," June said.

One of the storm windows was cracked, and I pointed it out. My brother had convinced her, once they started trying to get pregnant, to give up her job at Hope House, so she'd filled her time tracking down vintage crystal doorknobs across Minnesota, reading *The New Yorker* cover to cover, keeping the fridge stocked, rating school districts, and so on. Between that and the house projects to manage—the security system, the locksmiths, the plaster guys and the roof guys (there was a leak in the ceiling someplace), the cleaning people—she'd literally started an Excel spreadsheet to keep track of it all.

"Put it on the spreadsheet," I said.

She laughed. "According to the spreadsheet, this week I'm supposed to go back in time to January and call plumbing contractors to come give us a bid on the bad water pressure upstairs so it can be done next week. I don't wanna be doing this crap. I heard something on the radio about the Philadelphia Sound, from the '70s, you know? I don't even know what it was. Instead of maintaining a spreadsheet, why aren't I buying CDs from the Philadelphia Sound? Huh? Huh?"

I shrugged.

"You're no help. My grandmother told me to marry a guy who makes me forget about chores—now I have one who loads me up with them. Lately it's shmutz shmutz shmutz—all he sees is shmutz. In the morning you say 'Good morning, Carl,' and he says 'Good morning, shmutz!'

"Well," she said, "you can talk to me anytime about this. I know Carlton's not the best commiserator."

"Yeah."

"I mean, we're all family. But we're family family. You come first over Carol Ann. And I promise I won't tell you to dump her like I did that time in New York."

I laughed.

"We can just blab like school girls like we always do."

"I blab, you mean. I'm the blabber and the blubber."

She raised her beer to that and drank.

"Anyway, thank God for it," I said. "Because I'd either be here or sucking down beer at Nora's." This was my favorite bar in town, where I had gone for more than my share of solace from Carol Ann. I patted my stomach. "And fatty doesn't need the beer."

"Speaking of," she said, "you want another beer?"

I sighed and rubbed my face. "Of course."

I slept on their couch that night; Carol Ann was not a fan of me coming home drunk and angry, and I'd put myself into a position where I was both. I remember my brother getting home late and checking my pulse, then laughing his way upstairs. Then, in the morning, he descended to ask if I wanted heart-shaped pancakes or regular. It was Valentine's Day.

Chapter Three

The rest of that Friday night steak dinner went fine, except for my behavior, which began with assessing everyone through the bottom of successive gin and tonics and went downhill accordingly.

The guests were Bob and Angie, friends of June's, mismatched in age if not values, whom my brother was trying to hit up for investment money, and also Terry, who used to live in June's group home, and his mother, a small, straight-backed woman wearing a pine green cardigan she had obviously knitted herself.

I'd met Terry only once before, at the group home before June and Carlton were married. His love for June was matched only by his awkward fixation for my brother, who called him "the kid." Well into his twenties, he was no kid, only kidlike—small and easily distracted, with a bird's chest, delicate and hollow, and a scruffy beard, pointy at the chin, with high brows over open eyes that went from mildly startled to calm and back again. June had never told me what exactly was wrong with him—when he was a kid, his parents never delved into the ins and outs of it, thanks to a chaotic, living-beyond-their-means lifestyle that ended in divorce. It was all they could do to send him from special ed class to the group home.

No one even knew Terry could paint until June started her art class. But he had a talent for it, was prolific, and had gotten some press a few years ago—a newspaper article that compared his development of figures and forms to "life arising from the primordial ooze." It even earned him patronage from a couple deep pockets in the outsider art crowd. I'd never seen his work, but June said he hopped from style to style, and subject to subject, a range of emotions and tones, probably because his amygdala—the nugget in the brain that determines base emotional response—was underdeveloped, and so he was prone to fits of intense wariness and outright fear. Scrawny as an alley cat in his puffy Cubs caps and mismatched Salvation Army clothes, he'd happily go with your flow until his amygdala decided to incapacitate him. Come to think of it, he was pretty much your basic artist.

His most recent success was a showing, all his own, at a local gallery. There was to be an opening reception the next day. Impolite, I had dug into my steak immediately; its juices oozed inside me as I watched everyone catch up. Wine glasses became fingerprinted, steak knives ambulatory. The wine was from Montana, of all places. Bob had found it in Coon Rapids, which he called Minneapolis's version of New Jersey. Something about all this confused and soured me.

Terry's mother was trying to tell us about her son's new apartment—his first stab at truly independent living.

"He has two bedrooms," she said, "so one can be used for art only. There's a wonderful agency in town that helps DD adults live independently. They check on him every day, for now at least."

I butted in to ask Terry what his favorite painting was.

Terry looked at his mother. He was wearing a plaid sport coat, too small for him, and a pristine yellow T-shirt underneath. He began to bob a little in his chair. "For however long he needs them to come," she said.

"I go for walks by the river and everything," Terry said about his new independence. He said it to Angie, whom he was clearly sweet on, "I have a walking stick and ten shoes."

"Tennis shoes," his mother said.

"Come on, your best painting," I asked him, "the one you like the most?"

"Oh," Terry said. His sport coat seemed to straighten itself now, but it was his mother doing it.

"We'll see it tomorrow at the gallery," Carlton said.

"My favorite of his," Mrs. Nolan finally answered me, "is a study of his father's swimming pool. His father lives in Phoenix."

"But what about the river?"

Terry was still on the pool. "I like to look at things real close," he said. "Real close is where it's on."

"Where it's at," June corrected him.

"Oh," Terry said.

"I would have liked to be an artist," my brother said. "If I could go back. I mean, I sort of am now." He said this last part to Bob.

"I'd paint my father's pool," I said, "if he had one. But he'd probably have Mom's body in it, propped up on a floating cushion, like *Weekend at Bernie's.*"

This was supposed to be a charming joke, but, well, if you don't know my father and his devotion to Mom, it lacks something. Namely charm, and joke.

Terry laughed, then looked at me, then looked at his steak.

"Artists shouldn't shy away from anything. Dead moms, whatever. That is," I added, "if you're really an artist. Otherwise, you might as well start sketching bucktoothed kids at the fair. On skateboards."

"Oh," Terry said.

"Terry, you are a real artist," June said, "and you can paint whatever you want. Anyone who says otherwise can shut their talking holes." This last part, obviously, was thrown my way. June had had her share of the Montana red, so I didn't worry.

I poured myself more wine. It was ridiculous, wine from Montana, but at least it wasn't polluted by that stupid oak that Californians love so much, lord knows why, probably because they think that's how the Frogs do it, so we have to too, only double! Everything in America is double. My country, twice as good as yours. My kids, twice as cute. I've heard they actually flavor the wine with oak, pour it in like liquid smoke in a barbecue sauce. Only Americans would invent liquid smoke. Only in America can retarded artists get gallery showings. And all this somehow tied to Carol Ann's "it"—some largesse I wasn't privy to, some shared vision of Togetherness that made everyone comfortable in their skins. And I, pushover, agreeable as a screen door, swung along, like born-again Christians, living in all of it, but not of it. I used to study literature, which made it somewhat okay, but now what? Now I proofed someone else's study. It showed up via courier and two weeks later I called to have it picked up along with my invoice and a Post-it saying, "Thanks so much—I really enjoyed this!"

I smiled at June, who glowered like Nixon, and said, "Art notwithstanding, I've decided to move to Montana."

There! No one saw *that* coming. It surprised even me. I'd thought of moving to Montana before, but only in the way poor people think of putting in a Jacuzzi. Saying it now, however, sounded right on the money. Montana. Where no one knew me, I wasn't married, and no one asked me "so what?" Mon. Fucking. Tana.

"After you finish the bathroom?" Angie said.

"What part of Montana?" June said.

I had no idea. "Mountainous part?" I said.

Bill at least was up for the bit. "Why not Mexico?" he said. "Much warmer, and costs less."

I dismissed him. "Too many Mexicans."

"Running away won't solve anything," June said, "no matter where you go."

She had sipped her wine down to the tannin residue, and she was stroking Carlton's arm with her fingernails while he perused his catalog shoot of a living room.

"Oh but I think it will. It's remarkable what can't be done to you when you're not around. Anyway, it will give me one thing for sure: peace from other people." I meant other people's control over me, but that sounded, in my mind, too whiny to actually say, and I'd rather come off a misanthrope than a *nebbish*.

"You can't have that," my brother said. He got that professorial tone he sometimes took—if he wasn't hammering, he was enlightening.

"You're Jewish. You're one election away from Kristallnacht. And we learned as kids that every time we went out, we were representing not just ourselves, but our family, the family business, and most importantly, all Jews."

"Every religion beats that into you," Angie said.

"No," I agreed. "It was different with us. I carry it around all the time. For instance, when calling a female friend of mine, I'm always sure to address a hello to the husband if he should answer the phone first—there's nothing more annoying than hearing one of your wife's male friends say, 'Um, is Carol Ann there?'"

Carlton sat up in his seat. His face steamed, ruddy and sharp, and full of Meyerson hospitality. "That's right," he said, smiling, "because it's not just you calling but all Jews."

"That's right," I said. "And see, it's impossible that all Jews could be sleeping with your wife—one of them would rat!"

"They did at Auschwitz," Carlton said. "There were informants and snitches everywhere—if it could score you soup or an extra slice of bread, why not? And if the ratted out guy got killed, odds are he would have died anyway. If you survived getting off the train, with the beatings and—"

"Stop," June cut him short. To me she said, "So why are you giving up now?"

"Because fuck 'em. I want to be oblivious. Put the world's husbands on alert—Bob, nothing personal, but by definition that means you—I and all Jews are now officially trying to sleep with your wives."

Angie smirked like "Yeah, hit the gym first, Hymie."

Bob said he believed we all had a plan in store for us, but God gives us choices along the way. "You can choose your way into a new plan," he said.

"So I choose Montana," I said. I looked at my brother, who was chuckling. "There's room enough for all Jews," I explained, "and everyone's wives too."

June declared this wonderfully insightful, then stood and took her wine glass into the other room, and a bright patch of halogen

light winked off Bob's bald spot. We sang June "Happy Birthday,"
and my brother asked Bob and Angie if they had any liquid assets
they were looking to get a 10 percent return on.

Chapter Four

The next day was warmer, and lovely as a hundred dollar bill. The gallery showing Terry's work was a narrow storefront space sandwiched between an eyeglass store and an antiques shop, but it had nice big windows that let in lots of light, so much so that I had to keep my sunglasses on. With them and my baggy jeans and a vintage western shirt under a ratty orange sweater, purchased off its owner's back for a just-opened pack of cigarettes back in Old Grinnell College, I could easily have been mistaken for blind.

We'd come late, and the party had already begun: about fifteen people milled about, eyeing each other and carousing the white-aproned table of finger food that stood in the middle of the gallery, tilting a little on the uneven pine-plank floor. A slouchy bartender poured wine in the corner. A few people were looking at the art, jaws munching crackers and heads thrust over paltry cocktail napkins to catch the crumbs. They were in general a slovenly, homely crew—some guy was wearing overalls, another a tight little felted white cowboy hat.

Terry stood in the back of the space with his mother, near a collection of some other artist's pottery—at least I hoped it was someone else's, as I was jealous enough of the kid. He was talking to a man in jeans and a blazer, who was taking notes on a little pad. Probably a reporter, or an emissary from the MacArthur Foundation. "Developmentally Disabled Artist Wins Genius Grant"—isn't that what we all need to hear?

My brother said, "Oy."

"Stop," June said.

"What? It's good. I mean it. They're really good. Don't you think so, fatty?"

I oinked.

The piece closest to us was small and bright with primary colors. It was a backyard scene, cartoonily out of scale. Two enormous teak lounge chairs sat rigidly on either side of a cement-lipped pool the relative size of a bathtub. Behind all that were two red pots sprouting sickly palms, and behind that was a black fence, a mandarin semicircle of sun, and a blue sky thick with angry brushstrokes. It was uninformed surrealist realism. The cement felt like cement, the chairs unused, the objects overlapping their boundaries and infecting others, the way they do. He already *was* painting what he saw, and it was both dreamy and imprecise. I felt a flush of shame for how I'd treated the kid. I sighed.

"You can say that again," my brother said. Coming from his Daddy-wannabe outfit of pressed chinos and a suede jacket, it sounded dismissive of the piece, whose power was undeniable. Even so, it came out of nowhere, and so felt a little vacant. Vacancy is as vacancy does, perhaps.

"I need a drink," I said.

June turned to us, for a little troika of castigation. "I don't see what the big fucking deal is for you guys. He's an artist, and you two just can't handle it. Especially you, Drunky Montana," she said to me. "If you had any decency you'd go over there and apologize."

I sighed again, and June went to say hi to Terry, whose face brightened at the sight of her. She hugged him, though he didn't hug back, just rested his chin on her shoulder, smiling. June was the only person, other than his mother, he let touch him that way. I watched Terry's lips, which were so thin on the edges of his beard that they disappeared altogether when he smiled. He had a little niblet of something in his beard. His face had a way of going momentarily blank, like a computer monitor between Internet pages.

A guy near us, hands limp on the stroller in front of him, had just given his kids gummy worms to eat. The kid asked if you fished with gummy worms, would you catch gummy fish? "Depends," the guy said. "Are you in freshwater or sugar water?"

My brother was still looking at Terry's big pool picture. "Sugar water," he said under his breath. To me he said, "Maybe only the really screwy people can make art. Like, they are the only ones to have the right commitment. Will power. Like, I took a film class and was going to make a movie. I was going to make a movie about people in the park, and then about Rabbi Zabin. But I was only interested in those things. I didn't have a point. You have to be screwy to think there's a point."

"There doesn't have to be a point."

"And anyway," he went on, "I figured I'd never make a movie as beautiful as *Nebraska.*"

"You mean the album?"

He scowled at me. "Yeah the album."

"Hey Boss!" I put on my best Jersey accent, which wasn't very good, to say, "I got your movie right here!"

"You can joke," he said, "but you have to think big. I've always wanted to do some big project, something that means something to people. Like a movie, or an installation."

"Or toys," I offered.

He swiped at the air between us, mumbled something, and went to the treats table. It was the usual, and free, but he sniffed over it all like he was choosing between two fennel bulbs at the co-op. He poked at the last prosciutto-wrapped date, and then June was waving me over.

Terry's mother was holding her purse in front of her, so I thought it best not to offer my hand. I did take off my glasses, though. The old lady looked me in the eyes and said, "Hello again."

Terry was talking to some buddies from the group home. He was wearing a suit, very out of style, the high slacks exposing his white-socked ankles. He didn't have his Cubs hat on, but a little round pin on his lapel kept the faith. Next to it was a button that said "What Would An Artist Do?" I didn't call him on the capitalization.

"What a day, huh?" I said.

He beamed, and said how it was very exciting. He'd remember this a long, long time, he said. The day, he said, had great color, and hope.

"Listen, Terry. I'm sorry about getting on you last night."

He looked confused, then ponderous. He could have talent as an actor, too.

"I was just kidding around, but it wasn't funny. And your art is really good." I waved my arm, trying to be beneficent. "You should be proud, and I really mean that."

"Oh," Terry said.

"Well that's very nice," his mother said.

June smiled at me, I made a little repressed grin, and our party was joined by three guys who were obviously from Hope House: short, uncertain, and buzzing with ambiguously directed energy. One guy was wearing a skydiving helmet; June had told me he was afraid of head injury. The tallest one smiled and looked as if he had spruced up for this event, but the third one scowled, his sharp cheekbones set with a vague disapproval, and kept his hands in his windbreaker pockets. The three of them nodded at Terry, who bobbed a little. They said no more than strangers waiting for a bus together, and I got the sense that this was how they liked it.

"We're gonna try our hand at being artistic tomorrow," June said. "We're making a shower curtain out of gingko leaves. Hank's going to help me."

"I am?"

"You make the leaves stick by using Mod Podge. You just brush on the Mod Podge and it makes the leaves stick, and it dries clear over the leaves."

"Wow," Terry said. "I'd like to see. I've never made a shower curtain before. That would be cold."

"Cool," June corrected.

Everyone agreed this was true enough, and when June asked me to help her go next door and pick out some glasses, they started in about shower curtains at Hope House, and the tall guy made everyone crack up with some inside joke I didn't get. Even the scowling guy got a kick out of it. Terry told them there was going to be an article about him in the *Star-Tribune* in a couple days, and that they should cut out the article for him, because he doesn't get the *Star-Tribune* because he lives in St. Paul now, by the river.

June took my hand.

"We know where St. Paul is," the scowling guy said. He was back to scowling again.

"We'll get you a copy of the article," Terry's mother said to him, but he made a face like, "well, we'll just see about that."

The glasses shop was small, but we were completely ignored. Some South American music purred from a back office. Amoebic shelving held the tiny titanium wonders that were hip at that time, with no "men's" or "women's" section. I guess you were just supposed to figure it out. In the middle of the room was a low rectangular island unit with an open top filled with groomed white sand, a few well-placed frames rising up from it.

"What's with the shower curtain?" I said.

"You're going to help me. You went all Martha Stewart on that one you did for Carol Ann."

She was referring to my attempt to spruce up the bathroom, way before we decided to rip it out completely, and the memory of Carol Ann's indifference to my effort made me slouch: "like putting a Band-Aid on a sunburn," were her exact words.

"But it's your birthday tomorrow."

"Yes. Carlton's going to the studio for the day. I want some time for myself, and the shower curtain is something I want to do, and since you haven't gotten me a birthday present, you can help me."

I nodded. Really, how would one claw out of such a logically dictated demand? You'd need Derrida himself.

"Are you looking for Carlton?" I asked her.

"He's back at the gallery, talking to our friend Jim."

"No, I mean glasses."

"I know. I was making a joke. You never get my jokes. No, I'm looking for me. I need them to read."

"How much do these things cost?"

I had slipped a pair onto my face. They were round and prudish, and they made me look Charlie Chan squinty. I struck a pose for June, who simply said "No." She took them off me and replaced them with a more substantial pair, tortoiseshell brown, that made me look like a Web designer. She smiled.

"My hard drive isn't big enough for these."

She laughed and flashed me her old Jewish comic routine: "You're a funny kid," she said.

She seemed disinclined to try anything on herself, turning her nose up more than once when I brought a pair for her approval.

Finally she plucked a small square pair with almost nonexistent frames and slipped them on. "What do you think?" she said. "Carlton's taking me out for my birthday tonight, but I don't think he's gotten me anything yet. It must be a Meyerson genetic thing." In the mirror, we considered the frames, both of us suddenly serious in consideration. June moved her bangs out of her eyes and tucked them behind an ear.

Finally she said, "Well, you've redeemed yourself."

"What, Terry?" I said. "I do what I can. No, wait. I do what I'm told."

She patted my sternum like a puppy. "Good boy. Let's go outside so I can smoke."

It had gotten chillier, and I was glad for my sweater. June had her leather coat with the thin shearling wool lining, warm enough to leave unzipped. We were around the corner on the far side of the building, where the wind wasn't so bad and no one leaving or entering the gallery could see us. June brought a cigarette to her lips and lit it with a small, thin lighter that snapped an almost invisible flame. It was a clove cigarette.

"These make me sick. I can't smoke more than one at a time," she explained. "It's my sad way of making myself cut back."

"Do you realize you're wearing those glasses still?"

"Yep," she said. "Let's see if that gets their attention, because they didn't seem too concerned with me when I was trying to be a goddamn customer."

"True. And Carlton can afford bail."

"True," she said.

The clove smoke drifted past me and tumbled along the brick wall we had our backs to. A hole in the clouds ladled out some sunshine. I watched June smoke. In the glasses she looked like a disguised woman, playing it cool. To inhale, she'd turn her face sideways, and squint into the light. She picked something off her tongue with a pinch of her cigarette hand's pinky and thumb. It was complete affectation, but on June such things didn't wear thin. There was nothing shabby or common about her. Some people are just born with it.

"So what's your Master theory?"

She demurred. My brother's abuse, maybe. "No, now. I want to hear it. Maybe I'll go back and get my PhD, and this'll be my break-out study."

"You'd steal my idea?"

"In a heartbeat."

"Well I just think she was nuts. I think there was no Master."

"Who was she writing letters to, then?"

"Beats me. I think she got frustrated with her effed-up attempts at romance—that guy, the biographer?"

"Sewall."

"He showed how men were baffled by her, cuz she was so smarmy and inscrupable."

"Inscrutable."

"So I think she was frustrated and just created one guy who was all the guys wrapped into one."

I did remember, in one Master letter, how dramatic Emily was, asking her Master to open his life wide for her, or something like that. Something if you did write to an actual person would only read as sweet nothing, or maybe code.

"They burned all the Otis Lord letters they found in her room—"

"The judge she had an affair with? Master wasn't him. I've got it all dog-eared in the Seward book."

"Sewall."

"I can show you tomorrow after we do the shower curtain."

I frowned at the idea. "That damn Emily Dickinson. I didn't understand her at all, and never will. She made everything up, it was all personal—every word means something peculiar to her. It's like a twelve-year-old's diary, only intellectually over my head. Way over."

She raised an eyebrow. "We'll just uninvite her to our Mod Podge party then."

"It's nice of you to include me in that, and I want those duckies gone as much as the next guy, but you don't have to spend your birthday—"

She frowned, wrinkled her mouth to exhale away from me. "I want you there. Anyway, I don't know from Mod Podge."

"It kinda smacks of girl time."

"Well," she puffed, "dance with the one that brung ya."

After a minute she said, "What's this Montana bullshit? I'm assuming that goes in the same bullshit bin as your treatment of Terry."

"Yeah, about that. I'm really sorry."

"You already said so."

"Not to you."

She smiled, and nodded that it was ancient history.

"But I don't know. Montana sounds kinda good. Light out for the territories. Start over. A clean break heals better."

"Hmmm."

"You're dubious?"

"Can you blame me? Besides, I'd miss you. I'd be down to only one retard in my life."

"Ouch. I don't know. It's a pipe dream. It's not an answer, like you said. There's plenty else to do instead. Finish the bathroom is one. I could hit the effing gym, too."

A couple rounded the corner and approached us, arm in arm: he trim and dark with a Roman nose, she thin and be-scarfed and simply dog-paddling in earnest ardor. June blew smoke at them as they passed, but they were oblivious. A little down the block, he pulled her to him, his black lawyer's London Fog coat opening cape-like to receive her. He whispered to her, his nose in her ear like she was a complicated wine, and he was detecting maybe hints of currant and bergamot.

"You should be loved like that," June said. "You should be having sex," she added.

I felt the bricks through my sweater. "Ah, it's overrated."

"Carol Ann's damaged you. Do you think you could ever get back to normal with her?"

She looked at the cigarette in her fingers, the way smokers sometimes do, like they're having a Stockholm syndrome moment.

"Sure," I said. Then I remembered Carol Ann in the basement, under the flow of water from my bowl, and got it confused for a moment with the mean duckies on the shower curtain in my brother's place, and it all made me sad. Maybe it was a good-bye hand job, a going-out-of-business sale.

"I mean, no," I said. "Probably not."

"Men are funny. You can be emotionally hurt by a person and still let them yank your dingy."

Carlton must have told her. Or she had an uncanny way of mind reading.

"You know why I did?"

"Why?"

"None of your business, that's why."

"Well don't be like that. I'll tell *you* something." She tossed her cigarette to the ground, where it log-rolled, smoldering, over the curb. "I went back on the pill."

I bit my lip.

"I'm not ready. It doesn't feel right."

"But—"

"It's not a debate," she said. "And I haven't told him yet."

She aired out her lungs of the last of the clove smoke. There was something defiant to her I didn't like.

"I won't tell. I got enough, like, betrayal to deal with."

"But with her yanking your dingy, you must be making up."

"Yeah, that's why I want to move to Montana. For the big Montana make up convention held every year in Make Up City, with a hike up Make Up Mountain and dip in Make Up Lake followed by—"

"I get it," she said. My face must have looked a lot like Terry's at dinner after I'd laid into him. I couldn't change it before June touched my arm. "Sorry," she said. Then: "Don't you think it's strange, how we can say anything to each other?"

I shrugged. The bricks stayed put behind me. "Mishbucha."

"Wouldn't you miss it? If you went to Montana?"

"You? Of course."

She smiled like, "Damn right you would."

Then she said, "You'd miss your chance to join the family business too."

This was a joke of ours, ever since our trip to Toy Fair. There had been talk of me coming on board permanently.

"The business doesn't need any more family—seems to be doing just fine without me."

She sighed. "Sometimes I don't know. I'd like to know what the new toy is. He won't tell me, ever since I predicted Rocktopus wouldn't do well. Sometimes I wonder if he's even working on it at all." She mock gasped. "Maybe he's having an affair!"

I rolled my eyes.

"You're right," she said. "But I almost wish he would."

This seemed to come from far left field. Were it a baseball, it would have hit me in the face. Which wouldn't have been unusual.

"I think you probably want to reconsider that."

June waited. The wind came at us again. "Never mind," she said. "Go to Montana or make up with Carol Ann. Just don't let me

Mod Podge a shower curtain alone on my birthday."

Back inside the store, there was still no one to buy the glasses from. "Hello?" June said.

"Just a second," a guy called.

We stood there, and soon Carlton came in. "Christ," he said. "Where have you been? You left me with that Jim guy I hate. And you were smoking. I can smell it. It's disgusting."

"Hi honey, having a good time?" June said.

"Are you buying those?" Carlton asked June. "They look expensive."

I said I wanted some snacks, which for me meant wine. The wind at the open door frisked me through the holes in my sweater. I heard my brother yell, "Hey hello? You wanna sell glasses, or what?"

Chapter Five

I went home and putzed into the night with chores and more putzing. I called June and Carlton's place. My brother answered.

"We just got home from dinner," he said.

"Right, right."

"You're on the train," he observed.

"I'm sober as the day you were born."

He said sure, right, and that he'd jog over and take me out to sober me up. I wasn't one to object.

We took the Jetta. He lurched us onto the freeway ramp headed toward Wisconsin. My Jetta was not one of the shiny new ones they try to sell you with Nick Drake soundtracks and a free mountain bike—my Jetta was circa 1986, the last year they still made them in Germany, but was nonetheless pockmarked and rusty, a symphony of undiagnosed noises and straining motor mounts. Metallic nuggets rattled, the clutch stuck, undefined systems whined, various flanges and manifolds perspired oil and power steering fluid, and every once in a while I'd make a sharp turn and a piece of something or other would skitter across the pavement, never to be found. Other mechanicals failed periodically, like the passenger-side door handle—for anyone to ride with me, I had to open the door for them from the inside. Worse, I'd neglected its interior to the point that I could have been accused, in the backseat at least, of driving a trash car. Copies of the free Twin Cities weekly paper yellowing from sunlight, wrappers and pen caps, mugs and the muffled clankering of beer bottles, forks and baggies and Velvet Underground tapes and sticky stains of freestanding grit. Worse, it was all dampened and molded by the half-gallon mote of standing water that had found its way inside via an as-yet-undetected gap in a window seal. Still, it was mine, and it ran like a champ—a carefree, German-engineered metaphor for lord knows what. Maybe, like my old man would say, it was just apt.

Suffice to say, the driver's seat was the only place my brother could bring himself to sit. He accelerated, and the poor thing complained. "It doesn't like to go over seventy," I said.

"Hell of a car," he said. "How do you get the sunroof open?"

"It's automatic. All I have to do is crank this handle here"—I reached up and grabbed the recessed knob—"and turn it, even just a little, and the sunroof opens. *Automatically!*"

Carlton ignored me. I left the sunroof cracked a titch, a sound like our grandfather whistling through his dentures. After a while, we were still on the interstate, and when I reminded him the Jetta likes it at 3300 rpms tops, he told me to shut up, and he took the next exit and headed us into the country, down some darkened Jew-killing road. A few stop signs and a left turn later, we were pulling into a state park, the ranger office of which was dark and quiet. My brother steered the Jetta along the road into the park, leaning into the curves and leaping up a little as we pulled out of small dales. Finally there was a parking lot.

I got out of the car and stayed warm by leaning against the bumper and heated hood. Carlton stood erect and thin as a young tree in nothing but running shorts and a hooded Nebraska Cornhuskers sweatshirt. He slipped a little LED light over his head. When he flicked it on and turned to me, I had to squint. His face was darkened. "Stop it," I said.

"Come on," he said.

We took a paved trail past picnic benches and a bathroom and a scenic overlook, then took the old railroad right-of-way rail until eventually we found a set of suspicious wooden steps leading down to the St. Croix River. The river was calm and wide here, which was why the town a few miles north was called Stillwater, but the current could be deceptive. We descended beneath a half-moon onto a haven of sandbar beach that arced into the river, then cut back upstream before spindling out into a long point of stones and trees. Downstream the beach ended abruptly in more dark trees. After our hike, it was a small relief just to be quiet on the sand and watch the dark water hold itself together all around us.

We stood quiet until my brother said, "What do you think of a small rabbit, or chicken, who has a chip in him that can recognize motion, and you magnetize him to your fridge so that when you come to open it he says, 'Hey, Brando, how about a jog?'"

"Is this the big new toy? It beats the spelling teeth." The last idea he'd told me about was a set of fake teeth with different letters on them, which were re-arrangeable to spell out "Bite me" or "I luv you Donald" or something like that.

"You know it's not. It's an *idea,* something I've been fiddling with. That's the way it works. Ideas are their own beings, coming and going. A part of our own brains is always coming and going, totally out of our control. Isn't that interesting? I bet you've already thought of that, probably in grade school. Remember Mrs. Steiner? She hated me."

He looked at his thick black runner's watch, the headlamp turning it into a lurid silver dollar of light.

"Hey, I don't normally treat June like I did yesterday and today at the glasses place. She always wants to put me in my place, it feels like. Ever since we've been talking about fertility treatments. She doesn't even want to go, not even the test. It's like we're playing on different teams."

"Thank God you didn't team up on me in your kitchen."

"I don't mean that."

"Most people don't think in terms of undermining—like 'Oooh, I'm going to undermine Carlton now.'"

"Who said anything about thinking? Ninety percent of life goes on without anyone thinking a damn thing, that much I'm sure of. Like my toy ideas. They just come. It's a debt we have to pay to our people who died without having time to write down their ideas. That's the greatest tragedy—they were tricked into thinking they were going to a place where they could at least have time to think. But no. In 1942 at Treblinka it was 20 cars an hour, with 170 Jews in each car. That's 3,400 an hour. They had to give the train drivers vodka. We owe it to them to not think too much, and get the most out of life."

"Jesus," I said.

"You said it."

Up in the drizzle of stars, nothing moved. Not even a twinkle. Then, all of them did.

My knees were starting to shake, my lower jaw clattering. But my brother seemed warmed by his own generator. His knees didn't even have gooseflesh. A small breeze sent us some waves, and knocked around the various tufts of grass that sprouted like mullets up and down the beach. A drone of a boat engine sputtered somewhere upriver, someone getting a jump on a season of hardcore pleasure-crafting.

"Do you really think I'm being a pussy?"

He shrugged. He was close enough to me that I could feel it more than see it.

"I don't even know what to say to her anymore," I said. "Talking to her is like talking to a sister, or a dorm mate. She knows me so well, like what I do and what I say and how I fart and stuff—so she assumes I never have anything of value to say. A lot of people assume that, but it hurts most when A) it's your wife, and B) she's fuckin' right."

What did my brother have to say to this? "Did you know that Treblinka had a zoo?"

Finally, it pissed me off. "Just where do you get off being so morbid? What right have you got?"

I could feel my brother fuming. June told me once he threw a whisk at her; she showed me the dent in the kitchen plaster from it.

"You don't know," he said finally. "You don't know what I've been through. You were off at college, being smart, while I was limping around University of Fucking Omaha nursing my knee. And when Mom died, you had Carol Ann to run to. I had zilcho."

His knee had been the reason for his quitting Hutchinson and baseball in general. Ostensible reason, that is. A few years ago, it was "I could have been pro, except for the knee." Always with the knee.

"That means you get to talk about the Holocaust all the time?"

"You want to talk about something? No one's stopping you."

"I've talked enough for tonight. But you don't know what I've been through either, so I'd prefer it if you'd keep your fucking opinions about my pussiness to yourself."

He didn't say anything, which left only the waves talking, and theirs is an awkward language, not languid like people think. More like a couple's argument, seductive only in its sheer monotony. The modern lullaby, which I'd heard in its entirety. Plus, the day's alcohol had sieved through me by then, leaving me sour, and my lower back was killing me.

"Look, it's freezing balls out here," I said. "We're lucky we're not dead. Take me home, or I'm leaving you here."

He muttered something, stripped off his sweatshirt and T-shirt, then kicked off his shoes and shorts and underwear and ran into the water. It was apparently quite shallow off the beach, for he was running a long time, lifting his knees high to reduce the water's drag on his stride, his ass white and dimpled at the hip sockets. Even in the water, he ran effortlessly. That old thrilling jealously, him tucking the football into his abdomen and lowering his head into the Gentile scrum, made me salivate. When he dove, he sank completely out of sight, then emerged with a gasping whoop, something self-congratulatory but otherwise unintelligible under his splashing.

It's funny the things brothers remember. His view of when Mom died: he had zilcho, I had Carol Ann. It was a little more complicated than that. The spring of my senior year in college, Carol Ann was talking wildly about marriage. The situation with her poor unmarried Aunt Jeanne had her riled. "It's *men,*" she said, "men who just want to dip their toes. Men are afraid of real intimacy. And she's wasted half her life waiting."

I went home to Omaha around this time to surprise my mother on her birthday. I took the Greyhound, straight shot down I-80, and it was a normal enough weekend, my mother on cloud nine to have me there—and without, I suspected, Carol Ann. I brought her no present. I probably talked, as best I could, about my widely acclaimed paper on the critical responses to Kate Chopin's *The Awakening* and the theories behind them. I'm sure I talked down to her, to them all. My brother especially, who by then was taking classes in something or other at the University of Nebraska, Omaha (UNO—University of No Opportunity). I don't know what specifically, whatever ex-athletes lean on when their knees give.

I try to go easy on myself for all my uppity-ness. It was generated out of love for my college life. The hippies smoking dope cross-legged in a sunny oval on south campus. The precisely spoken professors quoting Homer—Homer! The hardcore feminists who learned to laugh loud and grow their armpit hair. The women's rugby team performing beer calisthenics on Mac Field. The giant oaks barnacled with squirrels; the drafty brick dorms, coed down to the bathrooms. The anarchy of bikes, squeaky polemics against materialism, chained to listing racks in the south campus loggia. Think of it: I went to school at, and thereby spent the majority of my time at, a place whose architecture included a loggia. I went to school where they had an award called the Beulah Bennett Loring Prize for Excellence in English Literature—a prize I would win without even knowing it existed! Me, in my shlubby corduroys and shlubbier attitude. I went to school where people *tried* to be shlubby—with help maybe from a J.Crew charge account, but still. I went to school where darkened parties might turn naked at any moment, where bands like Soul Asylum and Uncle Tupelo played dorm basements, and as long as you weren't a Republican or a pervert, you were welcomed in and handed a beer. No, that's just a joke—the perverts got in just fine.

It wasn't Nirvana, but it felt like it. To me it felt sophisticated in an uppity, torn-jeans and stacked-syllabus way, and I exploded onto every computer terminal and classroom chalkboard. I couldn't understand the students who didn't want to study—come on, we're taking philosophy, and taking it seriously! And Chaucer. I loved every word that guy wrote, even misunderstanding them as I did, and even though I got a B-. For the record, it was my only B-. But in my family, no one even knew who Chaucer was. If forced to guess, they would have said he was a dog, a famous one in old movies. Maybe Abbott and Costello's dog, the one who unravels the mummy. A regular cut-up, little Chaucer, always chasing his Canterbury tail.

Anyway, Sunday night after Mom's birthday, I was to catch the bus back to Grinnell at 8:15. Mom took me downtown to the station since Dad had to exercise off our big Sunday evening meal. Carlton was lord-knows-where.

We parked across the street at a meter and walked together to buy my ticket. I had only my backpack, stuffed with books and toiletries and the day before's pair of underwear. The ticket agent told me the bus was close to capacity and that I might not even get a seat. No one seemed to know for sure, even the driver, whom they rustled up via radio. But never fear, there was another coming at 10:15, only it was a local—it would take Highway 6 and stop in every hick town that had a post office. Oy, Greyhound, I miss you not.

My mother and I sat to wait. Sitting and waiting was something we did well.

Susie and Daniel Meyerson, I'd learned long ago, were a package pair and, on most everything, presented the sincerest of united fronts. Yet she could calm me like he couldn't, and often gave in where he held firm. It was a matter of reading where things sat and just playing the odds. I'm talking about small stuff like having ice cream or staying out later than curfew, but it held true for larger life moments too. And sitting in the orange-upholstered chairs of the sketchy bus terminal, I was about to have one.

"Mom," I said, "you don't have to stay."

"I'll stay."

"It's late. And I'll get on one way or another. Eventually, I mean."

"I'll stay for the 8:15, then we'll see."

"Okay Mom," I said.

I sighed. I was antsy to get back to my real life, and the chaotic terminal seemed to mock me. There were two exits to the street, and some cat or another kept finding reason to open, step through, come back through, or otherwise shout out each of them. The 7:30 from St. Louis was late, but I didn't think that accounted for all the commotion. Didn't these people have GEDs to study for? The station was already cramped with a Lysol-scented oppression and vulnerable-looking travelers scuttering duffels and such over hyper-waxed linoleum. We all had one thing in common: none of us really wanted to be there.

My mother's calm made it worse: the loose way she wore her purse over her shoulder and kept opening it to rummage, and the way she crossed one leg over the other and bounced it liberally, her Tretorns bright as fresh paint. I was very sensitive back then about my class position, which seemed to me to be precarious, as if every working-class person I encountered was as outraged as I was on their behalf and was looking for someone to hold responsible. This is ignorance at its height, but back then I sort of rolled in ignorance. It kept me from sticking anywhere, like a dusting of fresh flour on kneaded dough.

"If I'd married rich," Mom said, "we could hire a helicopter."

"We'd *own* a helicopter."

"Someday you'll publish your novel and buy us one."

This was our family's perennially favorite game: "When you kids get rich…" First it was Carlton's baseball career, then my potential to be a doctor or lawyer, which certainly I had. Now that it was plain I'd be a literary stupe for life, the hopes had been pinned on some novel I was supposed to write. It would be tragic and intelligent, but also a mystery, or maybe a legal thriller—because only those kinds of writers could even hope to own a helicopter.

"Of course," I said.

"But I wasn't smart enough to marry for money. I was too young."

This was a joke, since my mother had clearly married for love—her knight in shining armor rescuing her from the drapes salesman's total eclipse. But since the origins of their marriage were rarely discussed, the drapes salesman banished to Silence City, it was an intriguing comment. Weighty. Had we been another family, we might have gone on to make comparisons between our situations, hers then and mine now. How *did* you decide to marry Dad? How rough was it to overcome the drapes salesman? Do you think I am more or less prepared to take a similar leap than you were? Can someone as young as me even *be* prepared? Is it okay to be this uncertain? Should I be up at night worrying about it?

But my mother wasn't a talk-it-all-out girl. She was a sitter. So we sat.

I sighed.

"Big sigher, you are. When did you get so serious?"

I chuckled and slid down in my seat. "I don't know. Am I? I guess I just think too much."

"You always did that. Something would happen in the world, something bad, and you'd go into your room and close the door to write about it."

"That sounds about right."

"Do you remember scratching 'Help Me!' into the underside of the basement table?"

"Yeah. I was playing some pretend game."

"You always had guys after you. I'd say, 'who?' And you'd say 'guys, Mom, guys!'"

"A boy needs friends."

"Carlton got more attention, I know."

I winced, re-crossing my legs. I saw myself sulking in the Burke High bleachers watching my brother burst from first base to steal second, springing nearly out of his cleats. He would ask the ump for time to brush himself down, then set his chin low and menace the pitcher with a ridiculous leadoff. But rather than cheer, I'd clamber down and sludge my way home. The little torpid failings that family is famous for—few of us ever outlive them.

"Yes!" I wanted to say. "He sure goddamn did!" But then I remembered him at Mom's birthday party the night before—sullen and unusually quiet, and when he did talk, it was too loud and showily brash, giving Mom a gold necklace with no drop or anything and then showing her how to wear it, like she was a teenager or a whore—and I thought, "He's a loser. My big brother the baseball star. He's turned into a loser."

"I don't think 'help me' was about that," I said to Mom. "I was a pirate, I think, but a good one. A good pirate in a world where people think very poorly of pirates, and most pirates prove them right. You can see my predicament."

"What are you going to do after graduation?"

This was a little abrupt, even for Mom. I went glib. "I'm looking at opportunities."

"Still want to be a professor?"

"Eventually."

"Take your time. It's hard to see you grown up, you're just a baby to me."

"Mom, why are you being so emotional?"

"I don't know." She made her face, her pursed lips and wrinkled nose. Then it was the sighing and the quick shake of her head to clear it away. I'd seen it hundreds of times, and considered it my inevitable inheritance, seeing as how she hadn't married for money— I'd get an overwaxed but otherwise immaculate Chrysler Le Baron, a mountain of debt from Kidsville, and this look. "I don't like bus stations," she said. "Your father does. He's much more practical than me. He appreciates people more."

"I don't know about that."

"He doesn't show that side of himself much, not to you boys. You," she chuckled, "should see him at the food shelter." As a couple, they donated food and volunteered at least once a year. Usually it involved some Kidsville employees too, so I'd always thought of it as a marketing PR stunt more than anything, but that was simplistic and cynical.

"Mom, I think I'm going to get married."

"I know," she said.

I could only laugh. "You what?"

"I can tell. It's all over you."

This didn't sit well. Two guys were hooting about something over at the exit, stepping in and stepping out, then back in again. Everyone else had found a seat by now, and had enough dignity to keep up the depressive shtick bus stations are famous for.

"Well," I said, "this isn't the official word. Just a heads-up, or whatever."

The 8:15 had arrived, though all I could see were its headlights in the garage, and the agent, in grey mustache and starched blue company necktie, was giving us the signal that he would check to see if there was a seat for me. It was if he were auditioning for the role of station agent.

"Well," she said, standing and tightening her purse strap to her shoulder, "it's good to know that at least I get a heads-up. I must be moving up in the world." She punched me lightly in the arm.

"It's just an expression," I said.

"Why don't we talk about it some more before the 'official word' comes down from on high? And you can give me more heads-up about anything. I won't bite. I'm your mother."

She smiled. She gave me a long hug, so it was a good thing there was room for me on the 8:15—exactly one seat—or else it would have been awkward to have to go through a second good-bye. I pulled myself away, gave her the confident smile I knew she was looking for, and trotted over to the idling bus. All the way down I-80, cramped next to a snoring Latino who smelled of lavender, I marveled at her: a mother knows. *My* mother knows, and she won't bite. All these years I'd been wanting her to bark, and here she was promising not to bite. Still mothers run deep. The old man was a barker; to put it literarily, he was bureaucratic text, all directives and blunt memoranda. Susie, my mom—she was turning out to be a more nuanced read, a richness I never gave her credit for. My world that night, in the humming jitter seep of bus-window darkness, became something I never thought it could—as generous with backward potential as with forward. It moved me to tears.

But I never called her—not with anything more than the usual patter, at least. After all, I had a big study of modernist novelists to complete, cinching my lock on the Beulah Bennett Loring Prize for Excellence in English Literature, and then there was graduation with all the Mom and Dad routine of "can we get extra programs for the scrapbook" and "you should wear a tie more often," and then there was finding an internship at a literary press, which I did, in Minneapolis. And finally the actual move to Minneapolis, and signing a lease with Carol Ann.

Just in time for the big bang. Mom was in her LeBaron, in the left lane of a major four-lane thoroughfare in Omaha called Dodge Street, apparently waiting to make a left turn. A guy in a pickup coming behind her was trying to switch lanes to get around her, rather than get stuck waiting behind her like a stupe. We are a country of people who don't want to be stupes: when drivers merge onto the interstate, immediately they get out of that slowpoke right-hand lane, no matter what traffic's like. Why? Because they don't want to be stuck with the stupes! Going slow-pokey like a stupe? Not gonna catch me stuck going the speed limit, no fucking way. None of us want to be stupes, and especially not the pickup guy, caught like a pussy behind some woman turning left—not him!

So Mr. Pickup looks over his shoulder to check the right lane, looks back too late, and suddenly he and a Monte Carlo coming the other direction are mashed up in a Mom sandwich. That deep, crushing sound no one can quite believe, the screech and scutter of hubcaps. I don't know if it would be worse to have seen it, lived it, or have to imagine it. But we don't get choices like that, for better or worse.

She died on impact, relatively untouched, thanks to her seatbelt, except for massive trauma to the head. The Monte Carlo driver had to have several bones bolted back together and a cheek rebuilt, but Mr. Pickup-Not-a-Stupe walked away with a broken collarbone and, because the DA deemed the whole thing merely a tragic accident, a citation. To him I say, would it have killed you to wait for my mother to make her turn? A few extra seconds out of your day—would it really have been that hard on you? As hard as, say, not having a mother anymore?

Oh well. The point is, it was only a few weeks later that I took a walk one night up Hennepin Avenue to the Walker and back, got a hot dog from the vendor who tried to make a go of it there for a while, squirted mustard onto my T-shirt, and came home in tears telling Carol Ann she was my whole world and that I wanted it that way forever. I told her where else was I going to go? What else was I going to be? She was all I had; she was my world.

Carol Ann cried too. Her nose leaked onto my shoulder, standing in our new apartment that was no bigger than a dorm room, really. It smelled dormish too—a brew of sweat and storage-basement must and Pine Sol. We'd been there two months, but still there were unopened boxes stacked against a wall, and one supporting the TV. There was a pile of laundry to do by the door. The world doesn't stop abruptly in Minneapolis just because your mother does in Omaha, and Carol Ann was living proof. I'd returned from my walk to find her skinny in her jean shorts and tank top laying new contact paper in the kitchen cabinet shelves, and this got me going more than anything. Our little apartment, cramped with this huge life lesson on opportunities lost in a split second, my mustard stain—it ignited in me a reverence for life, the life I'd created: Boxes in a corner, fresh contact paper in the cabinets, a lovely woman to come home to who understands your sniffled revelations. It was a life of new apartments and still-unmarried aunts and Beulah Bennett Loring Prizes for Excellence in English Literature and *Little House on the Prairie* reruns and pesto pasta sauces made on the cheap with walnuts and coffee shop jobs to support our true youthful passions—and more and more to come! More of everything to come, Carol Ann, I can just feel it. So marry me, Carol Ann, marry me. I won't bite.

Carol Ann held me and said how much she'd been wanting to hear that. She told me to take off my shirt so she could soak that stain. Then she said that she needed to think about it. Just, you know, it was a big decision. She'd let me know in a couple of days.

When my brother, still damp from his swim, pulled us up to my house, my house lights were on, each goddamn one of them, it seemed. Must have been from all my putzing. Putzing needs light.

"You're having a party," Carlton said.

He was out of the car before I could tell him he should go ahead and take the Jetta to drive himself home. He'd already had enough hardship—the cold water, which he said was a "Polar Bear Club" thing he'd gotten into but had been too wimpy to actually do this winter, so he'd started in the relative warmth of spring. He had sand in his toes, which was unavoidable but bugged him into a sulky silence the whole ride home. He didn't like admitting to being a wimp, either.

"Look," he said, "I don't care what you do about Carol Ann. You're not a pussy. I just want you to be happy. I've never known you not to be happy, and—and it makes me upset."

I nodded. Steve barked from the house, once.

He reached to his face and flipped on the miner's light, a blue flare literally defacing him in shadow. I thought I saw him smile though. Maybe not. He turned and ran off into the night.

Chapter Six

On Sunday morning I woke to rain. Thank the lord, too, for there is little more depressing about a Sunday morning than waking up to midday sunshine flooding the mayhem of your life. Little ATM slips and credit card receipts in the cubby of a bedroom shelving unit, socks, coins, stacks of paper, books unread, files unfiled—somehow a rainy day lets you off the hook.

Our house was a one-story, with a mansard-roofed 18 x 15 room tacked on as an upstairs—whose floor we had sanded but whose wainscoting we never got around to repainting—and a cramped fifties kitchen leading to two back bedrooms the size of cut-rate cruise ship cabins. There were none of the built-ins that bungalows are famous for, no buffets or mirrors or tiger-oak archways between rooms—Carlton's place had all those, but ours did not. We'd invested in a good two walls' worth of houseplants, and done some accent tiling here and there, and painted the front door purple, but otherwise we'd kind of abandoned decorating, and ignored upkeep altogether. Paint was peeling here and there in the living room, which was big and airy but ran the width of the lot and felt wrong somehow—probably bad feng shui—and had little of the nice light of Carlton's place due to the recent upward expansion of the neighbor to the south. There was an amoeba-shaped water stain on the ceiling (what other shape do they come in?) from an as-yet-undetermined roof leak, and the floors were wood but worn gray here and there, and warped elsewhere. As a whole, the place was snagged with the random layabouts of a life sort-of lived in unison: hats and gloves in all three drawers of the chest we got at a garage sale—I'd talked the woman down from twenty-five bucks to eighteen—threadbare pillows in disarray on the couch; the day's day-to-day purchases slumping in their plastic bag against the wall and baseboard; plants and extension cords and speaker wire and scratches in the wood and burned down candles and dishes in the sink, and beneath the sink scouring powder and vinegar and old boxer shorts used now as rags; a serving platter overflowing with mail and keys and Post-it reminders, floppy disks and file folders meant to mean something in color code. The baseboards had been over-scuffed, and the moldings bulged with loose nails and a half-inch layering of paint. The windows were streaked with Steve's nose juice, the sills if not rotting were giving it some good thought. The back porch listed. And don't even get me started on the backyard, friend only to Steve and her bladder.

It was Steve and her bladder who got me out of bed, whimpering and amber-eyed at my bedside. I went down with her and let her out, watching her track-and-sniff her way to an acceptable spot. On her way back she stopped to sniff a moldering Kit Kat wrapper that had blown over the fence. Or maybe I tossed it there. I went out to get it, feeling the damp chill of loneliness.

These are times we should leave well enough alone, but that's hindsight talking. Steve went to her bed in the living room to lick the damp off her, and I followed to the couch. With the rain having let me off the hook, I decided to get back on by calling Carol Ann's hotel room.

I could envision her there, still in bed due to the time change. Overlooking her notes from Saturday's sessions so she could make smart connections at the postmortem later that day. Thinking about cantaloupe for breakfast, and also pleased with herself—how much better it is to be on her side of the mirrored glass, the chummy side, the in-the-know side. She'd always told kids in junior high "secrets don't make friends," but really they do. A quick delicious lick of memory is all she allows then, just enough to validate but not engulf. Her hands trying new caresses, and her reward of an honest-to-Pete orgasm. The repulsive pride of "I did that, I went that far." The abyss of self-ignorance, in a hotel with lime green walls. She and her lover had never done it in a hotel room, which seemed to her like a saving grace, a line she hadn't wanted to cross. Never in the house, either. It helped, some, with the marsh of guilt inside her, like trying to jog after Chinese food.

In her bag, unpacked, were two options for the day's outfit. She'd be trying them out in her head, fighting a latent fear of choice, which had never served her well—always choosing from options that themselves were already poisoned—when my call rings her phone.

At first it was pleasant enough—I told her I'd pick her up at the airport later that evening, and she told me her focus groups were going well. All these different women she'd gotten to watch, via a one-way mirror, as they interacted with a moderator and an array of would-be snacks—it satisfied her voyeuristic and professional curiosity. These women, they weren't necessarily snacky—they were just the primary "family managers," whatever that meant (some had jobs, some no), of households with median incomes over seventy grand.

"There was this one woman," Carol Ann said, "Irish looking, with a bad haircut."

"Bad how?"

"Too much face. She was tough to read. Always looked ready to cry."

"Snacks are powerful."

"It's amazing how the big-boobed women do most of the talking," she said. "They talk with their boobs, honestly. They stick their boobs out, and it's worst when they're trying to talk over someone else."

"So," I said, "you're alone?"

"Hank, please."

But she owed me, so I waited.

"Yes, of course I am," she said.

"Carol Ann?"

"What, baby?"

"Was that a charity hand job?"

"I won't fight with you over the phone."

"No, no—"

"No, *you* no—"

"No I mean it. I really—I want to know. Because it's important. It shouldn't be charity. Maybe you need the opposite of charity, a passion. Or maybe you need a little charity yourself. Who doesn't? Things aren't as simple as my old man's day. He just decided, you know, 'Okay, I have a family now, God bless them. Now where's the cash register?'"

"But it doesn't matter."

"Well, that's *your* opinion. Or your lawyer's."

Only a small pause, but it was enough of a mea culpa for her to dive nose first into. "My lawyer doesn't tell me what to do, and she doesn't matter. What matters is why you're not forgiving me."

She started to cry. I could see it all: her lower lip puffed out, her face slick, and her entire body slumped into some hotel room recliner with spastic upholstery.

"I really really really didn't think you'd feel like this," she went on. "I thought—it's hard to understand what I was thinking. I wasn't."

I realized then that I was still holding the Kit Kat wrapper. What, do I have Alzheimer's? Am I a glutton for trash, for the spent and discarded?

"Not forgiving you?" I said. "Not forgiving you?"

"Don't get mad at me."

"You get to not think, and then I'm the bad guy for not forgiving? You know where that leaves me? Holding your Kit Kat wrapper."

"I know, baby."

"You don't," I said, and I hung up. I tried to do it hard, but on a cordless phone it's just a button, so I flung the thing across the room and, slumped as I was on the couch, kicked the lamp next to me, battering it to the wall and down to the floor in a satisfying crash.

Steve was up off her bed, alarmed and cowering. She came over and sniffed at me. "Well," I said to her, "she doesn't."

"Of course you're angry," June said. "Fucking A right—you should be angry. You have to be angry before you can forgive."

"It scares her. She'll leave me."

"So what?"

"Togetherness, that's what."

"You can't mandate happiness, Hank. You have to let it come."

"Let it come!" I said. "Who's stopping anybody from coming? Let anyone who will, come."

She leaned out over the shower curtain and drooped her head to laugh. We were kneeling by it on her living room floor, but were at this point only positioning the gingko leaves, trying them in different formations, and so there was no Mod Podge to get in her hair or anything. A gingko leaf did, and I plucked it free when she raised herself back up again.

Outside, it was an unusually warm April day. The clouds were making their way toward Wisconsin. All bad weather moves east eventually. Another reason to go to Montana.

If that doesn't make sense, it might be because June had the classical music station on, and we were stoned.

"Well, you're finally dressed for the occasion," she'd said when I showed at the door. She meant I looked ready to work, since I had on the same slop I usually wore.

"You didn't tell me this was going to be work!"

This she'd understood as a joke, and laughed, a smooth sound in a house that was as still and quiet as I'd ever seen it, not even the backyard maple tree cracking its knuckles. When I put my clean clothes down on the dining room table, I saw a little baggie of small white pills. Not birth control pills.

"What are these?"

"Oh," she said. She gulped a giggle. "I shouldn't have left those out. It's Percocet. Once in a while I take a few and watch *Friends* reruns. It's wonderfully boring."

I looked at the bag, which was the kind its manufacturer would call heavy-duty—plastic as thick as your credit card, almost, it will be in a landfill for thousands of years. I rolled a few pills between my forefinger and thumb, gawking like an orangutan.

"Are you going to study them," June said, "or take a few?"

The first thing I noticed was a weakness in my knees, and I don't mean figuratively—they felt as if from mere walking, my lower legs might snap off altogether. But when I'd finally mitigated this sensation through the taking of small steps—I decided small steps were better anyway—I came into a feeling of well-being. As poor uninvited Emily might have said to her Master, I was *plashless,* the normally sharp world around me blunted by pure goodwill. The new shower curtain, for instance, when spread on the living room floor, had a comforting slickness, a pleasing acrid aroma of new plastic, and even the little hairs and dust motes it'd picked up, which surely would get lodged into the Mod Podge, seemed there for a purpose. I was without comment, and soft, and Styrofoamed, and slow. Slow was way better. Whatever happened to that op-ed piece I was going to write when President Clinton allowed states to raise the speed limit? "A Literature Lover Makes the Case for Lowering the Speed Limit." Yeah, that would have told them. Another "so what?"

June laughed at me. Primed, we settled to the project.

One hour later, the die-cast pewter alarm clock on the armoire above us had only ticked off fifteen minutes. Maybe it was an hour and fifteen. How should I know? Like Carol Ann said, I was taking my own time.

I laughed at my own non-joke, which didn't need to be uttered. "This is good shit," I said.

June was studying the schematic of our shower curtain, spread as it was like a bed sheet or picnic blanket. She had given up telling me to get angry; for the next couple of hours at least, anyone getting angry was very unlikely. We had knelt ourselves at a corner of the square, pondering the layout. The gingko leaves were flat and yellowish, which was good because if they were green they'd rot under the Mod Podge. My shower curtain for Carol Ann had done exactly that, which of course she'd noticed, aloud, which of course made me throw it out.

"Terry has a fucked-up immune system," she said, "sometimes he breaks out with shingles. It hurts him, so they give him Percocet, but—"

"Whoa. You get this from Terry?"

"Yeah. That's not unethical, is it?" We laughed good and hard at this, and then she said that he didn't like them because they made him squirmier than he already was.

"Not me. They un-squirmy me."

It was time to affix the leaves. No turning back, since the old curtain was already in the trash, June said. She produced a cheap, wide paintbrush, and Mod Podge that she'd poured into a plastic sour cream container. White and milky, it looked like sour cream, too. I assured her it would dry clear as a sunny day.

"Funny," she said, "but I figured you'd ramble on about something or other. When you took the pills, I mean. I was like 'Oh boy, here we go.' But I have to trust you. We know one another pretty well. Trust is key to that. Anyway, the worst you could have done is bitch about A) Carol Ann, or B) The Project."

"As to B," I said, "if it doesn't work, I'll just hire a team of illegals to finish it off. I'll claim they are relatives. 'Jose, you are my *tío*, right? Jose, I need you to be my tío on this. *Entiende?* It's *muy importante* for you to be my tío this week.'"

"See," she said, laughing, "you're worth the risk."

"Obviously, or you wouldn't pump me with pills and hand me a paintbrush full of Mod Podge in your living room." I sat back on my knees and looked around. "Christ, I just might Mod Podge the shit out of this place."

She was bent over to affix the first leaf, and she shot her head my direction, sideways and low, cracking up but trying to keep her body solid so she wouldn't flick Mod Podge everywhere.

"Mod Podge the walls, the kitchen floor, the couch, the dining room table—" I said. "Do the Mod Podge in a nice square," I advised, "because when it dries you'll still be able to see the Mod Podge some."

She was still laughing, but she took my advice. Her tongue was sticking out of her lips a little. "Please please please stop saying Mod Podge," she said.

I made a little bow, though she wasn't looking at me. "Princess, your m-mod is my p-podge."

"Anyway what happened to 'it dries clear as a sunny day'?"

"It's just a little opaque, but if you just slap it on, it looks white trashy. That's what Carol Ann said. Actually, she didn't bother with the grammar. She said, 'It looks white trash.'"

Just then the clouds broke, and the living room flooded with light. The bay window was downright dewy with it. Outside beyond the porch, the enameled Brinks Security sign flamed with it. I could smell it in my throat. Even the radio's Bach concerto—Bach, mind you—took an upturn with it, foaming into a sunny cascade of chords. It was too much. June already had three gingko leaves painted onto the shower curtain.

I imagined the old shower curtain in a city dump heap, eaten by battery acid, bloody with pizza sauce—the sad limbo of our non-biodegradable trash. "Poor duckies," I said.

The gingko leaves were perfect, the simplest, most elegant shape I'd ever seen. I plucked one from the bowl and let it flutter to the floor.

She laughed and shook her head. "One time he said to me, he said, 'It's not special if we do it all the time.' I mean sex. And off he went into the bathroom to beat off. I was *right there in the bed,* and off he goes with a *GQ.*"

"*GQ?*"

"Winona Ryder was on the cover."

I made my rabbinical palms-up shrug.

"You too?" she said. "Ugh. I don't get her. All the boys like her."

"We like her because with her, there's actually a chance of doing her."

"You like 'em bitchy is what I think. And I don't bitch enough. I ought to bitch more. Look at Carol Ann. You won't leave her, even with what she's done. I should bitch more."

"Well, you might as well bitch now. When else will you get the chance?"

"Okay," she said. She didn't seem to switch gears any, just steadied herself over the shower curtain and kept painting. "He eats like a pig, Hank. He snarfs it in. Have you noticed? The way his jaw shakes when he's raising a fork to his mouth? It's like he's feeding a machine."

"Coal down the chute. Dad does it too."

"And everything is against him, nothing goes his way. Like he'll come home from reading and brainstorming at the coffee shop and complain that they were taking deliveries the whole time, with the truck idling and fuming and the delivery guy coming and going and slamming the door, and how it ruined it for him and how that always happens to him, and how he couldn't even think straight because of it. So I'll say, 'Oh that sucks, I'm sorry, baby,' and he'll look at me like I'm an idiot and say, 'I didn't say I was a baby, and anyway it's my fault for going during peak delivery time.' Like he's been in the coffee shop business all his life and should know better."

She had her face all screwed up, and relaxed it now to breathe.

"Oh more," I said, "please!"

"We were in bed once, and I was trying to start some action, and he said…you know what he said?"

"No."

"He said, 'You know what turns me on? A clean fucking house.'"

What do you say to this? Neither of us had a clue.

"And he doesn't admit being out of line, ever. We've gotten used to the Holocaust thing, but when you think of it, it's weird. Always just bringing it up, for no reason. This many Jews died here, or how soup was better eaten frozen than lukewarm. Always talking about it, out of the blue. Bone sediment in the Vishla River or whatever. And *I'm* the weird one for wanting to watch a George Clooney movie?"

She stopped again to breathe, still bent over the shower curtain. Gingko leaves were getting placed and Mod Podged with seemingly no effort, as if the words tumbling past her lips simply made it so.

"And always on the phone with your father—I cannot even come close to understanding what that's all about."

"Business."

"Yeah, maybe."

"Has to be. What else is there? I'm not on the phone with either of them all the time because I'm not in business. I don't do money. I spend money, but that's it. Carol Ann says I should get a job, start thinking practically."

"She's afraid of paying you alimony."

"Ha! I should make her."

"Did you know that he's been to Catholic Mass a couple times? Communion and everything."

"What?"

"Yup. He says it gives him a sense of peace, and he can just come home from it. It's not as weird as working with retards, he says."

"Don't you go to hell for taking communion if you weren't baptized?"

"He was."

I stared at her.

"What?" she said. "You didn't know that? You were too. Your biological father was Catholic. Carlton did the research."

"Holy shit." I knelt there. "*Holy* shit."

"And see, he didn't tell you, did he? Secrets! He's got so many secrets. He holds himself back, and that's not what I expected when I signed on, whatever it was I was signing on to, I don't know. I wasn't expecting passion, but I wasn't expecting this, either. His own brother—never told him he was baptized."

"Maybe my bar mitzvah cancels it out," I said.

She grabbed my arm then, at the wrist. Nearly all the gingko leaves were affixed by now, and I hadn't done a damn thing but enjoy myself. June looked up at me. I was expecting her to say, "Do some work!" or something, but instead she looked close to tears.

"Don't tell him I told you about the birth control pills. You won't, right, you won't?"

Ripple on the face of June. I couldn't have spoken fast enough to smooth it, even without the Percocet. "Sure," I said. "It can be our hobby. I need a hobby, like Carlton and his Polar Bear Club."

"His what?" she said.

The only thing the Percocet really did was unfold the day like a picnic blanket in the grass. Quietness, smoothness. A crisp square of us. I know for sure that the Percocet did not make me say things I wouldn't have otherwise. June had been right—we could say anything to each other. I could have filled her in on Carlton's cold-water swimming, and probably some other things, but what did that matter? She didn't particularly care to know about it, and rightly—at the moment it was beside the point.

"Anyway," June said. "He's not as bad as all that. He's just nuts. He told me he went nuts after your mother died, but I figured he was just being dramatic. He was trying to get me to marry him at the time. Do you know what happened to him when your mother died?"

I shook my head.

"More secrets. Anyway," she said again, "he must be nuts because he thinks you're in love with me." She wiped something from her eye with the back of her wrist. "He says, why else would he still be nancying around with Carol Ann? To divorce Carol Ann, or even fix things up, means starting over, but he doesn't want to start over because he has it pretty good, right where he wants to be. This is Carlton speaking," she added, "just to be clear."

She looked at me. "Let's hang this up to dry," she said.

In the bathroom, I remember June's hands were nimbly working the new curtain onto the curtain rings—the expensive, smooth-rolling kind, of course. She was on her tippy toes, her T-shirt riding up her torso and her jeans pulling down to reveal smooth, honey-colored skin puckered by a small scar. I was next to her doing pretty much the same thing, only not on tippy toes, and not honey-colored, and not nimbly. The rings unclasped awkwardly, and threading them through the new curtain's holes required laughable precision. My arms floated with ache, my hands more like hooves.

Then the curtain was up. It was the outside curtain, the one that wouldn't touch water, and this was good because the Mod Podge wouldn't stand up to it over time anyway, water being the most powerful thing on earth.

We laughed at it, wrinkled our noses at the petroleum plastic smell. We laughed at ourselves in the bathroom mirror—our fleshiness, our satisfaction, our hands on our hips. We were suddenly in such good moods. The past, our Mod Podged gripes—none of it could touch us. There were no more clouds passing over the sun, but each moment we stood there was like the sun coming out again, fresh, into the bathroom's lone window, even though it was an eastern window and by now the day was well into afternoon. Bach was still on the radio—it must have been a symposium or something, a teach-in on Bach. Was it Bach's birthday? It had recently been Lou Reed's; I knew that because we used to have a party in his honor back at Old Grinnell College, with side billing for Jon Bon Jovi and Mikhail Gorbachev, who also share the date.

I'd like to know when an action begins. With the movement of arms, with a feeling in the fingers? Or before that, the neuron-snap of the brain commanding movement? Or before that even, back to the start of the day, the opening of the eyes, or the arrival of the weekend, the departure of an airplane, the conception of loved ones, the conception of ourselves, the conception of Jon Bon Jovi? Impossible to tell, really, as is the way of most things. For instance, who closed the bathroom door, and who turned on the shower water? I couldn't possibly have done both. No way. I was already quaking in the knees and prattling on about how my original conception of a master's thesis hadn't been that bad, because as different as they were, both Dickinson and Ed Ruscha ended up in similar places. They each took words and reinvented them, completely, until they were brand-new things, things never heard or seen before. They each framed themselves in and then violated the frame, over and over and over. And then I was saying how my brother couldn't be all that dumb, because after all, I was over here all the time, and when I wasn't here I was usually thinking of here.

"Meaning you," I said, and after that it was all I could muster to touch her cheek, and her hair, and allow myself to fall toward her for those first kisses, which seemed as wobbly as my knees and my hands as they helped pull June's T-shirt over her head and unbutton my own shirt so that it dropped to the tile floor with, suddenly, everything else.

That was it. A look up, and there was June, smiling at me, bare and serene and unburdened, biting her lower lip and scratching lightly at some itch below her breast, then feeling the water with her left hand, her right holding onto the new shower curtain, perilously close to one of the not-yet-dried gingko leaves. I moved, at that point, only to guide her hand away from the leaf, because it really would have been a shame to ruin even a smidgeon of our hard work, but June took it, my hand, and, holding herself steady with it, said, "Thanks" and got into the shower, her skin disappearing behind the smiling gingko leaves and the double layer of clear plastic, her hand still holding mine and now pulling me in with her, the water pop-hissing off us while I kissed first her fingertips—they were fragrant with Mod Podge—and then up her now-wet arm, her dented elbow, her shoulder, chubby but toned from hauling around the lion's share of her life, then her neck, smooth and patient, her chin so small and perfect, her mouth. It was like honey, or ice cream—it was as slow and fat and delicious and as free as a long Saturday afternoon during her namesake month, when everything, at least up here in the great high Midwest, finally begins to grow.

Of course, all this is from the guy fucking his brother's wife.

And is there any other way to say it? Lovemaking? Expressing our passion? Consummating a connection sparked long ago? Sure, yes, and yes again. But I remember laughing and kissing every part of her face. I remember the distinct feeling that just kissing would be enough, though standing naked in the shower pretty much made sure that wasn't going to be the case. I remember her small, flat feet, and her damp brown pubic hair dripping a soapy stream, her tender drapery of hips, and the somehow distinct sounds of hissing water and the jangle of shower curtain rings and the squeaky rub of flesh against 4" tiles. The water that pooled at the solid seal of our pressed-together breasts. The steam and soap and hands.

Percocet or no, the steamy space leapt with actuality—which is just a master's-thesis way of saying it was a dream. My face at her slick neck, my hands running the length of her, the little fumbling struggle for a coitus that shouldn't have worked but did.

It wasn't just fucking my sister-in-law. It was something different. I knew what it was.

"I know what this is," I started to say.

But she didn't want to hear it. I should have quoted my favorite Emily Dickinson line to her: "The Creek turns Sea – at thought of thee." But no. There wasn't space for words. Even toweling ourselves dry, laughing and patting and kissing and toweling some more—we were like an established couple with a fit and healthy and down-to-earth routine of habit-forming happiness. It was us, as it seemed we always were and always would be, in our towels and our dampness and our giddy parsing through the clothes from the pile on the floor and our endorphined plateau and our reticent looks toward the steamed-streaked closed door—the door on which there was now a knock.

June leapt back to the window, placing a hand on the sill to steady herself. She whispered that it couldn't be him, that he couldn't be home this early, that he never comes home this early, but I had the sharp impression she was simply saying these words to give them some kind of authority, an authority that another knock at the door belied. We had been giggling and frisking, and he certainly had heard us, both of us. Was the door locked? It didn't look to be. June was stepping into her jeans, then her T-shirt, whereas I was still in my towel, resolving quickly not to attempt a Hanky defenestration, nor to cower, nor plead—but to face my due, my accident of fate, and let it be.

"It's okay," I whispered.

"Fuck fuck fuck," she said.

I couldn't blame her—my voice was about as urgent as someone asking directions to the bathroom. But it wasn't the Percocet. It was my right. There are no fates, no Olympian meddlers in our lives—we simply do shit, and maybe do it again or maybe do something else. In a *Charlotte's Web* world, we are Templeton the rat, stuffed to the gills with the trash we love so much. There's nothing metaphysical about it, Emily Dickinson notwithstanding, and I say that we'd better get used to it, and get our share. Carpe trashum.

My right! My brother's knock had intruded on my right to happiness. He'd told me to get to it, and the "it" wasn't Carol Ann or even Montana. It was this, this truth: my brother wasn't a brother— he was an interloper, a freak. Taking communion! He'd gotten lucky with June, and then he'd gotten lucky with the goddamn Roller Rings. They weren't even a toy but jewelry! Perfect dumb luck. I had nothing to fear.

June was behind me. I was still in my towel. I reached for the brass doorknob and felt it shock my palm with cold, and the shock was enough to carry forward the act of turning and pulling and opening the door.

Standing there, agitated but bright of face and clean of neck beneath the sharp blue Cubs hat, was Terry.

"Christ!" June said. She brushed past me and put an arm around the kid, leading him into the living room and cooing at him that he wasn't supposed to enter people's houses like that, even hers, etc. etc.

I closed the door and put my same clothes on—the clean ones I'd brought with me were still in the dining room, where I'd been putting them all along during The Project. Normal. My heart was in my chest, walloping from fear and from June. I felt sick in some distant way, nothing you could pinpoint, like heartburn or ennui.

When I came out, Terry was saying he'd knocked a long time on the front door and that he'd walked all the way here, but it really wasn't far, just from the river when you think about it, and to me he said, "Hi Hank." But his eyes ignored me for everything else in the room and out—it was still a squinty-bright day outside—until he finally settled on side-by-side framed pictures of Carlton and June.

"I was psychic to see the shower curtain," he said.

"Psyched," June said.

"Right."

"Of course you were," June said, "but then it's time to go. Maybe Hank will give you a ride home."

He thought this over a second. "I think Hank's too selfish," he said.

She looked up to me with gray eyes not yet free of panic, and there was some of the un-indicted co-conspirator in there, too, but then she started to laugh at Terry's honesty. "Yes a little, he is," she said, "but we still love him."

I was laughing too, and the kid started to smile. "I resemble that remark," I said.

By the time we got into the bathroom, we were all giddy. Relieved and steamy, the three of us stood there, the kid between me and June, the bathroom still streaking, all of us happily short breath. My body was limp and inoffensive, scooped of something deep.

Terry pushed his Cubs cap off his head briefly, like a contractor considering a job, and then pulled it tight and low again, taking a full moment to set the brim straight, the way he liked it. There was a small draft from someplace, and he fingered the slick plastic curtain at one of the now-dried squares of Mod Podged gingko.

What are we to do in these moments, when life unfolds without precedent?

Finally Terry let out a sigh, a weighty one, the kind people like him aren't supposed to know how to give. He put his hand to his beard and rubbed it, then put both his hands behind his slight back, Einstein style. He wanted to say the right thing, and smiled at us. We smiled back. I put my arm around him.

"It's good," he said. "It's a beautiful thingy."

PART TWO

So Nice, Montana,
All the Peace and Quiet

Chapter Seven

The barn I rented was south of Helena and had been converted and refurbished with drywall, molding, salvaged oak doors, double-pane windows, and close to an acre of R-30 fiberglass insulation. The landlords, Jeffrey and Tom, crowed about it all with that vulgar pride of do-it-themselvesers, but it was fine by me. Up till then I'd been living above an aikido studio along Highway 12's low-rent retail lobe west of town—I shared the place with the sensei, and the sensei snored.

The barn was a labor of love, and of Tom and Jeffrey's defiance: gonna build ourselves a goddamn gay fortress, put our hearts into it and more money than we'd ever hope to recoup, paint it pink, and rent it out to some poor unsuspecting son of a bitch in dire straits. I only wished they'd offered the place furnished so I could sit my dire straits down. But no. I had one open room downstairs for kitchen, living, and eating space, and one almost-as-large room upstairs, my bedroom, and all of it was empty as sunshine, except for whiffs of large-animal urine, and also mice, who appreciated the warmth as much as me and left little teardrop turds of thanks.

Thirty minutes or so from Helena, I made do on the fifty bucks a week I spent at the Albertson's, occasional trips to town to get a latte and gawk at the housing stock, and charity conversation from my landlords. Jeffrey I saw less often, as he didn't have a job and so was often puttering around doing something or other at the Big House, which was what they called their home two football fields or so up the hill from my barn. Jeffrey was memorable for saying that redoing the barn, on the budget they had to work with, was like stretching a Chiclet to the moon. But he stopped bothering with me once I told him the barn wasn't "dawn rose" as he'd called it, but in fact pink. Tom, however, I saw quite a bit more of, since he owned a small print shop and wannabe ad agency in downtown Helena, and was my boss.

I'd wandered into the agency off the street, having seen his small wooden "Big Sky Print Productions" sign, and asked for a job application, like it was a Starbucks. Tom must have admired the chutzpah, or been a poor judge of character, because he gave me an interview right there on the spot. I hadn't even shaved; I wore a fungal two-o'clock shadow like a dare.

"Let me get this straight," he said. "You move here on a whim, you have no plan and know no one, can hardly even find Helena on a map, you've got no experience in printing except for the fact that you've read books—"

"Lots of books," I added.

"And that you once worked at a publisher that specialized in poetry. Sound about right?"

Arms folded over some scribbled notepad of paper on his desk, he was thin in the neck but still substantial, almost stern, with a trim beard and rich brown eyes clouded by a quiet exhaustion—a guy who's been through one of life's various wringers but hasn't let it stop him from trimming his nose hair. He'd raised his almond-sliver eyebrows during his indictment, higher and higher, till now they were prying up one of the ceiling panels.

His office was the only walled space in the Big Sky mélange of cubicles and color correction tables and printer paper and laminating machines and copy machines only slightly smaller than the letterpress Tom had salvaged and refurbished himself. It sounds cramped but was actually quite spacious. Lots of high-gloss pine, lots of streak-free glass—one whole wall of it for Tom alone, so he could see what was what in the rest of the office. Facing it, he'd installed an old farmhouse dining table as his desk. His personal effects were the usual, including a framed BA diploma and a small snapshot of Jeffrey in sunglasses overlooking some magnificent mountain vista. Someplace a printer or fax machine hummed, then adjusted itself. I could feel through my Clarks the cranking of the screen-printing shop next door. The plaster in this office was extraordinarily smooth. On the two bookshelves, a brigade of papers, books, file folders, blue lines, stuffed manila envelopes, and the like toed the same line to the millimeter. I needed to up my cred.

"I do have a master's," I said. "I wrote my thesis on Emily Dickinson."

Tom sighed. "Tell me that means you can proofread."

"Oh, right. I've actually been a freelance proofreader for four years now. Chicago Manual, the whole deal."

He cocked his head at me.

"How's that relevant to your line of work?"

He was the first Montanan I'd made smile.

Our town was hardly even that: three paved streets' worth of necessities and indulgences, a splattering of homes laid out like a deck of playing cards tossed onto a staircase, and arterial forest service roads stitching their way up some creek bed or gulch into the wilderness. The kids had to bus it to another town's school, and, in fact, most activity involved driving, usually to Helena or Boulder. What we did have, though, was enough for me: a seedy bar, a church, a seedier bar, a little smokes-and-Gatorade convenience store, a post office, some hand-me-down businesses with their signs rusting and often outright wrong (John's Small Engine Repair was really a taxidermy and antiques shop), and an old jail no one had bothered to tear down. The jail was where the two or three renegade teenagers slept when they came down from meth, for warmth and also because, like most everyone else, they were afraid of Sugar.

Sugar was a dog. By the looks of him, he was part Bernese, part shepherd, but wild and wooly as a wolf. He was owned by one of the locals, up in the hills above town, who believed that if someone was dumb enough to stray onto their hill-hugging sprawl of property, getting mauled was that someone's own damn fault. These were the same people who rampaged against taxes and environmentalists, and had enough ammo stored in one of their outbuildings to take care of both if they thought they'd get away with it and if the mine hadn't given them these goddamn migraines.

Neither was Sugar's owner keen on upkeep, as in repairing downed fence, and Tom had seen Sugar out on the prowl plenty of times, once even harassing and wounding an old, sickly deer before being scared off by a passing truck. One Saturday, in the last light of an afternoon hike, I myself came upon the leggy hump of him. I've never considered myself to be much like a deer before—I'd put on a good twenty pounds, for one thing—but at this moment I was frozen wide-eyed by Sugar's headlights. Exiting the narrow trail, I had just put boot onto gravel, and there he was, standing broadside across a disturbingly empty forest service road. He stuck his nose down in the dust a moment, then looked at me in a way that evolution has taught us to fear. I picked up a rock, though Sugar didn't register it as a threat. He merely stood, flipping the Rolodex of his doggy brain. He licked a paw, tongue jabbing from his big Jell-O jowls. It was his nonchalance that was most frightening, his doggy inscrutability—if you live with a dog, you think you know the species, but then you meet a Sugar, and you might as well be facing the gestapo. Sugar looked me in the heart, did a little two-step in the gully shadows, and went on his way. I ran on mine.

Not that I had much to run to. Alone, exiled, forgotten, left to sup on my fate in the wilds of Montana—it was all very dramatic, despite its self-infliction. My Montana that May was proofreading for Tom, then coming home to a barn as bare as a roller rink—I let out a slight gasp every time I opened the heavy front door, as one would a cathedral—and watching the blackbirds mingle and mock in the field of echinacea and black-eyed Susans and big bluestem between my place and Tom and Jeffrey's. Then there were books and the addictive Montana AM radio and, of course, my suffering—and my suffering liked to eat.

So on those tart May nights, my fat elbows bitten by the Formica edge of the kitchen table I'd found at the See-n-Save, my life became a one-man buffet. I ate to no purpose save filling up— each meal a shipment to be warehoused. It was a second job, a full late-shift. Daytime it was finding the "teh"s and "tat"s of a Quark file; nighttime it was food to be gulleted. Canned peaches with half a package of sliced Jennie-O turkey. Nitrated hot dogs with Oz-green relish. French press coffee with cream thick as semi-gloss paint and two loaves of truck-stop banana bread. Vanilla bean French toast and a bowlful of butter-sautéed ramps bought fresh from Mennonites on the side of the road. Chew chew swallow, chew chew swallow.

All in a night's work, but instead of someone there to say *kaynahorah,* all I had was whiskey, and a good stiff dose of how I got here.

After June's birthday weekend, I'd spent the rest of April in a kind of ether, foggy and light-headed. It was a sloppy, pinheaded myopia, and I called it love. The power of it pushed out of me like crab grass, and life began bending to my will. Steve was newly obedient. An editor at the U of M press suddenly had work for me. My brother eyed me warily, Carol Ann even more so.

June wouldn't talk to me, not a word. I mean, more than she had to. No *talk* talk.

Our peonies bloomed, our rhododendrons thought about it. I retackled The Project and got all the way to tiling and grouting the wall around the gleaming new tub—though when Carol Ann came home and inspected my work, she announced that she hated the grout color, which was a sandy brown. Actually, the word she used was "unacceptable." I told her she was unacceptable. She said everything with me was unacceptable lately, worse than ever, and I said then why don't you call your fucking boyfriend, who always accepted you before? This she found truly unacceptable, really Hank, so I said, you wanna see unacceptable? Huh? And I took a bag from the closet, filled it with clothes, threw some miscellaneous shit into cardboard boxes, put it all in the Jetta, and started driving.

I thought I'd break down, both literally and otherwise. But no.

The North Dakota prairie gave way to the creepy, lanky incisions of Teddy Roosevelt National Park, then the spectacular nothingness of eastern Montana, and finally a choking crawl up and down the mountains. I fell in love with the Flying J truck stops and their spacious bathrooms and empathetic nods from the homely help and the eclectic selection of cassettes, from Tammy Wynette to George Carlin. In honor of my brother, I even bought *Nebraska,* but I threw it out the window when I couldn't stand the guilt. I made up for it with a great pizza in Bozeman. Then four beers and a breathtaking drive up Highway 69 later, I parked the car in downtown Helena and went apartment hunting. I don't know why—I guess I was tired of driving, and I've always had a fondness for state capitals, and they had a few streets downtown where cars couldn't drive, and everyone I encountered had their shirtsleeves rolled up.

It didn't feel like a catastrophe. Even with the memory of June's whispering "It was a mistake, Hank, sweetie, it was" when I finally got her on the phone a week after our Sunday together—it felt like a vacation.

Chapter Eight

During my first months, Montana found me terrorized by the telephone. Both the black 900 megahertz cordless in my barn and the quaint block of dusty buttons stationed in my cubicle brought to me a steady nightmare of transactions and transgressions, beratings and brick walls. Conversations with Carol Ann were particularly bizarre.

"Thank you for the mortgage money."

"Don't be silly. I'm not going to stop paying my part of the mortgage."

"We actually have more money this way. Isn't that weird?"

We paused to honor the prima facie stupidity of that last bit.

"But," she sputtered, "but what's your plan out there? I'm lonely. I cry all the time. I can't just stop knowing you. I never figured—"

"Don't you think you stopped knowing me when you wet our bed with your boyfriend, and then did it again and again and again and—shall I go on?"

Not much of a conversation, actually, but exhausting. So sometimes I'd say, "What's my plan? Sit here. Get really fat. Then maybe go feed Sugar the dog." Which made little sense to her but was enough, at least, to get her to stop calling and leave me to feed my suffering.

But the thing about suffering is it has to *do* something once it's been fed. It can't just sit around. It's gonna get antsy. It's gonna say, "Hey, goober, what *is* the plan?" And it will not take "We're gonna be miserable and pathetic" for an answer. No, it's gonna want to put your fist through the barn's new drywall, or hurl your whiskey and listen to the ice scatter, or rip pages out of books at random (starting specifically with a Stegner I'd inscribed, "For Carol Ann on her 28th birthday…"—now why had I taken that?), or scratch the CDs she'd given me (Sarah McLachlan?—who'd know the difference anyway?), or one of the thousand other mutilations handed down from the annals of love's labors lost.

Maybe a little more whiskey, with fresh ice.

What I was trying to tell Carol Ann was that the only real plan I had was for an exit strategy: I could drive up Macdonald Pass, which still got snowy in May, and glissade off into oblivion; they'd be finding oily remains as far as Beacon. Or I could stay closer to home and merely walk out into the wild and expose myself to hypothermia and Sugar the dog. Sugar doesn't care how you got here. Sugar just wants you to tilt your neck back like a good little adulterer and kiss your ass good-bye.

How simple it would be! All I needed was to let him find me, maybe stuff my pockets with bacon. And sometimes I could swear I heard him, prowling and pawing the barn, his treading paws amplified in my whiskey glass. I could smell his randy pelt. He also appreciated the insulated warmth, no doubt, and would like to click his claws across the pine floorboards Jeffrey himself had planed, and maybe curl up for a good nap after tearing me apart. So maybe I wouldn't even have to go to him—he was there, ready to come inside, a little scratching at the screen door. He could sniff the dust bunnies and my stale, fat-guy-with-closed-windows funk.

And if after a month or two Sugar hadn't gotten me, or I hadn't stumbled off a ledge, I could always just go down to the Copper Cowboy, the more lively of our two town bars, and tell everyone I'm with the government and would like to get up in their business, because there are some welfare queens back East who needed Kit Kat money, and of course guns that need to be confiscated, so please extend your cold dead hand and let me fingerprint it, or I'll even accept your hard Montana cock because I'm also giving blow jobs in accordance with my grant from the National Endowment for the Arts.

Sugar would be last in line.

Coming to Montana, I took the stupidest shit.

I took forty-one CDs, mostly jazz. I took two lamps, half my clothes, the garish afghan Carol Ann's great-aunt had crocheted us for our wedding, another blanket, two sets of sheets, three plants (a wandering Jew and two spider plants), the good nonstick pots and pans, out of spite, and a fucking half-bag of charcoal. Also a teetering stack of mismatched ceramic bowls, each hand-turned or whatever in some potter's studio—some orange, some celadon, some black. The steak knives. Two pillar candles and all the tea lights, I guess for instant ambience—ambience for one, that is. I took exactly half the pictures hanging on our walls. I took a pack of coasters with fake cork on the back of them, which I had found ironic in a Stephen Greenblatt way. I have a thing for glassware and so took all the highballs, the martini glasses, the four juice-sized wineglasses I stole during my brief stint as a waiter, and all seven of the plastic cups with the red-scarfed penguin, which they give you when you get a large Freezie at our local convenience store. The latter were the only practical way to drink anything healthy, so I was constantly reminded of Carol Ann's infatuation with Freezies. I used to take her, and she'd suck till her brain froze. She'd go into Freezie zone, where she was literally incapable of conversation until she finished her mad, frozen dash to the finish line. Slurp, scutter of straw, and she'd look at me with a mouth red as pomegranate, and she'd as likely as not say, "I think I'm gonna be sick."

I hated taking her. I hated her slurping, hated being ignored until the slurping was done. I hated her red mouth, her sugar high, her inevitable headache or crash, and what it would do to her body. But come on: why the hell not take her to get a goddamn

Freezie? Is that love, ignoring what's bad for a person and giving it to them anyway?

I found a book of James Wright poems Carol Ann had purchased on a Barnes & Noble spree—it was right before her affair, and I remember her finding me in the store's café to show me her purchases: a travel guide on Italy, A. J. Liebling's *Between Meals*, Temple Grandin, John Donne, a husband-and-wife cultural history of China. Surprises! How life can restart itself, lick its parched lips and smile—a person who shares your life but doesn't, too. I was astonished, and it offended her a little. "I read, I'm smart," she'd said. We never went to Italy, and she hadn't ended up liking the James Wright poems—they were too sad.

I had to admit, in Montana I missed Carol Ann, the daily of her, the way we sidled around each other, the dance of it. Her ire and self-doubt. I never lived a day with her when I felt alone, that's for sure. Lonely, yes; alone, impossible. In bed you'd think it would be me who weighted the mattress more, but no—I'd wake slumped onto her, my shoulder rising with her every breath.

This is a question: what does your life do when it leaves something loved? Many things loved, rather. What replaces love's statutory code, which determines all decisions? And what was there before it? It's like the big bang theory, which works great until you ask what came before the big bang. The suffering part, naturally— old Emily Dickinson spilling her guts in a labyrinthian ball-of-string metaphor that would never, could never, be requited. In Montana, I felt a similar eddy, caught and foundering. I couldn't even say I was lost, for I knew exactly where I was. You have to wander someplace to get lost—all I'd done is driven to Montana, stopped for a spell, and stayed that way.

Just look at my living quarters. I'd supplemented my Montana trousseau only by what Jeffrey, with a timid knock on the door and a nice hard-jawed smile, would occasionally foist off on me: a coffeemaker, a coat rack, a Japanese scroll hanging, silverware. Tom had told me Jeffrey was a big animal lover, a real Mr. PETA, and that he didn't care much for niceties, other than what's necessary to dump off old furniture on the poor fat guy in the barn. When he left, I'd turn back and look at the mishmash of my life, like a sad Polaroid of someone's moving day, and ask myself, "Well, what the hell did you expect?"

Chapter Nine

My father was obsessing over the *why* of my Montana move. He would call me at work. Our receptionist, Claudia, would answer the phone, ask very sweetly if she may say who is calling, hit "hold" with a puffy stub of knuckle, and yell, "Daniel Meyerson for Hank on line one! Hank line one!" This when there were four of us, total, in the office. Sometimes she wouldn't hit "hold" and my father would say, "Jesus Christ, does that woman screech like that all the time? She's an elephant, it sounds like."

But then he would always get right to the point, which was, namely, how much I was hurting everyone.

"They'll get over it."

"What in God's name are you doing out there?"

"It's nice out here. You can gamble at the gas station."

He considered this. "What, blackjack tables?"

"Slots. The video kind."

He muttered.

"But I just mostly sit around and eat. I've been for a couple hikes, couple of summits." This was an exaggeration. "But mostly I cook."

He himself liked to cook, having become, in the years since Mom's death, something of a self-made gourmand. It's a relative term: his meat was marinated in Catalina dressing from a jar, and he tended to overindulge in trendy ingredients, as in "The recipe called for two cloves of garlic, so I put in five!" He shopped willy-nilly because it was a challenge for him—sometimes he'd find radishes in the fridge and rejoice at having no idea what the hell he was going to do with them.

"But it's nothing like your cooking," I said.

"Well, I have a few years on you."

"I can make a mean enchilada. I make the sauce from scratch."

"So," he said, "enchiladas. That's what you're doing—do you know what your brother's doing?"

"What Dad?"

"Feeling terrible, is 'what Dad.' He thinks he's insulted you. Listen, all he was trying to do was help you get your head on straight. And with what that girl did to you, who can blame him? Yes, yes," he cut me off, "he told me all about it, and it's nothing to be ashamed about but nothing to run off about either, leaving everyone to mourn for you like you're deceased. And now your brother won't work. He won't show me what ideas he has, no prototypes, no nothing."

"Ah, I see. Prodigal son should come home so that Dad can make the scratch again."

"Don't be ridiculous. You'd be coming home to your life. What are you out there, a proofreader?"

"I was a proofreader there too!"

"You could teach."

This produced in me a shutter that shook the phone, probably enough for him to hear. Teaching: the dry cracked feeling of my hands after class, from chalk dust and sweat and sheer, unabating terror. All that chalk dust! What the fuck was I putting up on the chalkboard anyway? Logical fallacies? How to free-associate on a paper topic? The relevance of jazz to James Baldwin? Christ, I should have just given free time and an A to anyone who showed up. What the hell did I know about making sense? And my students—desperate or plain, troubled or intent, friendly or sulking like bags of rice propped into those little Tonka Toy desks—they were worse than Sugar, if only in hygiene.

"There's no school."

"There's always a school!"

Poor Dad. He'd loved the idea of me being a professor. I might not get paid like a neurosurgeon or get interviewed by Charlie Rose, but I'd been plucked from the English department's pool of 327 applicants and deemed intelligent. That's right, 327 applicants. This had impressed him most—"Can't argue with numbers," he'd said.

"Nevertheless," I said.

"Nevertheless nothing. Couples go through things. Me and your mother, we fought."

"You yelled at her for not vacuuming the blinds right."

"And she agreed with me. But that was bickering, not fighting. We *fought* fought over things that mattered, and then we worked it out. You kids these days, you think it's supposed to be handed to you. Everything's me me me—"

"It's capitalism, Dad. People want what's easy because capitalists are so good at finding ways to give them easy."

"It's not capitalism. Capitalism sent you to college, don't forget."

"Nevertheless."

"These days you just move to Montana." He said it like a Montana yokel would, though it sounded more Texarkana. "Is that it? When your mother died, and your brother was a wreck—"

"What kind of a wreck was he, exactly? I hope he was a complete goddamn raving lunatic, because I'm sick of hearing about what a wreck he was, or is! What a wreck am I? Aren't I a wreck?"

"You're a wreck too, but I'm telling a story. It would have been easy for me to sell the house, move out, get an apartment someplace. But that's not how I was raised, and you neither. You were raised—"

"Whatever happened to Charlie Tuna?"

"There's no tuna in Montana." He was clearly relishing the sound of the state, like this one word was enough for a jury to convict. "Montana? Where you have nobody? It doesn't make any sense."

"Would you rather me live in my room forever, like Emily Dickinson?"

"I don't know from Emily Dickinson."

"Mom would understand."

"Don't make your mother choose sides here."

And this of course made me feel awful, which Dad had a way of pulling off. When we were kids, his brooding morning routine eclipsed the sun and made me feel small right up until the garage door closed and he was safely off to the store. And in the evening his shadowy balloon of darkness returned with a mealy, manly five o'clock shadow that even then I knew I would never be able to match: I'd always be mediocre, and pointless. It's hard to describe how literal I am being about him eclipsing my morning. With Mom off to teach by 7:30 and Carlton always seemingly involved with something before school, it was just the two of us, but he'd say little to me. Maybe a "Hi Hanky." I'd just hold my breath, wondering how I would explain myself, and not even knowing why there was explaining to do. But he made me feel there was a justification to be given, for my very existence—one July morning he showed me the electric bill and told me 90 percent of it was from air-conditioning my fat *tuckus*. And I remember feeling that the right justification from me, the right spell of worthiness, would alter us both, raise his spirits and his tent flaps too, if I could only pull it off. But both of us knew I couldn't, and when he left for the store, I'd exhale and wonder how I'd pull off another pointless day of letting the kids at school call me fat. As an adult I can see that he simply hated his job—but back then I was pretty sure he hated me.

"The point is," I told him now, "I'm here. I like it. I'm well fed. And you're probably not going to understand."

"I understand plenty," he huffed. He breathed into the phone a second, worked up, figuring the odds that he was right about there being no tuna in Montana. "And your brother," he finally said, "he's a wreck."

Good old Dad. He'd done the questioning and the answering both, as was his wont—he'd reminded me that my distaste was not necessarily for my Hank-ness but for my Meyerson-ness, the punch-drunk tentacles of it.

When my brother called to guilt me more, I told him, "There's just no room for me there. There hasn't been since the day you moved to Minnesota. No, since before that. You and Dad took it all up and ate it for breakfast. You're never gonna understand, so just don't try, and stop hectoring me. That's it."

"You're a fucking idiot," he said. And hung up.

For a while, it felt good, walking around enrobed in an ahistorical hostility. I was becoming one of those estranged family members some people have, one who was grievously wronged and remains righteously enraged accordingly, but no one knows why. "Yeah," the rest of the family says, "I got a brother in Montana, but we aren't close. He hates me. But I don't know what I did to him. June sends him a Hanukkah card, but I don't even know if he's Jewish. How can he be Jewish in Montana? Well, I did all I could. What more can I do? I'm not gonna beg him. You don't beg people to be family."

It was the same shit when we were kids. Until my father could no longer afford it, he kept a social membership at Fairheights Country Club, the predominantly Jewish one in Omaha. One of the reasons I love my people: Exclude us from your country clubs, and meh, what do we care? We'll build one just as nice, with a monthly minimum to make you *plotz*. Anyway, there was a pool and a dining room and of course a golf course, but for me the entire thing meant tennis.

I was the kind of tennis player that made my brother scowl: I slapped at the ball ping-pong style, loping and lunging like a simian Swan Lake. For him to play me was a struggle of principles more than anything, and he'd show his disdain with a "Why did you do *that?*" or even a "Don't you dare!" when I managed to lay a crossing shot onto the sideline. What bothered him most was that I was actually pretty good—it was all in the wrists, and with them I learned to generate a wicked spin, sticking balls to the cement like bean bags, or else scuttling them rabbit-like past your knees. I relied on those slapping Genghis Kahn slices so much that I never learned to hustle or reposition myself like you're supposed to do—which meant I could play lots of tennis that first year of junior high and still be chubby.

By summer my weight had our old man mystified. How was it possible, he wanted to know. Do you play for cheeseburgers? Do you have Alfredo sauce in your water bottle? After quizzing me and getting only sulky shrugs, he'd turn to Carlton, who proved poor intelligence. He was always off playing basketball or at the swimming pool or palling around with an increasing harem of non-Jewish friends now that he was a freshman—all things I avoided, especially the pool. I'd rather die of heat exhaustion on the court, where I had a modicum of physical grace and would probably be pounding some poor Hebe half my age, than find myself stuck at the pool, alone in the shallow end and taunted to tears. Palms to their faces, they'd fatten their cheeks and summon up a character created just in my honor—"Chubby Wubbenstein." Even the *girls* would go at me. "Duh, wuhmp a keesh, Chubby Wubbenstein?" I'll tell you, if the Messiah ever comes to declare the Peace on Earth promised us thousands of years ago, when asked why he waited so long, I have no doubt he'll blame Jewish teens.

So I stuck happily to the courts, even happier when my brother deigned to join me. One day we were awaiting our turn to play, watching two flailing sixth-graders display a stunning lack of skill.

"Look at those nancies," Carlton said. He shook his head, arms crossed next to me.

There were four courts at Fairheights, but one had a doubles match scheduled in half an hour, and the other two were, to Carlton, unacceptably cracked. We chose to wait on the bench outside the pro shop, because inside was cramped with a colicky air conditioner, sordid tennis gear on nickel-plated display racks, and Pro Charlie himself, humming along to bootleg Grateful Dead tapes and restringing rackets. We were each drinking a can of orange pop, the Whistle brand with the slogan "Thirsty? Just Whistle!" We were in no hurry, soaking up the summer heat, which was already making me sweat.

"Fuckin' nancies," I said.

My brother had Charlie's boom box on his lap—the one he let us play outside, on account of the Grateful Dead inside—and was cranking Van Halen in the sixth-graders' direction at inopportune moments. Inopportune for them, that is—we found it quite charming. The song "Jamie's Cryin'" became "Nancy's Cryin'," with my brother narrating about how Nancy'd been in love before, and he knew what love was for—it should mean just a little more...THAN ONE NIGHT STANDS!

Plunk—right in the net.

My easy cackle made my brother happy, I think. Thing is, I liked losing to him. I liked the surety of it, the routine of his unchallenged supremacy. I'd get four, maybe five games from him in a set, each of us holding serve, but then the net would turn eight feet tall on me, and the court on his side skinny as a sidewalk, and he'd break me and that'd be that. Off he'd go to the pool or the arcade, leaving me to take out my aggressions on the practice board or some bucktoothed fifth-grader who wanted a piece of me.

He fast-forwarded the Van Halen tape. "I want to hear 'Ain't Talkin 'Bout Nancy,'" he said.

"Sweet."

He nodded at the nancies. "Who are these kids?"

I didn't know. The boom box spooled along quietly. It was a good boom box, made before electronics companies started going disposable.

"I think his name's Nancy," Carlton finally said.

"First or last?"

"Both. Nancy McNancy. He's got a bit o' the Irish in him."

"Hey Nancy," I called, in a vague British accent. "That be a nice forehand ye be displayin'."

"What are you now, a pirate?"

I shrugged. "A Jewish pirate," I said. "That'd be something. We'd sail the seas and board your boat just to tell you about our boat, which is a nicer boat—you've never *seen* a boat like this one."

This made my brother laugh, his eyes slitting like cheerful scars, which was so infuriating when aimed at me, but not now. His polo was green and too tight on him, the little polo player beige but lustrous in the sun. "Yar," I said. "Fetch me my yarrrrr-mulke. I'm lookin' for the circumciser what gave me my peg leg."

My brother was laughing when he took his drink of Whistle. At first I thought he was spitting up out of laughter, but something wasn't right. His can of Whistle had been sitting on the bench beside him, and the wasp must have crawled inside for its own waspy reasons because Carlton never saw it. He merely drank, pitched forward with a sickening retch of "Hnnh! Hunnnh!" like a sleeper having a nightmare, and started spitting. The boom box fell to the cement with the solid 1-2-3 landing of a paving stone. The fast-forward button depressed, and the AM radio came on in a loud static.

I never saw the wasp either, but we knew it was a wasp because of its size and the fact that it managed to sting him three times before he could spit the thing out: once on the tongue, twice on the fleshy lower left cheek wall. Regular bees can't do that shit.

While the nancies finished their match, Carlton sat with his elbows on his knees and head between his elbows, spitting and spitting onto the cement. The AM radio fuzz kept on until my brother kicked the boom box to make it stop. It took three kicks.

"Do you want another pop?" I said.

He shook his head.

"Some water?"

Again with the head.

"Should we tell Pro Charlie? Maybe you need to go to the hospital or something."

"Christ," he said, "shut the fuck up." But he spoke laboriously, cotton-stuffed, and it came out "phlut thhh phluck uff."

When the nancies finished, my brother got up and went onto the court.

"You still wanna play?" I said.

He unzipped his racket. He looked close to tears, his face red, his bangs pushed up and back from having held his face in his hands so long.

"We don't have to play. I feel sick anyway." He began to practice his serve, hitting too hard and mostly into the net, while I stood by the gate with my racket in my crossed arms. "Come on, I'm hungry." I'd followed him, but now I tried backing out the gate, like he was a loose puppy to be led home.

To this he uttered the bee-stung, cotton-mouth equivalent of "Fuckin Chubby Wubbenstein."

That's when I got furious: not because of what he called me, or that he needed to beat me to feel better—I don't know why for sure. I can only say that fury simply became me, transformed me, such that I was more precise than ever, and unbeatable. I'd follow the ball's trajectory at me, foresee what it was going to do once it hit the cement, angle my racket into position, and shoot it back. So intensely did I watch my racket that I could see the strings bend and snap, geometrically controlled right back at Carlton's backhand. It was like the racket face was ten feet wide, and I was nimble and loose in every joint. I worked him left, then worked him right, then right again for fun. I placed the ball at his feet, and if he faded back, I dropped it mere yards from his side of the net. I had command of backspin, topspin, even a right-left spin I never knew existed. And it wasn't like, amazingly, Carlton's game was suffering from his stung mouth. Maybe his concentration some, but he was trying hard, and motherfucker if I wasn't just flat out beating him. I enjoyed it, too. "What?" I'd say when he tried to call the score before his serve. "Oh, my ad? Sweet." Rattled, he started double-faulting and then, to compensate, since he himself had told me tennis is a game of losing less, not winning more, he abandoned any heat on his second serves, and when I smacked my returns right at him, or sent him scampering cross-court, I'd offer a smarmy "That was a really nice try," or even "How's your mouth? Still okay to play?" I took long, pre-serve moments sopping my forehead with a wristband or finding a dry spot on my shirt to clean my sunglasses or picking little pieces of shmutz off the court—while he plucked his racket face, fingers wide and tense, arranging and rearranging his strings as if it mattered.

It didn't. I took the first set, broke his serve right away in the second, and went on to take that one too, 6-3. Two out of three sets, that's what we always played.

I was sweating, of course, had been the whole time, but my brother, standing there on the other side of the court in his miserable disbelief, was out-and-out wilted. I'd run him like a dog playing fetch, without sympathy; even when I hit him in the shoulder the one time he made the mistake of attacking the net, I'd aimed for his face. But now, drooping over his racket, which he'd chucked against the fence after the final point, his polo stained to his chest, he said, "Best of five." His diction had recovered some, but he was huffing, so it was all he could get out.

"Nah," I said. "You played such a good game, I'm tuckered. I think I'll go cool off in the pool."

When he came around the net, I thought fast how to protect myself against punches, as he himself had taught me to do. "You've got those pudgy arms," he'd said, "put them up to your face and tuck your elbows in to your liver, and no one will be able to touch you." So at first he landed only a few on me, mostly glancing blows as I backed away and he pursued. Then he got to my kidneys, my tender ears, my liver, my sweaty throat, wherever he could. I remember his face, not angry or crazed but simply intent, focused on hurting me, and when I got tired and dropped my hands a little, he had his opportunity: a quick snap right to my nose. I felt the cartilage give some, then just a pressure and a panic, and I fell to the ground to get free of it. I was right by the net, and I covered up as best I could, taking only two or three more punches before, finally, there came a sharp "Cool it!" from Pro Charlie, who had my brother by the collar. I heard it rip and thought I would be blamed for it. I saw my blood on the court, a small sparkling red puddle I hoped would leave a stain. I wanted to get up, but I was too weak for anything more than a leisurely one-armed leaning, as if at a picnic. From this position, high on adrenaline and coagulants, I said, "On second thought, I'd be happy to beat you best of five."

Carlton lunged at me, but Pro Charlie held him fast, surprising us both—we'd never seen the guy employ more strength than it took to lob forehands at a hyper-tanned Mrs. Finkel. He held my brother and shot me a scolding look. "Namaste, dude," he said. "You'd better quit while you're ahead."

Around this time my father had discovered exercising and joined its cult. No joke, it was three hours of swishing nylon and grunty straining every night after dinner and often extending well into late-night television: stretching and leg lifts and push-ups and quad-strengtheners and hundreds upon hundreds of sit-ups, all performed like a temple ritual, and often after a four-mile run.

It's tough to explain this obsession. Maybe he knew Kidsville was not long for this world and wanted to go down ripped. Perhaps he daydreamed of a final showdown, him challenged by the CFO of Kids "R" Us to a push-ups contest. Because it wasn't like he was homely or physically lacking. He wasn't tall, but if asked to gauge his height, even people who knew him well would probably overshoot it, and he had a way, when reprimanding you, of standing shoulders forward, legs akimbo, like he was just dying for you to take a swing at him. I don't know; maybe seeing me chub out scared him. He had once been beefy himself, his senior yearbook photo was more future frat boy than athlete, and maybe he was trying to exercise for the both of us, setting a good example—he certainly made sure we knew about it, since all of us could hear him in the living room after Mom had gone to bed. From my bedroom I'd listen to him grunting, grunting—for the love of God it was nonstop with the grunting, and the wheezing and the turning over, and the clearing of the throat, the cranked-up TV blaring *Back to the Future* or *48 Hours* or some other cable staple we knew all the lines to! Nick Nolte: "And if Ganz gets away, you're gonna be sorry you ever met me." Eddie Murphy: "I'm already sorry." Ha! That's good bedtime theater, even better for pumping the quads. At least I had the decency to hide my shameful behavior—my un-kosher snacking and my beating off, both of which I kept to the privacy of my own room, quietly and with a precise fastidiousness that even the writers of *Murder, She Wrote* couldn't have imagined: all clues, including the wrappers and wadded tissues, would be stored in my backpack under my bed until I could dump them in one of the trash cans at the Sinclair station on my way to school. That's the way you handle your shame—not stretching it out every evening on the living room carpet and leaving matted indentations for Mom to vacuum. Not adjusting your gray, red-striped briefs with a twist and snap that could only be called pornographic while your son sits with his friends on the couch sipping caffeine-free Cokes and waiting for your okay to go out for the evening.

Anyway, two nights after the fight at Fairheights, he was at it in front of the dark-stained entertainment console that held the TV and VCR and videotapes and some framed pictures and the little wicker elephant hiding M&Ms for guests. I was watching too, from the worn-shiny blue couch, tethered in pain and feeling sorry for myself. My nose was still bandaged, having been broken in a way that required not resetting, but a leathery tolerance of suffering—yet my brother was out with friends at a movie, and hadn't been grounded or anything. But I kept my trap shut, letting my brother's sore-loserness speak for itself—that's what Björn Borg would have done. And anyway, it was a time in our culture when whining for recompense was considered pretty nancy. I blame Rambo.

My father was at the end of his last routine: bicep curls using short bars with flat metal discs slid onto the ends, held with tension clips. He rocked through a steady stream of them in thirty-rep blocks, planted tank-topped before Johnny Carson. Johnny's couch was spastic with a bug-eyed Rodney Dangerfield, who even then was like loose gravel poured into some dead Jew's skin. Only funnier. "I'm ugly, I'm telling ya," he sputtered. "My proctologist, he stuck his finger in my mouth." My father didn't laugh or miss a rep, the barbells clinking between grunts.

My mother from the bedroom: "Danny, you should go!" Later I would learn what had precipitated this remark, a telephone call from a concerned parent, but for the moment I neither knew nor cared to. With our family, just like TV, you could tune out a while and pick up with the plot later on no problem.

My father didn't say anything back to my mother. Perhaps there was no point, and anyway his breath was scarce. He finished his reps, bent at the bony knees to set the barbells down, stretched his back by shooting his hands up toward the ceiling, and shut the television off. He stood a moment, his shorts creeping with dark curls of hair at the small of his back, and he watched the dark screen in the quiet. No asking me if I was enjoying Rodney Dangerfield, no nothing. He went back into their bedroom and came out pulling a big gray T-shirt over his head. His running shoes were on, flashy as a freeway sign. I asked where he was going, and he couldn't say, because he had mouthwash in his mouth. His cheeks puffed with it like Carson's. He waved that I was to come with him.

We took the company van, which my father used for moving merchandise from store to store. It had seats only in the front, the back just a cave of furrowed metal, two humpy wheel wells, and a small window in each of the back doors. Stopped, waiting to turn onto Pacific Street, my father rolled down his window, spit out the mouthwash in a luminous green-white jag, and rolled the window back up. After all, the AC was on. I think this might have been the greatest reason my mother loved him, besides his rescuing her and her two kids from single-mother oblivion. He was more than willing to spend gas on air-conditioning to keep everyone comfortable. This to my mother was the chivalrous good life. "Blast us out, Danny," she'd say, whenever we sizzled ourselves into a hot car, and he always did.

He drove us west, and the night was a filmstrip of adolescent suburbia: well-roofed houses in shades of beige, an alpine-inspired apartment complex advertising free first month's rent, a park or ball field, the occasional dark crick or gully, Millard North High's empty parking lot with "Congrats Seniors!" on the unlit marquis, and, soon enough, the watery quiet of corn, defaced occasionally by the lights of an Amoco. The lights felt harsh in the summer darkness, prickling like nettles down in Trendwood Creek.

My father said, "What do you think a mother's looking for when she's buying a sled for her kid?"

You had to be on your toes with our father. He could angle at you from all directions, and usually there was some sort of testing involved, since he wanted, naturally, to come off as teacher to my student. Usually I demurred with an "I dunno" that left him shaking his head, but this night, maybe because my nose and my indignation made me unafraid of being further wronged, I met him head on. "Depends on the sled," I said. "What kind of sled?"

"A Flyer. The wood ones, you know, with the metal runners. How's your nose? Talking hurt your nose?"

"It's fine," I said. It hurt, but only some. It cramped my voice, boxed it somehow. I hadn't realized how much I liked my voice. I'd been practicing for my bar mitzvah day and night, and I was getting good at even the more warbling Talmudic chants. Cantor Fetterman was as approving as his cold-cuts face could be. I was just happy that in Hebrew I didn't sound so chubby.

"I like the plastic ones," I said.

"Why do you think she wouldn't like them too?"

"I don't know. She wants the real deal, maybe. The brand name."

He didn't say anything.

"And anyway, what does she know about sledding? You go faster in the plastic ones. The Flyer'll probably end up hanging on a wall."

"She wants her kid to go fast?"

He had me there. You could control the Flyers better. They might even have had brakes so you didn't have to drag your feet.

"It's the brand," he said. "It's an emotional thing for her. If she doesn't just go and grab a plastic one right away, she's looking for something else. And the something else is always one of three things: quality, prestige, or brand loyalty."

The whole topic didn't sit well with me. "I'd do better," I said, "selling her Ho Hos."

My father laughed. He still had a young face, a little like Robin Williams without the shtick, and when he smiled it was all you wanted to look at. But it could snap back, too, sharpen and shrink like someone at the wrong end of the telescope. This was what Kidsville did to him: blinded him to most joys. For instance, most kids grow up thinking snow days are the bomb: no school, make a snowman, cocoa and cookies and all that, smoke some dope in the snow fort, whatever. But if you had any sensibility at all you'd know that snow days are days parents probably can't get out and shop. Jump up and down about a snow day, and you might as well be jumping up and down on the old man's grave.

I thought this was why my father went silent again as he turned the van into one of the newer, just-plotted housing developments, one of those cut into the cornfields where the houses rose like landed UFOs, all overlit with mysterious self-assurance. But then after driving a long, winding, sidewalk-free lane barren of trees or even, in spots, sod, we pulled up to one of these barns buzzing with teenagers.

My father sighed. He put the van in park. He looked at the party, the light from the house slicing the night with the flat sounds of reverie. A trio of kids tromped down the front yard in a way Carlton and I were forbidden to do on our own grass. With each of their hoots and jaggy laughs, my nose pulsed. They looked our way and lowered their voices.

"I think your brother might be in there," my father said. "He's supposed to be at a movie."

Someone yodeled from inside the house. That guitar riff from "Money for Nothing" came next, muffled but still rich with surliness.

"I don't think he'd do that," I said.

My father smiled and patted me on the knee. His hand was small, he couldn't palm a basketball, and the wingspan of his old softball glove barely covered my head, but his knuckles were bulbous and strong. He patted again and took his hand away, and we were both glad for it. "Go get him," he said.

No one looked twice at me as I walked into the party. I was wearing mesh basketball shorts that drooped to my knees and hid my upper thighs pretty well. My T-shirt was something an uncle has given me, printed with "Let's get This over With" in a scratchy typeface, my running shoes appropriately scuffed. If I'd had jeans or Genera shorts on, I'd have fit in just fine, except for the bandage over my nose. Finally a kid with a crew cut and bulging buckteeth said, "My warrior bud," and he held his hand up for me to slap it. "Beer's in the kitchen," he added.

Carlton was in the kitchen too. He was sitting on the stove, listening to a story about somebody at some other party. He laughed and stood and made a chicken-flapping motion with his arms, which I didn't get at all but everyone else found very funny. These kids were older than him, and none were Jewish. There was a thin girl with half a box of rubber bands around her wrist. A guy in cut-off jeans had a long scar down his calf. Another girl smiled at me in the dopey, dreamy way of an effortless beauty who has not yet learned to pluck her eyebrows. They were all laughing at my brother's bit.

When he saw me, he salvaged himself from the chicken flap, but his face continued to savor the moment. "Hanky," he said, as if I'd been there all night, "we'd better get you home."

He finished the Coors Light that had been beside him on the stove, and he made his good-byes. The dopey girl said to me, "Come again," and I smiled and turned my back and hoped I wouldn't hear her add "Chubby Wubbenstein." Even "Rocky" or something along the lines of my bandaged nose, but please not Chubby Wubbenstein! Each step down the hallway I expected to hear it, but finally, at the approach of the fake wood front door gleaming with brass hardware and a half-moon of glass reflecting ourselves back at us, I stiffened and went cold at the new worry of actually going outside. With my hand on the door's handle, I said, "What are you going to do?"

"About what?" He cocked his head back and considered me from under heavy eyelids. His face was slack and very boyish, even a little girlish. He was so pretty, my brother, with his red lips and fine blonde hair and delicate cheekbones; if it weren't for his athletic body and cocky squint-slanty eyes, he'd be a drama fag for sure. Now his face was sliding ever so slightly off his skull, and he stared hard at me but like I was an insect on a twig. I knew little of such things, but any human who's ever watched daytime television could tell he was loaded.

"Dad's in the van!" I said. "He's going to fucking kill you. He doesn't know you're here for sure—why don't you go out the back, and I'll tell him you weren't here?"

"Don't be a daisy," he said.

"Nancy," I said.

"Sorry," he said.

"But—"

He walked out the door. It was a sort of betrayal—we could have gotten away with lying, and he could dash to wherever he was supposed to be that night. Instead, I followed him through the grass, skulking like I was the one in trouble.

It wasn't a pleasant ride home. My brother lay prone in the back of the van, not even bothering to spread out the blanket kept back there to protect merchandise from a ding that would cost him 20 percent—a lot of Jews shopped his store and could spot "as is" from three aisles over. No, he chose the cold hard metal to take his medicine. Our father worked himself into a lather, the pigheaded irrationality that would get him through Carlton's rebellious freshman year and, eventually, get Carlton onto the Burke High baseball team, batting upward of .365.

It was the usual tough-guy dad stuff, and I was not spared. Here's a snippet: "You think people respect smartasses, losers? You think losers can support a family, buy a house, go to college? What? You think you can go on fighting and farting around like kids? Huh? Huh Mr. Big Beer Drinker? And you," he said to me, "Mr. Ho Ho, rubbing yourself blind in your smelly bedroom. Disgusting. Some bar mitzvah you're going to have—you think I'm going to stand up there with you and say you're a man?"

One of Carlton's punishments was to work at the store, weekend mornings, for minimum wage—first in the stock room and then later on the floor. One day several months later, the *nakhes* of my bar mitzvah safely behind me, I biked over to see how it was going.

Carlton was with a customer, a woman, and they were looking, of all things, at sleds. It was still early to buy sleds, but my old man had decided that to be competitive he had to be first with the good stuff; if you can't do more volume, you can do smarter volume—this was his most recent slingshot against the ever-growing Gargantuas.

I never walked into Kidsville like the son of the owner—I skulked in, ashamed for some reason, trying not to trip over my family ties. I didn't deserve to act like I was some big shot; I didn't even think I deserved the smiles I got from my father's employees. So I kept my mouth shut and never even looked at all the toys that some other kid might have considered his for the taking.

I didn't want to bother my brother while he was making a sale, so I went right, toward the clothes, and down the stairs to the furniture department, behind which was my father's office. But only Sheila was there—his secretary—lighthearted, over-rouged, and always whispering. "Upstairs," she said.

I went up again and found him at the cash register, where he was alone, counting the checks in his drawer. The store was as quiet as five or six people shopping can be. I heard my brother laugh—maybe he was telling a sled story from his youth. We used to construct ramps to jump off of, heady with the joy of leaving the old man's doom back at the house, so we never had Flyers but the plastic sleds because they were faster.

My father kept counting checks. "Did you rake?" he said.

This was my penance—a farmlike list of chores I would perform to earn my keep, as my father put it, and lunch money. Any additional funds would have to be requested on a "what do you need it for?" basis.

I told him it was done.

"Because if there's one leaf—"

"I did it!" After a minute I said, "Did you tell him how to sell a sled?"

He stopped with the checks. He'd have to go back and recount or whatever, that was clear from the way he laid the counted pile on top of the others. He looked down, then back into my face. Though not technically broken, my nose would never heal well and would crag my otherwise baby-smooth face. He looked at me hard and sad, his mouth a small line. He turned and saw Carlton with the early bird sled buyer—he was showing her how the front handles of the Flyer turn to steer the thing.

My father re-stacked his checks, made them a crisp, neat deck again in his hand. He licked his thumb with a motion quick and birdlike. "No," he said, before he began counting again. "He's a natural."

Chapter Ten

Memory was a constant irritation, a clattering ceiling fan or pine-sappy fingers. Its prickle and odor reminded me of my ersatz existence: Steve for Sugar, a house for a barn, a wife for a coat rack, moral outrage for a spell of wound-licking, and a brother for two landlords who pitied me—uncloseted in Montana, and *they* pitied *me*.

But because I cleaned a lot, they also loved me. They would breeze down on weekend afternoons sometimes, after laying new gravel on the walk to their house or power-raking the field of its flowers ("had to be done," Jeffrey said, "what with the rain we've had"), to offer me a dinner of wine and roasted chicken and such up at the house, making me the preferred pet charity of the backwater do-it-yourselfer homosexual set. But I steadfastly declined their offers, even though I figured I might learn a thing or two from them, given their lives. It took me a while to realize Tom had money—homes with renovated barns just don't appear in your portfolio one day—and the relative facility that comes with it. But the story he told me, one day at work, gave me a new appreciation. Tom had been a model Montanan and happily, unsodomizedly married when Jeffrey moved in down the street, an event that kicked off a torrid, erotic summer of backdoor shenanigans that even one night included Tom's wife, to obviously disastrous results. But soon all parties recovered and became happy little churchgoers again, in their separate ways—Tom's way was to dress and act straight, and serve his Jeffrey as protector, provider, and grantor of whims.

We were in his office looking over my work when he sketched all this out for me. Some of his clients paid him extra for creative work, so they didn't have to go to an actual ad agency. Tom did all the work himself, in Quark, but recently he'd thrown me some bones: a few headlines for a senior center's promotional brochure that were needed after a sudden redesign. My head tilted once toward the plants on one wall and again toward framed examples of Big Sky's work on the other. He had the deck open to one of my better lines: "Stately Maturity." He put the printout down and put his legs up on the desk. It was almost time to go home, but still bright as noon.

"What's *your* story," he said, "is the question. You need us to fix you up with someone?"

I felt honor-bound to tell him I was comfortable with my heterosexuality.

"Ha!" he said. "That much I get. You're a guy's guy."

"I used to decorate shower curtains. A real Marty Stewart."

"Yeah?"

"And I'm technically still married."

"Well, marriage is somewhat emasculating."

"You seem to handle it fine," I said.

"Maybe that's why you don't seem interested in women, either," he went on musing. "Maybe you fancy yourself a eunuch. I used to."

"We'd be better off."

This elicited only a small nod, a wise little knowing admission with downcast eyes. He scratched at his beard, then rubbed the back of his neck, leaning back in his creaky office chair.

Claudia came in then and dropped something on his desk, a binder-bound sheath of papers. "For Tanya," she said. "That'll settle her hash."

I enjoyed Claudia—her husband had a lazy eye, and according

to her, it wasn't just lazy anymore but had gone on welfare. She said their home life was about as interesting as an airline magazine, but at least those came with barf bags.

Tom pulled the sheath closer to him, if only to acknowledge receipt.

"You getting to the bottom of him?" Claudia asked, nodding at me. "Find out if he owns a shirt that *isn't* stained."

She left without waiting for an answer, picking up her purse on her way out for the day. Her computer keyboard was covered with plastic, like a typewriter.

"You," Tom pointed at me, "have an albatross. All these people calling for you, your own kin, as they say, and you put them off."

"I don't want to abuse your long-distance."

"I have unlimited minutes. It's the business plan."

I just looked at him, so that all he could do was shake his head.

"So tell me," I said. "Can I write copy, or what?"

"Yeah you're all right," he said.

"No I mean, may I? As part of my job?"

"If you proofread it too."

"Then I'll need a raise, and business cards."

He kicked up an eyebrow. "Anything else?"

I leaned back, folded my hands where they fit so well, over my stomach, beneath what would have been my pectorals, had I any. "Would it kill ya to set some mousetraps in my barn?"

"They'd have to be shrew traps, and no, it wouldn't kill me—but it would my man. That guy loves God's every creature."

"He'll never know."

"Still," Tom said. He started packing up his leather shoulder bag with printouts, a few Zip disks, and a few books on geriatrics, which he looked at a moment before handing over to me, apparently because I had just weaseled myself into writing more copy for our client's new site. "No," Tom said, "what you won't do for someone you love is worse than what you will do. What you *won't* do is what kills ya."

To this I had nothing to say, and he noticed.

"You know a little something about that?" he said.

"Used to," I said.

The anxiety was like a blindfold: the barn gone dark, my body kidnapped in bed, and one move would snap me into my own mouse trap. It must be what a primate or other intelligent animal feels in a cage. A gorilla! Who in their right mind would cage up a gorilla just to watch him? Or worse, a dolphin? Humans, that's who. Humans are the great cagers. We'll cage anything. Lesser creatures, lesser humans, gorillas, dolphins—shit, throw the gorillas and the dolphins together, we don't care. We can always claim biblical superiority, and budget cuts.

But it wasn't just anxiety. I was in love, and every time I thought about it, which was always, on its heels came the guilt. The shlameel to suffering's shlamazel. Lying in a borrowed bed, guilt rapped a tappa-tappa on the inside of my breastbone. Its tapping served as alarm clock, torturer, inquisitor, and mother: How could you? Who the hell do you think you are? Your own brother, your own suffering sister-in-law? And where could such a thing have taken you, either one of you? You think you will get looks of loving kindness, benevolence bowed up and boxed like a wedding gift? Would they not be tainted, no matter what your love? And what exactly do you know about love? Big expert in love, aren't you? Nice track record you got there. Fell for the second woman you sexed, held on to her as slave to master, and are now headed for divorce.

Tappa-tappa, tappa-tappa.

It was a rhythm that arrived daily, catching me spent and beaten by a depressing day of proofreading or a hangover or, more likely, both, and unable to muster the strength to rationalize and defend my behavior. The tappa-tappa brought high heart rates and a panic unlike any I'd ever known, even those from the hours I'd spent torturing myself with images of Carol Ann on all fours with her lover. No, this was a pure panic of the "oh why oh why?" kind. It felt like a murder had been committed, and though this was dramatic to the point of hyperbole, it still *felt* that way.

When this feeling came, whatever I was doing, I'd be forced to stop. In the Jetta, *tappa-tappa*. Bent over a manuscript of backcountry survival techniques, *tappa-tappa*. Lying in bed in the barn having crossworded myself into a droopy-eyed anesthesia, *tappa-tappa*. The naked image of naked June at the shower curtain would come up into my mind like a screensaver—and I'd sit up straight, rigid in my body as if shocked, zappa-zappa! I'd look around, turn myself over or reach out as if to stop myself, assume a different position, or run my fingers through my hair and cough, like a person chronically in pain. I felt it down in the alveoli, the tight, inexorable vacuum of conscience.

It was an affront, this tappa-tappa, because I was used to walking with the righteous, the martyred—as the younger, less successful brother, but also as a pumper of Jewish blood. For Jews, righteousness is a sort of shield, a badge, a source of both heroism and caricatured foolishness—from Freedom Summer volunteers and Golda Meir, to my father demanding a better table at the Outback Steakhouse. An abused people, a despised people, who fought through it nonetheless—it's funny how such a mindset can settle at your core. People take to you, you become convinced that because of this moral standing, your two feet perched on Moral Mountain, you'll never be knocked down, when in reality you can be pushed down quite easily—ask the soldiers in the West Bank about it.

But oh to be a soldier in the West Bank! There's at least a mitigating ambiguity there, because that ten-year-old Palestinian *could conceivably* be carrying a bomb or a shoulder-fired rocket launcher into the kill zone, and the same goes for the ambulance that comes to treat his wounds. It's war, sort of. Whereas my situation was more black-and-white: I'd taken advantage of my lonely, drugged-up sister-in-law, out of pain and frustration and zero self-worth, but still. I'd recognized an opportunity and taken it. Her reaction to my return was showing the whole thing for what it was—the basest of egoisms, an attack on decency by lust's pernicious insistence, an of-the-moment debasement that would have made even your free-lovingest 1969 hippie cringe, get a haircut, and call Charles Schwab.

Tappa-tappa. Tappa-tappa.

Would that it were real—some uniformed authority rapping at my barn door, some polizei for moral frauds and those in over their heads. But no. For better or worse, America doesn't work that way.

Chapter Eleven

Down at the Copper Cowboy, I was welcomed. "Oh yeah, renting the gay barn." Everyone knew me but didn't bother with my name. They could see I had misplaced my life somehow, and that was enough. And anyway, the TV was always broken, and when you're fat and pathetic and new, people tend to tell you their stories. For a little while that summer it salvaged me, pulled my blood along in the right directions.

Les, for example. He stopped at the Copper Cowboy most every night except Mondays—burger night at Ting's Bar in Jefferson City—and nowhere but at the Copper Cowboy would he and I become friendly. He was just over fifty with a hedgerow of black hair and Johnny Cash good looks. He called me Tiny, and when he told me, "Tiny, the best drinking buddy is a guy with a bad memory," I said, "Right. Who's Tiny again?" From then on we were thick as thieves, as Mom would have said. When I told him where I lived, cringing at my landlords' sexual orientation, Les said, "Hey, I got no reason to judge nobody. You wanna paint your barn pink, what gives me the right to say boo?" Turns out, this was Les's credo, as he had put a man in a coma with a roundhouse kick to the head—he was a black belt—when he was living in Yakima, Washington. It was over a woman, obviously, and the story as Les told it involved such ambulatory altercations—at his house, at her house, at a bar, and finally in a Conoco parking lot—as to make retelling it almost impossible. But the point to Les was that if the guy didn't come out of the coma, they were gonna give him manslaughter.

"I gave the guy two swings," Les said. "And one of them even hit me! But the judge said it was Washington law that I needed to give him three swings." He held his pinkie, ring, and middle fingers erect in front of my face. "Can you believe that shit? I went to jail for not letting that asshole hit me a third time." He lived in Montana now because Montana law takes a more self-defense-friendly approach in requiring only two charity swings. Unless you have a gun, and then you can just shoot the fucker for looking at you wrong.

"Judge said," Les continued, "that if I was that good at martial arts, I should have given him ten swings. But I really ain't all that good—I just know enough not to get hurt by the idiots. But I'll tell you what, Tiny—don't ever get into a fight, because it ain't worth it. Ever."

"Right," I said. "But who's Tiny?"

That had him laughing so hard he called Bartender Bill to buy me a drink.

The other bartender was Sharon, the smiling beauty with a sweet heart who fended off patrons' pawing and proclamations of love with jokes like: "What drives a lesbian up a wall? Crack in the ceiling." Les would flirt with her, telling her he'd fight every guy in the joint for just one night with her, and though she declined with a head shake and a "pretty good offer, but…" he was about the only guy who stood a chance, because women loved him. He said so himself—facts are facts. But he said he deserved everything he got, good and bad, because his father was poor as dirt but always found a way to make money, once by salvaging spent cigarette stubs from the urinals, drying them, reconstituting the tobacco, and reselling them as whole cigarettes. Stories like that just fell from him, and then, even though there was no way in hell your history could possibly be as interesting as his, he went ahead and asked you anyway. No wonder the women loved him.

"Oh my family is a piece of work," I told him. "My brother is a toy inventor—made a quarter of a million dollars in gross sales on a ring that rolls on, with ball bearings, like a condom. Our old man is his rep."

"One brother is always the clearer success," Les said. "No offense," he added.

"None taken," I said. "I slept with his wife."

What a treat to see such a thick-chested guy's guy like Les buckle over with laughter—and then figure out I wasn't kidding.

"Hmmm," he said. "So he tried to kill you."

"No. He doesn't know a thing."

I half-expected him to say "What's the problem then?" but Les was a more sophisticated guy.

"Right," he said. "Now who are you again?"

But it wasn't funny, so he went on. "Do you love her?"

"I'm here, aren't I?"

He nodded, in the way of a man who barely knows your name, has no idea what you do for a living and couldn't care less, and yet knows your deepest secret, just like that. I won't say it only happens in bars, but wherever else it does happen, I don't think I want to be there.

In any bar, no one is your best friend forever. People have to get up and mill around, bullshit, play the jukebox. It's a bar, for God's sake—there are calls to be made, cigarettes to be purchased, kids to be checked on, stories to be told. It's the pedestrian preposterousness inherent to any opiate, and I took no small solace in it to be sure. Oh that it would have lasted. Maybe if I'd decided to blab my heart out on some other day. But no—I blabbed on the day I did, and got my solace cut to the quick. To explain how, I need to convey a little about the Copper Cowboy regulars.

First, there's Karl, who never really said a word to anyone, not that I saw at least, but then would buy a round out of the blue, and everyone would say, "Thanks Karl!" Sharon told me he was living out back in a lean-to literally chicken-wired to one of the Copper

Cowboy's storage sheds for the summer; come winter he would start hitchhiking south again. The rumor, unconfirmed, was that he used to be a ballet instructor in Los Angeles, and from the elegance of his parted and greased hair to his long fingers cupping his vodka tonic at the end of the bar, I believed it. But you didn't want to ask him, for it would be a violation of his ghostly privacy. He sat there, watching, sometimes reading a thin hardback without the dust jacket, straight-spined in a black tab-collared Members Only jacket, minding his own business.

Then there was Tiffany, or rather Tiff, the village skank. Drunk one night at the Copper Cowboy's new jukebox, she showed me her appendectomy scar. She'd been saying how it was her and only her who'd made sure they put the really *good* songs on there, like "Do You Really Want to Hurt Me?" and Kid Rock and "You Shook Me All Night Long" and that one that goes "Don't hand me no lines, and keep your hands to yourself" and, ooh ooh, "Billie Jean." She said she didn't care if he was a pervert—Michael'd get you dancing like no one else. She often wore only a halter top and women's high-waisted jeans, and she was excellent, she said, in a crisis. This one time, she'd been slapped by her ex-boyfriend when he came to get some stuff from her apartment, and so on his way out the door, she threw a salad plate that shattered and sent a shard right into his eye. "He was all bent over goin' 'shit shit shit my eye my eye!' and I just walked up to him and peeled his hand back and fuckin pulled it out like that," she said. "He slapped the wrong woman." To which I said it sounded like he slapped the right woman, one who can hurt you and then save you, and this made her screw her eyes up at me and tell me I was pretty slick. That's when she unbuckled her belt, parted her fly, stretched her purple thong, and showed me her scar.

Then there was A.P. He had a voice like a breaking wineglass, and he'd use it to spout off about one thing or another, most often environmentalists. He asked me if I was an environmentalist the first time he met me. He was a short guy, puffy from neck to belt buckle, and, drunk or sober, he would cock one eye at you and throw his gut at you; the two of us face-to-face must have been a sight to behold. I told him I was no environmentalist, and he said good, because he'd shoot one in the head if he thought he wouldn't get caught. "Pop pop pop, wouldn't fuckin care." When I said, wow I can't imagine shooting anybody, except maybe Hitler, he said, "They *are* Hitler!" I'd once seen A.P. so drunk he had to get Tiff to write out his check for him, but man, he was a talker—which was why his wife locked him out of the house so much. He was one of those guys you can only nod and smile at while he's talking, which creates the myth that he's appreciated for his wisdom, when really he just won't stop talking. In New England that might get you a CEOship or the vice presidency, but at the Copper Cowboy it gets you a bar tab you only have to pay quarterly.

On the night I unburdened myself upon Les, A.P. was in with this woman Paula—his girlfriend—and he was louder than ever: "Who the fuck you waving to?" when I tried to say hi to greasy-haired Ted the stoner. "Can we turn the fuckin' jukebox up now?" to Bartender Bill, and also, "What the fuck's the point of a jukebox if you can't hear it?" Paula was even shorter than A.P., like almost dwarfish, but she held her own with him at pool and at drinking, standing by his barstool, nestled into his crotch. She smacked gum she kept on the rim of her beer glass. She had a big face that was pretty if you looked at it in the reflection of the pizza freezer behind the bar. Finally she said they needed to get home to "check the laundry," wink-wink, and when Bartender Bill said to A.P., on their way out the door, "Do it once for me," A.P. said, "Pussy! I'll do it once for you, once for myself, then once for her!" I was one part repulsed, one part empathetic, and two parts jealous: until back they come into the bar, butting their way in, Paula first, scuttling backward, then A.P., who had his hands up in a pleading appeal to someone who hadn't yet shown her face—who turned out to be his wife.

Mrs. A.P., looking like Ma Joad in jeans and plain gray hair pulled back in a bun, waddled her way into the Copper Cowboy carrying what looked to me like a rifle. I mean, it was a rifle, clearly, since she had it cocked into her shoulder, finger on the trigger, and one squinty eye leveled at A.P.'s heart. I ducked behind Les like a little girl, and when Mrs. A.P. started firing, I figured my adrenaline-fuelled head, or my cowardice, was clogging out the sound. But no: there simply was no sound. It was a BB gun, and BBs were now spraying and caroming across the bar, off bottles, into the pockets of the pool table, up off the foam-board ceiling panels—everywhere the skizzing clink of small metal.

A.P. yipped and contorted, like a man swarmed by wasps. Someone started laughing, even as the BBs were still flying, but it wasn't until A.P. and Paula had scampered their cursing way out the back door and Sharon, quick as a whip, had snatched the gun from Mrs. A.P.'s face that the full revelry began. Mrs. A.P. was quickly enthroned on a barstool and given her favorite drink, the bar's signature copper cowboy, which she drank stony-faced, proud, with maybe a little curl of smile there when someone slapped her on the back. She fixed her bun, and the copper cowboys lined up for her like fans wanting an autograph.

Les said to me, "Don't see that every day, do you?"

"Hope not," I said.

"Tiny, you were scared?"

"Weren't you?"

He hesitated, then nodded.

"So," I said. "Any advice?" We were still, I hoped, on the subject of me and June. I hadn't talked about it with an actual human for so long, it was a relief I didn't want to relinquish quite yet.

"Would you take it?" he said.

"Maybe."

"Well, my father said you have to put down your Bible to tie a noose."

I nodded knowingly. "What the fuck does that mean?"

"I don't know," he said. "I was hoping you would."

I must have looked despondent.

"Look, you got two choices, as the Missus over there made plain just now. You either forget the whole thing, or stand up and face the consequences."

"Thanks," I said.

"Don't mention it."

It was then that we noticed something going on at the end of the bar: Sharon was handing Karl a napkin, and then fetching a clean towel, wetting it, and telling him to hold to his tilted-back head. His face was calm, his mouth grim, his highball glass jagged with the shards remaining from one of Mrs. A.P.'s unluckier shots. "Glass in his eye," Sharon said. "Glass got him in the eye."

This was when Tiffany, having gone back to feeding dollars into the gone-quiet jukebox, shrieked out a concussive "Don't touch it!" She stormed up to Karl, only to be held back by more than a couple pairs of arms while it was discussed whether or not Karl should go to the hospital. "Bullshit!" Tiffany huffed. This was her moment, when her gift for crises was needed. Her calling. It was only because Sharon had been closer to the shooting that it wasn't Tiffany herself to take the gun out of Mrs. A.P.'s hands. Tiffany had been headed right for her—she'd been shot with a BB gun before goddammit, and everyone there knew the boyfriend story. So Karl agreed to let her have a stab at him, as the closest urgent-care center was in Boulder—who would drive them, as even Sharon had been drinking?

So when the bloody towel was removed and Karl turned his face to the light for Tiffany's inspection, and Tiffany tipped her tongue through her lips and said, "Okay now—wish I'd gotten a manicure," for once my stomach gave out and I decided I'd learned enough about Montana's brand of crisis and suffering for a night.

Poor Karl will have to remain in that submissive state forever, his body monk-calm, the bar quiet until "Do You Really Want to Hurt Me?" came on the jukebox, because despite my best intentions and more than a few cravings, I left the Copper Cowboy and, for that summer at least, never went back.

Chapter Twelve

At dawn, if I were to get up and hike about a quarter mile, I could watch the sun rise over the Elkhorns with a soft purple-orange ascent like the train to Jordan coming around the bend. The sunsets had more of a hardness, not petulant but not tranquil either, as if to suggest we didn't get enough done today, because today is what matters, not tomorrow.

The mountains here are somehow different than the Colorado ranges where the Meyerson family used to vacation every July. Montana's mountains feel, if less magnificent, more omnipresent, a constant surprise of fisted stone. And more personal too, approachable and intimate. You can get into them, on top of them, and be part of them. Take a nap under a Douglas fir, and it's your mountain. Each breath feels like you've sucked it off a high, hard spine of rock.

So with the Copper Cowboy off the itinerary, I'd go try to out-hike my suffering, having saved enough for a nice sturdy pair of Vasque boots. Out in the Elkhorn Mountains, there was acre after acre of pristine, untouched loneliness. I forced myself over every scrabble of it, one foot in front of the other, with a map in my back pocket, as if it mattered. At the top of Crow Peak I found, sure enough, crows flitting and flapping and soaring around its summit with a plumage and grandeur far above what crows are supposed have—imitating eagles, these crows were, and enjoying themselves, playing, fornicating as much as any lover, caressing the high drafts and plummeting when the thermals beneath them cut out. When I took in the view, the topography spilling away from me in all directions, I saw the folds of June's body, the tight, smooth saddle like the small of her back, the luxurious ridges and hidden dales. But the fucking crows would have none of it—they laughed and mocked, in the way that only a creature who'd recently disemboweled a jackrabbit carcass can. And I was too out of breath to retort.

Which is to say that during that summer, it became clear to me that I was not one of them, Montanans. When would I ever be? People here don't walk around with their heart exposed like a bone in a dog's mouth. Love is more a fact, a force of nature, something you do on Saturday night. People here act, and I needed action like a hole in the head. Action is what brung me, and I didn't want to dance with it.

Chapter Thirteen

But by August the cement was hardening around me: I'd stuck with Big Sky and now had something of a mini-career, about which I could tell Dad with less upbraiding. They even knew my orders at the cafes and sandwich shops up and down North Last Chance. I'd bought some 1x12 white ash boards to make myself a bookshelf. I plugged my phone back in, cut back on my drinking, and heard through the grapevine that Karl's eye had healed just fine. I was cooking myself healthier meals with some actual fiber in them, and I didn't even chafe too much when the crone in the See-n-Save sold me a used sofa for $155 because "It can't be Jewed down any more than that."

It was that sofa, actually, on which I was lying when the world went upside down again. It started with the phone. It always starts with the phone.

"Hello?"

"Hank."

I had imagined that I would play it cool when the moment came, but what can you do? Steve McQueen, I've never been. "Holy fucking shit," I blurted, "I've missed you!"

June laughed, a sound so normal, you'd think I'd been talking to her daily. "Holy fucking shit, I miss you too."

"So you're coming to see me? I've kept the place all clean like you like it."

"That's all you got for me?"

"I got a coat rack. It's very charming."

"How is it charming?"

"I don't know, it's stupid and simple. Like a daisy, or a Bennigan's."

"Ha."

"So what more could you need?"

"I need you to come home."

I was sitting on the sofa now, face lined with the impression of its herringbone upholstery. The thing smelled, I realized. Not like an old sofa but like me.

"I'm there," I said.

"But let me tell you why."

This was a dream, obviously, what I was hearing—I must have fallen asleep on the sofa. But I could hear my heart race, and I felt my turnip face and knew I was awake.

"What's wrong?" I said.

June sighed. She gulped down a breath like the last of a muffin she'd been chewing. "Your brother had an accident."

He'd been jogging, at night, she told me, on the pedestrian path that hugs West River Road, which at times takes exercisers right up to the trees and the underbrush that plummet down to the river basin. This was where my brother lost his balance and fell.

He tried to mitigate his fall by grabbing at branches and by planting one foot on something—ground or tree trunk or bush bramble—but there was nothing, and when his extended left leg finally made contact, it was locked up and got mangled something good: severely broken ankle, ligament damage to his knee that may or may not require surgery, and some kind of socket damage to his hip. The rest of the fall beat him up pretty badly too, breaking a couple ribs, cutting his lip and ear, puncturing his palm, and giving him a concussion. He managed to climb back to the road, where a middle school teacher on her way home from her fiftieth birthday party stopped to give him a ride.

The ankle required a cast. June had waited two weeks after it'd been set to call me, though at first she didn't say why.

"How is he now?"

"Not good. He's morose, bitter."

"Sounds normal."

"Well, it's not." She paused, sighed. "He's moved out. Sorta."

He'd gone to live at his studio was what she meant. He had a futon and coffeemaker and everything, except a shower. So he was home a lot too. It was strange, she said, but no major freak-out blowup or anything.

"I'm there," I said again.

She didn't say anything. The phone line's connection was oppressively clear.

"What?" I said.

"We're not splitting up."

"Sounds like you are. A separation is a sep—"

"It's not a separation. I just can't deal with him right now."

"What's he doing?"

"Just being him, but like, amplified. He's just a nasty little shit sometimes. It's just this new toy. And our finances are running thin."

"Like what, what's he doing?"

"No," she said. "That's the point. I can't say—not to you."

"Sure you can—"

"You know what I mean."

"Sure I do."

"If you come home, and I want you to, do it for him. He doesn't have anyone, and I know he's hurting, but he won't tell me how, and I'm afraid for him to—"

"For him? You can't talk to me about it, but you can ask me to come home for *him?*"

"Of course."

"For him?"

She obviously didn't see the issue, no matter how often I repeated her words. Still: "For him," I said to the coat rack.

"Your brother is hurt, and feeling rejected, and he wants to see you."

"Did the fall affect his ability to use a telephone?"

"You banned him from calling."

This was true. June was huffy now, and I'd lost the chance to say the things I'd been building up in my head to say. I crossed my legs, and the sofa sagged beneath me. Turns out, it *can* be Jewed down a little more. It was getting windy outside the barn; the sun gone now, replaced by the browbeating gray of a coming storm.

"I don't want to go there for that," I said. "I want you to come here."

"You can't have that! This isn't about you and me."

"Well then if it's about my brother—"

"Obviously—"

"Then I can't come. I won't come."

"You're a Ted Kaczynski out there now?"

"No, I've just come to realize that I don't even *like* my brother, or my old man! They're parasites to me. I have nothing left! Besides," I told her, "he'll be fine. This'll be just the kick in the pants he needs. He doesn't need me to do it for him."

Her response was quick and sharp. "What if I need you to do it for him?"

I was not so quick. I was ridiculous again in my pink barn, childish as a puppy. "Maybe," I said, "that's something *you* can't have."

Chapter Fourteen

I didn't hear from her again. Montanans were guzzling the last of their summer like cans of Rainier. I worked on the Carroll College Millennium Fund brochure. I carpooled with Tom when I could, the Jetta putzy in the altitude. Sugar the dog menaced a ten-year-old boy riding his bike, but the subsequent community outrage got nowhere, then fizzled out altogether. Nobody called to update me on my brother, or anything else. I wasn't worried. I wasn't really anything.

It's funny the things that get to you in such a state, the underbellies exposed. I unearthed a night crawler while planting tulip bulbs at Jeffrey's request. I thought it was as a tree root until I saw it throbbing to escape me—at least eight inches long, sucked away into dirt like a wet noodle. Then tackling the "to be recycled" cardboard pile, I discovered a pizza box that had harbored a shrew flophouse, a littering of little turds tumbling down the accordioned cardboard.

Both incidents sent me inside in tears. I can't say why.

Stand up and face it, Les had said, or forget it. If I kept up this way, my choice would be made for me.

The Friday before Labor Day Tom stopped by the barn. Faced with my mystifying return to hollowness, neither Tom nor Jeffrey had said very much to me of late. Sensible people know better. On some pretense or another, Tom would sometimes check in on his barn, look around at his handiwork and maybe see if I was up to no good or something, and I would complain about the steroidal spiders—seriously, Montana's like a goddamn spider Venice Beach—and the wasps that make themselves at home because what are you gonna do about it but give them your iced tea, and maybe the rest of your omelet too?

But this time was different. He knocked, and when I opened the door his back was turned to me. He was in jeans and boots, very rural. He complained of the heat, then asked how it was in my place.

"Fine," I said. "But if the window fan and the ceiling fan were ever to unionize, we'd be in trouble."

I got nothing from him. Just a small smile, then a sigh. He was squinting in the sun, goatee glistening with little beads of sweat.

"Do you have anything to drink?" he said.

In my kitchen I offered him juice, water, Vernor's, but he cut me short. "I mean to *drink*."

Well why didn't he say so? He himself had turned me on to the alluring irony of the Happily Married Liquor Store.

I poured us whiskey with lemon and sugar and a little Cointreau, my own special creation. Tom eyed it but drank a good long sip. He lowered his head sheepishly.

"You okay?" I asked him.

"Oh sure. Just procrastinating."

"Tell me about it."

"I don't want to go home to the love of my life...isn't that weird? This day's been like a dream, one of those stupid ones where you're just going through the motions but everything is weird."

"I once dreamt I was folding sweaters in my closet. That was it.'"

He drank again, then sucked air like he'd hit a sore tooth. "What *is* your story, Hank? A young guy like you shouldn't be so miserable. It must be a woman. *Something* has set you off, the way you treat your brother, though out here brothers are as likely to beat each other down as hug. But you don't need to talk about it. Just—hell, going into town and trying to get laid might do you some good. There is a world outside the Copper Cowboy. Montana doesn't need another hermit."

"Maybe."

He waved as if to say "No, no maybe." He looked around the place, frowned at something up near the ceiling, then said, "Have you ever killed something, Hank?"

"Just crickets," I said. "When I was a kid, they lived in the driveway's retaining wall below my window, and they'd keep me up. I'd be out there with a can of Raid, inching toward them, because if you just walk right up, they stop screeching because they know what you're up to."

Tom swished his whiskey around in the glass. "You're a weird one, that's for sure."

This rankled me. All my life people have been telling me I'm the weird one, and I guess Montana wasn't immune. But they didn't know the half of it. The quarter of it, even.

The sugar in his glass had settled, but with his swishing it now spiraled back to life. Tom had small, shallow eyes, with chocolate brown irises—unnaturally rich, really. It softened his face and put you at ease. He finally laughed at my cricket hunting. How could you not?

He said then that it's sort of a way of life out here, killing. "Most people who live outside the city have killed something. It's in the air, or the trees or whatever. Don't tell anyone if you see a mountain lion, by the way—they'll form a posse."

"Noted," I said, though I'd never considered the possibility.

"Things have a way of taking care of themselves out here." He considered this and added, "God I sound like Governor Bush. Some good ol' boy."

"Come November he'll be Good Ol' Boy in Chief."

"It's just that that dog was on a train, Hank. He was going to hurt someone, and really there is nothing that can be done about it until—"

"You're talking about Sugar?" I had to say this out loud, because before Tom's knock I had been thinking about Steve, and of course Steve wouldn't hurt anything but squirrels and someday maybe somebody's bumper. I had been wondering if she still likes having her paws rubbed.

"Yeah," Tom said. "Sugar. A good name for a bad dog. I shot him today." He looked up at the ceiling fan. He crossed his arms, then uncrossed them to finish his whiskey. "That's a good drink," he said. On cue, I refilled our glasses and stirred them with a fresh spoon. The spoon was pointed and had a viney pattern etched in relief up its handle, I assumed to honor Bacchus. They came with the barn, since I hadn't packed any silverware at all. "Those were my grandmother's spoons," he said. "Cynthia never much cared for them. Cynthia's my ex."

Oh that word! It's vague and yet dangerously mysterious, like shards of glass wrapped in white tissue paper. And something about it will always make me start in on the palliatives. "He was a scary dog, a loaded gun on paws."

Tom nodded.

"And you can't go up to those kind of people and speak reasonably to them," I went on. "That just doesn't work, and the situation goes on unchanged. The larger picture—"

"Yes, yes. We can drink to that."

We clinked our glasses. The ex's spoon lay on the kitchen table with a little puddle of whiskey winking sunlight.

"Was it hard to do?"

"I don't like to kill things, Hank. He was just a sorry animal, raised poorly, didn't know any better." But as he said this, Tom seemed to see something else, a terror he slowly shook his head at. "The way he kept coming toward me—I got him first in the chest, and his front legs were, like, not working. He was pushing himself forward with his hind legs."

"Christ. It's like something from Hemingway."

"Worse. I got him again when he was ten feet from me. I didn't want him to suffer."

"And what did you—"

"Put him in my truck, dumped him in the woods. But see, Jerry has an insanely bleeding heart. He believes in reason. He believes in rehabilitation. He hasn't lived here all his life. Jerry's a—a lover, I guess. He's a lover. He thinks love can solve everything. He'll be furious with me. No, no—he'll be 'disappointed,' like I'm a kid or something. He's going to give me that look."

It took me a minute to realize that this Jerry he was talking about was actually his partner-lover, Jeffrey. The whiskey must have made him slip, I reasoned. Why was I so stubborn in my errors back then? Why did I insist on them the way tasteless people insist on decorating their homes themselves?

"Jeffrey," I said, "will understand. Tell him what you told me, and take the whiskey with you."

He blinked at me. "It's Jerry," he says. "Not Jeffrey." He barked out a laugh, a sharp-edged sound I didn't care for. "Christ, Hank, you've been here almost four months and you don't know our names?"

"I must have misheard."

His laugh tapered to a sneering sigh, then fell away altogether. "Oh shit," he said, wiping his face. "Being drunk isn't going to help this situation, either. Maybe I'll tell him first that he's known as 'Jeffrey' down here, to get him laughing."

I leaned back, bobbing from this small shame. "Tom and *Jerry?*" I finally said, suggesting that he might still, somehow, be wrong.

"Yeah. Perfect, huh? You can bet people had their fun with that one. And here all this time I just thought you were being tactful not to make some little joke. You like to make little jokes, don't you?"

"It's adds up to one big one, I promise you. But listen, don't tell him about Sugar. How's he going to know? Isn't the larger picture the issue?"

"That's not the way it works," Tom said. "You seem like someone who'd come to see that already. Sometimes you have to do the hard thing and carry it through. I lived a long time thinking what Cynthia didn't know wouldn't hurt her, but it's a hard road, and one I don't like. I had to do it, and Jerry won't like it, but we're still gonna be lovers, and all those things can fit together in this world just fine."

"Says who?"

"Says me." He made a little Vanna White wave of his arm. "My world, I make up the rules."

This took the wind out of me. I don't know. It wasn't like weeping was a stranger, but its suddenness titled me back, a speedy conflagration choking my sinuses. Tom looked at me, stood, and through my erupting weepiness his face took on a birdy insouciance—the dark, shallow eyes, the soft inquisitive forehead, the sharp nose transformed to the gleam of observant beak. He cooed something about being sorry to have unburdened one like that and to please please forgive him and also keep the whole dog-killing thing to myself so we don't start our own Balkan Wars here, and then smiled and circled the barn a moment, skittish, stealing a look out the windows, as if for Sugar's ghost. Then he found the still-open front door's rectangle of light and flapped out it, slapping his jeans of dust, steadying himself briefly on the first of my three steps, suspended there like the sugar in our whiskeys and squinting up the road that led to his house and his lover and his world, for which it looked like he was making rules at that very moment. But then no, he finally shoved off quick as light, carried by his own air current, because he was caught by his own rules and really couldn't wait any longer to go tell Jeffrey what he'd done.

Jerry, I mean.

Chapter Fifteen

One thing I had plenty of time to do in Montana was think. Probably too much. Thinking is best left to the professionals, like librarians and theoretical physicists. But I couldn't help myself. With Tom gone, and Sugar too, and the whiskey-Cointreau opening doors in my head, I had no choice. I didn't just think—I inhabited. It was a talent I suddenly discovered in myself: thoughts not just my own, but of those I loved too. I rooted in them, riffled them, played all the angles, as if each fired neuron was essential to the calculus of this Montana disaster. Which it was.

This is what I thought about, while Tom was up facing his lover's kind-hearted wrath: a night, way back during my first month of graduate school, when I took Carol Ann, Carlton, and June to a party thrown by my new peers.

This was before I soured on academia, or vice versa, before my spell of barfing from the anxiety of teaching, and I wasn't yet afraid of the crowd in the backyard, all slouching in varying degrees of ironic seating. June and I were yucking it up with them, even—June was saying that she'd had a dream where her mother and Pamela Anderson were making out in the laundry room of her parents' home in Kansas, and June had been there too but was doing the laundry, and her basket filled up with folded whites and she couldn't see her mom or Pamela Anderson anymore, just hear their slurpy kisses.

Carlton and Carol Ann were off playing quarters, so there was no one to temper June's enthusiasm for describing the kisses. She got more than a few cringes, even from the most dedicatedly blasé of my colleagues. I sort of cringed too, wondering if this was the kind of thing that smart people found hokey—and not the good kind of hokey. But June had powers of attraction, obviously, and someone picked up her enthusiasm and said Pamela Anderson was one of those awful stars you can't help but look at, like a car accident.

"Yeah," I'd said. "A car accident you really, really wanna fuck."

It was the first time June ever touched me. She'd been sitting next to me, outside in the backyard of this party, her in a gingham picnic chair and me in an inflatable Garfield pool raft, and she grabbed my arm, laughing. I saw the back of her throat in the tiki torches' flicker. I didn't know her from a can of paint. She'd been together with my brother about three months, and he had, during the last of those months, made her a standing offer of marriage, which had sent everyone into a tizzy that grew each day June remained undecided. Dad counseled caution but seemed more proud than anything else—his Carlton had become a buyer for A Passionate Childhood and already had the beginnings of the Roller Rings idea, but still—that he might be in a position to get married was a coup.

The backyard was surrounded by a six-foot wooden-slat fence. The only light came from the candles and the house windows and the screen door. There was one tree, a medium-sized maple that needed pruning, off in the corner near the kitchen window. Up in its branches, a murder of crows was ignoring us, except for one or two of them rustling down to the fence slats and back. If we were keeping them awake, I figured it was their due, since their early morning kvetching did the same to humans all over the world. Or perhaps, being scavengers, they were waiting for one of my big-brained colleagues to kill off another—already it was happening, with a woman in pigtails and dark blue jeans calling a guy next to her "disingenuous" for saying he wouldn't fuck Pamela Anderson. "I'd totally fuck Pamela Anderson," she announced.

June saw me looking at the crows. "In Wamego they roosted in a tree at this one woman's house, a friend of my mother's, an ancient woman, in her nineties at least, in this big, nice old house on Vine Street. She wouldn't let anyone touch her crows. People offered her money to get in there and go after them because they were such a nuisance. But she wouldn't let them. 'I'll sue!' she'd say. She told us about how intelligent and misunderstood crows are, how she'd seen them soften acorns in the birdbath to make them easier to crack. But when we visited her she'd let my sister and me scare them away so that we could watch them fly back. We'd run underneath them and say 'Get on now, git!'"

She looked at me, drank some of her beer. "Then one day she died," she said, "and the neighbors baited the crows with squirrel carcasses dusted with arsenic."

"Quoth the raven, 'Nevermore.'"

"Fuckin A right."

She knew this would make me smile—her casual cursing was starting to charm me.

Inside, Carol Ann and Carlton were still at it with the game of quarters. "Who do you gotta blow around here to start a game of quarters?" Carol Ann had said, which was one of her standard raunchy-isms before the professional world got into her skin. You'd think some big-brained theory guy would be smart enough to say, "You're looking at him!" or something, but instead they just pulled out the dining room table and filled the glasses.

June and I could hear the occasional whoop when someone plunked a quarter into a plastic cup, and once or twice Carlton's voice in a mild argument. Carol Ann and I had been fighting that weekend about getting a dog—i.e., Steve—and the sound of her voice whooping was intended as punishment, I was sure. Oh Christ the suffering of her soul because I didn't want a dog too! When our wants didn't coincide, it literally hurt her, and confused her too—like being chastised in a foreign language. It seemed I was always playing the pessimist to Carol Ann's optimist, the practical to her impromptu, the downer to her upper—or, she had often accused, the one trying to keep her down if she was down already. The stick-in-the-mud. The responsible one. And this from a kid of twenty-five, an otherwise sky-is-blue reveler in the passionate art of literature, who just the month before had re-read *To Kill a Mockingbird* and wept when old Atticus held his head high as a corrupted jury condemned his innocent client. I was Mr. Can-we-afford-that? Mr. Isn't-having-your-parents-cosign-a-mortgage-a-bad-idea? Carol Ann both depended on me for this and hated me for it. It made her sometimes abrasive, sometimes quiet as stone.

June didn't seem to notice the quarters playing. "Crows have it good," she said. "Nothing gets to them, it seems. They're like the annoying roommate whom nothing annoys. Some people are like that, but most aren't. Like you—I bet you have a thousand pet peeves."

"Me? Just Pamela Anderson."

She laughed again, then squeezed my arm and let her hand drop.

"Speakers that buzz," I said. "That's tops." I readjusted my weight in the Garfield float, and the new-plastic smell rose up and comforted me. "And shit rolling around in the Jetta's trunk. Too much Togetherness. The morons at *Granta*. Jogging, and not jogging. Tailgaters, big time. Soggy french fries, melted ice cream. Oh, and hunger, poverty, injustice, etc. You?"

"What do you think would happen," she said, "if we just started making out back here?"

I sat on my Garfield. I smiled.

"Like all gross and grabby."

I laughed. "What could they say?"

"They'd think Pamela Anderson—"

"Exactly," I said.

She hit me in the arm. "You don't even know what I was going to say."

"Yes I do."

Someone approached from behind us. It was Carol Ann, dark-faced with the lit house at her back. June and I turned to look up at her. The crows in the trees rustled. She looked us both in the eyes: me, then June.

"Kids," she finally said. She lifted her plastic cup to us, downed it, then pursed her lips, grinned, and tongued out a quarter. It was small compared to that nose of hers, but still—it lay on her tongue shiny as a full moon, then fell over her lips into her palm. A very sexy thing to see. And, shame on me, I had the thought that if I just gave in about the dog—big, slobbering snout muddy-nuzzling its way through my paper-grading!—I might get some action.

"Your boyfriend," Carol Ann said to June, "sucks at quarters."

From inside the house we heard a dull metallic ping-and-clatter, and then another, and another.

"He's practicing?" June said.

Carol Ann nodded. "And drinks when he misses. He tried telling that Davey guy there's no 'I' in 'TEAM.' And Davey told him there's no 'U' either. That's awesome."

Carol Ann shook her head in that way people do when they're telling you something you won't possibly find as amusing as they do.

My brother flung the back door open then, swinging it wide and fast and smacking the house's wood siding with a slap like a car backfiring. It made us all jump, even the pigtails. Up in the elm tree, the crows had had enough. They rustled, bellyached, and flapped off into the night, a flustered cacophony.

Carlton watched them and made a face. "Sorry," he said, but he didn't mean it. June smiled and rose from her chair. She watched the last of the crows slope into the darkness above us and dropped her cigarette into her beer bottle where it made a small hiss. "Time to go home," she said.

But that wasn't the end of the night, far from it. The next morning, in our little dawning corner of the earth, at least three events were still playing themselves out. There were more, sure, but these are simply the three I am aware of, as best I can reconstruct them, having eventually become fairly intimate with the principals involved.

1) At June's apartment, she and Carlton were lying in an awkward, post-coital quiet. Having managed any coitus at all, given his alcohol-slogged system, seemed to my brother a feat of biblical proportions, and he lay moldering in pride and satisfaction. The

rarity of his lovemaking with June, rather than shameful, added a kind of chaste indulgence, a tickle of healthy living, and he found himself promising June he would drink less, maybe even not drink at all. Would that help her see herself as his wife?

Drinking, he was admitting to himself, had already become not really a problem, but more a management issue. It wasn't the same as before, after Mom died—that was a lapse, a crack into which he'd fallen. This current bout was merely lazy overindulgence. That's what happens to the lazy; they don't get rich, and they damn sure don't get women like June. He'd embarrassed her last night, and she wouldn't tolerate very much of that kind of thing. Carlton knew this, and he told June so, there in bed. He told her he knew a lot of things she probably didn't think he knew.

He told her about the time, for instance, in the darkened store basement one night during the Kidsville "going out of business" catastrophe, when the old man tried to pay him for his work—$500 in folded twenties. It was a cold little bundle in the guy's hands, which were shaking, and Carlton didn't want it. But when he said so, the old man hardened in the jaw and barked, "Take it!" So he did. It was money, after all, and he had earned it. Maybe he could buy a nice video camera and see if he could make a movie that was actually worth a damn. But see, $500 wasn't a lot of money, insubstantial in the context of what the store had cost, not to mention the actual hours Carlton had put in helping him close it, but that wasn't the point. Five hundred dollars? Carlton's plan was one day to spend that much money at a ball game, or at dinner. On a fucking bottle of wine, if June wanted. He'd had this same plan even back then, getting sidetracked only by his knee, but he took the money anyway, a lump in his back pocket—he took it because his father wanted him to have it. It wasn't $500 but a wad of something else, and he took it because of what it meant to the old man, who then retreated into his dark office to compose himself.

Carlton knew, in other words, what it means to be a family.

2) June lay in bed in the uncurtained window's wan light, the sheets and her grandmother's Lettuce Quilt ("Lettuce give thanks…"

"Lettuce prosper…" "Lettuce dance a polka…") furrowed among and between their bodies. She had never heard that story before, about Carlton's father closing the store and the money. Something about it unsettled her: no one had ever handed *her* a $500 wad of twenties, not even for college. Not one fucking dime, her parents gave her. Not a dime! It was all her. She'd gotten herself a full-ride scholarship to K State, thanks to her ACT scores and editing the yearbook. Did anyone jump up and down? No.

When she wanted to pull out and go to Minnesota, *that's* when the jumping up and down started. But she couldn't be deterred— moved herself up here in one trip, got a job at a Sri Lankan restaurant that eventually earned her residency, then scratched together small scholarships and loans and work-study aid that lasted only a semester, but still: she paid her own way. Okay, they'd helped her buy the car, but she'd paid them back last summer.

Moving to Minnesota showed June one thing she will never forget—how the world tends to grow around you, like the small section of chain-link fence behind Woodrow Wilson Elementary that had been wholly subsumed by the bark of a maple growing next to it. It takes time, but it happens—the metal just taken in by the bark. It's the way of life. Things fuse. Your world solidifies, expectations build on top of you, braced and joisted like a small house getting a second floor. It becomes a struggle to move anywhere but inside yourself, and that wasn't enough for her after that first year at K State, thanks to Wyatt.

Wyatt was a goat-legged philosophy major, a junior but barely bigger than her, physically. Wyatt wore a beret and had weasely, yellow teeth, that was the sad truth. He was smoky and bespectacled and raw and not even handsome except counter-culturally, and she was ensnared by him sexually pretty much her entire freshman year. Sometimes, at times like these, when she's in bed, with Carlton chumming in his sleep next to her, or maybe on the bus or in the car, she'll think about it and her hands start to grip whatever they're resting on: a kneecap, the steering wheel, her purse. His house on Juliette, rented with a bunch of other guys, his beaded, batiked bedroom with the mattress on the floor—oh it's probably happened to endless women in college. The thrill of an upperclassman who's smart and rebellious-looking, the satisfaction of being at Rusty's Last Chance and getting asked, "You wanna get out of here?" Then the stumble out of Aggieville, the making out in some sleeping family's front yard, the losing of your ID—and suddenly you're in his bedroom and he's taking off your pants on his mattress on the floor while you pull at the tassels of his area rug to get yourself in position. And then it's over, it's morning, and you get up with him and go have breakfast.

Weeks later you're coming to his house every other night. He never calls you, nor introduces you as his girlfriend—you just show up at 10-ish, watch some TV with the guys, pass the bong, and go upstairs. The occasional bar outing, and more breakfasts, and offers to do his laundry with yours, or drive him to the Kansas City airport. Sometimes he takes you up on it, but that's not what he really wants. What he really wants is to sit on that mattress and spout off about acid jazz and DDT and the internship opportunities that make you feel unaccomplished—and then have you go down on him. If there's such a thing as sin, it's listening to that idiot talk and talk, and then unbuttoning his army surplus pants and pulling out his little erection and kissing it like it was a puppy. A self-sin of stupidity and debasement, even if you think it's love.

It's this idea of sin, performed all winter long, that brought June to the campus All Faiths Chapel. The chapel itself was too large for her tastes, too drafty, and too prone to intrusion. But its secondary chapel, on the north side, was small and perfect. With its heavy door, foyer of cardboard boxes, and apse crowded with double-stacked piano benches, it smacked less of group worship than personal storage. The details seemed second-rate. The pews were padded with gaudy purple cushion, and the knee rests too. And the stained glass windows each paid tribute to a triptych of great Western figures, religious and otherwise: Noah, Galileo, and Christopher Columbus to her left; David, Moses, and Clara Barton to her right. Who the hell was Clara Barton?

So June sat, and asked God to put aside her sinning for a second. It was as close to confession as she'd come since precociously abandoning the Catholic Church at age eleven. She sat alone in a pew and asked for her sinning to be not forgiven, but understood, by herself at least—she wanted an awakening, or strength, or merely insight. Anything to help her stave off the rank indifference she seemed to have for her self-respect. It wasn't like she was praying to make Wyatt love her—the idea was ridiculous, and she knew it even then. She saw it like an easy calc question every time he stopped talking and leaned back against his smoky purple pillows to have his dick sucked. No, what she wanted was a solidity, to help her cope with the undertow of her love. Theologically immature as it was, this favor of self-improvement, that's what she asked Clara Barton for.

Thirty minutes of quiet ardor and stained-glass sunshine through her eyelids—and she felt nothing. This she hadn't expected. No epiphany, no descending awareness, no precipitation of any kind. Well no wonder she let Wyatt do as he pleased—what was going to stop him? Noah, with his pebbled white beard flared by flood-winds? Apparently not. The truth was, there was nothing in her, and nothing descending from on high. Just the sun through stained glass, lighting the chapel's high, exposed beams, which were stained dark like a Southwestern *iglesia*. Then she looked down at her purple bench cushion, which not far from her was ripped at its edge, the piping white as exposed bone.

It was a feeling of almost perfect loneliness. And she knew that if she didn't get out of Kansas, she'd return to Wyatt's floor mattress night after night until he barred her at the door or otherwise made the whole thing unbearable—what would it be, what awful thing would he ask her to do? And then after him, wouldn't it be someone else?

The inscription etched in metal inside the chapel read, "Dedicated to the Worship of God and the Prayer that here, in communion with the Highest, those who enter may acquire the Spiritual Power to Aspire Nobly, Adventure Daringly, Serve Humbly." Okay, she thought, well said. Besides the fact that there was no Highest to commune with—she was certain of this now—the point was still valid. Just like Clara Barton was still valid, whoever she was. Aspire, adventure, serve…God had nothing to do with it. God was the exposed piping of a church pew bench pad—the rest was up to you. And if you had to pray about it, fine, but prayer was simply giving yourself a talk and making it sound like someone else.

Up in Minneapolis, men were wary of her. Being perpetually surrounded by retards probably didn't help. But it was more: they could see in her face that she had welcomed a Wyatt into her life. Oh not all of them saw this, but certainly they wanted what he wanted. Out shopping for Halloween costumes, they watched her all around the store. Even at the Ragstock, even at the Walgreen's. They clutched a furry purple pimp's hat and a package of vampire teeth, and looked her up and down, and if she was holding something they'd say, "You'll look good in that," or "Where're you gonna party, princess?" Their chubby frat faces and their frayed denim—even Wyatt would laugh.

And the worst part: if you gave those guys the choice—success at their pickup lines or a wadded $500—they wouldn't flinch. Cash money.

Carlton didn't want her like that. And the sex they had wasn't about getting what he wanted, or even, for that matter, passion—he climbed on her more like she was a staircase, or an amusement ride he was scared of but wanted to show he could withstand. No, it was something else. He wanted *her,* and he wanted her enough to humiliate himself with this open offer of marriage that he knew she might very well decline. This was a powerful thing for a man to do to himself. And let's admit it: he had great, beautiful arms and a strong chin and some kind of confident dispossession—a man for other women to covet. He was tall, too. Lying next to her like this, he had so many places to hold on to. The quilt panel that curved around his shoulder showed a head of lettuce bulging out of the window of a squat house; it said, "Lettuce never outgrow home." All she had to do was shake him a little, and tell him she didn't want a big wedding. Maybe twenty people, tops. She thought it would be fun, though, if he wore a tux.

3) At the Meyerson-Cooper home, up in our one-room second story, Carol Ann was in a fit of weeping. She was sitting up in bed, arms folded to her abdomen, hard, like she had cramps. "Just seeing you two," she said "*looking* at each other."

She meant me and June. It'd been this way for fifteen minutes or so, since she'd woken up, silent, facing the wall.

"It was like I was intruding on some couple, like I was bothering some couple at home when they weren't expecting company."

"No, no," I said, with a sincere, concerned indignation learned at Old Grinnell College. "June and I, it's *ridiculous.*"

She shook her head and squeezed her eyes. The soft morning light, dappled through tree branches, was coming in the window. Our socks and slippers were scattered around the bed, other clothes too, and stacked magazines and newspapers and drinking glasses and the like. Co-mingled clutter. Ours was an unkempt Togetherness.

"It's not that," she said. "It's not. It's us. We aren't like that. Someone pops over at our place, it's—it's fine. More than fine. It's a relief."

What is there to do when a person you love says something like that? Who among us would prod, or debate, or nosedive into the implications? Very few: stronger men than me, with bigger brains, frontal lobes lit up like Tokyo.

No, I could only pull her to me and kiss her damp shoulder, and the strengthening light of morning seemed to ascent, and to promise something, a continuity. Continuity! The sun will always come up, and there will always be earth beneath it. We merely need to awaken and take it in. We merely need to make a home of light. A little Togetherness. Right?

I said, "Honey. Let's get up and make breakfast." She nodded, and smiled because she knew what I was going to say next. It's maddening, the accidental obviousness of our selves, for which we slave, voluntarily, and at which we throw everything we have, all our muscle and will and audacious youthful rapacity for doing the right thing, even if you have no idea what that might be. It's maddening to try to be in love.

"Then we'll go to the Humane Society," I said.

She lifted her chimpy eyes. She sniffled.

"You know," I said. I gave her a squeeze. "Just to look."

If I'd been hallucinating through all this memory, my own and not my own—and anyone who's had Cointreau with whiskey will know it's entirely possible—then it had to portend something. Some vision quest I was supposed to translate. My own shaky roots. My brother's fall, June's opacity. Sugar's tumbleweed of neglected fur, pierced and torn by a .22. We who are born wily and puppy-eyed, how life denudes us into monsters.

Somewhere around five in the morning I packed a bag, made some coffee and five or six fried-egg sandwiches, found the tent Tom had given me (I'd said I might enjoy camping because all you did was lie around) and packed it all into the Jetta: splendid, overheated box of rocks—would it survive another trip?

And it would indeed be only a trip. I'd go, climb some Crow Peak to eat what crow I could, and show my best hangdog face like Lucy with some 'splainin' to do. I'd get my brother to buck up and get the toy done and even patch up with June. In this way I would create for myself a redemption. If I thought I'd slow-death myself into one out here, or even luck myself into a spectacular martyrdom they'd talk about at the Copper Cowboy and beyond—I was fooling myself. Out here, people go to their deaths like a trip to the toilet. No one says boo. I'd be just another guy to venture mapless into the national forest and lose himself to the hills and tangled gullies and abandoned mine shafts darkly yawning in the rock—just another bit of local lore not much more remarkable than the disappearance of Sugar the dog. The stupid son of a bitch renting the gay guys' barn, is what they'd say—you know, one of these newcomers who doesn't understand, doesn't get it, gets flattened by a train or lost someplace high up and freezes to death or falls asleep at the wheel or just cracks. Never heard from again, and not particularly missed.

At the Belgrade Flying J, I bought myself some country tapes and a six-pack—with how long I'd been up, my body clock was hitting happy hour. And anyway, I had a feeling it was going to be that kind of trip.

PART THREE

The Duck of Annunciation

Chapter Sixteen

Nancy!" he said.

I'd walked up, and there he was, on the porch, lost in some scribbling he was doing on a clipboard. He hadn't even looked up until I pulled the screen door's handle.

I was in his arms now. Not a big hugger, my brother, but here I was, like a tree he'd climbed to escape a bear, or flood. It was only 11:00 but already hot, hotter on the porch. The drive in that morning had caught me in some mysterious Labor Day traffic, cooking me in the Freon-challenged Jetta. Lying in the backseat waiting like a coward for June to leave hadn't exactly helped. My T-shirt was spotty with sweat down my chest and probably back too. My brother was still squeezing me.

"Christ, enough," I said.

He stood back and grinned. It was tough to look at him, his injured self so different from his usual winner's aura: he'd put on some pounds in the face, giving it a puffy, punched-around look, and his broad shoulders heaved with a dry, unhealthy coolness. He took shallow breaths. The cast on his left leg went from his foot arch to the top of his calf and was gel-cap white, like he'd been waxing it—his toes, though, were filthy.

"June told me she called you," he said. "She went to the store," he added. What good not having her there was doing me I didn't know—maybe it just let me confront my brother with a little less guilt, or at least one guilt at a time.

On the loveseat with the thick paisley-covered cushion was the clipboard he'd been bent over when I'd knocked on the tight screen door.

"What is that?" I said.

"Instructions for my funeral." He nodded twice, then laughed. "No, ideas. They're coming lately like, like the funding's back. But forget it. Welcome home. Come on, sit down."

He tossed the clipboard aside and sat in the loveseat. I took the matching wicker single opposite it. A fickle breeze slithered its heat down my neck.

"When did you get in? You look like shit."

"I got in just now. And thanks—I've been driving two days straight."

"How'd you go?" He said this like he'd been doing research and would add my answer to some graph of data points.

"Took 94 into North Dakota," I said. "Camped out a night, then from Fargo—"

He leaned back. "You *camped?*"

"I'm not exactly made of money, you know."

"You're not exactly made of Gore-Tex either."

"Listen," I said. "I'm not in town long. I came just to see how—"

He held his hand up, closed his eyes. "How I'm doing. Yes, fine. You're going to stay though. I can feel it. Anyway, I've never been better. I've been lifting, bench press and curls. And working a ton."

"Dad said you weren't working at all."

"What does he know? I haven't said word one to him, so he assumes the worst. He's tightened up on the money, too, but I don't need it. No, I'm working just fine. The fall shook something loose up there."

"Another screw?" I said.

"Ha! Right. Another screw. Totally. See, that's why I'm glad you're home. You keep me honest."

I leaned back in my chair until my hair caught a scratch of window screening behind me. "So. Why are you here? I thought you were living at the studio now."

He bobbed his head, ledged his lower lip out some. "I was. Not good. But I'm home now. We seem to be doing okay. You just have to get everything out in the open." He made a choppy horizontal cut with his hands, like a referee signaling an incompletion. "Don't tell Dad about it, by the way."

I nodded. I couldn't resist. "So what came out into the open?"

He locked his lips into a smile. "Sorry, none of your business."

I nodded. More hair into the screen behind me.

"I'll be getting back home then."

"Shut up, you shit. I need you here still. Listen, I've thought about what you said, on the phone, right after you went out there, and it was tough, but yeah, I haven't been a very good brother. When we were kids, I had everything my way, and it stayed like that. I had a knack for it. I always thought you needed that tough-brother thing. You know, since Mom died. Then the thing with Carol Ann…but I think I misjudged you. You've got a kind of strength. And now I need some. It's just not what I'm used to." He stretched back in the loveseat and put his bum leg up on the glass-topped coffee table between us. It clunked more than I thought it should have. "You're deceiving that way," he said. "But now I'm starting to see a lot clearer. Crisis mode, I guess. Fight or flight.

"Hey," he said. "You know the Jewish myth of the golem. It has nothing to do with *The Lord of the Rings.*"

"I kind of do."

Some shimmer seemed to pass over him, something in the humidity, and he became a pontificator. A thinker.

"I've been doing some reading. Research. It was a creature created by the top rabbis in Prague. They made him out of mud, and then wrote the Hebrew word 'truth' on his forehead. And he came alive, just like that. They wanted him to help roust out the anti-Semitic plots of city officials. You know, that shit was happening all the time."

I nodded.

"So the golem does all this great work cuz he's small and can make himself look like a lump of mud. Then one of the rabbis' wives has him help her with the picking up, and the cleaning, and gathering firewood and all that. So suddenly he starts to wonder—what the hell, dude? He's basically a slave. He confronts them, refuses to work. Demands his rights. A regular Rosa Parks. You know what they do?"

"Give him a TV show?"

"No, they tell him okay, okay, calm down. They say they'll re-write the word on his head so it will read 'freedom,' and he's psyched, but then the rabbis just etch out one letter, changing the word for 'truth' into the word for 'death.' And the poor bastard dies right there in the kitchen."

He picked up his clipboard and put it back down again.

"You have to break free in this life, one way or another. So when I got done being royally pissed at you, I applauded you. You opted out. We can't be slaves."

"June keeps you a slave?"

With a squeak of wicker, he shook his head and smiled. It was a kind smile, like I just didn't get it. And I wanted him to be right.

"June and I talked about how it must have been for you, when we were kids. I got a lot of the attention. You must have felt overlooked."

He crossed his arms and dropped his cast to the porch floor and crossed his right leg over it. The floor was painted brown and had been recently swept clean.

"I've been trying to create a toy for that kind of kid," he said. "I think it's important. There are many kids like that out there. You know, Mom wasn't tops in the hugs and kisses department."

"She did fine," I said.

"Yes, fine. But to you, enough? We always called you mama's boy, but there's no shame in it." He tapped his forehead. "Drop ten feet and hit your head on a stump, things get clearer."

This was not the reception I had envisioned. My bother heavy with contrition, the white cast like a buoy keeping him afloat. And the two of them talking about, of all things, how hard it had been for me as kid. Damn right—it *had* been hard.

The breeze was gone altogether, and I was suddenly wretchedly hot. I realized I was home, in part, to tell him the truth. That was the idea, at least. Where would all this Hank-sympathy be then? Montana, if I were lucky enough to escape Minnesota again. It was one of those sudden dour truths made weightier by how long you've willfully ignored it, like a warped clutch or the fact that David Letterman's just not funny anymore.

My brother, sure enough, saw it coming. "Come here," he said.

I got up and sat next to him on the loveseat, the wicker seething at my gall. I sat there with my arms crossed and tried to compose myself. His bony shoulder against mine held me in place. He put his hand on my knee, which was hot and clammy under jeans.

"It's good you came home," he said, "we've got some brothering to do."

I honked out something unintelligible, and that was all we said until June got home, and I stood. She was smiling, holding a bag of groceries, the tip of something green brushing her face—fresh parsley or fronds of fennel.

June could see I'd been emotional. "Welcome home," she said.

"Don't hug me," I said. "I'm all sweaty."

"Are you ready for a fried candy bar on a stick?"

I wasn't expecting this, and laughed accordingly. It's good to laugh at the mysterious.

June laughed too. "We're going to the fair."

"And you're coming," my brother said. "It's the last day."

The Minnesota State Fair has at least one wonderful thing going for it: after meandering through any of the separate animal showing barns, and after taking a few moments of olfactory relief, you can usually consume a representative of the animal you've just cooed over. Well, not the horses, unless you count the Purina pet food booth over in the Pet Center building, but almost everything else.

Pigs? There's pork chop on a stick a block away. Lambs? At least three gyro stands. Milking cows? Line up for a milkshake. Turkeys? Shaved breast on a bun right outside the barn door. Rabbits? Ask around discreetly, and one of the 4-H kids will know a guy doing up a couple in a turkey fryer out behind his trailer—they aren't blue-ribboned for charisma, you know. Add to that the cotton candy, fried candy bars on a stick, Juanita's Fajitas, ice creams, mini donuts, fried green tomatoes, corn fritters, alligator sausage, corn on the cob, etc...and a guy like me can do some serious damage. I tend to go for the meats, not being a sweets person; there's already enough sugar in the air to make a diabetic nervous, and after two hours or so of inhaling it, a fried candy bar on a stick sounds good only in theory, like libertarianism.

The only two drawbacks are the arteriosclerosis and the fact that you have to wait in line to get it.

But in such a morass, especially prodding along an overstimulated developmentally disabled adult, such worries dissipate. You gotta go with the flow. Which is exactly what my brother refused to do. He had an agenda, gleaned from visiting the fair's Web site and from the experience of his past visits, that would route us to all the major hotspots and still leave time for sitting and people-peeping, as he knew June and I loved to do, and also for riding a few midway rides if Terry was up for it.

Terry hadn't changed, but my brother treated him now like a member of the family. His bearded chin stuck out with a kind of pride, his heated face red with the excitement, his crooked teeth clattering away about it all. Carlton stopped when he did, answered his questions, tapped his toes to a beer garden band thumping out "Play That Funky Music." The two of them perused a booth where you could get a belt branded with your initials for only fifteen bucks. The crowd ate us alive, digesting us with the dust and trash and heat and fried sugar and candy-bright awnings and small human dramas like a parade.

So I just got a beer, and some french fries and a corn cob dipped in butter and a fried pickle on a stick, and then resigned myself to watching from behind a pair of very dark glasses I had bought at the Police Union's booth. If there was one thing Mom and Dad had taught us, it was how to shut up, eat, and have a good time.

First order of business was to see the painting Terry had submitted to the fair's annual art contest. After a quick stop to see the butter sculptures of young women vying to become that year's Princess Kay of the Milky Way, and also to learn why nuclear power was such a great choice to provide the energy needed to keep the butter princesses chilled below melting temperature, we found the Fine Arts building. Terry called it "the art barn," and he wasn't wrong: it was indeed a barn, cement-floored and stifling.

All this time I'd been ignoring June, which clearly wasn't going to work. I took her hand and held her back a moment. She was in pigtails and overalls, her annual fair getup. I leaned to her and kissed her cheek, feeling her tense up, stone-faced, even as I pulled away. "Hi," I said.

Then her crooked little mouth went into a smile. "Thanks," she said.

The first piece we saw was a portrait of Hubert H. Humphrey rendered entirely in agricultural-grade seeds; his halo of hair was hued with flax. Terry stormed past it into the heart of the big, airy building, demanding of it something he didn't put words to.

It took a few minutes to find Terry's painting, a self-portrait. The fair staff had taken care of the hanging, so even Terry hadn't seen it yet. There he was, thin-lipped and silent, looking off to the left. Everything was watercolor except his beard, which was pieced from brown floral wallpaper fussy-cut around the petals. He had his Cubs cap pulled over his eyes, and he was wearing some kind of suit—dark brown or maybe black—but in it his arms and legs were cartoonish, straight and flat as a paper doll's. The background behind him was bright orange, grading to a tangerine color down at the bottom. It was titled "Everyone's Smart." I liked it immediately and said so.

"It's great," I said. "Really really."

"Really," Terry said.

Terry said it wasn't a real museum, everyone knows. Real museums have actual floors, and guards. Like the mee-ah.

"He means the MIA," June said. "The museum."

"I love it there. It's the real deal."

"Good," June said.

"But no one takes me, and they asked me not to come by myself."

"Hank'll take you," June said.

Terry nodded.

"What?" I said.

"The art institute," she said. "The big one."

Terry looked at me, kept still. He didn't show any "say yes!" anticipation—maybe he never learned how to. He just had the insistent patience of sculpture.

"Okay," I said.

No one said anything. Carlton nodded at the painting like someone had just given him instructions. "Well," he said, "one thing's for certain." He squished his lips together and put his arm around Terry, who squirmed but let it stay put. "I can't do anything this good."

After a minute, he led us back outside.

Carlton limped Terry off to ride the Ferris wheel, saying he'd let "you sisters" catch up. June and I got sno-cones and sat on a quiet bench facing the midway madness, as long and broad and manic as Times Square. And thank God! The people gave us something to look at, and talk about. Short, fat, tall, skinny, broad, low-centered, haughty, inscrutable, aimless, pumped, horny, drunk, blissed-out, edgy, inches from violence, or sleeping it off on a patch of grass—they gleamed like fool's gold, burbled like farm animals. Everyone seemed to be wearing a sassy T-shirt. "Simon Says You Suck" or "I'll be in Electronics" or "Bald to the Bone." One large-breasted woman with a top-heavy hairdo sported the saying "I am my own boss—in and out of the bedroom."

"That just makes no sense," I said.

"You'd think she'd be worried someone from work would see her."

"It literally makes no sense," I said again. "Basically it means she's a masturbator. It would be like me wearing a shirt that said 'I go to bed with my Shop-Vac.'"

June laughed. "Ouch. Can you do it with a Shop-Vac?"

"It's a special attachment. It's called The Violet."

She considered this as if it were in the realm of the possible, which made it funnier to me.

"I heard the new fair food this year is spun pork." She shook her head. "Steak smoothies?"

"Everything has to be on a stick."

"I'm not on a stick."

"So this is what we're doing?" she said. "Going ahead and talking like we normally talk?"

"Sure."

"You say it like it's no big deal."

I nodded at a guy aimlessly following his brood of smear-faced kids, the whole gaggle led by a stout short mom in Ray-Bans even darker than mine. The hubby's T-shirt said "My kids think I'm an ATM."

"Now that one's just sad," I said. "It's pure mindless pre-packaged expression. The wife saw it and said to herself, 'Oh how funny, because they do, they *do* think he's an ATM.' And as he unwraps it she says, 'See sweetie, isn't it funny?'"

"What's sad about that?"

"Well, what a corner it paints him into. He's now 'put-upon dad.'"

"He doesn't seem to be complaining."

"All the sadder."

"What you don't get is that people choose their lives. Not everyone stumbles around like you."

"Is that what it was, stumbling?"

"What?"

"You know what."

She sighed. "I thought we were going to talk normal."

"Normally, normal normality normalizes normalcy."

"Okay." She sighed. "I'm glad you're back. But it's got to be this way: you've got to ignore that."

"*I* can, but what about you and him—"

"He looks fine, but he's been awful, until now. Moody and down, then it's like he had an injection of something. It makes me worry—"

"He just makes a drama of everything. His ego is so big, it barfs out onto everyone else."

"Well, he can barf it on you for a while."

I let that go, but the ATM guy and his kids, still straggling not far from us, all turned their heads, piqued, until Mommy Ray-Bans led them away.

"You want to hear about Montana?" I said.

"No."

"But I've got some great stories. I've hiked on trails marked 'rattlesnakes have been spotted'—in my sandals! And I was shot at."

She looked incredulous.

"With a BB gun," I said. "But shooting is shooting."

She shuddered and shook her head. She took a minute to re-secure her pigtails. I could smell her shampoo, something minty and cool. I almost reached to help her.

A breeze came up, throwing a fistful of fair smells at us. Fried cheese, dust, drying beer, large-animal manure, Old Spice. We watched the people go by, chuckled at the wailing kids and the fashion-challenged teens and all the bared-skin virility. A shirtless dude carrying a huge Foghorn Leghorn got us to smile again, and I held out my hand for hers, which she held and dropped well before my brother reappeared, leading Terry out of the crowd. He was drag-stepping his cast just a little more than he'd been before, but he waved to us broadly, getting Terry to join him in unison, like extras in a Broadway musical.

Terry had new cowboy boots, cheapy-shiny ones, black with gaudy turquoise diamonds outlined by yellow stitching. He showed them to June as Carlton explained: After the Ferris wheel they'd come upon a sheep-shearing exhibition, and Terry hadn't seen anything like that before. He "went nuts" for it, and there was a stand selling boots right outside—duh—and so there you go.

June seemed pleased. She asked Terry if he'd said thank you, and the kid turned back to Carlton and nodded.

My brother nodded back, then noticed June and said, "We got you something too." He held up a stamp collection of midway tickets. "We," he said, "meaning me or Hank, but probably not Hank, are going to win for you," he gestured here to the midway, as if he owned it, "the stuffed animal of your choice."

His game was pool—one of the "true games of skill" spicing up the midway that year. On a regulation-sized table, you were essentially playing yourself. You started with a rack of four balls, and after your broke them, you could shoot them in any order, but one miss meant no prize. Carlton and I were to take adjoining tables and compete. From the thickness of the ticket book he'd purchased, it looked like we'd have all night, if we needed it. The prize would be determined, and thereafter owned, by June. The logistics of it all had to be explained to Terry several times.

Toni Morrison says in one of her books that the third beer is the one where your buzz becomes commonplace and somewhat sour, after the satisfaction of the first and the elation of the second. I disagree wholeheartedly. The third beer is when you meet your true self: will you keep going, or taper? It's a decision that belies the essence of life, and hence infuses you with life; you inhabit it with a magnanimity and optimism that, well channeled, can serve you well. Poorly channeled, it can be disastrous. I didn't really think all that: just made a mental note that everyone seemed to want me to act normal, and I was third-beer happy to oblige.

My brother was a pretty sharp pool player. All the Meyersons were—even our color-blind grandfather, who shot with the cue supported between his first and second knuckles because of shrapnel still in his hand from fighting Germans in France. I myself was mediocre, with flashes of brilliance—I once held a table for eleven games—but there at the fair, with three beers in me, I was guilty of both overestimating my talents, and really, really wanting to win.

"This is dumb," June said. "With what you paid for those tickets, we could have *bought* a Foghorn Leghorn. Two."

"Where you gonna buy a Foghorn Leghorn?" my brother said. He smiled at her and gave her a little kiss on the forehead.

You wouldn't call the guy running the pool game a carnie—he was too respectable, waiting with hands behind his back. He was not a barker—you came to him—but he sure scowled like a carnie. He racked the balls for us, side by side, with a sharp, aggressive precision that suggested we'd have to take our Foghorn Leghorn over his dead body.

My brother gave a countdown of three-two-one, and we broke. My break was terrible, but I had a two-pronged strategy I knew would serve me well: Number one, ignore my brother completely. Number two, since we had a ridiculous cache of tickets, why monkey with the hard shots? If a shot was hard, go ahead and miss and pay the man again and break anew. My brother's skill and old-school competitive arrogance would never allow him to do the same; he'd force himself to line up shots and study where to leave the cue ball and all that. I would be the guerrilla warrior to his be-medaled general.

I missed my first shot. Terry cried out. It didn't seem a taunt, but June shushed him anyway.

"Rack 'em," I said.

My third break actually sunk a ball, the twelve, leaving the fifteen right on the lip of a side pocket and the other two balls in the center-south of the table. I sunk the side-pocket one first, figuring it would at least put some pressure on my brother, and also because such an easy shot gave me a better chance of setting up my leave. Whether I achieved the former goal I don't know, for, like I said, I was ignoring him, but definitely by making that shot I left myself well-placed: a straight shot at the thirteen in the corner pocket, which I sunk with enough backspin to leave me a cut at the fourteen into the side pocket, which, if made, would mean victory. It would also mean that I would never shoot pool with my brother again.

A pool table doesn't know you're fat. A pool table is more like an open-minded lover: it don't matter how big or small you are, she says, as long as you know how to use that stick, and you play all the pockets. This was more or less what Carol Ann had repeated throughout most of our marriage, until the tune changed and suddenly the stick itself wasn't enough—it was the putting together of the stick, and the brushing of the table, and the drive to the pool hall, and the night before the drive to the pool hall, etc.—*those* are the things that really mattered. You know, the shared-vision thing. Togetherness. All things that, for me at least, required time travel to fix.

Still, pool was the game at hand, and I leaned now on the table and felt my gut cede space to the faux-mahogany edge, then collapse around it for an airtight seal. Part of me was actually dipped into the corner pocket over which I was leaning, as if in solidarity, or maybe to show the fourteen ball what to do. It was the first time in a while that my body felt on the same team as its occupant. Maybe once or twice apexing some Montana crest, and of course last April with June. But still: my body and I were suddenly copasetic.

I heard my brother take a shot, and by the way the carnie moved behind me, I knew he had missed and was forced to rack again. So I tried to concentrate, and my body's subsequent betrayal, as my shot hit its mark but also sent the cue ball straight into the far corner pocket for a negating scratch, was tortuous.

"Eff me!" I spit. "Rack 'em."

I didn't have that good a setup again for another two breaks, and when it came, I was ready for it. No farting around, just me and my body and my disdain for this whole stupid idea, the entire pastime of pool altogether, and of course Carlton, and even June. "This is the guy you begged me home for?" I was saying as I banged in shots with disregard for leave or anything. "Your husband the shmuck, and you know what they say: 'he who beds with a shmuck is also a shmuck.'" I'm sure it's in the Talmud, someplace.

Finally facing a solitary ball and potential victory, I was rounding the table to set up for it when I heard my brother say, "Hey chubby!" I should have just gone ahead and bent to the shot anyway, but the river of our brotherhood had cut too deep a channel to be leapt out of casually. So I turned to him, and he was lined over his last shot too, smiling at me: his last ball, the four ball, sat perched on the lip of the corner pocket such that even a whimper from Terry might tip it in. Without looking back to the table, smiling at me, in fact, he fired his shot, sinking the four and leaving the cue ball lolling in empty green.

I made my shot too, chose a Foghorn Leghorn almost as tall as me for my prize, and carried the damn thing all the way to June's Subaru, stopping only to down a beer and to endure the bar maiden asking me, "What's Foggy having?" On the ride home, Foghorn rode in the hatchback space because in the backseat were me, a body-odor wafting Terry, and the smiling purple Barney that June had chosen as the prize her husband had won for her.

Chapter Seventeen

I insisted on getting a hotel room. My brother didn't object too much, June not at all. I knew there was one by the university, but when I got there it was too Day-Glo, and astonishingly pricey. I asked the young woman if the rate included a valet, and she suggested a motel down University Avenue, which ended up being much more to my liking, meaning it was a shit show—the type of one-level kitsch that would, in a few years, be demolished and reincarnated as a convenience store or copy shop, of which the world never seems to have too many. But it didn't disappoint in terms of cost, especially when I took the weekly rate that the kindhearted manager woman made up for me on the spot. So I thanked her with the smart slap of my one good credit card. It was 2:30 in the morning when I pulled the Jetta around, room key in hand.

Seth's Motor Lodge. The identity of Seth was a mystery, but the joint had a new asphalt lot stenciled with sharp yellow parking lines, and I had my pick of them right in front of room fourteen. It was supposedly a nonsmoking room, and all in all a perfectly fine place, once you overcame the aged carpet and general scummy depravation. On a trip to Wyoming once, by not making reservations ahead of time like Carol Ann had asked me to, I'd managed to trap us into the one motel that had vacancy, and at dawn Carol Ann woke up screaming because of an enormous cricket crawling up her leg. It was a test of sorts, and soon enough I was made well aware of how hard I'd failed, even up in the Bighorns, hiking, when I tried to hold her hand and she told me I had a cricket's chance in hell of making up with her and so should just stop trying. Fucking cricket.

The bed was a queen, with a navy quilt and a taupe-colored headboard that was sticky and mysteriously dark in spots. There was a shellacked pine side table holding a bedside lamp with a beige shade that wobbled precipitously with any small tremor—it had a glass body with fake flowers in it and a rusting brass base. In the drawer beneath it I found Gideon resting atop a Domino's Pizza delivery menu—I breathed a quick prayer that I would stoop to neither.

There was carpet everywhere, including the exceptionally clean bathroom, where the window treatments were actually old white terry bath towels. The toilet paper roll's end sheet had been folded to a triangular point like in the fancy places, and the sink and tub looked like they'd been sandblasted. The mirror, not so much. The blonde pine paneling in the main room turned blonder in the bathroom, and because of my relative success with The Project, I let myself admire the woodwork, which was true and soundly cut and free of dust, before I settled into watching the tiny small TV—seriously, it was like fifteen inches, tops—which they'd mounted on a bracket up in the corner.

But it was pointless, as I was exhausted.

I closed my eyes and listened to the air conditioner, constant regurgitating companion. I thought about June in her pigtails at the fair, then about making love to her with her pigtails splayed out on some bed. This bed?

When I had her there, in her house, I should have sent Terry home and held on to that moment as long and as fully as possible. I should have gripped her and made it unforgettable, an inevitability, not a mistake. But humans fritter. We never live as fully in the moment as we wish we had. Hindsight is gluttonous, and rarely satisfied.

In the morning, meaning noon, I had some phone calls to make.

I decided on Dad first. Get it out of the way. He was in St. Louis for a sales-team rally. Most of the season's selling was already well finished, driven as it was by huge, preplanned marketing packages. But the smaller stores had been stalling, and getting them to write their orders was the topic at the St. Louis meeting. Twist a few arms, threaten, sweeten the pot, whatever the reps had to do.

The specialty stores, the mom-and-pops, the general gift stores that still carried fun kids' toys, all those poor struggling bastards living on borrowed time and a clean-swept storefront walk—for them, deciding what inventory to carry was a gamble, not the no-brainer it was for the big chains. So they tended to put off ordering as long as they could so they could test items and feel out their customers—all the while asking their reps to hold inventory for them. And my father could hardly blame them, he who'd walked many miles in their shoes: If you buy too big or overestimate a trend, it could put you under. But on the other hand, there's no worse feeling than going cheap with the inventory and watching customers walk in and walk out with no registers ringing in between.

Our father had simmered these kinds of accounts into a nice little gravy. Sure, he had his share of dependable urban accounts and some regional chain operations, but otherwise he worked the hinterland of Oklahoma, Kansas, and Nebraska like a maestro, consistently bringing the strong items needed to lure eyeballs away from the Wal-Mart. Thus he turned a *bubkes* relationship into one that wrote a minimum $300 order every time he visited, so that with his cut, 25 percent, he at least covered expenses.

The headaches kept him kvetching, to be sure. Places with names like Mary's Heart of Hearts or A Giftin' Time. Owners scared stupid, who sing you a hick-happy "See you Tewsdee" on the phone but then demand to see and feel your samples, not read about them in a catalog you lay out for them, and also sales history, *local* sales history, never mind if it's a brand new item. And when you finally sell them, they write an order for five units like it's putting your kids through college. Still, my father identified with these guys. He kept their best interests in mind, and also in his trunk, along with their samples. His heart sank for them every time some sharky guy from corporate slapped him on the back and asked him, "How's the sticks, Danny?"

In St. Louis he'd checked himself into a hotel on the edge of downtown. He had a per diem from the company, but they made sure it ultimately came out of his margins—it was all *Glengarry Glen Ross* that way—so he still had to watch costs and stay where it wasn't so nice. If he mentioned the place, it was okay; if he didn't bring it up, you knew it was a dump. This particular stay he mentioned only that he could run to St. Louis's great arch and back, no problem, on actual paved jogging paths, too. He'd just finished doing it when I reached him.

"Good for you!" he said when I told him where I was. "That's fantastic news. I knew you'd get your head on straight and go home soon enough."

"It's a visit."

"Fine. You call it what you want. But your brother can use the extra hand, I know. He's working that hard. I've worn my share of casts, and it looks as bad as it is, trust me. This is fantastic," he said again. "You help him get around, be a good brother like you are, and we'll get this new idea done in no time. Then I'll come up, and we'll celebrate."

"Shouldn't he have had this great idea done by now?"

He laughed. His cell's connection warbled the sound and cut it in two. "He's taking his time. We Meyersons are stubborn. We do things at our own pace. Why's he so tight-lipped right now? I got no idea. So you let me know what's what—be my spy, right? Then I'll come up, and we'll all go to Ruth's Chris for steaks. You'll see. You boys'll figure it out just fine. You've got your mother's good sense. Her good looks, too."

In the video of my bar mitzvah party, there's footage of my mother in a long, baby blue dress, slow dancing with her husband in her Princess Di hairstyle. She had at least two inches on him, especially in heels, and yet she clung to him like Fay Wray on King Kong's leathery finger: she'd had a hard road, from deadbeat drapes salesman to bar mitzvah beauty, and Dad was her hero. I didn't know where that tape was now, perhaps in the old man's safe he kept in the closet of his basement office at the house in Omaha—the combination to which he'd given to Carlton for safekeeping.

"Okay Dad," I said.

"You bet okay. You're home with Carol Ann?"

"No, I'm at a little joint called Seth's Motor Lodge."

"What? I treated that girl like a princess! Now, she's no Angus steak, I know that, and I know what she did was terrible and hits you right where your rooster crows, because if it's one thing you are, it's loyal. It's a fault of yours—a not so bad one, but still, a fault. You're a pushover. I used to beg you to think of Hank first. Remember the Giving Tree, who for his trouble got cut to a stump—"

"Why did I call you, again?" I said.

"No one begged you to call."

What a piece of work. A big bullying dump truck of familial unfunded mandates. In the old peoples' home, he'll be the guy who mocks your false teeth, or your spotted-banana hands—perfectly ignorant of his own. He'll die in his sleep, dreaming of jogging routes. Or else he'll die in the middle of a sentence about how he certainly isn't going to die before you, with all the trans fats you eat. He used to squawk about leaf-strewn lawns and other slob mentalities, and people who buy chotchkes at the Cracker Barrel, and people with no retirement plan. But for family he reserved the more ensnaring barbs. "Not taking *seconds*, Hank? I'd think you were on a diet, if I didn't know better." He was a remarkable multitasker: laughing with you and at you at the same time. And if you called him on any of it, he'd pout like a ten-year-old girl.

"Okay Dad," I said.

"All right, then. You're my eyes and ears, now. Stick with him, check him out—and give me a full report, okay?"

My father in St. Louis didn't need to wait for me to answer. He started pushing buttons on his phone until he found the one that disconnected our call.

It about did me in, and I fell asleep again for most the afternoon.

Chapter Eighteen

Carol Ann agreed to meet me at a bar that evening. Her hair was still short, but she'd dyed it blonde, and she'd recently discovered whiskey. I told her that's what I'd been drinking in Montana.

"Let's do Jameson then," she said, both to me and the waitress.

After we'd had a couple, things started coming out. I apologized for leaving like I did, and she waved it off for now. She had taken up, of all things, boxing. For some reason, this news made me apologize again.

"No, you did us a favor," she said. "Look, we were sitting there falling apart, stagnant. Because of my affair. But now, instead of feeling guilty forever, I can feel rejected. Which is kind of intriguing," she added.

Carol Ann's tortured logic somehow put me at ease. The bar helped too. Nora's was a homey neighborhood place popular with both the Let's-get-a-burger-honey and the Wutter-you-lookin-at? crowds. It had a long mahogany bar with one central brass tap, all backlit with track lighting tinted a mild red for ambiance. Here and there crudely Sharpied signs announced "No checks!" The walls were nailed with clusters of framed sports memorabilia—Twins jerseys, Vikings greats, newspaper articles on memorable

U of M games, old North Stars nostalgia, somebody's hat. At the bar, guys bullshitted and told stories like they do, while back in the booths couples and longtime friends and adventuresome older ladies chuckled and munched. Circuiting through it all were two or three blithe, unflappable servers delivering the goods with tight Scandinavian smiles. It was no Copper Cowboy, but probably that was a good thing.

Carol Ann and I were at the tall tables just off the bar, in between the dart machine and the popcorn cart, because Carol Ann thought the booths would be sticky from the humidity. We could see our reflections, along with those of the seasoned drinkers, in the bottle-stacked mirrors behind the bar. We were filmy, all of us, and needed a cleaning.

"Oh, you'll appreciate this," Carol Ann said. "We did more focus groups last month in Portland, and when the moderator asked what they're looking for in a snack, this one woman says, 'Well you have to consider the modern human condition.'"

"Ha! People love to feel smart," I said. "Tougher to actually define the modern human condition."

"Oh but she did. She said it was 1) lack of time and 2) a desire for well-being."

I gave a snarky chuckle but was impressed. "That's better than I could have done. I would have said something about always being tricked into believing the worst part's over."

"Snacks can help that."

"Yeah." I patted my chest. "Help me right into a coronary."

"That used to be my biggest fear," she said, shaking her head. "That you'd just up and die. Not because of your weight, but just any reason. A car wreck or you'd cut your arm off with the circular saw."

"I almost did."

"And in July I had a dream that you'd come home, and everything was going to be okay. It was early in the morning, and I heard your voice in the kitchen, but when I came down you weren't there. There was a little sparrow on the windowsill. I thought it was a sparrow at least, though it was yellow and green. It opened and closed its wings like a butterfly, and I was happy for you and scared at the same time."

Carol Ann blinked hard, like she had shmutz in her eyes. Her irises went right and left. She touched the back of a knuckle to her eyelid.

"I once dreamed," I said, "that we were in the Jetta's backseat trying to make out or whatever, and suddenly the Jetta just started driving. Pulled right out into the street and down a hill and past a cop. You were like, 'Just play it cool,' but I was like, 'Oh yeah, like they're not going to notice that no one's driving the car.'"

She laughed, and sniffled. "That's sad too. But that's us. Was us. No one was driving the car."

"Hmm."

She couldn't look at me, only at the Jameson in her hands. Her fingers were long and weak-looking, a musician's fingers, atrophied. In fact somewhere in her Eastern European genealogy was a Serbian concert pianist whose performances were boycotted by Croats. Foreign hands—fingers of controversy and conflict. I couldn't recall an actual time I'd held them in my own. Probably when the judge married us. Then she lifted her head and gave a brave smile, and our food arrived. Burger for me, and chicken burrito for her, both in wax-papered red baskets.

The modern human condition? It's taking one for the team, smiling through your frustration, and doing it all again at some later date. At least, that's for us pampered Americans. Most of us experience no great epic, no wild catastrophe, none of the murder and insanity and incest that always seems to win some shut-in a National Book Award. The truth is that most of our lives are of trumped-up significance: we suffer small feelings, we calculate losses and accruals, and we try to make ourselves feel better with latest Hollywood gossip. And in between, if you're lucky, somebody drops by with banana bread.

I'd had enough of Jameson and was drinking beer with my food—Summit, a local brand. It sat placidly, carameled and bubbly in my glass, like beer should. The Twins were on TV, trying to get into the wildcard race. Over in the booths, a well-postured grandma type raised her voice to say that Brad Radke did have a nice ass and she didn't care *who* heard her say it. Local beer, local ball, local conversation. Chewing and wiping my hands, I got off my high stool and looked underneath it, and sure enough, the stamp in the wood said "Borgen Stool and Chair Co., Minneapolis, Minnesota."

"What are you doing?" Carol Ann laughed. There was a nibble of someone's chicken strip on the pocked black-and-white linoleum under her feet, and a soggy french fry off against the grimy baseboard. Not pretty, the underlife of a stool.

"Nothing. Remember that time you had to take a stool sample to the Grinnell Hospital?"

She'd had an unexplained anal itch, and the nurse behind the desk had made her repeat "stool sample" three times, each louder and louder. Just small-town pettiness, but in those days such things were liable to break Carol Ann in three. She used to be reticent like that, like a person ordering a smoothie in a dive bar. Now it's Jameson, and boxing.

"Good times," she said.

"So what the hell with boxing?"

"Oh I love it. It's great. I go to a gym especially for women. Well, there's like two men, but they're gay. Do you know how good it feels to get hit in the face? It's like communion, which you wouldn't know. But who understands getting hit more than Jews?"

"A lot of Jews were boxers back in the day. Basketball too. Whatever black people are doing now, Jews were doing then. Except hip-hop."

"There's a, something, to getting hit. It's so simple. You get popped in the face, and you're like, okay, and then you try to keep it from happening again. The other day I was moving around with this girl in the ring, and it was just pop after pop after pop. I'd jab, and she'd follow with her right, because I wasn't bringing my jab back high enough. Bam," she said, putting her left out there in a pretty good jab, not a girl jab at all. "Bam. Like she was trying to break my nose. But you know what? Everyone there *loves* one another. My sparring partner, my trainer, the other women. There's a camaraderie. I think men take that for granted, growing up with sports and circle jerks and roughhousing. But for me, it's new."

Carol Ann had grown up dancing ballet. "Have you actually had your nose broken?" I asked.

"Of course not," she said.

"I have."

"I know."

I pushed my burger basket away, with all its coagulating grease and ketchup. Knowing there was more of the same inside of me was almost enough to inspire a Carlton-esque 10K run at midnight. Almost. The server eyed it but saw that Carol Ann was still eating. She was wearing a Gophers T-shirt. Another server smiled at me as she carried two cases of beer up from the basement. I blushed and looked away.

"Are you nervous? To be around me?"

I shook my head. I shrugged.

"I promise not to cry anymore, tonight at least." She uncrossed and crossed her legs. She saw me watch, via the mirror. She seemed to be chewing her burrito carefully. She cut it into pieces with her knife and fork. No bulging cheeks, no lippy embellishments.

She wiped her mouth. "I think you used to think there was some button on my body that would make it work," she said. "Sex, I mean. Like getting candy from a vending machine. You push E and then you push 4 and then the little spiral spirals and you get your E4. It's not like that."

She ordered another round, on her she said. When it came, she raised a toast at us in the mirror. Her Jameson was the color of her hair, the ice little melting pools of light with alcoholic outlines that shimmered like her highlights. She wasn't wearing a bra. She rimmed her glass with those long, delicate fingers, now used for making fists. Sitting slump-shouldered and dumbfounded by the changes in her, I gave up and tried to just enjoy them.

"I'm saying," she said, "that we didn't know what we were doing. You know? We had no idea. There is no E4."

"But maybe there is. The modern human condition, after all."

She shook her head, and with it a little more Jameson. "No,

there isn't. You create it by trusting. I mean, you make every button E4. That's the idea."

"No one trusts anything anymore," I said. "We're not a nation of trusters. We're a nation of…of ass-kickers and conceal-and-carriers. SUVers. How else do you explain Senor Ranchero running neck and neck with Gore?"

Carol Ann jumped on this. "We trust all the time. You trust when you eat a burrito. You don't know what's in there. You see an onion and a pinto bean or whatever and you go with the odds, which are good, but still, you don't *know* know. Could be brains in here. Could be squirrel."

She wiped her mouth again. "But not you and me. There should have been an E4, but…We just—couldn't."

"You could."

She was sitting with her back very straight and her right shoulder pulled back away from me some. I was just realizing this must be a boxing stance when she reached across the table and jabbed me in the face. Not the nose, but below, in the lips and chin. It was a nice sharp punch, like Carlton had told me jabs should be—more a typewriter stroke than a baseball pitch.

"Sorry," she said.

My lower lip was inflating already. I tongued around for blood. I gargled something unintelligibly angry.

"I'm sorry," she said again.

I held my mouth, whined like a little girl. "I thought you said I did us a favor!"

"Well, maybe. But it hurt. Hurts."

Our waitress finally came by to clear my burger basket carcass. Great timing she had. She didn't let on that she'd seen me get hit, but after gathering napkins and pinching an empty glass with her free hand, she said to Carol Ann, "I hope he deserved it."

"Maybe we should get the check," Carol Ann said.

Carol Ann, because of the blow she'd given me, felt it was very important to have me stay at the house, which she called "our place." That I'd already paid the weekly rate at Seth's Motor Lodge wasn't a valid argument. I agreed to at least stop by, to see Steve.

The reception I got from that dog fondued me with joy. In the living room still graying in the floorboards and still water-stained in the ceiling corner, she simply would not stop barking. Paws up in my chest. And when I wrestled her down to the thin Oriental rug we'd inherited after Carol Ann's parents redecorated their house, she clambered with toothy vigor, submitting and licking and chomping on my arm and ear and chin until I headbutted her in the ribs. This is what dogs were made for—a dog you can't headbutt in the ribs isn't worth leashing. I was slick with saliva when Carol Ann brought in the sheets to make up the couch.

But in the dark that night, me on the couch with a blanket discarded to my feet, Steve couldn't decide where to sleep: up with her mommy or down with me. The jangle of her collar, her clicking claws down and up the stairs. Her cold nose at my elbow. I tried to make room for her, but it was pointless, and habit eventually wore her down. I heard her jump into bed with Carol Ann. I heard Carol Ann call her a good girl.

I couldn't sleep and was gassing up the living room. Burger, onions, and beer—it was awful, spawning memories of times I'd been ogreish, which is to say, most of our marriage. Or so it felt. The night we got home from that trip to Wyoming, when I'd checked us into Cricket Motel, which admittedly made Seth's Motor Lodge look like Trump Towers, I chose to sleep on the couch, just like I was now. I'd thought Carol Ann was asleep, and I started crying just a little, feeling sorry for myself. But she wasn't asleep—you never know your intimates the way you think you do. Things are rarely as you think. She came down and made love to me. She must have felt bad, but if she did, she didn't apologize. She straddled me on the couch and smiled through the whole thing, like a goddess or a benevolent whore. It was creepy. I should have said "Get the fuck off me!" but I didn't—I was too baffled.

Once just before a Thanksgiving trip down to Omaha—we were

literally in the car—I had to run back into the house for something, as is my scatterbrained way, and I left the driver's door open. This was not the Jetta, mind you, but the Honda—her car—and it had great heat, but the fact that I left the door open exposing her to the cold November sunshine, the fact that I hadn't even considered her temperature situation at all while I was rummaging inside the house for whatever the hell it was I'd forgotten—this was thrown into my face as I settled back behind the wheel as unconscionable. "You don't seem to worry about my happiness," was what she'd said. My defense was to blurt, "Happiness? Your happiness? Everything I do is for your happiness! What the fuck!" This kept her sulking and silent all the way to Mason City.

Yet, this is undeniable: Why *wouldn't* you want someone you love to be warm, amount of time having nothing to do with it? Why wouldn't you think of them? I was the one who, not four months before the affair, had refused to buy Carol Ann the modest diamond ring she'd hinted about for our anniversary. She more than hinted—she left the catalog open on the dining room table. I honestly had no recollection deciding against it. I wasn't cheap, nor contemptuous, nor resentful. I just wasn't thinking.

But boy was I now. How can a body sleep suspended in the agar of such memory? The house sagged with it, Carol Ann with her blonde hair and E4 buttons heavy overhead like a wet quilt.

Chapter Nineteen

I left a note for Carol Ann and went back to Seth's Motor Lodge. My brother's Volvo was parked and puttering between two yellow lines in front of my room. I pulled up next to him, got out, and bent down to the passenger window he had opened to talk to me.

"I was about to leave," he said.

"I was out with Carol Ann. She wanted me to stay there."

He nodded.

"What's wrong?" I said.

He shook his head and made a reassuring squinched face. "Nothing. I was just working, and now I've got insomnia. I'm antsy. Let's hang out." He held up a can of soda and swished it back and forth for me to hear the liquid inside. It was a strange-colored can of soda, because, I realized, it was actually beer.

"Off the wagon?" I said.

"Don't be a downer, and don't tell your sister-in-law."

"I've had plenty to drink already."

"You nancy! It's one night. You keep your trap shut about it, and we'll have some fun like we used to."

"It'll be last call soon."

"El Volvo is never closed." I heard the car unlock, so I got in.

The door closed with a deep, solid slap, the enviable comfort of money well spent.

"You got kicked out again, didn't you?" I said, but he ignored me. He handed me a can of beer; he had his own between his thighs. His ankle cast was shockingly white in the darkness at his feet.

He had already gotten us onto the interstate, headed for the St. Croix River like we had that spring. He checked his mirrors for cops and took a cautious pull from his beer can. My brother wanted to swim, but of course he couldn't, so I was going to be his surrogate. "Unless you want to try to fit in a quick game of pool?" he said.

"Fuck off and drive."

"That's more like it," he said.

I made up my mind to give swimming a shot and not get pissy about him commanding me what to do. After all, it was still pretty warm, and the drive was about a three-beer one, so by the time we reached the darkened state park entrance, I'd reclaimed my pre-punch good cheer and was ready to dive into anything, pretty much.

We parked, and my brother affixed the blue headlamp onto his forehead, fumbling with the Velcro behind his head a good minute, with his elbows up like he was trying to put himself in a headlock. The injuries he had sustained in his fall didn't seem to be bothering him, except for the cast—and that gave him instability more than discomfort.

He looked over at me, then down the path, then back to me. "What's up with your lip?" he said.

I brought a few fingers to my mouth, felt the cocoon there. "Um," I said. "Domestic violence."

He wrinkled his forehead.

"Carol Ann's learning to box, and she hit me. We were at Nora's."

He nodded like that kind of shit happened all the time.

"But not in a bad way," I said.

He nodded again, and we made our way to the river, him limping but brushing me off when I asked if he was okay. He really only had trouble with the steep wooden stairs leading down to the river—we took them together, his arm around my shoulder, his jerking headlamp lighting our descent like a bad horror movie.

The water was lower than when we'd been there in April, meaning there was more beach and more vegetation. A southern wind blew waves at us, leaving a sine curve of black matter all along the beach. It looked unnatural to see waves coming upriver like that. But if you ignored that and just focused on the river, you couldn't help but get enthused. It was like a great prairie of water under the bright moon, and I stripped down to the nude and ran in.

The river was a salve to my skin: clean, pleasant, cool but not cold, and in it I was buoyant, at least in spirit. I was not a good swimmer—check that, I was not any kind of swimmer. Did some diving for the Jewish Community Center team as a kid, and scored surprisingly well too by forgoing grace and skill in favor of degree of difficulty. But swimming I never took to, and believed no one should: we humans mutated to supremacy by flapping around on land, not water.

But when I realized I could walk a good twenty yards out and get wet only up to my navel, I plunged. The world went quiet in that way that makes you feel like a kid. This is what swimming does to you, and why most people love it. I felt the day's sweat wash off me, the toxic whiskey afterglow too. The rest of my day's *mishegos* probably wouldn't go that easily.

I dog-paddled back to stand about thirty yards from shore. Waves pushed as high as my nipples—the iceberg exposed. My brother's pale frame stood in the sand, kicking it—the cast like his own personal Q-tip of moonlight. He folded his arms and looked out at me. He didn't seem satisfied.

"How's the water?" he said. He didn't have to yell. "I love how pure it is here. It's sandy and unpolluted. There aren't many places like this left in our country."

From somewhere downriver came a voice, faint but sharp. Then a door closing. Water carries sound a tremendous distance.

"Do you remember when Dad and I were studying once—"

"You were always studying."

"Christ, tell me about it! Every night, every book he made me bring home."

"You would have flunked without it."

"One semester," he said. "And then I would have gotten my act together, like I've been doing all my life. He's too paternal, which is ironic. That's the right word, right?"

I nodded.

"He treats people like that, even the penniless people he buys Hanukkah presents for off the list at Jewish Family Services. Anyway," he said, "we were going over biology for a quiz. Parts of a plant. And Dad laughed when you walked by and said, 'Let's ask Hanky—he'll *never* get this one.'"

"I don't remember."

"And he asked you what part of a plant stem carries water and nutrients up to the leaves. Solid high school biology stuff, no kidding. And you were like, 'Xylem,' and went into your room and shut the door."

"We must have studied it that day. Dumb luck."

He smiled, his misaligned teeth recently whitened. "No, no," he said. "You're just smart. And educated. Those are different things. You just have a way of soaking stuff up."

"Am I supposed to be soaking stuff up about you and June?"

"Nice," he chuckled. "No, it's none of your business."

"Okay."

He sighed. He crossed his arms. "I'll tell you all about it. Just not tonight. "

"I said okay."

Suddenly he snapped out of himself and took an easy, wide-legged stance in the sand. "Anyway," he said, uncrossing his arms to gesture at his long body, "don't I look fine?"

I had to admit, except for the cast, he did. I had been walking back to him as he said this, and now my feet were in dry sand, an uneasy feeling. I was dripping everywhere, naked and chilled. What is it about Minnesota that it's never the fucking temperature you want it to be? I cupped my hands over my crotch, why I don't know—protection from the elements I guess. My brother produced the towel he'd had tucked into his pants at the small of his back. It was a paltry towel not the quality kind June kept stocked in the house. I did my best with it.

My brother downed a beer and brought out another one from his sweatshirt pocket.

"Yeah, you look great, except for the limp. But you're drinking," I said, "and June said you were mean."

He big-eyed me, owlish.

"That's all she said, but still. That doesn't sound fine."

"But it is," he said. He smiled at my toweled hair, which probably resembled the wild grasses sprouting down the beach. "In fact, I'm so fine, I'll even let you drive us home."

"Are you saying I can hold my liquor better than you?"

"No question," he said. "I'm not at peak conditioning."

The sand in my sandals bugged me, but not much. I kicked them on the rocks at the base of the stairs, but on the car ride home, my brother kept eyeing them and frowning. He'd stowed extra towels for me to sit on, too.

"Stay a week at least," he said. "The old man's coming up, and I'm going to show you guys the next money-maker."

"It's ready?"

"No," he said. And he laughed out the window at the night.

Chapter Twenty

Wednesday morning, my little hovel was still postcard perfect, as I had yet to unpack anything but toiletries. I'd been watching the little TV with gusto—basic cable's humble hodgepodge of poker tournaments, trick-shot pool shows, cooking tutorials, celebrity insider's paparazzi, and the ubiquitous reconstructing of rapes and murders that keep you guessing whether or not the bastard went to jail. Then to CNN for a little election coverage: George Bush's big-eared "aw shucks" routine, while Al Gore stood like a man in a freight train boxcar talking to himself.

TV. The great succubus of suburbia. My father was one of its junkies; though to him TV was merely a tool of distraction while he toned his body. Probably he considered it his only option— what, was he supposed to read *Moby Dick* instead? Even if he could concentrate and keep his place, what would be the point—everyone knows the whale did it.

June called and asked if she was bugging me.

"Of course not. Just enjoying a poker game."

Silence.

"On TV."

"Oh. So are we going to see each other?"

"Maybe."

"Let's define, like, the rules."

I huffed.

"Carlton's not here, if that's what's bugging you."

"Nothing's bugging me. I'm going to be here all week. I'll see you. I've been occupied."

"Poker?"

"Yes, and trick bank shots. And how to make gnocchi."

She laughed. "Don't get testy."

"Listen," I said, "why don't you and I have lunch or something. But alone. A picnic lunch, by the river."

I could hear her biting her lip. "I don't think so."

"But why? It's normal to have lunch with your brother-in-law, isn't it?"

"It used to be. Now it's more normal for you to be there for your brother."

"Where's 'there'?"

"And Terry—you remember Terry? He wants you to pick him up at three."

We seemed to catch the Minneapolis Institute of Arts on a good day: no crowd, and the herringbone wood floor had recently been waxed. I could see Terry's Cubs hat in it as we walked into the main gallery area, having paid the "suggested donation" and gotten a map.

We didn't need a map. The kid knew his way around like a goldfish. He had a strange gait, Terry. It wasn't retarded per se—it just looked as if he might retrace his steps at any moment, like he was memorizing his way. Most of us walk without a thought; Terry walked like there was going to be a test. He held his hands tight to his sides, and his Cubs hat was so low over his eyes he had to tilt his head back just to see more than five feet ahead of him. He was wearing his new cowboy boots, too, which certainly didn't help.

"How many times have you been here?" I asked as we went all the way up the open staircase.

He didn't answer me. He eyed the big Chihuly sculpture like one of its brilliant yellow tendrils might reach out and stab him, which looked to be exactly Chihuly's intent.

We stepped off the stairs into a long hallway leading to European period rooms starting at about the twelfth century. Terry kept shuffling, his boots echoing with the sound of a plastic cup falling to the floor. He paused before one of the hall's enormous tapestries, worn out and faded, and I took a second to look at one of the displays of gilded china under glass, but in that second he was off again.

We passed wooden benches with beveled edges and security guards with more piercings than Christ on the cross—the comparison was easy to make, since almost every painting I'd thus far glimpsed in the galleries, if it wasn't a dour portrait of some mawkish matron or a beady-eyed bishop, seemed to be of Christ dying for our sins. Thank God Christmas has been secularized, I thought, because this kind of thing every December would be tough to take.

The security guards eyed us—sulky, malevolent, bored out of their skulls. Some had their arms crossed, some fiddled with their walkie-talkies, some played somnambulistic mental solitaire like we didn't exist—all wore navy blazers that were too big and too ridiculous, even with the little gold insignia you were supposed to mistake for authority. Where do they get these guys? How are they supposed to stop me from damaging a painting if they can't get down and give me twenty pushups?

"You must have a destination," I said to Terry, but he ignored me. Maybe he was heading to the café for a tasty sandwich.

A grouping of straight-backed students on a guided tour slipped into and out of the great room we were in like a collection of young ghosts. They were followed by a cute couple killing time with a set of in-laws, discussing dates of Dutch movements like it fucking mattered. "Wasn't it the nineteenth century?" "Oh, you and your nineteenth century!"

And I, I knew enough about art—thanks to all the Ed Ruscha and Pop Art research I did for my master's—to know that the better part of my education was ignorance. The best thing to do in a museum like this, then, is to embrace the ignorance. This meant that instead of movements and dates and influences and themes, I had to start with the noticeable details and see if I could glean anything from repetition or whatever and try to let a piece have some impact on me other than "That's a lot of Jesus."

So, entering the gallery room Terry had chosen for us, I first noticed the stuff Joe Twelve-pack would: a few black scuffs darting the floor, the demonic exit sign, a flat-footed retiree strolling out as we walked in, the maw of an air vent at toddler level, and each painting's pair of wire cables descending from a run of molding high overhead. Track lighting clinging to the skylights casings even higher overhead. Are we having fun yet?

Terry shuffled up to, and sat down cross-legged before, a painting in the corner. His neck angled up off his curve of back in a way that made my own neck hurt. With a small pang at the goodness of the world, I thought that in all probability, someone, somewhere had received schooling specifically to do massage on retards. God what a world! Preposterously teeming with goodness! So much so that it takes nothing short of an Eichmann every now and then to yank us from our clouds.

The painting that captured Terry's attention was small, relatively. But Terry was into it. It was simply framed in gold-painted wood, and even I could tell it was an Annunciation. There was Mary, in her red and blue cloak, piously kneeling at what the didactic called her chamber's "prie-dieu," while behind her the angel Gabriel was trying to get her attention. High in the middle of the painting, in an opening created by billowing gray clouds, was a small white bird, glowing deistically and shooting a golden ray of knowledge toward Mary regarding her soon-to-be birthing. There were some baby angels floating up in the corners too—can't forget the baby angels. All this was taking place in some nice digs, with a tile floor of big orange circles alternating with big green squares— apparently this was before the manger, when Mary was a little more flush.

"See her robe isn't moving," Terry said, "but his is blown all around?"

"Yeah," I said. "Yeah I do."

"This is my old-time favorite painting." He considered this a moment, then backed off it slightly. "For now," he said.

"What kind of bird is that?" I asked Terry. After all, he had clearly just established himself as the expert.

His head shifted slightly, and I could see his wheels turning. Maybe he'd never thought of it before. I should first have asked what he was looking at, what he saw, why he liked the damn thing—for all I knew, it was the frame.

"Gosh," he said. "What a question." He started rocking some, and put his palms to his beard like Macaulay Culkin.

"Probably a dove?"

"I don't think so. I don't think so at all. It should be a duck."

"Why a duck?"

"Because a duck would mean that something's going to happen. Ducks quack. They're very loud. You'd want a loud bird there. And it's too small to be a goose, and too white to be a crow."

"What's going to happen?"

"They say the baby Jesus."

"They say, huh? And what do you think?"

"She doesn't look very happy to me. That's the long of the short of it."

"Yeah," I admitted.

"If it was Jesus she'd be besides herself."

A gabber, this kid was! Emotional and headfirst when the spirit moved him, as it clearly was now before this painting, he was starting to grow on me.

"That's probably true," I said. "But why a duck? Paintings have things in them for a reason usually, though the reason is hard to see sometimes."

"Boy how! I would say it's a duck because something bad is going to happen, because she's so pretty, and the angel wants her to know about it. All that smoke means a fire. That's what I think.

The light is coming from the smoke. It's a smoke alarm. The duck is alarming her."

This got me laughing, which Terry didn't appreciate.

"Fires burn people."

"I'm sorry," I said. "So why do you like it, if it's scary like that?"

"I don't know scary. It's so pretty," Terry said. "I really want to paint something this pretty. Do you think I ever could?"

"Sure."

"I'd like to have a girlfriend, a lot. That's why I want to paint something like this."

"Maybe you will."

But the thing was, the painting wasn't even that good. It was by a lesser-known Italian from the mid-eighteenth century, Agostino Masucci, and it was squashed, cramped somehow, too small. Sure, it was touching the way Mary refuses to recognize what's happening, even with Gabriel's primped wings and his fingers pointing like "Hey, hello, see the duck with the laser?" But the overall composition was pretty static, and Gabriel was too pudgy and doe-eyed, the baby angels too frivolous. Actually, it was Christian propaganda, not art. It's only a magical moment if you know about all the fabulous tragedy to come, the loaves and fishes, the water and wine, the vampirification of Lazarus, all the *thou arts* and *my childrens*. Myth-makers have a way of knowing what strings to pull in your head and heart, all the praise and thanksgiving, and in that sense Agostino had succeeded. Made you want to fall for Mrs. Nazarene yourself, quote St. Paul's letter to the Galatians 3:12–17, and fill yourself with the Virgin Mother's redemption and self-sacrifice till you feel lowly as a mouse in the basement. I wondered if Terry could comprehend all this, assuming I could even explain it myself.

But I didn't have the patience—we'd sat there too long as it was. My back began to hurt sitting on the backless bench, and of course I couldn't leave him alone. The other paintings were just as propagandistic, some more visually interesting, some less. There was another Annunciation, a slithering Diogenes, a fabulously bizarre Titian called *The Temptation of Christ,* and also good old Salome holding the head of John the Baptist—in this version she looked impassive, neither dismayed nor triumphant, more like "all in a day's work." And there was a penitent Mary Magdalene, turning from darkness up to the sky as if the wrath of God were nigh—which, the painting seemed to say, serves her slutty ass right.

"Terry," I said. "Terry, we need to move on."

He nodded and hopped up, repositioning his Cubs cap, and left the room.

But nothing else interested him, except the gift shop, where he chose an El Greco print for his mother. Before taking it to the counter he brought a small phonebook of folded twenty-dollar bills out of his pocket. There had to be a grand there, no joke. "Holy shit put that away," I said, looking around like we were going to get rolled right there among the Dorothea Lange books.

"What am I doing wrong?" he said.

"Don't you have a check card or something?"

"A what?"

This made me want to kiss him. Those delicate lips, untouched by modern worries. Oh I knew this wasn't true—his parents were divorced, for Christ's sake—but the look in his eyes like "What new thing do I have to worry about now?" made me melt for him.

"I'm sorry," I said. "Just…put it away. That's too much money to carry around."

"I sold two paintings," he apologized.

"Really? Listen, just pull out three bills."

He did, and I handed them to the cashier, who gave me back change, which I funneled back to the kid's pocket. He raised his face to me, and it lit up as much as anyone wearing a hat from such a terminally ill team as the Cubs could, and soon we were outside in the bright sunshine, then back in my Jetta, and the guy wouldn't shut up. He kicked the passenger seat's nethers with his boot heels, then turned his attention to the hurricane of my backseat and made a joke.

"I could start a volunteer to clean up your car."

I laughed.

"It stinks in here," he said. "It stinks on heaven high."

"Roll your window down."

"What is it, fish? Hank, is it fish? I feel fish smells awful but tastes pretty good, and that's another strange thing there."

It had rained one night of my drive east, and there was some water on the backseat floor. I should drill a drain hole, I thought. That way the mold would die in ten years or so, instead of ten thousand.

"A friend could get lost in your backseat."

"You can clean it for me if you like. I'm fine with it just how it is."

Was that true? Couldn't I see the laser coming out of the duck's beak? I was odd man out. When I left this town again, it would be for good, and I would never love this way again. This week, it was all I had. For the rest of time, it was just me and the retard and a blessed, oblivious Virgin Mary I didn't even believe in.

Terry took a big sniff of the air in the car. He tried to roll down his window more, but it was already as far as it would go, the internal cranking mechanics having broken some ages ago. "That's pretty strange," he said.

Chapter Twenty-One

Dad got hold of me in my room. He said immediately that he was at the sales conference and that if he lost me it was because his cell had hit one of the hotel's dead zones.

"How did you get this number?"

"How did I get your number? Who do you think is paying your hotel bill?"

"Me and my Working Assets Visa card."

"I had the hotel credit your account. I'm taking care of it. You're my man on the inside, after all."

I grunted. I'd been all but asleep in the clutches of early evening lethargy. The little cloister was becoming spiritual to me. I tried to keep it as neat as possible, my life untouched behind drawn shades like a patient Nosferatu.

"Anyway, I got a better rate than you got. I've stayed in all kinds of places like that, so I know. They're not so bad, they're just people trying to get by. We understand each other. In Wamego, when I visit June's mom and dad, I stay at the Simpson Motel, with the deer heads and the cougar mounted in the office. That cougar always cracks me up. Anyway, the richies in town pooled their money and built a Super 8 right across the street. Isn't that terrible? There has to be a conscience someplace. There have to be principles."

He interrupted himself then, awkward and without cause, to ask how the new toy was coming.

"I haven't seen it."

"Well, what has he told you?"

"What has he told you?"

"Don't worry about that."

"He said it's not ready, but it will be. We're still on for Ruth's Chris."

"So he's good?"

"Good? He's fine. He's dressing a little more scruffily and might be growing a beard."

"He's working too hard. And you? Patching up with the wife?"

"Not exactly."

"Everything with you is not exactly."

"I know. That's why you went into business with Carlton."

"Ah, I never wanted that for you. You were built for smarter things."

"Really?"

"Of course! It's a racket, this thing. It takes a lot of handholding. You don't even know."

For a moment he sounded like he was going to confide in me, some cluck behind his words, like I wasn't his son but a guy next to him at the Copper Cowboy. But he stopped short. We were a family of stop-shorters. Mom too—right up to her last left turn.

"Anyway, you're still gonna do great things. You could be anything you want, always could. Sure you could have a nicer car, a nicer house, a stronger marriage, better teeth—but you're finding your way still."

"What's wrong with my teeth?"

He sighed, and told me the signal was breaking up.

"I can hear you just fine."

"Sorry about this," he said.

It's very difficult not to use metaphor. Try describing a lopsided sports victory without it. People love it because it's unique to us humans.

Maybe an ape or an artificial intelligence computer can say, "Please peel me a banana," or "The banana peel is yellow," but they can't understand "He banana-peeled to the floor," or "Is that a banana in your pocket?" Not yet, anyway. This is why the figurative is so enjoyable—it reminds us we are human, and more than literal. The literal can get old actually. Technical manuals are literal, and meeting minutes: noun-verb-direct object, noun-verb-direct object. I eat, I work for someone else, I pay back debts, I sleep, I screw my spouse. How liberating to say, "The debts are eating me, so screw work; I'm going to get payback by sleeping with someone else's spouse!"

But Jews of my father's generation and before don't like metaphors. I'm talking regular Jews, not the poets and rabbis and scholars. Literal language, that's the horse to ride—hard and fast words like *buy* and *golf* and *bucket* and *inventory*. Which is understandable: as a people, metaphoric feats like double entendres and creative comparisons haven't exactly served us very well. The hyperbolic descriptions, the inscrutable fine print, the ambiguous property laws, medieval Jews massacred by the thousands for "stealing the Host" when a family had been found celebrating Passover with a few crusts of matzoh, the editorial cartoons in the national Saudi newspapers depicting "Zionists" as heinous, hunch-backed, and hell-bent for world domination—they've all been used against us. "Arbeit Macht Frie" over the entrance to Auschwitz. The de-lousing. The women getting their hair cut short as if they were about to shower, for real—really, it's a shower, why else would we bother cutting your hair? There's good reason to be wary of anything but the literal.

So for generations we've stuck to the noun-verb-noun, and that's it. Business, law, medicine—real things in the real world. We say, "Oh Palm Springs is gorgeous, just gorgeous," and use our most earnest voices for emphasis, and also a few repetitions from the spouse ("Gorgeous!"); we do not say, "Palm Springs is my Xanax."

There's a joke in which an old Jew wants to take the train to Minsk. But first he walks the ten miles to the train station to find out when the train runs. The station agent tells him there is a train to Minsk every day at 10:00 a.m. "Every day?" the Jew asks. Yes, every day. "Each and every day, you're telling me?" Yes, that's right. "On every day of the week, there is a train departing for Minsk?" Yes, yes, a thousand times yes! So the old Jew begins to walk away, then stops, fidgeting, and finally pads back to the station agent and says, "Thursdays too?"

In other words, no joking around, thank you. Just the facts, *meshuggener*. Pick up that banana peel and put it in the garbage where it belongs. Oy a world of banana peels and station agents and wise guys and getting screwed out of 20 percent and "Arbeit Macht Frie"! Obviously, such a world is nuttier than peanut brittle, and he's a fool who tries to beat it at its own game.

This was the idle chatter in my brain that morning. Because my motel room faced east, the morning sun played Kabuki on the carpet—the shadow of a bird on a wire. He twisted his head, took some cautious hops, and finally lifted off for safer ground. Birds, always on the lam—their fear keeps them alive.

Birds, metaphors, the train to Minsk. Thinking wasn't getting me anywhere.

June answered on the third ring. "Hi," she said.

"What's going on there?"

"Oh, you know. Carlton's at the studio. Terry and I are doing a puzzle."

"Aren't we all."

She ignored this. "Hold on," she said.

There was a muffled transition of phone, then the kid's breathy voice. "Hello?" he said. He didn't wait for an answer. "I would like to thank you for taking me to the Mia yesterday. And we are almost finished with this puzzle."

"What's the puzzle of?"

He had to ask. "A train. A local motive."

"Locomotive," I said.

"Good-bye," he said. I heard him fumble the phone.

June said, "He needs to practice his phone skills. He gets all formal sounding. You okay?"

"Why aren't you talking to me?"

"Normal."

"There's nothing normal about this."

"Stop."

"Do you think we have souls?"

"Are you worried about it?"

"I don't know if 'worry' is the right word."

"There's no hell, Hank. How can there be? It's like, you're going to burn—but how? With no body, no nerves, no whatever. It can't be pain as we know it. If anything, it's ennui."

"Well ennui smart?"

"Ha! That cheered me up. Let's have lunch, out someplace, all of us. Tomorrow."

"Didn't you ask him to move out again?"

"Kind of."

"Everything is kind of."

"I'm not talking about it now."

I sighed. "I think we have souls, and the thing about a soul is, it shakes you. I felt it in Montana, and whenever I'm alone. It's not like other shaking."

"I'm going to let you decide when you want to see us, okay?"

"Right. You've got puzzles to do."

"Don't you?" she said.

Terry yelled, "Good-bye, Hank!"

When I went out for Thai food that night—one of the cosmopolitanisms I'd been missing in Montana—there was a note on my door, in Carol Ann's loopy, level script: "Where are you? Farting around? Why won't you call me?" There was a smiley face too, with a little tongue poking out its mouth.

Chapter Twenty-Two

Since it was already Thursday and I was apparently just farting around, I decided to do it at Nora's. A few beers might make me feel ennui smart, maybe get me punched in the nose again. Throw in some whiskey, and I was off to the races.

"The Duck of Annunciation waddles into a bar," I said. This was for the benefit of the bartender and a few waitresses, whom I was amusing. They'd heard all about the Duck of Annunciation by that point in the evening: how he waddles into a bar and makes his order and tries to pay the bartender with all this loose change and then storms out and goes back to God waiting in the El Camino and tells him they're going to have to go someplace else because it's horrible, horrible—that bartender guy wanted to be paid in *bills*.

Oh, and they'd also heard how the same Duck waddles into the same bar and says to the same bartender that he and God want to buy the bar, and the bartender says, well buying a bar takes some major scratch, so you gotta have something to show me you're serious, so the duck plucks off twenty or thirty of his feathers, puts them into a burlap sack, and hands them to the bartender, who says, what the hell is this? And the Duck says, naturally, "You moron. It's a down payment."

I made those jokes up myself.

So anyway: "The Duck of Annunciation walks into a bar. Same bar. Bartender says, 'Go on, beat it, you deadbeat.' Duck says, 'Calm down, cowboy—we just want a couple of drinks, and I got actual money now.'"

The waitresses were laughing. There were three of them waiting to hear how this one turned out, two with trays full of Captain and Cokes and the like. One of them wondered how a duck carries dollars.

"Shekels," I corrected her. "Anyway, the bartender is impressed and says, 'Well that's more like it—so what'll it be?' 'Two strawberry daiquiris to go,' the duck says."

"And what's with the drinking and driving?" another waitress said.

I shrugged. A Somali guy in a Cosby sweater and a corduroy baseball cap was leaning against the wall by the Golden Tee in his best Marlboro Man pose, right down to the Miller High Life propped in his crotch like a hard on. I smiled at him.

The problem was that I was making this joke up as I went along. "I guess God gets to choose what rules to follow," I said. "So anyway the bartender says 'Coming right up,' and goes to town, and it's taking a while because you know, it's a daiquiri from scratch—no pre-mixes for the Lord!—and God's out there blaring the horn on the El Camino, cuz they have places to go. So finally the daiquiris are done, and the duck pays in shekels, with a nice tip, and waddles out with the drinks in Styrofoam cups. But after a minute the duck waddles back in. He's got one of the drinks with him. 'Oy,' he says. 'This is embarrassing.' 'What?' the bartender wants to know. 'What, is it no good?' 'No, no—it's fine,' the duck says. 'It's just, He's very finicky…' 'What, what!?' The bartender is dying because this is God's drink we're talking about, and he made it extra-special good. And the duck says, 'It's no big deal. He's just got it in his head that he wants a virgin.'"

Thank you ladies and gentleman! I'll be here all night.

But I ran out of jokes, and audience. Left on my own on the barstool, I pondered myself in the dankened mirror behind the bar. My face sallow and frank, like a hollow mask, lumpy and blotched under the eyes. The face of a guilty conscience. I was a complicated man—which felt good somehow. Or maybe that was the beer. My lip was still somewhat swollen, and it hurt too. I could raise my hand to it without help from the mirror.

See, pain is a great locator, a regular GP fucking S. Pain puts you in touch with life—a trail map with a sheet metal screw right through your you-are-here forehead. And yes, I suddenly felt alive, sitting in that miserably cheery bar! And I didn't want to feel any better, didn't want "closure" with anyone, even June. Nora and Seth, and the great Duck of the Annunciation, and that would be fine by me. Fuck closure. Closure is the thing that puts an end to suffering, meaning life. That's the real reason why fairy tales end with "happily ever after"—the story's over, and you aren't supposed to give a shit anymore. There are no good stories in paradise. No, paradise, the reward for self-denial, is a flat numbness at best. And we Americans, middle-class and up, are about as good at it as any civilization before us. Paradise found, in a six-pack and *The Simpsons.* That's the modern human condition right there—snacks just make it taste better.

But this didn't cotton to my mood. Not even the swivel-sashay of the prettiest waitress did. There was a hipster party in the corner, guys and gals with hair perfectly mussed—they think that if they put their keys on a big key ring and use a carabiner to attach it to their belt loop that no one will think they use lots of hair product. Sorry kids, we know. Still, they were having a great time, the Minneapolis Department of Inspections had made sure that the popcorn they were eating by the basketful had less than five fecal parts per million, and there was plenty of electricity in this world of ours to keep their Amstel Light cold.

Happy people, who can carabiner their lives together, how do they get that way? Can't all be from Duck of Annunciation jokes. One way is probably just to shut your fucking mouth and simply be happy. But my father would offer other advice, if asked. I could see pilgrims making their way to his house, where he's doing sit-ups on the carpet gone dingy as airplane plastic, the same carpet Mom had installed just before she died. Happiness? he'd say, holding up one hand and bending his fingers to tick down the obvious: family, health, enough money to go out for steaks once a week, a clean conscience, and a cleaner car.

I told the bartender to save my spot, and I went outside to the Jetta, which was parked in a primo spot right in front of the joint, and I began to clean it out. There was a city trashcan at the corner, and I dragged it over to my car and began to fill it with my life's detritus. It was the river of my life up and through the present, like a ghost hand parting the curtain to a simpler me. There, for instance, was the instruction manual—in English, Spanish, Chinese, and, inexplicably, Dutch—for the tape player Carol Ann and I had installed upon buying this, our first car, from a stockbroker who didn't want it anymore because it was a stick and he couldn't drive and talk on his cell phone at the same time. There too were the empty power-steering-fluid bottles that were required because that particular system had a leak someplace and created a whiny grinding sound upon each turn of the wheel whenever fluid got too low. Snow-white Styrofoam packaging from speakers I had bought and installed myself. Pens and pencils chewed at the nibs by someone, possibly Steve. A single blue glove, a sock, a pair of scratched Oakleys I had inherited from my friend Lance back at Old Grinnell College. Coke and Sprite bottle caps announcing I was not a winner but that I should "Play Again!" and "Drink Coke!" Lottery tickets, peel-off plastic rings from milk bottles, leaves and unidentifiable papers and gas receipts, a waxy sleeve of Ritz crackers, and a fire extinguisher still in its damp, soiled box—I had purchased it for Carol Ann, actually, but she had laughed it off as just another damn thing rolling around in her Civic, and I had often of late envisioned her car bursting into flames as she watches helplessly on the side of the road, crying, "Oh Hank, I was wrong!"

I moved to the glove box. Carol Ann and I had never had sex in this car—evidenced by the calcified condom packages I now found myself holding. I'd had to peel them from under the small first-aid kit, meaning they were circa 1996, and I laughed a three-whiskey laugh at their optimism, and at how they were tucked in among the

Burger King handiwipe packages of similar size and shape. With my luck I would have grabbed the wrong package anyway, and Carol Ann would have shaken her head and said something like, "Well, if you'd rather go get a Whopper…" I tossed the squished packages at the garbage can like skipping stones, and when one of the condoms missed and skittered to the cement, a passerby quipped to his girlfriend, "Dude's going bareback!"

I started to feel sick to my stomach at that, though maybe it was from the memory of Carol Ann announcing, just a year before all this, that she was going on the pill—and we all know whom the beneficiary of that little pharmaceutical adjustment was. Are there any jokes that start "A bedwetter walks into a bar…"?

I was slicked up with sweat from stuffing myself face-first into the hot car. But I wanted to keep going, finish the job at least half-right, so I stepped around to the trunk. I opened it with the key, and raised it up, forgetting how angrily I'd jammed the Foghorn Leghorn I'd won at the fair in there—I'd folded him in half, beak to ankles, to make him fit, and now he leapt loose like a coiled spring. I screeched and slammed the trunk down, but his neck caught in the latch so it wouldn't close. I kept slamming, and Foghorn kept bouncing, until finally the latch caught, a scrap of mangled orange beak still bleating out. This was when my brother caught up with me.

"What the hell are you doing?" he said.

"Goddammit," I said, about getting scared by a cartoon plush.

He saw me teetering, and he seemed to be teetering too—maybe in sympathy, or because of the leg, but probably mockery. "Well, you're well on your way for the evening," he said, "so come on. I've got to catch up."

He wanted to swim. "How do you like the digs?" We were crossing the river not far from the university, and he nodded to his left—where the piquant Seth's Motor Lodge sign was somewhere blinking. He handed me a beer.

"It's great. The old man's paying for it."

"No shit? Maybe I'll come join you. You got room?"

"Let's just get a suite and put it on his card."

"Ha. Watch that, though—when he pays, he gets all in your bidness and it's tough to get him out. That's why I had to stop talking to him, make a few executive decisions."

"Well good for you."

"Yeah, good for me. I'm sure he's been grilling you about me?"

"Yeah, the new toy."

"You all can wait."

That satisfied me, so I focused on the beer. Good old big-brewery brand, in a can. After the whiskey, it tasted refreshing and hardly alcoholic. Driving and drinking with my brother, the stupid risk of it, brought him down to my level somehow, like we'd gone back in time. His chinos were wrinkled and vaguely soiled. His T-shirt hugged him a little too tightly in the gut, and he kept using it to wipe his face of sweat.

"Don't you have any clothes at the studio?"

He shrugged—the nonchalance of a man in the doghouse with the wife—and I can't deny that this also felt good. Fall, brother, fall. He'd be high again soon enough.

Out in the water that night, which felt so pure and clean I didn't know if I should drink it or swim in it, I tried to make a clean slate of my mind. Nothingness. I splashed and dove and hollered from the shock, even with the water relatively warm, then shuddered and calmed down. A few stringy ligaments of water grass swaddled my calves. I tried to float myself back to that pure state of suffering I'd inhabited during my first month in Montana. It took concentration. Pure, elemental suffering—pure, compliant water. In Montana I didn't have June, which was making me suffer, along, of course, with guilt. At least here I had June—sorta, as she might say.

Even if I'd been a good swimmer, floating on my back would be problematic. Humans just weren't meant to do it. Even a guy like me, with extra ballast shall we say, has to flagellate with the arms to keep aright. Little sputtering toe kicks too. And even with the comfort of a good quarter mile's buffer of open water in any direction, there's the panic of unintentional drift and the small waves tonguing water into my ears. The freckled aspirin of moon hung like an admonition. This wasn't pure suffering—it was wasting time. I stopped and stood up. I needed to see her. I needed to see her right then, but of course I would have to wait until the next day. If I didn't, I might as well go home—because, really why else was I here? Besides entertaining the Nora's staff with jokes and fat lips. Carlton certainly didn't need me.

As if merely thinking his name could make him appear, my brother splashed up to me, his long frame white in the moon. He dove under, then emerged head first, his chest going goose-fleshy, his nipples springy. He pulled water from his face. I just looked at him, then up at the stars.

"This is great," I said. He handed me a beer, then dropped the extras he'd carried out with him into the water, where they floated. "Even better," I said.

We cracked them, and the sound jolted me a little. I drank, felt the wake of his arrival dissipate, and then realized something.

"Your cast!" I looked stupidly to his feet, though of course his entire lower half was submerged.

He shrugged. "I couldn't take it any longer."

"I thought you had willpower."

"Willpower. That's something they give you," he took a long pull from the can.

"Who?"

"Financiers, and the like. The funding supports their work."

"What the fuck are you talking about?"

He shook his head. He smiled and gestured toward his cast underwater. "Nowadays they make them so they can get wet. It'll just smell like shit."

"Well," I started, but what's done was done. You can't un-soak a cast.

There was no current where we stood, just surface waves blown by a breeze seemingly no stronger than AM radio, but I guess water works on its own rules. I got goose bumps that were chased away by the warmth of stillness until my brother scanned the horizon, turned back to shore, dunked his head, and corralled the floating drowned soldiers. Couldn't sit still, my brother, worse than a dog.

Finally he stopped. "June's not happy with me."

"Obviously."

"She thinks the toy idea will flop, just like Rocktopus. She said so. And she doesn't even know what it is! She's bitchy about it. She says I keep secrets. She says I'm a shit."

"Didn't look that way at the fair."

He smiled and nodded. "Yeah, that was some mojo going on. I don't know how to explain it. Our pool game too. You should have beaten me." The memory of that missed ball, clanking off all the other missed balls in my life, stung. "Anyway," he went on, "I don't know what to do."

"Try not being a shit."

"I do, but I'm hardwired for it. I blame the drapes salesman."

I didn't want to ask this next question, but I had to know what I was dealing with. "Do you love her?"

My brother made a disgusted harrumph. He dropped his empty can into the water, and opened a fresh one. "I'd do anything for her. It hurts. You and her and Dad, always the same questions. Always chiseling me one way or another. Haven't I made myself clear?"

"I don't know."

"You don't know? You don't know. That's great. Maybe you've missed me working my ass off and raising our standard of living. Maybe you had your fucking eyes closed. Maybe you were asleep. That would explain a lot. You'd have to be asleep to miss your wife cheating on you."

I fished myself another beer too. I took a deep breath. When you grow up with snarly, petulant barbs of abuse, you learn to deflect most of them.

"See now, I can't for the life of me see why June thinks you're a shit."

"Just help me manage this, and then the toy will go out and make a killing, and it'll be high times again."

"How do I help you manage this?"

"I don't know. Talk to her. You did when she asked you if she should marry me, so do the same thing. Isn't that why you came home?"

I wanted to tell him I was good in a crisis, but Montana had relieved me of that delusion.

"I'll do what I can."

"There you go. Come around tomorrow afternoon. Don't bring that retard! He's not a part of this at all."

He was shepherding the two remaining full cans in the water around him, and the two empties as well. But he wasn't very nimble at it, and he just seemed to scatter them more. Then he lost his balance and splashed down into them, and the empties were off in the current. We watched them go until my brother whistled "Taps," and that was our night.

Chapter Twenty-Three

Terry got into the Jetta that morning without complaint.

"I like the Mia, Hank. I like the way it smells, and oh boy is it a rich place."

"You mean culturally rich."

"Yeah yeah yeah. I like these big doors and the archies."

"Arches."

"Yeah yeah. What kind of stone is it?"

"Limestone."

"I like having friends. I like socializing. Sometimes there's too much socializing, but then I just have to say I'm done socializing for today. Hello," he said, "you cleaned up your car."

"Yes. Just for you."

"I was cleaning the river the other day, and I found a hair scrunch—is it scrunch or scrunchy?"

"Scrunchy, I think."

He nodded. "And it had beads like eyeballs on it, and I hung it on the branch of a tree. The branch was dead and didn't have anything growing on it, but now it does. Then I saw the most beautiful red-winged blackbird in the world."

"I bet."

"I feel that people should pay to go in."

"The river?"

He shook his head. "The Mia. Things cost money. I've got plenty, so I like to pay."

But when we got to the entrance, he didn't pay for me, nor did I—it was a "suggested donation," after all, and I got the feeling we'd be coming here quite a bit.

Up to *The Annunciation*. Terry sat cross-legged.

Even a street sign or a milk carton, if you look at it long enough, will take on a humbling beauty, but that said, today I liked the painting better. Rather than cramped, it looked intimate. And I admired the narrative decision—you'd think anyone promoting the Nazarene would go for him as a baby with a crown on or something, or maybe addressing Judas, but this moment, it was before all the shit went down. And yet there was a human drama being told, as well as a divine one: Mary is obviously the picture of humility, but she also refuses to acknowledge the duck's nebula of truth. And yet, her turning away is also a covering up: she's already curving around her child, taking on the role of Best Uterus Ever. The billowing clouds, I noticed too, weren't in her part of the room—from her perspective, the room was whole, not floating off into ether. For the angels, and the duck, there is only divine ether. For Mary, there is only her remaining corner of the room. And the clouds—they were indeed dark, kind of nasty, like a fire, as Terry had said. But what I saw now was that they had a source—they were emanating from the bed. The bed is where normal people conceive children, in a blaze of coitus. Was Agostino saying that Mary was still somehow implicated in normal conception? Wouldn't that be blasphemous? Or was it that she turns away from the darkness of sin? But why would the darkness turn into the opening through which the duck makes his grand entrance?

Yes! A dark hole, built from a bed, penetrated by God, who shoots his holy semen into Mary's head. This was divine pornography. A virgin money shot. And Mary, looking placid and accepting, turns her face away, but only a little. She's the good girl whom

God seduced, really not a good girl at all—the virgin who takes it in the face, while at her studious prie-dieu even! That's a bad girl, rewarded with eternal virginity. A necessity becoming the mother of redemption.

Terry stirred not a molecule. That's rapture for you. But couldn't he have picked a different painting? This one cut too close to the quick. God's transgression was a net good for humanity. Mine was just a transgression. My sperm had spiraled down the drain. If I'd waited, I could have gotten her to kick Carlton out on her own terms. But her "Thanks" when I helped her into the shower—should I have turned my head instead of offering my hand to help her? Looked away? Walked away? Gotten dried and dressed at my prie-dieu? When it was right there for me, the thing I wanted?

Correction: *is* right there for me.

"I feel the Mary is pretty," Terry said. "I like her feet and the way she turns her head. Such a pretty face! Do you believe she really was pretty? Pretty as a picture? Not everyone is pretty, but God of all peoples would choose someone pretty."

"Hank?" he said. He twisted his back yoga-like and looked at me, then nodded his Cubs cap and went back to Agostino. "It's all right to cry," he said. "I'll sit here."

PART FOUR

Et Tu, Nancy?

Chapter Twenty-Four

My vacation at home wasn't always as eventful as weeping in the gallery. Some of it was errands, and floating listless through the fringes of daytime doldrums. That afternoon, for instance, between dropping Terry off at his place and arriving at my brother's, I hit the local grocery store—a sulfur-lit spree of razor-thin margins and convenience merchandising. Small talk with the grandmotherly cashier, for whom retirement was apparently not yet an option, and whom the bagger, a few years her junior, jokingly threatened to write up for her many infractions that day. Sharing a demure laugh with them like we aren't all in the same boat of pathos, I emerged with a ten-ounce top sirloin steak, a half-gallon of milk, a quarter-pound of organic coffee, some Carl Buddig deli-style turkey slices, a six-pack of Dr Pepper, and an impulse-buy *Cosmopolitan* for June. Another double-bagged mélange of pointlessness, another credit card charge that would earn somebody, somewhere, a healthy 12 percent in interest.

Well, at least I wasn't alone. It was what millions of regular people were experiencing with me, swimming through the last afternoons of summer's urban swelter. Drooping dogs with their tongues lolling out of truck windows. Towering sunflowers with leaves as big as elephant ears. Fading state fair promos on newspaper vending machines. Iced lattes in cups the size of Big Gulps. Slinky kitties who've lost their wherewithal. Air conditioners humming and blowing like the new band member, and dripping on your head, too. A condo complex's newly laid sod, parched into a clumped bristle of dog brushes. The curled leaves of rhododendron, like tongues without saliva. Sprinklers spiff-spiffing with a permanence and purpose I'd never be able to muster. It was a sadness, but only of the Walgreen's kind. As in, "Well, the day is shot—might as well hit Walgreen's." That should be the company's tagline.

It was a uselessness I hadn't felt since my last year of graduate school. The entire first three years of it had been a slow grind into oblivion. I'd struggled for a topic, foundered, and finally landed on Emily and Ed, with an advisor who was five years older than me at most. But the death knell was my teaching performance, the anxiety it caused me. One day that fall semester I barfed in the trash can. Their concerned faces, slightly mocking, which is their way, flushed me. I wiped my lips with my tie, which gave them the laugh they were looking for, then returned to the lesson. I was in the middle of a lecture on *Song of Solomon,* about Milkman's journey to the South being like a solo in blues music, and to illustrate the point I had them listening to Robert Johnson's "Ramblin' on My Mind." I reset the song, and the students turned quiet and appreciative, taking notes on the lyrics, and struggling to hear the sixteen-bar structure—while I was staring at the trash can by the door, wondering if I was going to need it again, and then considering the door itself. Its wooden jamb gleamed from a recent oiling, and the transom's pane, untouched for a good ten years, probably, listed inward like a grin. Mr. Johnson warbled about his feet on the road, and I left the room. Didn't even grab my bookbag from the podium's inner cavity; the zipper was broken anyway.

Take some time, the Lind Hall authorities said. Take spring to think things through. They were very sweet and had more than a passing familiarity with dysfunction. They recommended a therapist, just down the street at Boynton, and even dropped the casual suggestion of medication. What I would probably do instead, I knew even then, was give up my teaching fellowship, pay for two more semesters out of my own pocket, and walk away with my MA bookbag free.

In the process of realizing all this, I'd gone to New York City to help June and my brother hawk the Roller Rings at the industry expo, Toy Fair, held every February in the Jacob Javits Convention Center in Manhattan. The whole trip, my brother was professional, charming and seething in confidence. He'd quit his job, after all, with his boss's blessing. "You've got major balls, kid," she told him on his last day of work, "I hope someone reaches out and grabs them."

My brother spent the trip with his game face on, schmoozing the reps and buyers he already knew and catching the eyes of the ones he didn't. He didn't need to work them too hard: Smart buyers, he said, make a point of touring Specialty/Educational at least once, because when you work for a smaller store or for a catalog, one killer item can make a huge difference. They don't schmooze, they don't kibitz, and they can smell a dog four booths away.

By the end of Toy Fair, it had taken its toll on my brother. On our last afternoon, he'd been cooped up in Javits Center for three days, he was out of his giveaways, and he simply stood and said he had to get some air. June asked if he wanted company.

"No," my brother said. He was fumbling in his slick black jacket to make sure he had money. It looked like he was patting himself for cigarettes.

"No?"

"I'm going to walk."

"Walk with me."

"No, I mean I'm going to walk walk."

"Fine then."

But it wasn't fine. "You've been out and about in Manhattan every day, not me. You were just out all morning for Christ's sake. I think it's my turn if I like."

"I said fine."

"Then fucking mean it," he snapped.

He'd found his money in the jacket's breast pocket, fished it out, and inexplicably peeled off the jacket itself and tossed it onto his empty chair. He knifed into the crowd and was consumed.

Our booth neighbor had overheard the whole exchange, due to the fact that his booth was empty, which was itself due to the fact that his product, which he called the Lamp Bank, was possibly the world's worst kids' product: a lamp the shape of a bowling pin that helped a kid save up pennies, nickels, dimes, quarters, and dollar coins. Fill the slot and turn the little crank, and your coin dropped away to be displayed in the lamp's ovular viewing. All night long a child could stare at the 1988 nickel she'd saved last week, and sleep comforted by its soft shine.

During our dinners out, all planned by June from her daily excursions into the city, we'd mocked Lamp Bank Guy to death. He was one of these guys just happy to be here, cheerful from the top of his Polly to the tip of his Anna while he sat at a table bannered with "The One-Of-A-Kind Lamp Bank!" in a script similar to a Betty Crocker box. Because it was handcrafted by him in his garage, the Lamp Bank wholesaled for $45, meaning it would retail around $110. "People love handmade things," he said, "especially 'hand made in Arizona.'" But it seemed to us that he really hadn't thought through what "mass" meant—really, if some catalog buyer came to him and said, "I'd like to ruin my career by carrying this monstrosity—can you ship 200 by Easter?" the odds that he could pull it off were bleak.

Now here he was in the wake of my brother's pissiness, fidgeting with his lone sample so it would display a Sacagawea dollar. "Toy Fair's hard on the nerves," he said our direction.

I nodded and settled into my folding chair, which had a loose joint but not bad enough to bother requesting a new one. June was sitting a good four feet down our display table, arms folded, one leg crossed over the other, skittishly bouncing a scuffed clog. I couldn't hear. In the buzz and scutter of Toy Fair, she said something I couldn't hear.

"What?"

"This sucks," she repeated.

"Tell me about it! What am I doing here?" I said. "Am I going to be one of those guys who hangs around his relations' business getting paid to do nothing?"

"What?" she said.

I moved my chair closer, gently, on account of the loose flange, and repeated myself.

"He's paying you?" she said.

"I'm tapped out too," I said, after he was gone. "The whole thing just makes me sad. The slick guys, but especially the small-time guys. I'm too sensitive to be here pushing product."

"Sad?"

I shrugged. "Melancholic?"

"Alcoholic, try."

At that moment a very young buyer from some catalog approached and said he'd heard about us and was wondering if we had any more gloves—Carlton's admittedly brilliant marketing ploy was to give away several hundred cheapy cotton gloves splashed with the same design scheme he'd hired a small marketing firm to create for his booth and packaging. And of course each finger had Roller Rings printed on them, in all types of colors and configurations.

June had stood to tell the young man no, we were out. She'd been spending her free time back then recovering her slim figure after letting herself go some. Every day it was the YWCA or a run or something. Her arms were toned and sharp, her biceps taut as ferrets under her sleeves. Her hair was pulled back, too, and that always made her look striking. She wasn't wearing any makeup as far I as could tell, just the freckles and maybe some lip balm. Add to that her general at-ease expression and the way her tight camisole parted her lavender blouse, and if you didn't know her, you'd gawk.

The young buyer certainly was, in his way. I watched her explain Roller Rings to him, replete with sliding them onto her fingers to show the color combinations. He batted away a loose lock of his curly hair and laughed. He slipped some Roller Rings onto his thumb, all of them red. Out of the corner of my eye, I saw Lamp

Bank Guy hovering, hands behind his back, sizing me up for small talk. But I turned my shoulders, so that while June flirted away with the young faun of a buyer, both Lamp Bank Guy and I watched her the way an entourage watches its star sign an autograph.

The night before, June and I had left Javits early, Carlton saying he'd meet up with us at this Argentinian steakhouse June had found on Hudson and Twelfth. June and I cabbed it to the Village, then wandered. We stopped in a bar or two, just to have the feel of doing so. At the second joint, we hardly stayed long enough for me to eat a half-pound of peel-and-eat shrimp.

The Village's treescaped pleasantness and walk-up architecture and casual richy-rich elegance were welcome compared to SoHo's chaos of young people with too much disposable income for their own good—mostly Frogs and Krauts, as my brother called them. June and I were too late to shop, so we had to make do with window-browsing and in general making quips like we owned the place. We noticed a lot of New Yorkers wearing these pouches around their necks, instead of purses or wallets. When June wondered what they carried in there, I said if it were me, I'd carry half a pound of peel-and-eat shrimp. Passersby were good for other games too, like "There's Your Boyfriend," and also "Sober or Drunk?" It was that kind of thing, harmless, until we stopped in front of a hip luggage shop. We could make out some prices, and June said, "Hmm, I can go on a Jamaican vacation…or purchase luggage." I told her I should buy something for Carol Ann but that the idea made me nervous.

"You ought to dump her," June blurted.

I stopped short. "What?"

"I'm only going to say it once, because I'm new to the family and all, but you should." She wavered a moment, then stood straight again and jutted out her chin, which unfurrowed her forehead, to repeat herself. "You should dump her."

A pair of women walked by, underdressed for the temperature, stepping sourly around us into some remaining snow. One said, "Who does he think he is? He's a *bouncer,* for Chrissakes."

We were still standing before the window—two forms in reflection, no faces, and lots of softly lit leather. "It's a marriage you're talking about," I said. "It's called divorce, not dumping. And things aren't that bad."

"Don't tell me things aren't bad because you tell me all the time otherwise."

"I wouldn't say all the time."

I was doing my best to be offended, which I don't think she'd anticipated.

"Okay, that's it," she said. "I feel bad now. I will feel bad forever."

"Let's not get dramatic."

"It's just—it's a matter of how you see yourself. You're too smart to be barfing around on eggshells."

This was both mixed metaphor and simple truth. But it hadn't occurred to me that the problem might be Carol Ann. I wasn't ready to hear that, and wouldn't be until she found herself a boyfriend.

People had streamed by us as we talked in front of the window, but we were shielded from them somehow. It wasn't cold cold, not Minneapolis cold certainly, or we wouldn't have been out this long. It was hands-in-pockets cold, and we tucked ourselves into our coats and leaned toward one another.

"Let me put it this way," I said. "Look at that bag."

Staged on a perfectly mitered white wood box amidst a jamble of old weathered watchbands was the coolest bookbag I had ever seen. I'd noticed it right as we approached the window and stared at it as June voiced her attack on my wife. It was orange leather, with two discreetly zippered outer pockets of orange canvas and a gray mesh strap and a thin stripe of green leather that crossed the front and wrapped around the back. Very Euro, though humble and literary. It would hold a man's essentials, albeit a man very different from me: a dog-eared copy of *The Stranger* and a package of tobacco with rolling papers, and a Visa card, and maybe a notebook and pictures of the kids and the wife.

"I *love* that bag," I said. "That bag makes me feel like I could go make it work—graduate school, I mean, and teaching. That bag is beautiful enough to make me a teacher. But I can't have it because I don't have it. At some point you just have to accept who you are."

"I'm sorry," June said.

"Don't be. I can take my lumps."

"That makes me sad."

I shrugged.

"But it's none of my business," she added. She kissed me on the cheek. We stood there a second. Tears pounced to the back of my throat, and she had to hold my hand for the rest of our walk. Which was wonderful, but not very Manhattan. Manhattan, including my brother and the Argentine steakhouse that evening, told me to forget about it.

But back at Javits, June had other ideas. She managed to get the young curly-haired buyer to order a set of Roller Rings samples to be sent to his company's warehouse in Ohio before mentioning how happy her husband would be and that he, her husband, would be following up next week personally. The poor kid. He skulked off, grabbing a card from Lamp Bank Guy in order to keep from running.

"I got you something this morning," June said then.

She pulled a box from under the table. She handed it to me, apologizing that it wasn't wrapped. "I was too neurotic to ask," she said. "I'm from Kansas!"

In the box, of course, was the orange bag. There was a card, too. "For whatever your next grad school is! (Not a barf bag.)"

The white tissue crinkled around it like pure, sacred flame, which made me laugh at myself and my overdramatic imagination.

"Thank you," I said to the bag. I didn't want either of us to get embarrassed. "It's too much—" I started.

"Nuh uh," she said. "It was on sale."

"Liar." I fingered the green stripe, and then started unzipping like a kid at Christmas. I got up and paraded down the aisle and back, vamping like a fashion model, then strolling like a philosopher. Lamp Bank Guy chimed in that that was some bag, and it looked great on me.

I thanked him, made a face for June's eyes only. She laughed, then said I shouldn't tell my brother because he was worried enough about finances as it was.

"You should dump him," I said.

Chapter Twenty-Five

When I got to my brother's house, it was already after 4:00. He was on the north side of the house with the storm windows lined up along the foundation. It was a warm day, but he wasn't sweating or in the least spent. I handed him an iced coffee I'd picked up on the way—urban life, at its finest.

"Thanks," he said. "I thought you weren't going to show."

"Can I check my e-mail and print out some stuff on your computer? For work?"

"You work?" he said. He gulped down his coffee, shook the ice, then tipped the glass back again.

"A little early for putting up storms."

"Nah."

"How's the toy coming?"

"Fine. Worked all night."

He'd attached a bottle of generic cleaning product to the garden hose, which was lazy in the cement driveway at our feet. The product was supposed to cleanse the windows and then rinse spot free without you ever having to lift a squeegee. He'd already taken down the screens and sprayed the permanent windows. These storms were old-school, the kind that went in with more than a little banging and had thumb-twist closures to hold them tight. Several of the storms had fresh glazing residue that still had to be scraped off. He waddled to the row of leaning windows, which reflected sunlight into my face.

His cast was already brownish from the previous night's swim. He kicked it through the weedy grass between the driveway and the house. "Look at this goddamn creeping Charlie," he said.

I let him be and put my pointless provisions in the fridge then headed up to the computer room. Creaking upon the last stair tread, I saw that the master bedroom was neat as a showroom, as if propped to sell—a small bouquet of carnations in a green glass vase and a few Raggedy-Ann-type dolls on the rocker in the corner. The rocker was where June was going to hop out of bed at nights and nurse the baby, when and if one arrived. In the room with the computer, there were paint chips taped to a closet's jamb—one palette of pinks, another of blues. This whole fucking situation was one big cliché, like most of life.

Tom had been hounding me to do what I could while home, and it was the least I could do for taking, unannounced and unearned, vacation time. "You beg me to write copy, and then you take off," he had said when I called to inform him where I was. I told him my brother was injured. "The same brother whose calls you refused to take?" Didn't miss much, Tom. Entrepreneurs rarely do. This is because they're usually footing the bill.

I'd already written and sent, working on a public library computer and utilizing a Hotmail account created solely for this purpose, copy for a vegetarian restaurant's menu. I was glad not to be public librarying it again: the dreary brick, the triangular nooks, the overwhelming Anne Rice collection, the librarians eyeing me as if I'd chastise them for not having a Lacan section and thereby remind them of their original life ambition: to PhD the shit out of Jane Austen. Can't blame them—they're just one Republican away from getting zeroed out of their budgets and jobs.

My brother had a Mac, of course. It slogged its way to Hotmail. I had one e-mail, with a Word attachment, from Tom: "Hank, please proof. Hope brother doing ok. When you return?"

I fired back: "I didn't know you spoke Chinese."

The document was ten pages of content for a Montana Brain Injury Awareness booklet, provided by the client. Resources, sufferers' advocacy, dealing with insurance and hospitals, new drug treatments, general descriptions of brain trauma, first-person testimonials, recovery strategies, definitions of terms, stories of hope. I cringed and hit print.

I was left to wait, and how much *New York Times* can you read? I drew the line at the metro section and instead found the family's digital pictures on the hard drive. I opened up a folder called "Terry." In a folder called "More" there was a Word document called "why." I opened it.

"I just want to be won over. I want to be supplied with something I didn't know was coming. My orgasms are like train stops and that's not very satisfying, or I guess they are in the way that getting off a train is. The pleasure of getting there, arriving. Is that why they call it coming? They're empty, though—they're an ending and not a beginning. I suppose someone gets on a train at almost every stop, but it isn't me. I always get off, and it's always the home stop. Which means there's a sinkful of dishes to do or someone who needs me to say the right thing or sit in the right way. C's so needy that way. Everything has to be aligned. I'm just tired."

According to the information at the bottom of the window, there were 113 pages in this document. I closed it. I clicked the file and selected "Save to floppy disk." The animation made it look like paper was flying.

Shattering glass is a sound uniquely frightening. It's onomatopoeic, as sharp in your ears as it would be in the palm of your hand. Startling when you're minding your own business, it's doubly so when you've been snooping.

The sound was coming from outside. Sounds, I mean. First one shatter, then, as I took the steps three at a time, another and another.

Outside, my brother was still in his driveway. He bent to the neighbor's foundation, reached down to the red rock landscaping they'd installed after some work to improve their foundation drainage, and got into a pitching stance. He hunched into a windup, then pelted one of the windows lined against his own house, puncturing it with a small nebula of jagged empty space. Two of the other windows were similarly punched; five were intact. I saw that they were free of glazing—the blade he'd used to scrape them glinted on the sidewalk.

He bent for another rock, nearly losing balance because of the soft cast's lack of support. These were not what you'd call stones— not smooth and displayable. They were many-edged and small and might puncture your sole if you stepped on one barefoot, but otherwise were supposed to be harmless.

"What are you doing?"

He looked at me quickly, as if to see if I were leading off at first, then fired away. This one missed.

"Fuck!" he said.

"What are you doing?"

"Getting mad."

"Okay, but—"

He pitched again, and this one also missed. It was a tough strike zone.

"It's my house still. I own these windows. I paid to have them fixed. I can break shit if I want to."

"You can also dig up earthworms and slice them into little pieces," I said, "but that doesn't—"

Shattering, then another quick shattering as this rock rebounded off the foundation and punctured the window again. I recoiled, fearing for my eyes, but my brother threw his hands up in the air. "Double play!" he said.

"Cut it out!"

He looked at me, stupidly. He blinked. He turned his head and went inside.

"That's the last time I give you iced coffee."

We were sitting in the kitchen at the breakfast nook, munching chips and salsa. That's family, I guess—outbursts followed by snacks. June was supposed to be home soon, so I'd swept up the glass shards as best I could, then secured the remaining glass with duct tape and loaded them into my brother's Volvo trunk. He was appreciative.

"Never thought you'd be dealing with this, did you?"

"I don't even know what 'this' is."

He muttered an agreement of sorts. "I just get so mad," is what he finally said.

There were two benches in the nook, and both of us had our legs up, resting on cushions. For both of us, the salsa bowl was awkward to reach. He looked down his length, shook something off his cast. I hoped it wasn't glass.

"I hope the neighbors don't think someone was hurt."

"I'm sick of worrying about what the neighbors think."

This much I understood. I couldn't mow the yard without feeling like some Lawny McWeedsalot was looking out his window and shaking his head saying, "Look who thinks he's a big lawn mower now?"

Carlton chuckled. He recounted how he'd been walking a few Sundays ago and complimented a neighbor on his landscaping, because you gotta, and the neighbor's kid had said "Thank you very mulch!" Where do they come up with that shit, my brother wanted to know. He shook his head.

"Their parents," I said.

He nodded. "God only gives them to the deserving."

"You don't believe in God, do you?"

"Of course."

I used a heavily salsaed chip to register my incredulity. Humans seem to have lots of ways, verbal and non, to do this.

"You should get an apartment or something. Sleeping at your studio isn't good for you. All echo-y and alone."

"Hank, I'm not breaking windows because I'm scared of the dark."

"Hey, I've been there. I threw a mug of milk at the TV last December because the Vikes got a bad call. And I don't even *like* football."

"Did you break the TV?"

"What? No. It was a crappy mug. Bounced right off the screen."

He grunted.

"Your cast reeks."

Another grunt.

Twilight was coming. Over the summer June had painted the kitchen walls a chalky yellow, and in the fading light the room seemed to close like a flower. Life's petals, always caressing us, whether we notice or no. For the first time in ages, I thought about Emily Dickinson. She had a way of popping up like some bad thematic cliché, some trope the librettist just can't let go of. An Emily Dickinson opera—why not? I heard some fucker was writing a collection of short stories inspired by Bruce Springsteen's *Nebraska*, one for each song, so obviously anything was possible.

I told my brother about the book based on *Nebraska*.

"Sounds good," he said.

"I don't know."

"I'll tell you something you don't know. This will give you a little insight into 'this situation.'"

I nodded.

"You know how I was doing a lot of reading on the Holocaust and stuff?"

"Yeah."

"Kind of a mild obsession?"

I had to laugh at this. "Mild obsession? There was a month when you were a goddamn walking memorial."

"Well, yeah. But now I stopped. I'm researching other stuff."

"Good."

"But I don't know." He shook his head, sipped his whiskey the way you would hot coffee. My brother—he had no one way of doing anything. "What put me off it was the worst thing—" He looked up at me, gave me that little encouraging nod people use when they really really really want you understand. "The worst thing I've ever heard."

"Go ahead," I said.

He frowned. "You sound like Mom. Remember she used to get on us for getting upset over anything? She'd say, 'Why are you being so morbid?' What do you say to that, as a little kid? I was crying, for Christ's sake. I don't even know what about. Something."

He had me there. I *had* sounded like Mom. Poor Mom—she never got to grow, change, become a person who isn't cleaning up after us, tolerating us, or imposing some injustice. My brother and I would always think of her like mopey teens. I had my obvious mopery, Carlton too. I remember him more than once staying holed up in his room for a full day. Baseball was his antidote, or maybe revelry. Baseball is a depressive's sport, when you think about it.

"Sorry," I said. "Go ahead."

"Treblinka," he said. "It was a small place, I guess, built for killing Jews, and that's it. There was no 'prisoner camp' like at Auschwitz. Just a train platform and gas chambers. But this is the weird thing—they had to keep up the ruse, you know?"

"Yeah. Make them think they were going to be processed somehow, taken someplace for real."

"Yeah. So part of that was where they took the sick and the injured and the old people and orphaned kids. These were people you couldn't send to the gas chambers because they were slow and liable to gum up the works, see. It was like a factory—you had to have a way of dealing with rejects."

"Hmm."

"So they had a place they called the infirmary. It was down a path off from the one to the gas chambers. It had a big red cross and everything, but they had it fenced off with brush and barbed wire, like the gas chambers, and you couldn't see what it really was until you got there. What it really was, was a big pit, filled with burning bodies, burning day and night, and there was a little booth at the edge of it. Whoever was brought to the infirmary was made to take off their clothes, step up to the booth, and walk out onto a plank that extended over the pit. You had to stand on the end of the plank and face the pit. Then an SS officer shot you in the back of the neck, and you fell into the pit."

"Jesus fucking Christ."

"Even little children, they did this to. Little boys and girls who had no mother or father."

I had my head in one hand, palming my cheek and temple. Without thinking, I reached for the chips. I literally inhaled a crumble of one and gagged.

"I can't stop thinking about it sometimes," he said. "I mean, can you imagine?"

I had chips on my chin, some on my shirt.

"Standing over burning bodies, naked. That's hell. That's an utter hell. And I can't get it out of my head, and this is partly responsible for this situation."

"You've told June about all this, and she's unsympathetic?"

He contorted with incredulity. "Are you out of your fucking mind? I have told no one this. It's just there. And I'm trying to create a toy? Have kids? Gather round, kids!" He started laughing, so I did too. "Daddy's got a nice story to tell you."

So at least we were laughing when June arrived. She put her purse on the counter. Her hair was pulled back and clipped behind her head with something dark and toothy. "I don't even want to know," she said.

"Yeah," Carlton said, "you probably don't."

They padded around each other in the living room for a while, the domestic two-step that makes twenty-four-year-olds think they have marriage down to a science.

I went up to get my printout, and also my disk. When I came back down, my brother was dressing to go for the night. He gave me a reassuring look and said he'd leave us be. After all, he said, someone had to go make a living.

"Ish, that cast," she said. "Why did you let him get into the water?"

She had changed clothes for the grubbier: long cut-off shorts and a T-shirt from some 10K race Carlton had run. It was crisp white and screechy with corporate logos.

"Am I staying, or—"

"I'm sure we can just talk normal," she admitted. "Like before."

"Sure," I said.

We went out onto the porch. The wicker chair complained under my weight, so I resettled to really give it *tsuriss*. I put my feet up on the coffee table. "How's this for normal like before?" I said.

She laughed. "That looks about right. Except there'd be a drink in your hand."

I checked my watch. "Well, it is beer thirty."

She went inside and returned with a small bucket of iced Corona, a show beer that she kept in the house for herself and for entertaining. It made me wince. I should be honest with her about Carlton's drinking, just like I should be honest with Dad about Carlton's situation, and of course with Carlton about June—but there'd be time enough for honesty. Seemed like it, at least.

"Is that your Supervalu bag in the fridge?"

"Yeah. There's a ten-ounce steak for you, and a *Cosmo*."

She shook her head. "Well," she said, "this isn't so hard."

"Maybe we could do this forever. Just this."

She didn't say anything. A car lolled past, booming bass from a woofer, or a subwoofer. Then a plane overhead, a neighbor's phone ringing. A woman in power-walk gear came striding down the block, and we watched her, so she waved and smiled at us. She was Asian, possibly Thai, though of course when she spoke it was with perfect Minnesota English.

"Hey there!" she said.

June said hi back and something about her kids being in school. When the woman was out of earshot, she said "Isn't she beautiful? Two kids, great body. She was adopted. Her name is Kathy."

I laughed. "That must have been a moment: someone adopts a Thai baby and says to it 'Tran Truc Lu, you are now...Kathy.'"

"She's Filipino. Your lip looks like it's healed," she said.

"What a night that was," I said. "She just tagged me. Thing is, I didn't get angry. I was like, 'Okay, so that sort of makes sense.'"

"Does it?"

I shook my head, made my mom's face of distaste. "Probably not." I sighed. "Maybe it was just on her to-do list. Probably on her Microsoft Outlook calendar: 'punch soon-to-be-ex-husband.' It's good for her."

"So you guys are done."

"No one's said it, but…" Apparently I didn't want to say it either.

"You should call Bob—of Angie and Bob?"

"Don't you want a beer?" I asked her.

She shook her head. "Now here's a question for you." She was languishing on the wicker loveseat, arms folded. Bugs bounced against the screens. Carcasses of the same had collected at the porch's corners, with dust and a leaf or two. Death and imperfection wrinkle everything; all else is illusion. I thought about Treblinka, but just for a second—the only way you can.

"Do you think you'll ever get married again?" June went on. "Assuming you get divorced."

"I don't know. Maybe. But it'd have to be a whole different thing. I've been thinking a lot about it, and maybe I'm jaded. Don't laugh! It's possible I am jaded."

This did get her laughing.

"It won't be no bullshit wedding, that's for sure. Marriage vows written by Pam the Humanist celebrant? Snuffing out two candles after lighting one bigger candle? No way. I am my own fucking candle, dude."

"That sounds doable. You can carry around your own candle the entire night. You could write 'Hank's candle' on it in permanent marker."

"I'm being serious."

"I know," she said. "I know. You're protecting yourself. You *are* your own candle. Only, that's not very passionate. Sometimes you have to try to make passion where it might not exist."

"You—meaning me?"

"No. Me."

She reached into the bucket and pulled out a can of root beer for herself, the high-end kind only the co-op sells. It was wet from the melting ice.

"But to what end?" I said. "Why make passion out of nothing? Would you have me try that with Carol Ann?"

"No."

"Then why?"

"I'm not you, he isn't Carol Ann, and this isn't talking normal like before."

"Which before are we talking about? Before you kicked him out of your house, or before—"

"Both."

"I don't get it. If you're unhappy—"

"I can't talk about that."

"Well—" I leaned forward, then slumped back. "I'm going to tell him is what I'm going to do. And then we'll see what happens."

"You will not."

It was a command, and I didn't like being commanded.

"I might."

She got up and went into the house. At first I thought she was fetching something, like a rag to wipe up the pooling condensation from the beer bucket. But she didn't come back.

In the house, she was sitting on the sofa with a boxy blue pillow clutched to her gut. She didn't look up when I came in. She didn't seem to be breathing. A tear pooled, then shlepped its way down her cheek.

"No no no," I said. I went and flopped next to her.

"Don't you dare." She gave a sudden sniffle. Her little freckled chin creased, relaxed, then kept creasing.

"I won't. I just talk a big game. It's just—this is hard."

"No shit!" she yelped.

"Okay okay." But the tears were coming now, and nothing was going to stop them. It wasn't a moment for comparisons, but I felt strongly, all of a sudden, how different it was from Carol Ann's weepy protestations of Togetherness—funny how it never felt like she really wanted reconciliation. Carol Ann's tears were punitive, as if to show me the value of Togetherness by denying me it. Nothing

I said or did could make a difference; her despairing was complete, utter, and solitary.

But June was with me, something hard to explain but easy to feel.

"Listen, remember that party, with the crows?"

She nodded her head, tight-lipped.

"You suggested we make out. You said it. We could have, we should have. And—and this wouldn't be anything."

She sobbed.

"Okay, remember Toy Fair? You bought me the bag. Why did you do that?"

I was looking up into her eyes, the way guys who are trying to fix something in the grille of a car do. She looked off to the side, but not away. Her eyes gray as clouds, the way they must look from the inside.

"You bought me the bag because you love me."

She nodded again.

I had a meltdown then. The whole damn thing was a meltdown, but this one had me back at that Toy Fair nightmare. June was sobbing inches from me, but I was off wandering the Javits Center aisles on the ten-minute lunch break Carlton gave me. There was Lamp Bank Guy, so guileless and lonely, but braving a smile, fairly grabbing a buyer by the wrist as she passed unimpressed. And beyond him, oh the pointless shlock! There were Lunatwigz—moon-white glow sticks that connected to each other or a central trunk via magnets, or rather, magnetz. There were glowing balls and Frisbees and yoyos too. There were literally tons of plushes: plushes with voice recognition, plushes with lights, plushes with motion sensors, plushes that danced or rapped or hummed the national anthem, plushes that flew kites, plushes that hugged, plushes that didn't do a damn thing except sit and smile amid a pyramid of other plushes. There was sciencey stuff that you drop in water and it turns into goo, sciencey stuff that you blow with a hair dryer to expand into monsters, and more sciencey stuff that came with its own beaker, magnifying glass, centrifuge, and first aid kit. There were talking poker sets and inflatable kiddie furniture in the shapes of football helmets and flower pots, and do-it-yourself wallpaper with nontoxic stick backing, and all manner of things to hang on a kid's bedroom wall, from airplanes spelling out your name to a duck divided into two halves to make it look like it'd gotten stuck flying through your bureau. There were Purrrfect Catzzzz and Tiny Totz and Zooper Heroes and the worst of Z offenders, Coconutz Noize Makerz. There were characters known and not so known, the latter vying to become the next Spiderman or Godzilla—Uncle Buggus the Astonishing Insect Man (first name Gregor), or Captain Poofypants the Gender-Bending Superheroine. June and I had laughed hard at that last one. Laughed a big, hard, "what the fuck?" one entire afternoon.

I opened my eyes and saw June so close to me. I asked her if she remembered Captain Poofypants. She laughed. I kissed her, at first just along the cheek.

"Captain," I said, kissing. "Poofy." Kissing her mouth now. The tears were warm as shower water. They had wetted her mouth, so the taste of her kiss wasn't the honey of my memory, but salty, a little bitter. This is how it is, I thought, falling from grace. Bitter with indulgence.

We were on the couch now, snuffling for air, my knees cemented to the rug, holding me up. I couldn't move except for the necessary places—hands and face and bending of neck. I felt her fingers along my cheek, then neck, then ear, which now she yanked, and held the yank. She used to it to yank my face away from hers.

She wiped her mouth with the back of her hand and looked at the floor. "You have to go," she said.

And because it was more the truth than not, I did.

Chapter Twenty-Six

But why did I have to go? Because staying would cause pain? But lots of things cause pain—cancer, for instance. People smoke, and that causes cancer, and that causes people pain—people the smokers love.

People ride motorcycles, take excessive doses of barbiturates, scamper on wet boulder fields—it was all documented in the brain-injury text I was proofreading. They do all manner of things that put their gray matter at risk, and it caused a lot of pain—living with a brain-injured individual is apparently no picnic, even if they are functioning. The right kind of trauma can change personality, alter who you are—not to mention robbing you of your ability to tie shoelaces or remember to turn the stove burner off.

People do hurtful things all the time. All I was doing was trying to be in love. And anyway, pain's a great locator—so what's the problem here?

Everything in my room, every piece of kitsch at Seth's, seemed to agree. The cross-stitched aphorism hanging on the door, which read "Tomorrow is another day…but living this one puts you ahead of the game"—had an orange kitty in a red helmet throwing a green football. And the smoky bathroom mirror with the pine frame, which had been shellacked many times, over the grime and stains—small nuggets of foodstuffs, flicked from some traveler's dental flossings, stuck to the polyurethane. This is life, the enumeration of sins—only they aren't sins, just called that. They accumulate around the edges of our true selves. But to the next traveler, they cause no stir. Maybe a small shudder, and a resolution to next time use a travel agent. Otherwise, they blend right in.

I proofread into the night. I caught many typos. Classics like "thee" for "the" and "their" for "there," but also "bran" for "brain" and "mater" for "matter." Spell-check can't get everything, thank God. Brain injury was my Friday-night companion, mollifier, and narcotic. Even after going for coffee, it put me to sleep the way the portable vaporizer used to when, as a kid, I had congestion. The dangers, repercussions, and miscellany of brain injury in Montana—they were my Mom for the night, rubbing Mentholatum on my chest and telling me maybe I wouldn't have to go to school in the morning.

Terry was one hell of a listener. If he was bothered by my prattle, he didn't say so. Maybe because I was a veritable art gravy train for him: three trips in four days. But for whatever reason, all the way in the car, up the MIA steps, and to the gallery room I'd come to know like a wing of my own home, he took my rambles in stride. Eyes on his precious *Annunciation*, he eschewed the verbal tics and clues that people use to let you know they are either listening to you or bored to constipation by you, but that was okeydokey by me. He plopped cross-legged beneath his Cubs hat and green windbreaker and took it all like a champ. I was beginning to enjoy him—life is best when it's a little off. Only then do you really notice things, and only when you notice do you really enjoy. Think Owen Wilson's nose.

Agostino's Virgin Mary was as we'd left her: still prettily oblivious, as much so as her not-so-virgin counterpart across the gallery was afraid, and I said, "Make passion out of nothing? With him? If he wasn't my brother, I'd tell her she was nuts. Wouldn't I?"

Terry didn't know. Or at least he wasn't saying.

"I mean really, if you were to get to the elevator after your lunch break and push the up button and get on and the numbers tinked upward like they do, and then all of a sudden they start going in reverse, down past 10, 9, 8, and then faster to 4, 3, 2, 1, and while you're panicking and spilling your coffee all over yourself, would you be satisfied that you'd stuck it out? Would you say, 'Well, at least I tried to make passion out of nothing?'"

"Nothing," Terry repeated to the painting.

Two elderly women were shying away from me, clutching their purses, though, being of the artistic stripe, they tried not to show it. I glanced their way and said, "Hell no! You'd give your right arm for even ten seconds of the real thing!"

The duck was still shooting its spermy laser. Terry was still enthralled.

"I mean, is the implication that I should have stayed with graduate school? Stuck it out to get my PhD? Gone to parties where people call you Temple Grandin because you wrote an essay called 'Listen to the Cows: Poetic Silence in Sherwood Anderson'? Sat in seminars listening to some poor American Studies fart groan on and on about why *Too Late the Phalarope* is the most underappreciated novel ever written?"

"You shouldn't say fart," Terry said.

I laughed so hard a passerby would have had a tough time guessing who was the retard and who was the retard escort. And suddenly we had the best judges of such a distinction right there in the room with us: a tour of developmentally disabled adults, maybe five or six of them. Their shuffling footfalls came through the door behind us, with a shrill-voiced tour guide from the museum and two tall young men in jeans and sweatshirts corralling and cajoling. One kid walked on the outside of his feet; one guy resembled Roy Rogers, down to the ear-to-ear smile; one woman had glasses so thick I feared to think of her turning her face skyward on a sunny day; one guy wore a hockey jersey, autographed in black marker; a thin woman with a Times Square of curly hair obsessed that no one should touch the art, not even the frames. They dressed like any other Minnesotans, they spoke softly out of respect for the art, and they were in general having a hell of a time—only slightly off from the rest of us, like Canadians.

"Here we have more of the seventeenth century," the tour guide said. She was over-enunciating. "Again very religious. But more personal style, and some lightening of the, of the Roman Baroque. There are human emotions: Mary Magdalene in her hour of judgment, the cold Bishop of Naples, and Diogenes the philosopher—who was said at the end of his life to sleep in a earthenware jar—shown with owls, the symbol of the goddess Athena, and also of wisdom."

How I admired this woman. Here she was spouting off when most of her audience was mumbling to itself or fingering the dust along the corner piping. But what of it? I was here mumbling to myself too, and, morally at least, was no better than the dust, not to mention the flesh that fingers it. And anyway, to this woman, most of the world was in dire need of arts education; she probably made few distinctions beyond that.

Terry, I noticed, had taken interest. Intent and somewhat sour, he eyed them as they made their circle of the room and then got a move on, breaking off toward the twentieth-century stuff, which promised no doubt to be more their speed. Even when they'd left completely, Terry didn't turn back to his Mary, Gabriel, and duck. He looked at the floor, his still-shiny cowboy boots, and the fraying hem of his jeans. No, not true: he was looking at himself, his face, in the high-gloss wood floor, and his eyes were as big as if he'd seen a grizzly bear towering over him.

"Buddy?" I said.

"I'm tired of here, Hank. I'm kind of nerves."

"Nervous? Okay."

"I don't want a tour."

"You're not on tour. You're doing your thing. Inspiration, right?"

"I am." He said this as a half-question, but it really wasn't even that. It was a small truth. The modern human condition of Terry, as in "I am...what?"

Good question. In the end, at that final precipitous elevator drop, if "I tried to make passion out of nothing" isn't a satisfying chew, what is?

I looked up at the painting. The point of building a repository of beautiful things, if you can ignore the fascism of being told what gets in and what gets left out, is to connect with other humans: being moved by the human struggle for the divine and nudging your neighbor and saying, "Something else, huh?"

But Agostino didn't exactly have the something else I was after. His entire life was lived before the notion of romantic love, as we know it, even existed. His was a weightier, if theocratic, concern. How could he have known someone like me would be standing here with someone like Terry, both of us wishing, suddenly and mournfully, to be not an appreciator of beautiful things, but hung on the wall with the rest of them. Glorious love, the all-encompassing sensorial pursuit. Thanks a lot Wordsworth. Thanks a lot Walt Whitman. What do either of you have to say to a man who lusts for his sister-in-law? What do you have to say about the no-limit poker game that humanity has become? Agostino certainly had something to say: "I see your physical, and raise you a meta."

"Look at how the angels in the upper right don't even have bodies," I said. "They're just heads with wings."

Terry wasn't having it.

"Man, but this guy does wings like a motherfucker, doesn't he?"

Still nothing.

"You know what?" I finally said. "Maybe you should go home and paint." This got me a face-full of him. "You don't need any more inspiration. You're a painter. Paint an Annunciation like this one. You probably know it by heart."

He reset his ball cap, low and secure. "I don't feel it, though. Not like Daddy's pool."

"So, sometimes people paint to feel."

After a minute he tilted his head back and told me yeah, that was right, right as raindrops. And he was gonna do it, he said. But first he wanted to hit the gift shop.

Chapter Twenty-Seven

My brother's studio was downtown, in one of those old hotboxes of industry that mixed warehouse space with office space. He signed the lease when the Roller Rings started selling well, choosing a spot somewhat beneath his ambitions because he wanted a liability he'd be able to afford no matter what his fortunes were. It was in an old manufacturing building, the Sexton, down on Seventh and Portland, kitty-corner from Hennepin County Medical Center—ambulances screaming all day and night.

He had the northwestern corner unit on the top floor, the sixth. It had a phone line, though he never activated it, and two six-foot long radiators sitting under a bank of windows overlooking the river and the old municipal field house. He said it gave him a sense of citizenship, to keep a space—pay into the local economy, actually produce something useful, though I quibbled with his definition of useful. At night the soft violets and roses of a sunset seen only in the east would paint the windows and give a calm to the room. I know this even though up to then I had only seen the room once, empty, on the evening he signed the lease: we'd sat drinking Champale on the floor.

As Saturday afternoons weren't exactly what this part of town was zoned for, it wasn't hard to find a meter, and I didn't even have to plug it. My brother's building was seedy, but in a romantic way. Looking up at it, I found what I remembered to be his windows— the sixth floor, north side—but they were blacked out from the inside by something more substantial than curtains. I could imagine him barricading himself in, to avoid spying by competitors or just for the shit of it. A normal person would want as much natural light as possible, but, well, normal people don't have the gall to think they can make big money off of strings with ball bearings on them, either.

When I got to the sidewalk, several multiply pierced and tattooed young people came out the main door and scoffed past me—if they spent half the time on their art as they did on their appearance, they'd be Jasper Johns, all of them. I stood aside to let them pass, gracious as an invisible man.

My brother followed on their heels. He looked angry, coiled for some reason into a longish raincoat. His limp was pronounced, and the cast, by now peeling like birch bark, seemed almost a step behind him.

"Hey," I said. Only then did he recognize me. His body softened some, like a sheet when you shake out its wrinkles. "I came down to spy on you."

He took this literally at first, then cracked a smile.

"You want to report to the old man that all is well."

"That'd be nice."

"Well, you can wait. Trust me. I was just going to take a break. Drive around."

"It's getting dark."

"Yeah, well. You come. We'll have a party."

"The liquor stores are closed, so we'd better go up and see what you got in the kitty upstairs."

I started to go past him inside the building, but his fingertips on my chest stopped me. From his raincoat he produced a fifth of cheap bourbon. "Meow meow," he said.

I drove. We passed the bourbon. "You want to go to the river?"

He shook his head.

"My hotel? You can bunk with me."

"No thanks."

In the Jetta, I could reach out and touch him. Nobody does this when they're in a car. Lovers, maybe.

"Perfect," my brother said. He'd found the Swiss army knife I kept in the now-uncluttered tray behind the emergency brake. He tried blades until he got to the saw. Unused, since I had the thing primarily for the bottle opener and the illusion of preparedness on Montanan hikes, it was still sharp, if gooey from some spill or another.

He sipped from the bourbon bottle, without urgency or greed. A gentleman's sip. He handed the bottle to me, and I did the same. Its scratchy asphyxiation made me cough.

"Christ what a nancy you are." He bent to his cast with the knife.

"Nice," I said.

We were driving down Hiawatha now, south, past the grain elevators owned by ConAgra. Steep and ancient and lit only by squares of yellow in the boxy office building and cones of blue igniting the frayed brand logo, I had no idea if they were still in use. They were fairly anachronistic, to be sure. Grain ain't condos.

"If you get a call," he said, "asking if you've seen or talked to me..." He grunted at his work on the cast. The sound was like a plastic snow shovel on icy cement. His bangs hung in his face, and he raised himself up and flicked them back. "Don't tell them where my studio is."

"What, a collection agency?" I was joking, but he wasn't.

He went back to struggling with the cast. "Money's a little tight, but it's no big deal. Just a credit card."

"How would they even know about me?"

"I put you down somewhere on some form. It's fine. I think Bob wants to invest, but he wants to see the new toy first."

"Then it's unanimous. I bet Mike Wallace wants to see the toy at this point."

He lurched back up from the darkness at his feet. I couldn't even see the cast. Only smell it.

"Maybe the drapes salesman could pitch in."

"You can't be serious."

He considered this. He passed the pocket knife, still open to the saw, over his fingertips. "No," he finally said. "It'd just be nice. I'm a starving artist! I deserve a grant."

I took a left at one of the lights, which meant I was heading toward the Mississippi. I'd take River Road up north again and get us to Seth's, where we could stay put.

He took a deep breath and dove again to his leg. "Mother—" he said. More sawing. "Fucker!" he added.

"Stop here," he said.

We were on River Road, not far from his house. He wanted to walk the rest of the way. He needed some clothes and stuff, and then he'd jog downtown to get his car later.

I pulled over into one of the recesses they put in for parkers. The headlights caught a fat raccoon scavenging in the grass near a trash can. It scampered back into the dark brush.

"This is about where I fell," he said, getting out.

He leaned back down to look at me. He tossed his cast onto my lap. It was crumpled and heavy as a wet towel, revolting, trash-white and floppy with fibers I couldn't identify. It looked like an angel wing out of Agostino's *Annunciation*. I pushed it off me in disgust. He laughed.

"Tell the old man the toy's done," he said. "Come to the studio tomorrow, at like five, and you can see it. You'll be the first—maybe you can invest your inheritance."

I started to tell him I didn't have any inheritance, but he closed the door in my face. It latched with once-precise German engineering.

Chapter Twenty-Eight

Turns out, when you pay the improvised weekly rate at Seth's Motor Lodge, you don't get housekeeping services. I'd been making my own bed because that seemed fair enough, but then I noticed that what little trash I'd accumulated hadn't been emptied. Towels stunk. Leaves and other trackables marred the carpet. A fine layer of dust obscured my poker shows, and my dead soldiers stayed in formation in the corner, as if ignorant they'd been decommissioned. Fast food grease in waxy paper packaging crumpled like my aorta. Yogurt containers curdled in their recesses where the spork couldn't reach.

The phone rang several times, until I unplugged it.

This was my Saturday night.

Sunday morning, and Terry wanted nothing to do with me. He was painting Carlton's leg, he said. In a cast, with blood. I didn't have the heart to tell him there was no cast anymore.

I went to the museum alone. Or rather, I made it as far as the general vicinity, circling for a place to park. Something about the beautiful benches, the beautiful hallways, the beautiful staircases, the beautiful bathrooms, the beautiful gift shop with beautiful price points—the idea of them made me feel small behind the Jetta's steering wheel. I sighed, parallel parked in a distinctively un-beautiful fashion, and decided to go for a walk instead.

A museum's point is to place you on the gangplank between our species' clumsy lunging for the divine on the one hand, and our equally clumsy depravity on the other, our unworthiness. That is, the art is worthy; you are to admire it and shut up. How undemocratic! When will we rise up and smite them, they who tell us what to appreciate and why? Witness this city block I was walking down, with its myriad of frameable lunacies such as the sidewalk yard sale that I stumbled upon, stacked with whatnots I couldn't even bear to look at, much less browse. I made up an immediate theory about yard sales. I don't like looking at some poor earnest son of a bitch's detritus going all flotsam on some sidewalk with all the appeal of kicked-through mulch. And because of this, I was forced to walk by in one of two ways: either with a charity perusal, out of politeness, or with no perusal at all, like I was too good for this guy's shit or for yard sales in general. Of course, I wasn't too good for anything or anyone, but nor did I wish to be polite when I didn't even ask for a yard sale but was just walking down the goddamn street!

But who among us doesn't have junk on the street? Who among us is blameless? No one, and arguably, least of all Henry Stuart Meyerson.

But why? In the sordid history of humankind, in which our record is mixed at best, why would that one event, that one trespass, add up to anything more than an ant-squashing? Even assuming God exists, spermy laser and all, wouldn't such a judge simply laugh at my crime and subsequent suffering sincerity and Boy Scout's self-importance? I mean, compared to murderers and pedophiles and cycle-of-violence perpetrators and drug dealers and mob bosses and petty thugs and genocidal instigators and Bill O'Reilly? And, on the other hand, what if there is no Judging; what if the only Teacher gives lessons in a one-room wooden schoolhouse located six feet below a nice patch of grass and a stone with your name on it? Then what? All this hand-wringing over literally nothing.

Aren't we just struggling to be beautiful, worthy of the wires securing us to the wall?

And anyway, it wasn't nothing, my sin with June. It was love, and reciprocal at that. Yes, reciprocal! If June had looked appalled that day when we undressed as natural as sunshine, if she had stayed clothed, say, and laughed or left the room or furrowed her brow and slapped me in the face, I could understand. If she had said, "Because I'm *married*, Hank. To your *brother*. And this is our *home*." And even worse, if I hadn't acted out of this true well of feeling I know to exist, if I were merely a man on the make, striking out at a world that had drawn first blood—but no. No no no. There was love, I tell you! And the love was pounding away at me with memory—her freckles, her sitting with me at parties, the sulky team we made outside the glasses store, our running Hearts game, her jokes and train-wreck syntax, her piquant head-shaking, her immoderate smiles at the immoderate love for her life, her simpering whims that I attended with joy. And of course the shower curtain, the gingkoes, her smile in the steam, her honeyed kisses. Her thickened feet, her red-veined nose, her crease of scar on her upper arm, wrinkle of eye, drip of chin.

The way she kissed me back, just the day before, through tears, until pulling me away by the ear. And even that, I was now convinced, had been done with love.

I was thinking too much. Analyzing like I was still in graduate school. For a mere feeling of superiority or pointlessness, I once spent a whole day debating whether or not a dog's preference for one nap spot over another amounted to proof of sentience. Just my fix of distraction, I guess. Americans are addicted to distraction; it's the national drug. Try to sit for ten minutes thinking original thoughts. Good fucking luck. You're as likely to dredge up a Rolling Stones lyric or Kramer falling down on Jerry's floor or some seeping sense of self-loathing.

And of course, guilt.

I was back in the Jetta by now, hoping its idle would have some response for me. Without its trash, it felt a little soulless, a lipsticked pig. All it could do was idle over 1800 rpms every now and then, then dribble back down.

It's hard to describe the drive over to my brother's house that afternoon. I can't really say it was a hallucination, since it was so focused and isolated to the Jetta's passenger seat. My mother was there, wearing a black nylon tennis warm-up suit. She had fabricated some kind of flat cushion to sit on, too, not for comfort but to protect her outfit.

"Don't worry," I said, "I just cleaned the car."

"Drive careful, now," she said.

I took this to mean she had been traumatized by her accident. She pressed her polished fingernails to the dash in front of her as I made a right turn. "Okay," I said.

"Now, is this really the son I raised?" she said.

"What do you mean?"

"Why are you putting yourself in a position to sin?"

"Sin?"

"Well, what would you call it?"

"I don't know. Love?"

"You'd call it love. I guess that's good to hear."

"Mom?" I said. She patted her hair.

But then I looked both ways at a stop sign, and she was gone. I was parking in front of the house.

June told me to stay on the porch; she'd stay in the house. "We can talk through the window," she said.

"What? What the hell?"

"You know," she said. "I can't be making out with you, or whatever."

"You mean to tell me that you are forced to separate yourself physically from me to—"

"Don't flatter yourself. It's just better this way."

I sat in the wicker. The porch was remarkably sunny and pleasant. September in Minnesota. I slouched in the loveseat, not even looking at the window where June was now settling. I heard her take a drink of something but of course had no idea what it was.

"This is like confession," she said.

"Okay," I said. "I love you."

"You can't. We can't. I want you to stay here, not go back, because I want you in our life."

"Our life."

"But to do that, you have to give this up."

"And you can do that?"

"Yes."

"Well, you guys are perfect for each other. You say it and it's so, huh?"

"It has to be. And we aren't perfect for each other. Obviously."

"You're choosing to suffer."

"You know damn well it means suffering. I made a commitment, and no one's going to tell me how to nurse it—"

"Screw him! He's made his own goddamn bed."

"Just listen to yourself. This is your brother we're talking about."

"You said 'nurse it.' Is that what you want to be? A nurse? Let him go find a nurse then. You're not a nurse."

"No, I'm a wife—"

"Stop it! Stop using facts and storytime! You're in love with me, and you're miserable."

"No and no."

"So why am I on the porch?"

"For good measure. Until you agree to—"

"Oh for Christ's sake."

I needed to pace. I lurched forward and felt June wince on the other side of the screened window. The wicker beneath me nearly snapped, then belched me up. I had not come to do any of this, actually. I'd come ostensibly to compare notes on Carlton's finances—it seemed the prudent thing to do, but not now.

"As I see it," I said, "Carlton is vulnerable right now, and your willingness to suffer for him is admirable—one of the things I love about you."

"I didn't say I was suffering—"

"But treating him like a child won't help, like someone from your old group home. He'll get over it, and we won't abandon him—I'm his family too. What if it's just some big mistake, you and him, and in time everyone will say, yep, worked out for the best?"

"You do live in a fantasy land, just like your brother said."

This got me going again; stepping toward her window so quickly, I almost stumbled onto the loveseat.

"Me? Me! He's the one with creditors calling."

"What's that?"

I looked now and could see her face in the screen, pressed close. The screen bowed a little, shading the light into a halo around her face while also darkening her skin. It was creepy, so I turned away.

"See," I said, "creditors. He just told me, the other night, and he's never shared this with you? What kind of marriage is that?"

"Don't question my marriage. I can do that just fine. And I pay the bills—most of them. There's no one calling."

"Okay, okay." See, now I was the bad guy for even bringing up my brother's mistakes. I needed to stabilize the ship with some logic. "Let me propose a plan," I said. "I'm on my way down there, to see the new toy."

"Really?"

"Yes. And here's what we do. You're threatening to go north for a day anyway, so go. Tonight. Just for safekeeping. And I'll go down there and tell him about us, and let him abuse me in any way he sees fit."

"No no no. I will never speak—" She lost herself a second. Because I couldn't see her now, as I was pacing and looking through the screened porch windows at the sunlit neighbors, I wasn't sure if she was relishing the idea or breaking up. "I'll never speak to you again if you do that," she finished. "No matter what happens."

"But why? Truth is always better. This happened between us, and he's my brother too."

"Because I don't want to be with you. I want to be with him."

I was half a step from the front door when she said this, so I decided to go inside, thinking she didn't mean it, as I'd see when I could confront her. She was putting up some kind of moralist's fight, keeping herself miserable out of pure duty to misery. In this, she was worse than me! I'd had months of suffering in Montana, but she was still wallowing in the here-and-now.

Something about the brass Home Depot handle enraged me. It twisted in my hands, and stuck. It was locked. "Motherfucker!" I said. I began to shake the door, pounding with my right fist now. I growled like a fatty Jack Nicholson and saw my hands slapping the door like sides of ham, sea lion flippers, thickened with uselessness. But then my pounding broke one of the door's small panes of glass, and June yelped.

The glass remaining in the pane was jagged as a mountain range, too risky to reach through to unlock the door. Anyway, my hand was cut, a small but wide gash in my fleshy palm, and it had done a bloody Jackson Pollock on the white door. Fuck Agostino—now *this* was a painting! It too was biblical, announcing that this was a sacred home, and I'd better go before the cops showed up.

Across the street in my car, it seemed my mother was back, shaking her head. But no—it was just a bush I'd parked next to, nodding in the breeze.

And anyway, what could she tell me? I had an appointment with my brother, and she had always told me to keep my appointments and if I couldn't, call my regrets at least an hour ahead of time. It was 4:40. I was supposed to meet him at 5:00.

Carlton's building was one of those throwback six-stories where some floors had cheery paint jobs with the floor number in Art Deco typeface greeting you as you exited the elevator, but other floors were drab and scuffed, suffering under a general malaise of peeled paint and weedy carpet. The place was not without an air of proprietorship, however. The firefighters' standpipe in the stairway— I took the stairs to avoid the claustrophobic elevator and to work off some steam—had the freshest coat of paint in the joint, and the signs denoting the floor and "no roof access" were better placed than code required. The handrail was unscuffed, the linoleum waxed to the baseboards. You got the sense the super made more money than any of the tenants—either that or he was retired and just did it for pride. What he thought of the street-level massage parlor I didn't care to know.

In the stairwell, the tinny echo of my scuffling feet went right along with my panting. Six fucking flights! The stairs themselves, chagrined under generations of green paint, gave me up for dead as I emerged through emergency-red double doors. My brother was there, and he laughed at my huffing. "I heard you all the way down the hall," he said. He stood there looking like he wanted to tuck in his shirt, but of course it was designed to look that way.

"I'm good," I said. And when the dizziness left me, I was.

"What's with your hand?"

"Oh," I said. I pulled my hand to my chest, protecting it as much as hiding it, though I'd wrapped it in gauze from the Jetta's first-aid kit. "Cut it slicing a bagel."

He nodded. He might have gleaned the truth from his home's front door, but if I had the fortitude, I'd be beating him to it here momentarily.

As we walked down the hallway, his limping more pronounced without his cast, I began to appreciate the noir-ish personality of the place. The brass doorknobs were bulbous and stately, the big office doors mahogany-heavy with mysteries one would ponder while ambling the hallway's worn-bare gray carpeting, which kept a like-new diffidence along the warped linoleum baseboards. The thick-handled freight elevator, with door hinges the size of my foot, was where you'd dispose of a body, if you had to, and likely where any denouement would take place, with some anxious glances at the ceiling panels listing overhead, stained from watery accidents long forgotten.

The whole thing read like Philip K. Dick, promising dames with skeletons in their closets. I felt like I should be wearing a porkpie and carrying a piece. I asked my brother if the radiators ran on gin.

He laughed, and we turned a corner to his office, which was secluded down the end of the north hallway's dogleg, by the stairs. As he was fumbling with his key, I noticed his door. It was pretty much the same as the others in the building, but it had three metal bars across it, each with its own hinge to the right of the door and secured by a thick bracket bolted to the left of the door. Security, I assumed, but as he lifted the bars free, it became evident that anyone could do the same.

"What the fuck?" I said.

He said nothing. The door had thick rubber insulation around it that unsucked itself as he pulled it open. It was pitch black inside— he had indeed blacked out the windows.

"What are you, a vampire?"

He felt inside for the light, and took a deep breath. "Just stay with me for a second."

Imagine you've got a nice Christmas clementine in hand, small and round and secure in its rind, but when you peel it, curled inside, instead of white downy fruit, is a furry black spider. This is something like how I leapt when my brother turned on the light. His studio was not an office but some kind of industrial fantasy, completely empty and cold beneath a lone 100-watt bulb. My brother walked in, his footsteps a scuffling echo on a floor covered with 10-inch gray tiles, grouted and everything, that also ran halfway up the walls. The rest of the walls were still the building's plaster, painted beige. Where the room's windows had been was a wide metal door with no handle, circumscribed by the same thick rubber as the hallway door, which I still hadn't come through.

"Come in," my brother said.

It was impossible not to.

The ceiling was sheet metal, smooth and studded with screws sunk flush into washers. Weirdest of all, there were exposed pipes on the ceiling too, three of them running from hallway door to the wide door across the room, each with three showerheads, the wide-face kind that you see in the outdoor showers of the rustic temperate world we Northerners love to imagine vacationing to but rarely do.

My brother was impassive, with a neutral calm he almost never wore. It was almost peaceful, but resigned, and I had one of those time travel moments where you know what's about to be said just before the words hit your ears—so that when he spoke, I was already bending over to puke in a corner.

"It's Treblinka," my brother said. "The new gas chambers they built in 1943. The building was supposed to look like a bathhouse, and kinda like a synagogue too. And then they led you here and closed the door." He clicked the door closed behind us. Even its small latch echoed like a gunshot. "You okay?"

Throwing up in response to alcohol toxins has a sort of this-is-for-your-own-good intelligence, whereas throwing up out of revulsion and panic relieves none of the symptoms—it just takes you over, humping in your chest and throat. The spider in the clementine, already prickling up your hand.

Though I'd gotten some puke on my sandals, hence on my toes too, I'd landed most of it in a corner. But now the more liquid parts of it were flowing away from the corner, toward the other side of the room, via right-angle pathways of grout.

"The floor has a slight grade," my brother said. "I made it that way, because they did."

"You built all this?"

"Yeah."

"What the fuck for?"

My brother leaned against the door and slid down to the ground, which was when I realized I'd already done same, wiping my mouth with the gauze from my wounded hand. The puke smell took some of the staleness out of the air.

My brother was blinking. His chin, thick and stoic, bobbed a little. His blinking swiped tears to the corners of his eyes like windshield wipers. "It's complicated," he said. "To get it out of my head. It worked."

"You're supposed to be making toys!"

He said nothing to this.

I sunk into myself. The tile was warm now, from my heat, flattening my backside haunches like a wad of dough on a cookie sheet. I couldn't even feel it, really. I made myself feel it. Was the room creepy? Of course. But for me, it was almost a friendly creepiness. Certainly it needed no explanation—at least if you'd grown up going to Hebrew school, where they made damn sure you knew the basic mechanisms of the Holocaust. Jews were herded into an undressing area, thinking they were getting deloused. There were signs indicating as much—"Lice can kill!" and such. They were told to hang their belongings on a hook in the undressing room, and remember the hook number so they'd be sure to get their things back. All to avoid a panic, a scrambling melee that would require machine gun fire, which would gob up the works, slowing production, so to speak. This is the kind of shit most Jews know without thinking.

"There were ten of these rooms," my brother said. "Each could fit 60–70 people. They were about as big, actually, as this room. A meter or two off. Like 140 square feet."

"Seventy people?"

"Yeah, packed 'em in. You want to believe that, after the haircut and the reassurance about their personal belongings, that they were fooled up until the gas came on. It was carbon monoxide—they had a tank engine in one of the ten rooms hooked up to the pipes. Easy as pie. As the gas came in, people spread out, looking for air. They pounded against the door. The lights were off. People trampled each other, climbing for air. Heads crushed, children and old people ground to the tile. Twenty minutes later, that door was opened." My brother pointed across the room. "And the bodies fell out like stones. The Sonderkommando carried the bodies to the burning pit. These were Jews enslaved to do the awful work. What didn't burn was pulverized and dumped in the Vistula River."

Talking was helping my brother. Not talking was helping me.

"They started with the retards, you know. They'd take over an insane asylum, fire the staff and put a Nazi in charge, and experiment how to kill 'em. They took what they learned there and did it to us." He sighed. "Germans," he said.

"When did you do this?"

"I started six months ago, just tinkering, like maybe I'd do half the room or a corner or what the fuck. But then after you went I took it up a notch. It just made sense. If you could just go like that—it made me wonder about myself. Was I a good brother? Was I a good person even? I'd never asked that about myself. I mean, Dad didn't really teach us introspection."

I grunted.

"But we were lucky to have him."

Another grunt.

"When Mom died, I was convinced the drapes salesman had something to do with it."

"What?"

"Because we'd gone Jewish. I used to imagine he was watching me, down in Hutch. He'd come watch me play baseball, I just felt it. Once I even ran after this guy—ran back down to the river behind the stadium. I wasn't playing, of course. I never played. I ran down to the river because this tall blonde guy wearing one of those wool barn coats, you know, with the shearling inside and the buttons? But I lost him—there's a running path there, and it goes both ways, and a train trestle over the river. He could have gone anywhere."

Carlton laughed. "I spent ten minutes looking for him, and I was muddy and out of breath, and I came back to the dugout and Coach just looked at me and told us to pick up the chatter." He looked at me wide-eyed, shaking his head. "I mean, what the fuck?"

I wouldn't say this made sense—not *sense* sense anyway. But I'd imagined similar things about the drapes salesman. I've imagined being loaded into a gas chamber too. It's not illogical to think building something like this would be cathartic.

I raised my arm to it. "You did an amazing job."

"It's not hard. It's all real materials, from the Home Depot, but all for show. There's no functionality."

"Well thank God for that."

"This isn't easy for me. I could have shown no one, but I'm trusting you to see what it really means. It might look crazy, but it isn't. It's—I've always wanted to be an artist. But I screwed up that movie about Rabbi Zabin, and I can't draw or paint for shit."

He laughed through his nose. "It's been a total headache. June thinks I have a futon and espresso maker in here. And, a lot of times I had to actually get some work done. I had to carry my files in the trunk of the car."

I wasn't sure what to say. Sometimes the harder you look at something, the less you see. The forest obscured by the trees. But who says you were looking for forests in the first place? Who the fuck goes around looking for forests?

"You need to believe me," he said, "and trust me, the way I've trusted you. I did this to become a better person, and now you're home and are my brother again, and we've been drinking and the world hasn't fallen apart. This is just a thing—a badness."

He didn't look particularly okay, my brother. But he didn't look scared, either, just bone white on the floor, spent.

Our voices had flattened and drained the way they do in empty, hard places. It wasn't so bad, really. It was art, in a way. There are all types of obsessions out there—on the very day I got married, I did an entire Sunday *Times* crossword. Took me three hours. I was so, so proud. Me and my big brain—we were gonna hunker down and beat the odds, and when we needed more room, I got heavier. I could be fat and overeducated and still somehow manage to be extraordinary. In a crossword puzzle, the clue "make good" has a dizzying number of potential answers.

"I—" I said. "Look at this fucking thing. People should see this. It's incredible. It's a goddamn installation. It's art. You had a vision. It's a little macabre, but—"

"It's a lot macabre. But that's the point."

"Yes, yes. I mean, look at it. It's incredible. Where did you get the info? Did you just make it up?"

"Sent away for it. There are no pictures, just eyewitness accounts, mostly from Eichmann's trial. And they are more than happy to give them out. I should make a tape of the sound of the gas coming in, but you gotta know when to say when. And today is definitely when."

"Meaning?"

He raised his eyebrows and made a theatrical gesture with his right arm, indicating the entire sculpture he created. "Fatty," he said, "help me demo."

"What? We don't have any tools."

"I do. They're in a storage closet I built into that wall over there."

"Oh."

"The kitty's in there too, if you're interested."

He meant his alcohol. "I just puked, so no thanks. And anyway, this is tile—it doesn't just pry up. And I don't think you should touch it at all. It—this should be seen. You're like that guy who makes a grotto to St. Francis in cement and Coke cans or whatever. This is zeitgeist."

"It violates my lease."

"It violates a lot more than that."

"But you like it?" He seemed genuinely intrigued by the possibility.

I pursed my lips. They still felt slimy. "I'm impressed. It *is* art."

He smiled at this. It had its old effect on me. "I don't know. It doesn't feel like art to me, because it's not interesting. It's just a model. Hey," he nudged me, "get that toolbox in the corner."

I hadn't even seen a toolbox in the corner. I guess that's understandable.

"I don't feel like manual labor right now—"

"No no. Just get the box."

I pushed myself up, felt and stifled another wave of nausea, got the toolbox, and opened it. Inside was a soft, meticulously stitched gray furry blob with stubby Tyrannosaurus arms and a head hardly discernible from the body. It was about as big as a loaf of bread, and its eyes were agoogle, both in placement and in the irises. It had a perpetually open mouth, black and small.

"That's it."

I held the toy at arm's length. Its head was a beanbag that lolled over its body whichever way I tilted it.

"Hug it," he said, so I cradled it in my arms. "Squeeze," he said.

"Why?" I said.

He made a face.

I squeezed and the thing lurched a little. A yellowish fizzy foam belched from the mouth.

"I'm gonna call him Reinhard the Sick Puppy. He's based on you, kind of, your barfing phase."

I wiped the fake puke from my arm with the toy itself. He couldn't help but smile at that.

"Fifteen bucks cost—if my broker in China comes through and we buy a container-full."

"You're going to be a millionaire."

He nodded. We both looked at the room. The light was crap, that one bulb, naked and droning. But save for me and Carlton and the showerheads, there was nothing to cause a shadow. I took the toy and placed him in the middle of the room, where he slouched over himself like a thing waiting to be brought back to life.

I came and slumped next to my brother again. I felt his sharp shoulder bone cut into my flesh. He needed to eat better.

Some of my puke juice had made its way pretty much across the room by now, and Reinhard the Sick Puppy sat a good five feet from it, slumped and a little askew, ignoring it but somewhat wary too. Finally its heavy head tilted it over onto its side, one eye staring at us, the other at the puke.

"Now *that*," my brother said, "is interesting."

Chapter Twenty-Nine

Duck of Annunciation waddles out of a bar," I said on the sidewalk as they steadied me and took my Jetta key. "His beak is bleeding, and God is nowhere in sight. He has had too much to drink, yet again. He's depressed. 'Oh for the days,' he says, 'when I used to feel Mary.'"

I said this to the humming Nora's neon sign over my head. Humming neon signs probably give you cancer. A waitress and a barback who looked no older than twelve were outside with me, helping me wait for the cab they'd called. But maybe cabs give you cancer too, so I shrugged them off and said I'd walk home. And when a drunk decides to walk home, who's going to stop him? Who's really to blame, all things considered, if he never makes it?

Our house was very dark. I got close enough that I could see how clean the windows were, spotless and streak-free. I wondered for a moment if I had been the last one to wash the windows, but that couldn't have been—they were just too clean and I hadn't lived there for months. And anyway I was a lame duck around her, but not lame enough to wash her goddamn windows.

Minneapolis is essentially a residential town: start at downtown's skyscrapers and warehouses and institutions, any direction you choose, and in five minutes you come to neighborhood after neighborhood of plastic picket fencing, some wood and chain-link too, and shrubby buffers of lilac and rhododendron and spirea. It'll be a block of corner bars and auto body shops and insurance agencies and convenience gas stations and bakeries with their "open" signs on even though they're not—that always sticks in my craw— and then it's an oasis of dahlias in bloom, a few lilies still making a go of it, cottony dandelions in the yards of the less committed. Most of the yards are still green, but in these neighborhoods it's hit or miss, some trim and neat and bordered with interlocking brick edging or railroad ties or something, others tough and let go. A few houses had gone natural, with prairie grasses and coneflowers for a well-maintained wildness. The rentals suffered from neglect mostly, while the lifers gleamed with painted foundations, and all was trammeled with the endless hostas and evergreens, tree roots raising a cracked square of sidewalk to a fun-house pitch, flashing orange barricades guarding some municipal hole in the street not yet refilled and patched with a rectangle of tar.

Families asleep, college kids fornicating, the elderly conserving electricity to help save for property taxes. The scraps of paper and trash and municipal election signs—someone named Parks was running for the parks board. A car coming down the street then braking in a silent squeal of red to take the next corner. A cat tiptoeing the shadows, a threesome of munching bunnies. You can get a cat to look your way by mimicking a meow, and you don't have to be Frank Gorshin to do it, but a bunny will just sit still and munch. I saluted their uncompromising bunniness.

"I know you like bunnies," I told Carol Ann.

She had taken me in, drunk, late on a Sunday night, because she owed me, plain and simple. Yes, I'd failed her, but everything considered, my pain was of a greater degree than hers, and while this might lead me more thoroughly to my life—as pain is a great locator—that life was thoroughly falling apart.

"Why are you whispering?" she said. We were in the bathroom, The Project, on the floor. She was leaning against the wall and holding my head because my head wouldn't stop spinning, and I figured I'd need the toilet any time now. The toilet was new with The Project, the last thing I'd installed. I remember my satisfaction with it, fuelled by panic and love. It was a generic toilet, no personality or design, too white and also too mass-produced, a toilet made in Ecuador, probably. I guess one's biggest regrets in life are the economies, not spending the extra hundred bucks for a toilet you're proud to sit on. On my deathbed, there will plenty of thoughts like these.

"I'm trying not to yell," I said, about my whispering.

"You yell," she warned, "and I'm kicking you out of here."

"Hence the whispering."

Thus far, in my whisperings, I'd referenced the Duck of Annunciation, Terry, Rousseau's *Confessions*, Emily Dickinson's "The Props assist the House," Melville as a sex symbol, Minneapolis landscape design, the Final Solution, puke, ginkgo biloba, and the lone pubic hair curled up ashamed in the bathroom corner. Somehow it all made sense.

"I used to love it when you talked like that. It made *me* feel smart."

"Too bad I didn't talk sexy."

"Smart *is* sexy. Maybe you'll see that someday."

"I do now—Julia Roberts in reading glasses."

"But smart isn't enough for you. You always wanted to be— what was your word?"

"Extraordinary."

"Right. Better than everyone. A genius. And I was just sitting here."

"In the bathroom?" She shook her head. "You never just sit there," I said. "That's what makes you who you are."

"Oh believe me, for a while I was sitting there, waiting to see what kind of genius you'd be, and how I'd fit in. I worshipped you. It was like, if you were a genius, that would make it okay that you were ignoring me. Geniuses are known to do that, and I'm good at sucking it up for the cause. It gives me purpose."

"I'm no genius, and no one will love me. Who would love me, kitty?" I said. "Look at me. I'm pathetic."

"You're melodramatic."

"I'm a horrible person."

"You are not." She stroked my head.

"I am. I do things that should bother me, and I don't even care. And I'm not extraordinary. I'm me."

I touched her hip, more holding on than anything. It was with my bandaged left hand, and I didn't want to get blood on her.

"Okay, so we're both horrible. What if we made a mistake together this time? I've missed you. Haven't you missed me in Montana?"

"Sure," I said.

"So let's dive back in. Maybe we've grown, and learned— whatever we needed to."

"Do you have to work tomorrow?"

"Neither one of us has asked for divorce papers."

"It's only been a few months."

"But we can't go on like this. And you don't seem to have a girlfriend. And neither do I."

I turned up to her. I could see her nose hairs in her nostril maws. I raised my eyebrows.

"A boyfriend, I mean."

"Well, you're with lady boxer types all day, so—"

"Be serious a moment. I bet you haven't even gotten laid out there."

"You'd bet right."

"So neither of us are pining for freedom, are we?"

I didn't say anything.

"Are we?"

"Why did we paint it so pink in here?"

"It's peach."

"It's pinky-peach. It looks like pig flesh."

"I like it. This is the best room in the house. I still can't believe you managed it, with the new plumbing and the sheetrocking and all that."

"You're praising me now?"

"At some point you have to stop being angry."

"I'm incapable of anger anymore."

"Why? Tell me."

She was still stroking my head. The tiny room was so quiet, and the wood-grain laminate flooring so soft, I wondered if I could just lie there forever. It seemed simplicity itself, totally doable. It was a fantasy I was still crafting even as I told Carol Ann I was in love with June and probably always would be.

When we take stock of our lives, some of us are built to recall moments like these. We are not the winners of the world, generally. We are not the movers but, mostly, the moved. We are the ones who are kept up at night not by injustice and eternity, but by our human failings, when another heart beating in our presence went without communion.

What little claim Carol Ann had to despair, she invoked. She pushed me off, unfolded up and out of the bathroom. She tried to slam the door on me, but it was off-kilter some and could only be closed by lifting the handle a little, so slamming wasn't possible. That was the one thing I hadn't fixed.

I followed her up to the one room bedroom. The stairs were still narrow and slick, the floor up there still had that satisfying piney gleam, and she still had clothes strewn everywhere, strewn like cooked Swiss chard. The only light was from the stainless steel bedside lamp.

My head stung, my hand chewed, and even Carol Ann's soft duvet prickled me, but I kept talking, telling the story, or most of it, or some lie approximating it.

Finally Carol Ann turned off the light, soundlessly, and the streetlight did its best to take up the slack, and the room threatened to spin out of control. I had to will it to stop, eyes crunched closed and my body as hard and heavy as I could make it. It suddenly came clear what I wanted. "I want to be picked up at the airport with flowers."

Though she was turned away from me, I felt her nod. I held on to her and she didn't push me away but instead rolled to me and put her forehead to mine. Her breath was hot and cankerous, her face damp and sorrowful. But she put her arms up to my shoulders, and that small tenderness was how our night ended.

Chapter Thirty

The morning was Monday. Because of the heavy night, and, for me at least, the drinking, we were late to get up. Carol Ann did first. I heard the usuals in the kitchen downstairs: Steve plunging into the backyard and returning, then the house-shake of the back door closing and Steve waiting for a treat and then sitting and then getting a treat and then sitting again to get her breakfast and then going at it with a happy metallic slurp-munch. No marriage should underestimate the ecumenical power of a dog's morning routine.

Then Carol Ann calling work and leaving an "I'm sick" voicemail for her boss, followed by the slow squeal of the tea kettle. It was all too much. I needed to leave, but Carol Ann was clearly back on the practicality train—her strength.

I tried to still myself in bed, find a position that didn't hurt. Breath came wheezily, my carotid thumping with heartbeats I could feel in my fuzzy sternum. I stared at the wainscoted walls and remembered using a lit candle to find wintry drafts—like using a goat as a grass detector. We never ended up insulating, though as recently as my summer in Montana I idled away time trying to figure out how to do it with vermiculite.

Carol Ann would find somebody to do it. Someone would come along to love her. Rather, she would will it so—after all, I was spilled milk, really, and nothing to be cried over, certainly nothing to keep Steve from getting breakfast. I'd befouled myself with my sister-in-law; at least Carol Ann had chosen someone unrelated.

Then I heard the TV come on, and the sound of it was something I could taste on my thick tongue. Carol Ann and her TV, as natural as me with my hangover and wry thoughts. The TV was Carol Ann's lover until she found snacks. The sound of it, accompanied by her tea slurping, still had the power to dishearten me. My heart beat up into my throat, my liver a fuzzy star in my sternum. I swore, with the Duck of Annunciation as my witness, that I'd never drink again, and that I'd try not to say something catty about Katie Couric when I got downstairs.

But I fell back asleep instead, which was just as good.

"Hank," Carol Ann yelled up to me, "your brother's here."

I guess it made as much sense to see him parking at my forlorn front walk as anything else did. I was shaking from head to hamstring, Carol Ann was making French toast, and the day was autumn-beautiful—almost like a winter storm had come, and the world had gone quiet with white barbiturate of snow. I even said to Carol Ann, on my way to the front door, that we should go get the Jetta from Nora's because they might tow it before they plow the street. With the kind of night we'd had, she just nodded at me over tea and walked back to her French toast.

I blinked at my brother. There was no snow, of course, and the day was in fact pretty warm. But he had on a light suede jacket and looked cold in it, his hands piped into the pockets.

"I saw you in the window. Your car's at Nora's. You've got to take it easy on the booze."

"The booze needs to take it easy on me."

He shook his head and smirked, then shivered.

"You okay?" I asked.

He nodded. He said, "Hank, why are you here? Did you get back together with Carol Ann? It looks like it. I can smell breakfast."

Oh the pale, paltry moments among family! One thing we are good at, we human Americans, is calling people on their hypocrisies, their weaknesses, and their faults. People we love, people we want to see happy—how we run them through with our 20/20 vision.

"I don't see it's any of your business," I said.

"Did you have sex with her?"

He looked awful, his channel getting poor reception. He hugged into himself some more, and he looked me in the face, then down at the cracked cement stoop. A mild breeze found us, then thought better of it and skirted away. The pine tree in the front yard smelled unmistakably of pine tree. My brother's jacket was stained, a dark smear barely visible up near his right shoulder. He didn't raise his head to say, "Well?"

"I told you, it's none of your business."

I held on to the screen door's brass handle, a modest comma of solidity.

"No," I finally said. "Of course we didn't have sex. I came here drunk and—we talked."

"Okay," he said. "Do you want to hang out some?"

I must have looked wary.

"What, you afraid of me after what I showed you yesterday?"

"Don't be stupid," I said. "Come in. Carol Ann's making French toast."

"Nah. Let's go out someplace. Let's go to the river."

He looked like hell, agitated and constipated and bereft—he stood there drooping like a cut cable. Even his chino cuffs were frayed, though that was probably the way they'd come from the Gap, and his boxy black camp shirt, untucked, puffed out from below his jacket like a miniskirt and crawling with wrinkles.

"You don't look so good."

"Yeah, well, I've been under some duress."

"Join the club," I said.

I told him he might as well come in, because I had to wash my face and take a shit. But he just turned and gimped to his car. He was driving the Volvo, its white hide pearled and gleaming.

I told Carol Ann what was going on, and her reflex was to be hurt. Weren't we some kind of family still? Hadn't she called in sick for me? But it was a half-assed effort. "Maybe I'll go to work after all," she said. I snatched up a couple slices of French toast to set things better in my stomach, found my sunglasses and wallet, and went to the door. Carol Ann walked with me, then said wait a second—she went to the kitchen and came back with a Dixie cup of syrup for dipping. A Dixie cup of syrup against the tide of everything—we both laughed at it.

I hugged her. I told her I should go be with my brother, and she nodded, remembering why, and turned away from me. She didn't watch me leave or close the door behind me. Instead, she went back into the kitchen and then into the bathroom. I heard monkeying with the sticky door to get it closed tight.

My brother was down and, as it turns out, also hungover. For both of us, the world was coursing by on every other beat, illogical as a strobe light. I enjoyed the company—without it, the day's midday normalcy would have been too much. Red lights changing silently to green; airplanes surfing overhead and rock songs blurting sex on the radio; gas station clerks smiling or ignoring you according to their humor; and the great gear teeth of American life doing its lock and pull, lock and pull, as they have since Jamestown. When you're young, there's something wonderful in the idea that you can call out for pizza at 9:00 a.m. or stay home three days straight or get on a Greyhound with no destination or drive to Mille Lacs and gamble away your paycheck—and pretty much no one will give a damn. But at some point it just becomes sad.

"Working stiffs," I said to my brother after we'd gassed his car.

"It's a good reminder," Carlton said.

"What?"

"That we're just normal fuckheads like everyone else."

"Yeah, well—"

He cut me off to say, "But you always wanted to be extraordinary." He turned his head, slowly, like he was wearing an unwieldy cowboy hat. "Right?

I didn't turn to look at him; I shrugged. Something in the combination of the two put me back into that room, his studio cum death chamber. My skin crackled at the thought, and I decided I wouldn't think of it again today. There'd be plenty of time for parsing all that out, I figured. June would know what to make of it. It would help her forget my wolf-at-the-door routine. Hopefully.

It was an incredibly bright day, the sun high, everything clear as pain. We hit the freeway and cruised through the eastern suburbs, replete with dying strip malls and outlet centers and lake property and high schools and office buildings, 3M and others who didn't want to bother with downtown—they were mirrored and gleaming with ostentatious vulnerability.

"What I like about you," he said as we cut through it all, "is that you do what's asked of you. No one has loyalty anymore."

"I'm a patsy, you mean."

"That's a negative take on it."

He drove us to the St. Croix. The park's parking lot was empty— we had the place to ourselves.

Walking the wide paved trail, past the picnic benches and the bathrooms and the small pavilion with its tidy scenic overlook, it seemed to me that fall had arrived overnight. Not so much that it was cold, though certainly it was cooler than the days previous, but more that the light fell among us muted and heavy somehow, and the tree leaves had gone brittle. They pushed against themselves in the breeze with a sound like a baby rattle.

My brother seemed weighted. On the old railroad path now, he shrunk into his suede jacket, still looking chilled. He put his hands in his pockets, the football he'd brought for us clamped in one arm, and kept them there even limping down the stairs to the water.

It was an off-putting quiet on the beach. Little waves, from a southerly wind, glinted across the mile or so to the Wisconsin shore, but their light was more unified than I'd expected—until now I'd only seen them by moonlight. In daylight the water was more like a sheet of ice, a hard harmony, than actual water. I couldn't imagine either of us going in.

"No boats," my brother said.

"Monday."

He grunted. Without the boats growling, and of course without any plane traffic, you could hear the trees chatter. I could hear individual leaves clacking against their neighbors. Also terns and gulls, their calls loud as fire alarms, floating like buoys in the shallows. A white heron lifted into flight only to circle back into the trees on the point north of us.

"Here," my brother said.

He brought a bottle of whiskey from his jacket pocket. Johnnie Walker Red. I rubbed my cheek with the gauze of my cut left hand, which no longer hurt. I liked the feeling of the gauze on my skin.

"The kitty lives."

He took off his jacket and let it fall to the ground. Cantor Fetterman, who taught us both in Hebrew school, would not have approved—a coat is a precious thing, people have died for lack of coat, people beg for coats—and I said so.

"Fuck him," Carlton said. He spun the football in his hands, knuckling for the stitching. It was an action that since childhood has threaded me with anxiety, and I suppose it always will—I gotta catch that thing? I gotta throw that thing? Most American men carry in their gut a football-sized cavity of such distress.

"Gimme that," my brother said.

He grabbed the bottle. He winced his distaste.

He spat and trotted, as best he could, out to the end of the beach, the football spinning in his big right hand.

I took my dose, and our day began.

What I remember is the football punching into my arms, and holding it like a precious thing. And when I feared for my cut hand and the ball caromed off my skin into the sand, or when it stumbled off my fingers and fluttered end over end, landing nowhere near the pattern my brother had run, we merely laughed. My receptions took me into the shadow from the steep bank of trees behind me, and my tosses brought me back out. On my better throws, my brother giggled as he tipped the ball to himself, upping his degree of difficulty. Sometimes he even batted them down, playing defense. He gloated over vanquished opponents.

Everything had a strange hardness. The rocky downstream shore in shadow, the little stones and shards of driftwood lodged into the sand bar we were running on, the calcified goose poops, the swarming radioactivity of gnats at ankle height. Even the bombast of those terns. The whole place, which every season is re-shaped by the whims of water, seemed downright eternal.

Our shadows got longer, claiming more and more beach. We were interrupted by no one. An occasional boat puttered out in the swifter, deeper water, ashamed of its own wake. I began to take in the ball without fear of it. We kept the whiskey bottle midway between us, like playing keepaway—a few out patterns, a buttonhook, a pump and go, and then a quick huddle for a nip. We'd share the bottle wordlessly, soundtracked by some twittering insect off in the rasping grasses. My brother started quarterbacking, calling meaningless audibles for me, bantering. "Tallboy, Toronto, Bulldog, Hike!" My thudding in the sand, which I felt up into my body, filtered by the weight of me, my gut hanging over my shorts, the goose flesh prickling up my calves. We worked up a sweat, outwitting the inept defensive effort put up by the ganglia of grasses fluttering up and down the beach.

I soon had to stop and catch my breath. That's the way it goes. I was near the trees and the stairs, and my brother approached. Sauntered, really. The limp was gone. His scrunch too. He no longer looked cold, or withdrawn. It was me, had to be—I'd refashioned him, if only for today, pried free his recalcitrance, his suffering with June and his struggle with Treblinka, his efforts on the new puking Sick Puppy toy—I had removed it all and replaced it with that golden confidence. He was sunny, smiling with the whiskey bottle in his hand, and I felt a peacefulness about him and us and everything—an uncoiling into my body I hadn't felt since listening to Tom's story about Sugar. It was a stretching out into the true me, my destiny, as it seemed, fitting myself into my own skin, and it struck me as a truth that you have to *feel* fat to get *un*fat, which has implications for sin and redemption and all that, which was probably why Terry loved that goddamn *Annunciation* so much, and why I'd come to love it too, with it's puerile promise that if you just looked at things this way, the duck with the spermy laser penetrating the clouds, things could turn out all right, or at least you'd have sound reason to believe they would, which, in the end, is the same thing.

This was the bullshit I was thinking when I reached out for the whiskey bottle with my stumpy hand, and instead of handing it to me, my brother pulled it back, changed it somehow, and smacked it into the side of my head.

Stumbling to my left, my legs tangled, and I hit the sand in stages, like a controlled event: knees, then abdomen, then elbows, then face. I let myself lay, breathing heavy and cheeking small rocks and twigs no more substantial than hair clippings. There were little long-legged bugs in the sand, scurrying away from me and then leaping into flight. Why would they crawl when they could fly?

"That's for June," he said. "Just to get it out of the way. Because for the rest of today I don't want to be angry."

I'd landed next to a dead tree sticking in the sand a few feet from the others via exposed roots hard as the old lead pipe I'd cut from my bathroom. Carol Ann's bathroom, that is. The bark was brittle when I placed a hand on it.

The bottle hadn't broken; I saw it in the sand near me. He'd hit me high on the left temple, and it wasn't hurting very much yet. Throbbing. I felt the blood surging there, and the sickly uncertainty of its return. I fumbled onto my back. My hand was bloody, but it was the cut from the day before, reopened by the football. I spied the bandage down the beach, caught to a web of weeds. There are worse feelings, though. Let the bloodletting begin. It's about fucking time.

My brother lay down in the sand, at an angle from me, in the sun, and rubbed his sinuses. He held his palms up to the sky, stretching his arms. His muscles pulled at the T-shirt's seams. Even with them, he was a little flabby.

"I'm sorry," I said. "I love her."

"It'd be much worse if I thought you didn't. There'd be no logic to it then. Finding you there at Carol Ann's, like a fucking puppy, was almost the end of you."

We lay there, open to the pristine day. How the shit did this happen, when a few hours ago I was eating French toast?

Carlton sat up and hugged his sandy knees. "Christ," he said, "look at us. Pathetic, huh?"

I spit in the sand, a droopy spit that wouldn't quite leave my lips. I was anesthetized, sort of. My mouth felt Novocained from whiskey.

"Look, let's go home and wait and talk to her. She doesn't even—"

"Just shut up a minute, okay. Just be quiet."

I nodded. I still hadn't caught my breath. I felt like my mouth had been taped, like he had handcuffed me to this tree, and I started to panic, chest heaving, sweaty in the palms. The blow to my head must have been worse than I thought—these things happen: a guy hits another guy over a girl, like Les in Yakima, Washington, and that one punch causes a coma. I yelped a little with the idea of this, the weight of a big thing finally coming to pass—face it or forget it. This is how you die, I thought, falling inside yourself until you hit bottom, smashed beyond repair by your own craggy bones.

"Just breathe," he said. "You're gonna feel weird. I spiked the whiskey."

I must have yelped again. "It's gonna be fine. Just listen to me." He stopped me from protesting, raising his face so that his chin threatened. "Listen, listen to me. I've got it figured out."

My brother hadn't been sleeping, of course, while working on his Treblinka model. The more he worked on it, the better he felt, so it made sense. The Sick Puppy toy had been done for months now, except for some tinkering with the amount of puke that came out (4 or 5 foamy cc's) and some toxicology testing. But Carlton insisted it wouldn't sell. It's too much of a pain in the ass. Parents will turn up their noses, buyers won't want the hassle, and the price point's too high. It has no educational value, the specialty stores are too snobby for it, and no one at mass will want to take the chance.

"It will too," I said. "You're a natural. Let's just go home, find June, and you can see a doctor or something, or maybe you just need sedatives or something to sleep or—"

"What do you think's in the whiskey?" He watched me. "That's right—June's treats. I know where she keeps them. I know everything. Now don't you agree that the least you can do is shut up? You're going to fuck my wife and then try to tell me how to cope with it?"

"No."

He fished around for the whiskey. Swallowing, still hugging his knees and squinting out at the water, he said that this morning June went off on a little trip of her own, up north. One of the things married people do when they don't have kids and they're lonely. "And then," he said, "you know how things just come together?"

I shrugged.

"You do," he said. "But here's the thing. What it comes together *as*. The puzzle."

"I just think—"

"Shut up!" he shouted. "Shut up shut up shut up!"

I slithered inside. The cawing gulls down the beach took flight. The waves seemed to pause, then exhale back into sound. The day was hardening to a crackle now, like sun-dried mud. My brother pulled more of the whiskey.

"What are the odds all this would go down at pretty much the same time?" he asked me. "Showing you my work in progress, June going out for a little trip, Dad not able to come up, you fucking my wife—and that retard. He comes over today," my brother said. His tongue was out over his screwy front teeth. He flicked it out over his lips with a watery gleam. "He's upset over some goddamn painting, but also he's got the most interesting story about you and June in the bathroom for a long time with the shower on."

He shook his head. I held mine very still.

"Whatever," he finally said. "It's chickens coming home. I make people unhappy. I've been keeping it all in." He looked at me, getting more agitated. He flapped his hand around his midsection like someone saying "yummy" without words. "Right here. All inside. 'There's a taste in my mouth, and it's no taste at all.' That's Bowie. And it's true. That's who I am. So Treblinka is where you go when you finally get it." He chuckled. "That'd make our drapes salesman laugh his ass off."

He was breathing heavily, gulps of air that had nowhere to go in his tightly sprung body until he released his knees and flung back on the sand.

"It just sucks because I thought I was better."

"You *are* better." I had my eyes closed, leaning against my dead tree, with one of its angled exposed roots cutting into my lower back. It was always what he wanted, right? To be better than me? Than everyone. Fine, it was his. I wanted it for him. Right now, I wanted it more than anything. But opening my eyes I saw him standing above me with a rock the size of a softball in his tendon-strung hand.

"I'm not!" he said. "I'm broke."

That's when I finally saw that this ship was too big for me to steer. I was at his mercy, or rather at *the* mercy—of what, I wasn't sure yet. Whatever anxiety had been coiling in me while my brother talked now fingered into my lungs, up my esophagus, and around my liver and gutted me whole.

My brother sucked in his disgust. "Don't fucking cry like a fucking nancy," he said. "You wanted June, and what I'm saying is, you can have her."

I shook my head and wiped my face with sandy hands. Sand in my eyes now, to boot. "I don't want—"

"Oh you don't want her now, huh? Don't want her? That's why you're here and not in Montana? 'Came home to see how you're doing,' my ass. You came home to try to get her, to play mind games with all of us. Well, so, you're both fucked up. We're all fucked up. You can have her. You want my house too? My car?"

He shoved the rock down into his pants and fingered his keys out of his pocket. Something red on them, something bronze, a lot of brass, and the black hunk of Volvo key. "Go get it then!" he said. He danced a few steps and flung the whole set into the water.

He turned to me, seething, then back to the now-disappeared plop. He had to squint. He put his hands on his hips. He raised a hand to the breadth of water, and let it flap back to his side. "Aw crap," he said.

We didn't speak for a moment, me snuffling. His face in the sun was a stone carving, pale and chipped. It always had been. I had the creepy thought that somewhere, someplace, our drapes salesman might be wearing that same look, staring out over some body of water, or something else equally hard—probably, given today, a television.

"I'll go back to Montana," I said. "Everything can go back to normal."

He crossed his arms, gave me more of his broad back to look at. "There isn't any normal." He scanned the water, still pissed about the keys. "How can we go back to before you fucked my wife?"

He walked to me. When he got close, he was blurry to me. I wiped my eyes. My hand was hurting again, and the pain told me that maybe I could salvage things.

"I'm really," I said, "really really sorry. It was wrong. It was a mistake. She knows it too. But it's not part of some—"

"It wasn't a *mistake*. There aren't any *mistakes.*" He spit out the word, spraying my nose with its malice.

"Look at you," he said. "I hate you." He poked me in the chest. His breath smelled of mouthwash. "I was over it. I was done—all but the demo. And then you. I trusted you.

"I always get the bad break. If the drapes salesman had bothered to stick around, you'd be a computer tech or a librarian or something. No AP English for you, fatty. No Grinnell fucking College, because we'd have been poor. And me, I'd probably be in the major leagues because I wouldn't have had all Dad's Jewish bullshit fucking me up all the time, his strong-arm power bullshit, and so I would have actually played baseball instead of hating it. And I was fucking good!"

I needed to stand up now. I definitely needed to stand up. But he wouldn't stop squatting over me. It was like I was a work in progress or some curious laboratory specimen, his instruments waiting on a silver tray. I hung my head.

"I wouldn't have given a rat's ass about Treblinka, that's for sure. I would have said 'whatever' like everyone else. He was Polish, Hank. We are, I mean, by blood. Blonde, too. Aryan. Jew killers, not Jew stupes.

"I didn't fall while jogging, Hank. I jumped."

He sunk his head a little, scratching his chin on his shoulder.

"It was the right idea, just didn't quite do the job up to your satisfaction."

"Don't say that. I'm your brother."

"Why didn't you commit me, after seeing that, that monstrous thing I made? You should have wrapped me up!"

He said this last bit with a disheartening slur. "You're an artist," I said, very quietly.

He looked at me, eyebrows high, then waved me off, wrinkling his nose like he'd been hit with a snowball. He shook his head. "An artist. Maybe I'll be famous. Maybe I'll show 'Treblinka' at one of the Chelsea galleries." He threw his hands up. "New York City!" He looked at me. "What do you think my markup should be?"

I started to stand. I had the fuzzy idea of finding the keys and getting us out of here. There seemed little alternative. I guess I could have started shouting, but the Wisconsin shore was a mile away, and on it only modest docks on a rocky shore and a few houses peeking through foliage up the bluff. It was a day sealed in amber. "I'm going to find the keys," I said.

My brother shoved me down. "You don't go in the water," he said. He stood. He straightened his clothes. "I do. That's what it comes down to, all of this. What everyone wants. Besides," he pulled at his belt loops, "I'm the one with the rock in my crotch."

He grinned, more boyish than agitated now. He was sanguine, convivial, even when he turned then, and started walking.

"What are you doing?" I said.

But words had no meaning anymore. Goddamn words. They never add up.

So I stood too, and as my brother was taking his fifth or sixth step into the water, knee deep at best, his thighs splattering wet chino, I lowered, lunged, and tackled him.

At first my brother just punched me so he could stand again. With my legs dangling underwater, my arms around his waist, his wet chinos slapping me, everything offensively wet already, I barely felt it. A sound like china cracking, maybe underneath a towel, like the wedding glass under a napkin. I tried to hold on, but ended up down the ladder of my brother's frame, at his knees now, and gurgling water no longer clear but muddled with the sand and sediment we'd kicked up.

More cracking china, and we were farther out into the water. I went as slack as I could, actually getting some buoyancy in the water, still holding tight to the thick fabric of his pants, twisted now so that my brother had my cheek in his ass. One of his pocket rivets dented my nose, but I pressed into it harder. I was the barnacle on the whale, but trying to be the whale too. He could only go a few steps.

Everything gargled with cold water, a numbness, my clothes lapping it up. I concentrated only on making myself as heavy as possible.

"Stop!" he said. He laughed, then yelled again. "Cut it the fuck out! I just want to get the keys."

This was a lie—how did I know? My brother axing his ball-peen elbow into the top of my bent head.

Then I looked up at him, I don't know why. Maybe to strengthen my resolve—you're not getting in the water—or to gauge his. He seemed to have slackened some, too, but no: his elbow was still cocked. He squinted, saw the opening, and snapped another hit. This one like a gunshot, and I felt my eye move out of its socket. It was like my skull had sucked it in, tongued it, then spit it back out, not liking the taste. It's funny how you know where your eye is supposed to be, and where it's not supposed to be. It's not something anyone has to explain for you.

I slipped to his ankles. My face was below water now, my brother's legs bucking, scissoring. I had to turn my face up to get air, and I saw him say something to me, but I was half underwater, and with all the splashing I couldn't hear—I've always imagined it an apology for my eye, which if you saw it, even now, you'd probably apologize for it too.

His body was blocking out the sun. He was shaking his head a little, wincing up his face, eyebrows clumped, his shoulders already turning from me. His lips and mouth moving like a cow's. "Don't go," I said. Water in my throat now. His bone-white palm reaching for my face.

And with that, as it probably does in all people hanging on without hope, my strength just gave. No one willed it to happen. Everything in me just flushed, the plug pulled. I didn't even have what it took to grab the pant leg that flapped by my face, or the rock that could finally tumble out of them, now that I'd completely lost my grip.

When I could raise my head again, both elbows shipwrecked into damp sand, my face was lopsided with swelling, and I saw nothing in the river. Nothing that mattered at least. Green banks, some of them belted with sand, some not, and on the water that hard light, craggy as ice, unbroken across the many square miles between me and Wisconsin.

Chapter Thirty-One

All Terry had wanted to do, he would later tell us, was the right thing. The morning had a big problem to it, and when you have a problem, you ask for help. But at his apartment, there was no one for help, because that was living on your own. Mother had told him that, and June too—living on your own meant having less but more too. No one in your painting supplies ruining your brushes, but you have to make meals for yourself too, and turn off all the lights.

But when you have a problem, June had said, always always, you can come to her house. And always tell the truth about the problem because truth makes the problem easier to fix. These are always always the right things to do.

Terry knows he isn't smart. There are many things that go by the wayward side of him. He knows this. He does not know what most people "do for a living," as they say. No one bothers to tell him, usually, because they are too busy asking him questions about his life and his painting, but even when they do bother, he usually still won't understand completely, but he knows they are trying. Their faces take a certain look, drawn and slow. They talk slow, too. Simple. People used to call him simple. His father used to call him simple.

But he isn't simple. He knew, for instance, that the river looked very clean from high up on the Lake Street Bridge, but that if he were down next to it, in the sand or up in the weeds, it would be dirty with trash and other dirty stuff. It was a dirty river in many places, and living on his own meant he could go and clean it whenever he wanted to. That wasn't simple. And he knew that today had a problem sort of like the river's—he had taken buses to the Mia because Hank would not answer his phone, and at the Mia they said *The Mary and The Duck* had been taken for cleaning. They wouldn't let him see it. It was away. Away for cleaning. But how do you clean a painting? On the phone, Mother had told him not to worry; they are experts. But it's not like the river, not with a trash bag and rubber boots. And at his apartment the air felt dry and unbreathable, and he couldn't stop thinking about *The Mary And The Duck*.

He rang the doorbell to the Meyerson house, and it was Mr. Meyerson, and Terry started talking about it all. Mr. Meyerson had a cold, June had told him over the weekend. No, she had said it was like a cold. It might make him feel cranked. But he wasn't acting cranked now, or coughing or anything, which made Terry happier, since June wasn't home but up north for a small vacation.

Mr. Meyerson asked Terry if he ever wore anything but those boots, and Terry smiled. Then Mr. Meyerson told him to sit down and he would make coffee for them. Terry enjoyed coffee when it didn't make him feel too nerves. Half-caf, they told him to order. Half-caf mochachino with whip cream. Mr. Meyerson told him the problem in the painting was going to be okay, and that it would come back better and healthier. Like the river. Mr. Meyerson said it was the right thing to do, to come over, and to tell the truth about what was bothering him.

But then, in the kitchen, Mr. Meyerson was crying. Mr. Meyerson never cries. Terry sat on the couch in the living room. He didn't like to touch the couch too much with his hands because Mr. Meyerson made him feel that way, keeping his hands to himself. Like in the Mia, where you aren't supposed to touch anything— some things were okay to touch, but it was better to just make it everything in your mind. For sure not the paintings, though Terry had never wanted to touch *The Mary*. It was enough to touch it with his eyes. *The Mary* had a problem too that she was trying to find the right thing to do about. Terry didn't know what it was, but that was okay. Not understanding everything is okay. Kind of fun, actually. Painting Mr. Meyerson made him kind of fun, even with the cast. But the cast was gone now, which made it even stranger that Mr. Meyerson was crying. Terry looked to make sure his hands were clean, and they were.

Mr. Meyerson's crying made Terry think of the noisy radiator in his bedroom. The sounds were similar was what he meant. Both made him upset, which is different from sad. The right thing to do here was to not touch the couch no matter how clean his hands were, to try to make Mr. Meyerson feel better. Also maybe he could think about what problem he could tell about next.

That's when he thought about Hank in the towel.

Hank in the towel was a problem he hadn't thought about in a while, though he used to. He'd never seen any of the Meyersons in a towel like that, but it was more than that. When you're in a towel in a bathroom like that, you're supposed to be alone. Maybe with a spouse, because a spouse is someone who gets to be with you at times when no one else can, and gets to do things with you like sex, even though many people do sex without spouses, but really they aren't supposed to, not really really. But Hank was in a towel, and June was there with him, right beside him. She had wet hair, and he did too. It should have been Mr. Meyerson in the towel with the wet hair.

It was a pretty good problem, and so Terry didn't even drink his coffee when Mr. Meyerson put it on a coaster on the coffee table. Coffee on the coffee table made him feel okay to talk again, so he did. People have always told him he was a good talker, and at first it was good, because Mr. Meyerson stopped looking about to cry again and smiled, and he doesn't normally smile, so Terry kept on talking.

But something changed when Mr. Meyerson asked him, "My brother was wearing a towel?"

Terry didn't feel like talking anymore. But it wasn't the right thing to do to lie, and Terry had just spoken the truth. It wasn't even what is called a "white lie," which is sometimes okay but not really, like when people have sex without their spouses.

So, "Yes," he'd said.

And Mr. Meyerson had said, "My brother, Hank, was in the bathroom, and Mrs. Meyerson was in there too, and Hank was wearing a towel?"

Mr. Meyerson likes Terry to call June Mrs. Meyerson, and so he does, but not in his own head. Terry said, yes.

"And only a towel?"

Yes.

"And he closed the door right away?"

Yes.

And then Mr. Meyerson walked around the house and said things to no one. Most of it was things Terry didn't understand, because there are lots of things Terry doesn't understand. He likes to make paintings of things he understands, but then Hank had said to go ahead and paint things he didn't understand, and it made no sense at all until it did once Mother had explained it some more—how it could be kind of fun.

When Mr. Meyerson took Terry to the garage and took off his boots and used duck tape on his mouth and then guided him into the trunk, Terry had assumed that somewhere, at some point, he had been mistaken about the right thing to do. So he rode quietly, even when he heard Hank's voice, but when it was hard to breathe and he started to hurt—and June had told him that it was never okay to be hurt and that always the right thing to do was to say when you're hurt because she and everyone at the House loved him and didn't want him to hurt because that's what it means to love someone, that you don't want that someone to hurt, not even a little—so when Terry finally started to hurt in a way he thought people would call "real bad," he had to trust that the right thing to do was to bang and bang and bang so he could get out of the trunk and maybe find Mr. Meyerson and Hank and explain some more about how sorry he felt about making what people call a "big stink" about *The Mary and The Duck*, that it must be one of those things he doesn't understand, and also to say that Hank in the towel must also be one of those things he doesn't understand and that he was sorry for thinking that not understanding could be kind of fun. It wasn't.

It hurt his hand so much to bang that way, but he didn't have his boots on and so it had to be his hand. Even hearing one of the car's windows smash didn't stop him. Not even the trunk opening to daylight again, the man in the uniform telling him to calm down. Still Terry banged. He banged the daylight; he banged the man. He didn't have words for all this anymore, *The Mary and the Duck* and Mr. Meyerson and cleaning and Hank. They ripped off the tape; they held him down on the cement. And still he had no words. He only had banging.

Chapter Thirty-Two

My father woke that day in a hotel room in Wamego, Kansas. Since Carlton's in-laws lived there, he usually stopped for the night toward the end of his road-trip tour of accounts. After the Oklahoma triangle, then Wichita and a couple days in Kansas City, it was a final stretch of Lawrence, Manhattan, and Salina, plus all the rinky-dinks along the way. It wasn't so bad, once you got over the idea of an entire day only advancing you two or three hundred miles. But spending the time was what the whole strategy was all about—those accounts aren't going to kibitz themselves, and anyway, time he had. Time was his business partner.

That said, he was relieved that June's parents were on vacation, in Japan of all places. He could do without the visit this go round— it would pain him to make small talk with them and have it turn to his son and the new toy. What would he say? It didn't sit well with him that Carlton had kept him in the dark this long. It's not what a son does, and anyway it shouldn't be some big secret—it was a toy, an idea, and half the ideas out there flop. Then the kid calls Friday and says he needs his father up there over the weekend. Won't say why. The toy's ready? Close, he says. Well, I'll come next weekend. But next weekend isn't good enough; it has to be this weekend.

What's so special about this weekend? Can't say, the kid says, and gets choked up but acts like it's nothing, no big deal, come when you wanna come. Click goes the phone, and nothing since.

Always a prima donna, Carlton. His terms, his way. And so far it's worked well for him. But that doesn't mean Daniel Meyerson, the kid's father don't forget, is going to shaft his accounts and drive straight to Minneapolis like there's some catastrophe. It's his retirement he's working for, after all, and no one's going to pay it for him.

He still did the run that June's father had recommended on his first visit. He parked downtown on Lincoln and Fourth, then went east on Fourth through the older homes with wide porches and impressive profiles, then out Military Trail past the defunct Sinclair station with the old-time pump like a tombstone with a bowling ball on top. It's a nice, picturesque road once you get out past the ten or twenty acres of new-development housing, which he appreciated even less having been told about the leaky skylights and nasty covenant skirmishes. After that it gets rural pretty quickly along the flats of the Little Arkansas River.

Back at the car he was feeling good. He got a juice at the Espresso Hut, applauded Lincoln Street's irrational cheer, and got back to his hotel refreshed. The woman who ran the place, Candace, had been putting him in the same room since the first time he'd stayed there and had made the mistake of praising it. The décor was all white with a tacky seashore theme, right down to the wooden seagull wearing a triple-looped string of pearls, whom he named Sparky. There was a poor beat-up fake plant, and a luggage rack on the wall that looked about as sturdy as cardboard. But there was also an old chair, like something Susie's mother would have had, that was actually comfortable, and the armrests were well placed for reading. And the little side table had a candy dish holding seashells, but the dish itself was green and reminded him of his grandmother's candy dish, the grandmother his kids had been blessed to know before she suffered a stroke. The point was that this was *somebody's* candy dish, and somebody's chair, and the somebody-ness gave the room authenticity. Still, he always took the bedspread off, right away, because he knows what makes margins, and washing bedspreads every day ain't it.

Of course, he would never have tolerated a motel like this when Susie was alive. With her comfort to consider, he wouldn't be such a chiseler. Forty bucks difference to stay at the Courtyard Marriot ten miles away in Manhattan? Big deal. Love gives you high standards. Susie didn't demand it or kvetch about it—she just deserved it. But without her, there just wasn't as much of a point. Besides, he got to stick to his principles this way: mom-and-pop shops all around. He'd rather have principles than standards, plus a wooden seagull that cracked him up.

But now the shabbiness of his room was giving him pause. He felt constricted, conspicuous. He had five accounts to get to before home, which meant seeing his boys was a good week away. Sparky the seagull looked tired, and those pearls ridiculous. These accounts don't kibitz themselves, he started to explain, but that was ridiculous too.

He was well into Iowa before he realized his decision. Instead of heading west from Wamego into Manhattan, he'd doubled back east, to Kansas City and north onto I-35. The freeway creased through northern Missouri's sun-swaddled hills, bathing him along in green Midwestern waves. He made his calls, lied a little, but they understood. Everything could be done over the phone, if need be. Even kibitzing.

And the neighbor girl could watch the cats a few more days— she'd want the extra money for the new jeans her parents wouldn't buy. And besides, the world should extend itself for you once in a while, especially when you ask so rarely. Ask more than rarely, it starts to sound like a complaint.

It was against his principles to complain. Writing your own catalog headlines and item copy? Last-minute "partnership dollars" to pay for D4236 toxicology testing? The office won't let you do December terms? Fine, fine, and fine. He had the relationships, he knew his margins, he'd make it work.

But sometimes it's not so much complaining as seeing life for what it really is, and adjusting. He decided to make a list, not of complaints, but of lamentations. During the High Holy days, the congregation repeats, in unison, lists of *Al Chait*—we have sinned. It's a long list, which makes sense, trying to be comprehensive, and he usually intoned along like everyone else, but really—xenophobia? Idle gossip? Mistreating animals? They weren't for him. His list had some personality. His list was principled.

First on the list: when people asked if he didn't want to move to Minneapolis to be near the boys, maybe retire there, he said no because in truth he was scared. The house he hadn't changed since Susie died, not even the plates, was a sanctuary of sorts. Why? Because, though he occasionally went to shul and certainly respected God for his abundance and so on, when he prayed, he prayed to Susie. And the house just made it easier. Even the cats—they were Susie's from the start, but he kept on adopting them, running the Humane Society's 10k every year. Abraham the bearded intellectual, Tico the scrawny trickster. He kept their original names, the way Susie liked. She said it was more fun to find out who they are, rather than to make it up from scratch. Oh what a woman he'd lost! And what was he going to do, go on a date, to the Oakview Movie Complex with the stadium seating and the ten-dollar popcorn? He couldn't even accept the rabbi's invitation, offered once or twice, to come over for Shabbat dinner—what was he, too good to eat with a rabbi? Maybe he should get out more, knock heads with more than the regulars and the crazies at the JCC gym.

That he could decide on later. For now, the list.

Second lamentation: we are always, every man, woman, and child, at someone else's mercy. At this last St. Louis sales meeting, he'd run into a guy he used to buy from who had just joined the company from Mattel. Big Jewish big shot, the expense account they gave him, the office furniture allowance, and probably other deals not disclosed to compensate for the transfer to St. Louis. "Didn't you used to have a store in Omaha or some *gehockte* place like that?" the guy asked, straightening his tie. Didn't work out, Daniel told him. "Ah, it's a tough business for most people." That really salted Daniel, that "for most people." Oh, everyone has a needle to stick you with, and sharp too. And it only gets worse, until you're being told by some doctor on the bureaucratic dole that your bladder doesn't work.

Third lamentation: Somehow along the roads here he had forgotten that he was a man of great love and generosity. Great reserves, too. To shutter up Kidsville and go to work as a rep in the very industry that kicked your ass—talk about reserves. He'd gorged on reserves! And then right at the start of it to lose the wife he'd been lucky enough to find on the doorstep of his good-for-nothing youth. How he'd jumped at the chance of her—no, *demanded* it. Telling his father he was going to marry a *shiksa* and adopt her two kids, both blonde as Easter? That took guts. Taking over the store, too. Learning his management skills on the fly. Instituting changes, increasing margins, studying up on VOP and cost per square foot. He had lived in generous respect for the life that had been handed him, and he had wrung it for every return. He participated to the best of his soul's abilities, breaking it into submission and bringing his family—his family, he was proud to call them—every step of the way. When there was a mall fashion show, his kids were in it, in Kidsville clothes. TV commercials too—Carlton in a yellow turtleneck twisting a Christmas tree ornament to reveal a neon starburst "20% off!" So, stores come and stores go, but family mattered most. Someone goes to the doctor and finds out he has a brain tumor, who does he call first thing? His broker? His boss? This was why the consequences were so high with Carlton—he'd invested so much into the kid, and to questionable ROI, like a classic car, dropping in resale value with every piston thrust.

Daniel Meyerson didn't like cars. Ridiculously dumb inventions. So much steel and power with nothing but morality, common sense, and meaningless misdemeanors to keep the idiots from killing someone. And then when they do, it's called an "accident." You kill someone with your car, driving like Mad Max, and the police say, "These things happen" and send you home to your family. People have told Daniel that when a driver causes an accident like the one that took Susie, they "feel awful." Them? To hell with *them!* They feel awful until their wives bring them an iced tea at the end of a hard day. That's about as awful as they feel. Awful enough to remodel the kitchen and take a Mexican vacation and steal a long afternoon to make love. They may lie awake at nights, but eventually what do they do? They sleep. They sleep plenty.

He sighed, driving due north into the coming night. Humans— what a piece of work. Evolved our way to top of the animal kingdom, then created this magnificent democracy—so we could do what, exactly? Pie eating contests and get-rich-quick schemes and changing the definition of overweight and how to find the cheapest crib, even by pennies, no matter if the kid selling it to you can't tell you word one about it, can't even read the box, probably, or if the mattress was sewn by some Chinese worker chained to her machine just waiting to chew her arm off. And to what end? The toy they had him pushing this season, ho boy. A ten-inch Mylar ball with a floating cube inside printed with words telling the kid what to do with the ball. Bounce twice. Throw to friend. Bounce off knee. "Great for building reading and math skills," was the angle.

Carlton would understand this, he felt. He wished they could talk about it, just *talk* talk. How long would the kid have to rely on his old man for support and confidence. Wasn't that what the wife was for? How he was itching to hear the kid say, "Enough Dad! I can take care of myself." All those afternoons folding clothes with his mother and mornings making her blintzes. Daniel Meyerson never got a blintz. He got the business end of his son, teaching him a three-point stance and studying for pointless exams. Asking him where his homework was, and whether he'd done it, and the kid evading and making excuses, a regular Bill Clinton. Of course he'd been a star on the ball diamond. But there are physical and mental aspects to the game, which is why baseball players are on the whole so goddamn boring—you can blame the knee, but you have to be resolute, smart, and stable. So, he wasn't stable. Big deal. He's still a success. Daniel couldn't even recall a brilliant play from his son's

Hutchinson years, when not long ago his head had been like a movie screen of them: his graceful son, steely eyed and flexible, shooting the ball to left-center. The coach had even put him in for an entire second game of a double-header, probably because his father was there.

Daniel had to admit, he never went to Grinnell to watch Hank shlep into Burling Library and churn out a semester's worth of writing overnight. But Hank just needed to understand the difference—with brains comes responsibility. The capable suffer more. Just look at Auschwitz: the weak go to the gas chambers and are put out of their misery, while the capable work the factory and burn the bodies. And God help you if you bucked the odds long enough to see liberation. A lifetime of remembering insanity—talk about suffering.

And besides, it was more *tsuriss* with Carlton—just this past month, Daniel Meyerson had gotten a stone wall. When it was him who'd gotten the kid fixed in the first place! Recently widowed and slack-faced and over-starched, he needed that kid going off the deep end like he needed a hole in the head. Every morning, teary and mute. Hell of an appetite, though, and that's what gave hope. Daniel fed him left and right—ribs and fettuccine and chicken breasts on the grill and chimichangas and everything—and made him exercise, and just used good old common sense. Diluting down the vodka bottles in his room, hidden so carefully under the mattress, or so the kid thought, with half-water. This was Daniel's kind of due diligence, until one day his son's at the dinner table, sitting before thickly sliced flank steak and new potatoes and fettuccini Alfredo— he asks for seconds, then bursts into tears. But it was a different kind of crying. He was crying because he was clear now, and ashamed. And—and—because he'd seen cause and effect: he'd had a problem, and he'd let his old man fix it. What most kids take for granted, he'd never learned. Say what you want, but when there's cause and effect in your world, there's sanity. Where there's a father, there's hope.

This was why it was so important to be principled, all the way around the board. It was principled to stay in Candace's motel with the stuffed cougar instead of the Super 8 with the stuffed nothing.

But it was also principled to recognize that the place was a dumparino and he was debasing himself by staying there, and all the little other dumparinos too, just to save a few bucks and get a friendly hello and chuckle at the stuffed wildlife. It was principled to recognize that you were lonely and cut off and you'd never have let yourself be this way if your wife were alive. Where there's a father, there's hope, and you don't want to jeopardize that, and the truth was, he was jeopardizing it. Admitting so, driving all day and night like this to rectify it right away, was particularly principled, and it pained him like the truck-stop coffee he was drinking—so hot it spit *him* out.

Finally the traffic of the Twin Cities. The buildings of Minneapolis twinkling like flared targets. His boys would be impressed— it wasn't the weekend, but he'd still gotten here pretty quick, huh? And with his back killing him too, just a bear hug of pain. It was his burden, maybe, but he could carry it fine. He would simply show up, if they wanted him or not. Show up and do whatever it took, even if it's going for bagels. Get the toy finished, that's the main thing. After all, it's kids we're talking about—they deserve better than a ball that tells you how to play with a ball.

His cell phone rang on the seat next to him. He kept to 35W's right-hand lane, saw it was June calling from her cell phone. He had finally gotten all his important numbers programmed into his phone—a kid in the St. Louis office had whizzed him through it, and now he was even more thankful. He looked at what mile marker he was passing, so he could boast where he was, exactly, as soon as he pushed the green button.

Chapter Thirty-Three

Only children and people like Terry need hospital rooms explained for them. The rest of us, life teaches us, at some point or another. Besides, what's to know? You get sick, you go there to get better—which some people do, and some people don't. Best not to think about it.

I had only made it up to the old right-of-way trail before the park ranger found me—I kept falling down, and dimming out a while. Each time I'd start to think about the water, cold and white in my face, and that was when I'd try to stand up again and walk down the trail in a way that didn't hurt my head quite so fantastically. The ranger's quickening footsteps in the ashy gravel were the clatter-crunch of a confident man discovering a situation beyond what he'd expected. What a freaking weird day for him—ranger training probably hadn't covered a developmentally disabled individual taped up in the trunk of a Volvo.

Now I was being held for observation at the closest in-network provider, a Catholic hospital in downtown Saint Paul. The ranger had driven me, since the logistics of the ambulance ride were a nightmare and I responded appropriately to his smelling salts. The room in the five-story south wing was small and all my own. It just so happens they had an orbital-facial specialty team. I'd be seeing the surgeon in the morning.

Terry was sitting in the corner in a padded chair, but he shifted like it was hard plastic. He wanted to know why everything in a hospital was white.

"Not everything is," I said. "The TV is black."

He had already asked all the what's-that-do? questions, and I had admitted ignorance whenever possible. It hurt to talk still, but not nearly like it had before. He was just anxious and upset, and this was how it was coming out. There was a comfort to it.

"Does your eye hurt, Hank?" he asked.

"Not really. They gave me medicine for it."

They'd given me what they could, but no narcotics, on account of the Percocet-spiked whiskey in my system still. You'd figure that one would be tough to explain, but the admitting nurse just nodded like I was in to check my cholesterol. In the paltry bed I felt heavier than usual. Talking hurt like chewing tinfoil. It felt like they'd clotted up my sinuses with brambles and soap.

I didn't know what June had told him about me and my wounds. The search for Carlton had been called off for the night, making him officially a missing person.

"What's the name of this place?" Terry asked.

Believe it or not, I was ignorant of that too. "June?" I said.

June was sitting at the window, not in the wooden chair with padded upholstery the color of chewed gum, but in the ledge. Its inset silver heating vent ran to and under her ass. The window, black with night, held her head up. She was looking out, and crying, I was sure.

"St. Joseph's," she said.

"What was he a saint of?" Terry asked her.

I would talk for her. "Hospitals."

Terry squirmed. He kicked his legs up, one after the other. Then he inspected his boots for scuffs. There were none.

"What kind of tree was that at the forest that I sat under?"

The ranger had stationed Terry near the parking lot, telling him not to move.

"Mulberry," June said.

"But there wasn't any fruit."

At these words, my father burst into the room. I winced, and Terry flinched. The door leaned hard into its rubber stopper, the handle mechanics snapping. The fabric of our Q&A time fell from the walls and puddled around us, leaving Dad standing there like a clothed man among nudists. He was trying not to breathe too hard, though he'd probably taken the stairs, as it was only three floors.

He didn't like the sight of Terry. It was his nature not to like surprises, or folly. As a kid, I used to make tent forts in the basement with old sheets tucked into the couch's crevices and tied to curtain rods, or sometimes weighted on the mantel with Dad's barbells. He asked me once if a barbell were to fall on my head, how much would I like forts then?

He put his hands on his hips. His clothes had the appearance of being somebody else's. "What happened to you?" he said to me. "Why aren't we searching anymore?" He looked at June. "You said everyone's searching."

I understood why he couldn't keep his trap shut. With his adrenaline and concern and just sheer desire to lend his expertise, afford some stability to this situation—what was he supposed to do, sniff his way in like a field mouse?

"Who the hell is he?" He pointed.

Terry went straighter than the chair he was sitting.

"That's Terry."

My father nodded at him. He surveyed the room. That dawning of consciousness, that moment when you don't know yet, but you do, set upon him hard. He shifted his weight, and tilted nearer the wall, as if he were about to collapse. It's not something children should ever see in their parents.

"I don't get it," he said.

June would tell me later, much later, that she had been in a kind of catatonia during those hours. Her father-in-law bursting in, challenging her—she felt herself enraged at him without knowing for sure why, except of course the obvious. But she could neither move nor speak. Uttering the hospital name and "mulberry" had drained her.

The window she was sitting in faced southwest, and she could see the butt end of a church across the street. Its dual steeple was taller than our height on the hospital's third floor, and its fenced parking lot and squat stone outbuildings gave it the feel of a compound. Further west, she could see the broad side of the Dorothy Day Center. She could tell because a line of the poor, homeless, and otherwise destitute flanked around it—for admittance to the shelter or only a meal, it was hard to tell. They stood orderly, smoking, almost all of them men. They shuffled and watched the night, each in their own directions.

No body yet. He's a good swimmer was what she was thinking. Those arms, whose comfort was undeniable, though she had denied it—they had probably carried him a long way. He wasn't in shape, but he'd had this weird energy for months, and he had used it to accuse her of all sorts of sins. Whispering so neighbors wouldn't hear, he was so *mad* at her. Why didn't she want a child? And she must be in cahoots with the old man, or taken a lover—was that it? Had she planned this from the start, this sabotage?

Sabotage? Had he really said that? It seemed improbable now, and yet wasn't it the truth?

Every day it was the same shit, about the toy, the money, the old man, having a baby. He'd yell. Like, *yell* yell. And afterward he would admit he'd been talking crazy, he was stressed—the new toy, his father, the money, the baby. There were always so many stresses, always on him. One time she'd asked him, "What are they? What can I do to help?" He'd just hugged her, those arms like calamine to her skin, and said it was just stress. Let me make you feel better, she'd said, like I used to. Remember when I used to? Yes, you always could make me feel great, a king. You still do. He had loved her since he blew his knee, he'd said. It didn't matter if they didn't know each other then— it was a different kind of truth; time had nothing to do with it.

That's when they made love for the first time in a long while. At least she had that. Were his last thoughts, far out in the water, of that moment? Or did he swallow a mouthful of betrayal? It had to be admitted, probably the latter. To die rejected, can there be anything worse? No, she was thinking. There can't be any worse way to die than that, with the thought that it was for the best, for everyone involved—it was what everyone wanted anyway.

This kind of grief, it can't be shared, no matter how long it lasts. This was why Daniel Meyerson made her so angry, she realized. When he finally broke down—and he would: she could already see his proud face crumple, as clearly as she could see Carlton's going confused, underwater—she didn't want to be the one to hold his hand, console him. It was her grief, and she'd cling to it like a life vest or a windowsill. Consoling Daniel Meyerson—that was Hank's job. If he didn't do it, she would never speak to him again.

Not speaking had gotten her here, though. Not speaking to her husband about who he was, what he was feeling, what he was making her feel. There was quirkiness in every marriage, she'd told herself. Quirkiness. Every marriage becomes its own language—she'd read that. You create your own unique way of doing things, and a little nuttiness is bound to be included. That's what she'd said to herself. But maybe it was like Grandpa's dementia—no one wanted to deal with it, look it in the eyes, and in the meantime he's brushing his teeth fifteen times a day. Was it like that? Was Carlton so bad as that? All the things Hank had recounted, his ramblings on the beach before getting into the water—could they have been there all along? Wasn't it her job to see them and act accordingly? Good Christ, your husband begins acting strangely and you kick him out of the house? She should have seen. Talk about sabotage! She should have asked, nagged, talked around, taken charge. Isn't that what a wife does? Isn't that her job?

She'd never been confrontational. Running up here from Kansas to escape Wyatt—what did she expect? Abandoning her job just because it didn't make sense to Carlton. Then, of course, Hank. It was all running. Funny how you can think of it as standing up for yourself against a bully—someone whom you love but have to level the playing field with—and be so wrong. You were never bullied. You were selfish and deceitful. Sabotage.

Her head had started to vibrate then, a vertigo of ridiculousness, and she had to close her eyes, but that was no good either. So she watched out the window, all the lights of St. Paul—so many for such a homely city. They made for enough light to see a woman, a nurse or orderly, smoking in a doorway across the street. She shifted her weight, and her badge reflected like a burst from a flashlight. Down the street, parked at a meter, was a white pickup with rusting wheel wells and one tire very low on air. And then that line of aid-seekers at the Dorothy Day Center. They hadn't advanced at all. What if that's the way it was going to be from now on: all need ignored, all tenderness stagnant? What if we'd finally used up all the goodness, dried like a puddle, deflated like a tire? This made her close her eyes, finally—the lines of hurt and anger, betrayal and injustice, everywhere elongating, and everywhere dismissed. The shuffling bureaucratic endlessness of suffering. Hers began tonight.

I wish she had said something while feeling all this, though of course she couldn't articulate it. And when she could, for a long time, she simply wouldn't—forcing me to resort to reading that stolen Word document, which of course didn't have this day's thoughts, but still, it was enough. I read with the best of intentions and also with no small amount of self-flagellation. The long, illicit process of figuring exactly what it is you've lost.

But at this moment, I at least had a little more faith in humanity. The great thing about this human life we've created, for better or for worse, is that there's usually someone more committed than you, someone more compassionate and composed. Especially in times of crisis. My old man was on the phone with the Goodhue County sheriff right then, saying we needed to partner on this thing, maybe send just one boat to go out and shine its light into the bank brush, because his son wasn't like that—he might simply be disoriented or uncommunicative, because it had happened before, though he got better.

Then he was holding my hand, of all things, because somewhere there in the middle of all this I'd started weeping. "Shhh," he said. "Come on."

My father was dipping into himself in ways he probably thought he'd never have to again. People like him keep us on our feet. In the soup kitchens, in the hospices, in the boardrooms and church pews too—there's no end to the human struggle they're able to face. Go ahead, line up the suffering, bring it on by the boxcar. Someone will be there to shoulder it, for the time being at least. Until it's your turn.

It was a good three weeks later that my father and I went to my brother's studio. It needed to be done, after all. The survivors suffer.

I took the elevator, complaining of a headache still. My father chose the stairs and was waiting for me. My eye was still bandaged from the retinal reattachment surgery, and the sixth floor's hallway seemed dimmer for that reason, and less substantial too. My left eye gave it a valiant effort, then gave up, and I had to watch the carpet at our feet.

We stopped outside the door, reinforced with sliding bars to keep panicked, gasping Jews from pounding it down. Quite a strength some humans find—this the Nazis had learned and had adapted accordingly.

My father took a big breath. He had misjudged his son, overestimated him colossally. How colossally, he was about to see. No one would inform the authorities.

We'd requested a wheelbarrow from the super, and I'd rented a small Dumpster. Both were waiting out back at the loading dock. I'd borrowed some tools from the stash at Carol Ann's, and my father held the five-gallon bucket of them in front of him like a briefcase.

He sighed again as I fumbled with Carlton's key in the lock. It wouldn't turn at first, but then it caught a few tumblers and just needed to be jimmied the rest of the way. Cajoling a cranky lock and waiting patiently. These are among the innumerable things in life that no one tells us how to do. They perturb and persist, but eventually we just get a feel for them, each of us in our own separate way.

PART FIVE

Sick Like Emily Dickinson

Chapter Thirty-Four

I love to fly. Even with the security hassles and the bureaucracies thick as the Dutch East India Company, and even though it makes me queasy when my disability is waxing.

It's not a huge deal, my disability, but certainly a downer. It's a consequence, they think, of my second eye operation, performed six months after my brother's death. An infection. The surgeon wiped his nose, or I didn't posture correctly and the gas bubble went wonky. Or maybe it took hold, before all that, in the shallows of the St. Croix River. Who knows? Modern medicine is not so fancy. End result is I had some nerve damage and/or brain damage, and began suffering dizziness, depth-perception issues, numbness of the roof of my mouth, vertigo, some dyskinetic shakes in the extremities, and the farts. Though the farts are probably unrelated.

It tends to come and go on its own too. Sometimes I am fine, cheerful and ambulant as anyone; other times I struggle. And I am not foolish enough to think it should be otherwise. Still, a little elucidation would be nice—all they seem to do is advise against driving a car, and prescribe medicines that sometimes are worse than the symptoms. Headaches, drowsiness, some hallucinations, and all that. They're even starting to think maybe I have an autoimmune disease, my T-reg cells somehow compromised by the trauma in my retina—or as one doctor said, "Could be it was there all along, and the eye infection just kicked into gear." Which would be nice because then I could blame the drapes salesman.

It does have its entertaining moments. The drugs I take sometimes throw me some curve, turning a trick of light into a frontal lobe adventure. One time in an American Themes class, one of my students raised her hand, and when I looked her way, she was a chipmunk, slinky in her desk, bulged in the cheeks, and wholesomely furry. I was not alarmed. So, she's a chipmunk—what's to do? I just waited it out, smiled as she squeaked out a smart little observation concerning Saul Bellow's style and subject matter (i.e. his style *is* his subject matter), and soon enough she was a young woman again. A mere moment of annoyance, no worse than shmutz in the keyboard of my laptop computer.

To fly, though, I have to beg off the medication since I can't afford to fall asleep, or worse—it's one thing to have a student turn into a chipmunk; it's another thing altogether when the marketing shlep in 10B does it. And traveling makes me emotional enough.

Back at JFK, I was buying a *New York Times* in a little shop where the guy ahead of me in line—balding, gray-faced in a gray raincoat—was buying a mug. And what did the mug say, when he set it down on the scanner so that its red Helvetica Bold lettering could be read? "Happiness is being married to your best friend." Oh, you poor sorry son of a bitch: happiness *is* being married to your best friend, until, that is, you bring home a cheap-ass gift like that. See where the happiness goes then. But my thing is, he looked so *earnest,* this guy, though he wouldn't meet me in the eyes—his way of apologizing for my sturdy black cane, I suppose. The way his hands treasured the mug, his politeness with the clerk, the way he asked for gift wrap, the way he looked at his feet when he was smugly told that there was no gift wrap, like a script he had no creative control over. What are the darknesses that deaden our joy? Are they so singular, so idiosyncratic, that each of us must confront them ourselves, without help from society, government, or

Hollywood? Probably, and this is what air travel reveals—people at their thinking-of-you worst, ground up by gears too large to be seen in their entirety. But I didn't get to talk to him, tell him it's all right, even if he'd listen, because airports aren't supposed to be revelatory, and because I needed my *New York Times.* Mr. Mug Lover seeped away, into the sad semaphoric choreography of moving walkways and rolled luggage, like spilled water on an old gray deck. Oh well. Maybe I caught him on an off day or at the end of a particularly bad trip. And maybe the wife is one of those women who is quick to understand the humor in things, one of those rare people who trust your underlying goodness enough to see sentiment *and* stupidity. Or maybe he brings her home some ironic bit of crap everywhere he goes, some laughable trinket. Maybe it's a thing they do.

But that's me just trying to make the unknowable a little rosier. I spent several recent years trying, for instance, to understand my brother. Probably out of guilt, or some vague hope of solace. I'd pilgrimage to places he'd spent time: Hutchinson, Kansas, for instance. A fruitless town, home to salt mines and a state penitentiary and peculiarly bleak struggle. The campus is a wedge of squat buildings and re-sodded lawn just north of downtown. I ate lunch in the cafeteria, which was bright and chattery with student vitality—mostly jocks in sweatpants, boisterous in their rehashing of a particularly funny interaction with Coach. A few kids eating alone, looking around, smirking and then catching themselves in the smirk. The campus seemed to leave room for despair, if you were so inclined.

The town too. It felt disconnected somehow, with disappearing edges and interstitial meanderings where seedy, decrepit wasteland seemed to thrive—whole buildings with no tenants but a few water heaters crowding the cracked second-story windows. Businesses with hand-written signs offering you a great rate, or your first karate lesson free, especially for kids! Guys in work shirts slinking down Avenue A, hands in their pockets, caps low, headed for Salt City Automotive after giving me a glare. I went to the Cosmosphere and Space Center, which I know my brother visited at least once.

I went out to the baseball stadium too, which isn't on campus but southeast of town and paltry enough to make you cry for the kids who devoted their entire lives to baseball only to wind up here. Alone on the diamond—I had pushed through the fence's weak spot—everything has one—the towering light poles swayed in the wind with their lonesome cables clanking like the grommets of a forgotten flag. The parking lot didn't even have yellow lines painted on it. The press box was accessed by a ladder. I was thinking, you come here, you hardly get to play, you're Jewish and, just in general, a little weird and not as good as the other guys and fucking up in practice and smart but getting bad grades. I could see it damaging him. Just standing there damaged me.

But in truth, what did I learn from such a trip? Nothing. You can stand in a place, delineate its emotional geometries, and still find yourself lost. In the Cosmosphere museum, for instance, I could imagine all sorts of extravagant delusions—the exhibits explain the chronology of the space race, starting with the V1 and V2 missiles that the Nazis used to bombard London, and the whole thing is windowless and underground, essentially a curvy maze about as wide in most spots as a submarine and lit no better. Gizmos blink, pathways dead-end mysteriously, mission-ready seconds of satellites and space vehicles sulk behind glass, videos of presidential speeches are playing, recordings of Houston-astronaut conversations too, and there's acreage after acreage of ramblingly exultant didactics, rife with typos—it's enough to make anyone panic a little, and I could easily see Carlton feeling…what? I can imagine it, but I can't feel it. I can't substantiate it. The dead don't witness. Even at the Blue Dragon baseball stadium, cold and alone at second base—the dead just don't fucking witness.

This is why I never tried to track down the drapes salesman. Who needs him? And anyway, that was the whole point in the first place—there *was* no drapes salesman. Once he left, he was null and void—the damage done. Trying to conjure my brother conjuring him was like trying to understand Captain Ahab by going fishing. I even went so far as to call my father out of the blue—we had not talked in a while—to tell him that the drapes salesman may have weighed heavily on my brother's mind, but not mine. I've actually never thought twice about it, I told him. He, Daniel Meyerson, was my father, and my *father* father too. Period.

"I know that," he'd snapped. I don't begrudge him that—it was a rough time for him back then. And anyway he recovered enough to add, while I was still on the phone, "That's good, though." He sighed. "That's what we were shooting for."

Father father. Words, which used to be so paltry to me, now stab with power. But here's the rub: words speak, but the listener understands or doesn't or couldn't care less—those are really the only three options. Words only really exist inside us, in the dark wells where we go either to make our recognitions, or else to ignore them and weep for what we don't know—holding tight to our little mugs of "I love you."

Yes, airplanes make me melodramatic. The orderly shepherding of souls, none of us less humiliated than the other. The buckled-in buffet of strangers you may perish with. Not to mention the fact that, feeling a little wobbly at boarding, I had to be fetched by the attractive flight attendant and helped down the ramp. She was snippy about it, too, getting me to my seat behind first class, walking me like she held a racketball between her thighs. No one wants to be that guy. No one wants to be at the mercy of the thoroughly ambulant—the woman one row behind me, who can't seem to finish her orange juice before the plane jerks to a stop at the gate and she stands with juice and book in hand, spilling juice on my goddamn head. And get this: The book? *How to See Yourself As You Really Are* by His Holiness the Dalai Lama. There he is, on the cover, with the perpetual smile and the bad glasses, and I want to say, hey lady, I'm no expert, but don't you think that His Holiness would tell you the path to seeing yourself as you really are probably requires that you watch what the fuck you're doing?

And in addition to all this, because I couldn't make it onto the plane under my own volition, upon landing I have been classified by the new, improved Great Falls International Airport as a Type C1 passenger, which means I must be accompanied by some slack-jawed airline employee until such time as an authorized guardian, spouse, or caregiver can sign for me, no better than a bicycle in a box!

So, safely off the plane and wheelchaired in my Slack Jaw's care, I register my complaint by telling him I have to poop. Sharing such privacies is something I learned to accept a while ago, and anyway, since we're early, I want to clean up from the spilled orange juice and get myself as presentable as possible. Slack Jaw mumbles a lighthearted assent, and off we go.

One thing about my disability is that I move through time differently. Time is a collectible, as tactile as any other element. It enfolds me like sheets sun-dried on a clothesline, and I can always pull a handful of its calm freshness toward me and breathe it in. How else could I suffer the indignity of Slack Jaw wheeling me into the cold, bright restroom reeking of antiseptic, an indignity I'm as grateful for as I am disgusted? He guides me hand in armpit from chair to handicapped toilet stall, from whence I can manage on my own, to our mutual relief.

I don't bother to cover the toilet seat but just ago ahead and sit, turning myself with the aid of the finely lathed tubular guide rails. Now that I'm safely on the ground and under supervision, I can take my pills, so I do, without water, watching Slack Jaw through the stall door crack as he slacks his jaw in his stained white polo with the airline's logo at left teat. He has a flyboy crew cut—perhaps he has aspirations, and if so, good for him. I let loose some gassy stool with a sound like you'd imagine, and I see him wince and change position against the wall. But I can't be the worst he's encountered, can I, given his role with the airline? At least he doesn't have to help me clean my ass crack.

When I finish, and my pants are back up more or less where they should be, I take some moments. Remember what I said about time? It's not a metaphor—it's life practice. Slack Jaw can just deal with it.

Fuming, recapturing my breath, there with time bunched about me the way a moment ago my pants were around my ankles, I finally take my pills. And then I think of my brother, and Emily Dickinson. Unfortunately, for this trip at least, they have been yoked together.

I'm returning from a conference in New York City titled "Furious Burnings: Mental Illness and the American Literary Mind." I had submitted a paper to read, on Melville. He was our nation's first rock star—there were arguably more famous intellectuals of the time, such as Emerson, but no one had yet lived out that arc of meteoric sex appeal and success, followed by grandiose opus-fixation, followed by decline and bitterness, working as a drab-a-day customs official until death. It's a plot line right out of *Behind the Music.*

Anyway, a week before leaving, I took my first look at my actual itinerary. This is because Rose, the department administrator, spoils me—Rose who is as brainy as any of the professors she serves, only without the ten years of pointless education or the framed document on a wall. Rose even finagled the university into paying for my wheelchair, which I need sometimes, depending on the ebb of my disability. It's the dizziness, but also sometimes a numbness in my feet, a new symptom I haven't told anyone about just yet. So thanks to Rose's pampering, my hotel and transportation were details I didn't have to worry about. I knew The New School in Manhattan was hosting the conference, but what I hadn't known, and what took me aback more than a little, was that it would actually take place in the Javits Center's Special Events Hall, where my brother unveiled his Roller Rings idea at Toy Fair back in 1999, dragging my pathetic ass along as both charity and manual labor.

This had gotten me thinking: whatever had become of our booth neighbor, Lamp Bank Guy? And one thing I've got plenty of lately is minions—eager young graduate students who, because it's Montana, don't know any better—and I set them to work. All I had for them to go on was the name Lamp Bank, and the locale of Arizona, where he told us he lived on the last day of Toy Fair. After my brother left for his walk, huffy and spent, Lamp Bank guy had overheard it all, and taken note that Carlton had left without his jacket, and wanted to offer some consolation. I suppose he had to—it was in his soul, the soul of a Lamp Bank Guy. His booth was entirely packed up, which meant his banner and his one Lamp Bank sample were tucked into the black hard-shell suitcase grousing at his ankles.

"Well," he said, "I know the brain trust will find his way somewhere warm."

"He'll find a bar," June had said.

"Oh there are plenty of those—as long as he walks east."

This was a joke—the Hudson was the only thing west. "You've been here before?" I said.

"Oh sure. Used to live here. Up near the Cloisters." It was his attempt at seeming glib, but his stance betrayed him. He put his fists on his hips. In his cheap suit and trench coat and fraying tie and crisply barbered hair, suitcase at his feet, he looked like he was waiting for a train. "I used to be in theater," he added.

Then he held up his hands, which were already gloved to face the breezy Hudson cold. He held them palms out like a mime suddenly scaling a wall between us. It was an awkward thing, and June and I must have been embarrassed for him—we looked at our feet.

He just kept smiling, and when we looked back up, he wrinkled his hands. He gave us a look like we didn't get something, and he turned his hands to reveal the Roller Rings logo—he had snagged a pair of Carlton's freebie gloves. We laughed, and so did he.

"I live in Arizona," he said, "but I couldn't help myself."

Then it was "adios amigos" and he was gone.

"Well that was unsettling," June said, and we both had a nice little chuckle before the long wait for Carlton to return and rain on our parade, which was his specialty, it pains me to say.

That's all my minions had to go on, but with their knowledge of the latest Internet wonders, including archived pages from the past, and the world's seemingly endless concern for the back-alley trivia of our personal histories, they found Lamp Bank Guy. Whether his assertion that he had been "in theater" had any truth to it, they couldn't tell, but what they did find was that Lamp Bank Guy's name was Benjamin Hawkins, and he killed himself in 2002.

The script would seem to write itself—the garage full of unsold Lamp Banks, the creditors calling daily, the wife leaving him for someone more stable and productive. But no. Benjamin Hawkins did indeed have a garage full of Lamp Banks, but had also sold quite a few of them, only not to kids—coin collectors loved them, and coin collectors apparently had a lot of disposable income. He had just inked a deal to mass produce them, in multiple colors and sizes, and there were plans to alter the design to accommodate stamps and butterflies and other collectibles, when he gave it all up with carbon monoxide and a bottle of apple juice, alone in his Chrysler Sebring in his cramped garage.

The unfathomable nature of this act—suicide is hardly ever fathomable, but his seemed of unending depths—laid me out. I spent a day in bed, another journaling, and two more coming up with my new paper to be delivered at the conference: "Are You My Master?: The Psychotic Play of Emily Dickinson." In it I argue that Emily's life was all toying, but no toys. Or rather, *everything* was a toy, and everything was play. I mean play in the best sense of the word: the play of children, who know no separation between it and real life. To them, it is real life. This is why a bunch of sheets laid over the basement furniture is as much fun as a Tonka Toy or a Barbie. Adults eventually learn the difference, in order to pay the bills, but it was a difference Emily blithely ignored: for her, the moon can be a symbol of something, and yet still a regular moon, source of light and kind of boring. This much is true of many great poets, but for Emily every item in her life falls under this category, igniting her whole poetic world with mutually reflective possibilities, like a pond filled with broken mirrors rippling in the sun. When you look at her life this way, her "Master" can be numerous delusions and symbols and real people—all at once.

Flatly put, the woman was a functioning psychotic and had morphed all the men in her "life" into one composite lover—a figure who was eternally flirting with her but ultimately unreachable. Unreachable because he didn't exist. By combining together three or four men with whom individually she didn't quite have full relationships, she ended up with a man who could publish her poems, offer her spiritual redemption, tutor her in the ways of life and art, reminisce over past intimacies, and so on. Never able to actually contact this person, Emily cared not a whit—she just made him her God, and suffered under his hand.

It's a perspective that muddies the waters more than anything, I know, because it allows for multiple facts to be "true," like the Heisenberg Uncertainty Principle or the riddle of Schrödinger's Cat. But see, that's what makes her fun. Her life becomes like a religious text that illuminates through enigma, which is much more interesting than any Ten Commandments. If you say Master was Judge Otis Lord, a former Massachusetts Supreme Court justice with whom we know she had a love affair that was mysterious and contradictory and almost exclusively epistolary but also significant enough for both the Dickinsons and the Lords alike to take seriously even though no one can prove it was consummated in any real sense—when you say that, and start aligning her tropes that way, they twist themselves around, and you end up proving how much she loved Higginson. This was her real life, and it became a pattern from her first all-out love for her sister-in-law, Sue—her world was all jambled up into one miasma. It caused her pain and grief that eventually became transcendent. Studying her almost feels like operating on a patient without anesthesia.

This was the paper I read to my audience in the Javits Center's Special Events Hall. It was not original to posit a Master who didn't exist, but it was original to suggest that Master did exist and didn't at the same time, and that all her poems should be read with a similarly collapsed duality. My audience—thirty or so academics and a few mental health practitioners—was sympathetic, because of my cane and the way I leaned on the lectern, the way I drooled a little bit, the way I stared at them cockeyed, since I didn't want to take more pills and be cockeyed on the inside too. So they stuck with me, and I rewarded them by abandoning my paper altogether. I could go on, I told them, quote all the right quotes and reference all the right thinkers, but let's just assume for a minute Emily was as psychotic as I say. Is that a "furious burning"? No. It was a complete, overwhelming reality. It was her life, and it caused her much pain.

We are lucky she was able to employ it to craft such magnificent poems. But do the poems matter? Does Emily Dickinson matter?

At this point I told my audience what I had never admitted elsewhere: That I, Hank Meyerson, killed my only brother, who was suffering and needed me. Just like somebody somewhere killed Lamp Bank Guy. The logic of our culpability is unassailable, and cannot be mitigated. I killed my brother for his wife. It's an open and shut case—but like Emily's Master, and probably a lot of other things in her life, it's also just something I made up.

And for the hard of heart out there, I reframed the whole thing this way: For three years in the early 1940s, in a little train stop in Poland, German soldiers, with forced-labor assistance, stuffed hundreds of naked men, women, and children into square rooms to murder them with gas, then pushed the bodies out and burned them. Read that sentence again. This happened every day, day after day, as fast as humanly possible. In our world it's preposterous, couldn't possibly have happened, and none of us could possibly imagine it with any actuality. Yet it did. While Frank Sinatra was singing "Fly Me to the Moon." While Bob Hope swung a golf club on stage in front of ten thousand troops. While my mother was conceived, incubated, and born. It's a notion that should by all rights send each and every one of us blathering off to the funny farm. But it doesn't.

Does Emily Dickinson matter in the face of such facts? A brother dead for no good reason? Does anyone's furious burning matter, or make sense? No, I told them. Not a whit. But we should try anyway.

What followed was more than the usual niceties. Sincere applause, earnest handshakes, and cocktail invitations. Intimations of employment opportunities. People who wanted to connect about what I'd said, people for whom it seemed of imminent importance. All the smiling faces that conference, all the wrinkled noses and nodding assents, all the offers to please, sit down so we can talk more, and the delicate questions about my future—might I be more advocate than theorist?—I soaked it all in, all the stuff people do and say when you've just given the performance of your life, and probably ruined your career.

Chapter Thirty-Five

At the time they had seemed so true, my words. So real and alive. Like Emerson said of Montaigne's essays—if you were to cut the words, they'd bleed.

But now, still in the shit stall, taking my time the way Slack Jaw had told me to, it seems like sacrificial bullshit. Guilt! Carlton, charming me with "this is all going to be fine, just lighten up and help me out a little." Even the Treblinka model, I was led to believe, was the end of something, a corner turned, and not a cul-de-sac. And I believed him the way people do an addict, or the gambler who tells you it's all under control and after next Sunday's games, boy, you'll see, we'll roll in pay dirt then!

And I did nothing. Maybe there was nothing I could have done. Yet the facts, they remain. He was sick, delusional, and confused. And also desperate with betrayal. Rarely do I forget to add that part. Maybe he wasn't even crazy at all—maybe my betrayal just made him crazy for one day. It's a possibility, and even if I manage to make a career out of Dickinson, even if my Javits Center *shpiel* manages to get me tenure and not fired—it's a possibility that will remain.

I flush then stand and open the stall door and let Slack Jaw guide me back to the airline wheelchair so I can get myself to the sink and feel the water foam over my hands more like shave cream than actual water.

Slack Jaw sees me staring at myself and assumes, perhaps correctly, that though I've retrieved my comb from the backpack dangling behind me, I am unable to use it. My hands are too shaky, and the pills I took are only barely starting to take effect. So Slack Jaw steps up to use a little of his training. He takes the comb from me with a quick motion that brings it to the faucet's flow and to my head quick as the corner barber. Free hand protecting my ear and everything. I close my eyes, and the tines tingle deliciously. He pulls the comb slowly through, following with his palms to smooth things out, bless him. I've never had tangly hair, always fine as Lab fur, and the comb commands it into place. Slack Jaw's palms are as soft as the water from the sink, and I say thank you and close my eyes and he talks a little about college football. If you look hard enough at any play, he says, you will see guys holding. So many holding flags thrown! It's not football; it's pussy ball.

Then he asks where I'm headed.

"Here. Home."

"Do you have a drive still today?"

I shrug. "It's Montana, right?"

He chuckles because we all have drives. This state still has a surfeit of space and is reaping the rewards. Space is the commodity of the future.

"You get into the mountains at all?" he asks.

Bless you again, Mr. Slack Jaw. "Yes. Gotta love the mountains. When I'm not like this."

"Right," he says.

Because this is a depressing little jab of reality, I open my eyes to find a crisp, distinct part over my left eye. My scalp there is blaringly white, and every hair scuds like a tight school of fish toward one of my two temples. It's a goddamn continental divide, and beneath it I look like a cartoon character.

I want to tell him that I'm not always like this, that often I walk and laugh and fart around like anyone else, but no. "Perfect," I say, and he nods and smiles because it is.

He wheels me out to the airy terminal, and toward the baggage claim area, where everything seems clearer. Maybe it's the stabilizing effect of the pills I've taken—I have been reminded not to put off taking them out of some stubborn sense of independence, but I still do. That queasy lift in the groin that reminds me of desire and is equally comforting and exciting. I thank him again.

"No problem," he says. "I'll go wait for your bags, okay?"

Air travel, even with our improved airport, has its same-old same-old. You have to carry a bag, and if the bag can't fit in the cabin with you, it must be stored in the bowels of the plane and subsequently unloaded by salt-of-the-earth types and thrown onto some conveyance system and then delivered to you, forcing you to rush off the plane only to stand around watching like a puppy for the conveyance to begin, an infantry of Samsonites burping forth from a rubber-tongued hole in the wall. The only real difference these days is the luggage itself—brightly colored jubilations, none of this black and khaki stuff. Two carousels over, there's even a faux-fur one, the color of a golden retriever.

But I am not worse for the wait, nor am I particularly upset by it. When Carol Ann and I lived together at Old Grinnell College, our rented house's property line backed against the railroad tracks, and I'd be out hanging laundry to dry, walled front and back by squares of sunlit sheet and flapping plaid flannel, with the train's rumble and whistle so close I could feel the vibrations in my bones, and I would just stand there, clothespin in my mouth, empty of anything but goodwill and the eternity of my future. It's this kind of patience I'm trying to recover with Slack Jaw over waiting at the edge of the baggage carousel, his baggy trousers ruffled by the current of air off the machine. But there are no bags yet, and he folds his arms and totters on the balls of his feet while discreetly eyeing the nether parts of the females in the crowd—who can blame him, given his current duties with me, and the fact that our luggage seems to be taking a while? Go get 'em, Slackie—may you have many nethers in your future.

And besides, I am suddenly downright appreciative of the wait, because I've just recognized my mother waiting at a neighboring carousel. I see her standing there, off politely to the side, patient and alone but erect and proud: a standout in this crowd, with the simple majesty of the dead.

But she doesn't look dead. She has aged only a little, in fact, which makes sense, since she got the good Scottish live-forever genes, though they didn't help her in the car crash. For a minute I think, brilliantly, hopefully, that it was a hoax, the car crash—maybe some trumped-up thing she did, some crazy scheme to ditch the old man and change her life. Could this be? I wouldn't put it past her. Maybe she knew, somehow, what she was going to face in the decade ahead and just didn't want to deal with it. Or maybe her soul escaped for some traveling. She never did much traveling, after all.

Either way, there she is, and the excitement of it is unwound inside me till I have a tremendous *shpilkes* to move over to her and introduce myself, for she will hardly recognize me, I know. I begin to heat and sweat at my armpits and crotch. I get a hard-on, inexplicably, though it quickly dives back out the hole it came in through, and I falter. All I have to do is wheel my ass over there, but I can't for some reason. My hands are steady and trying to move the wheels, elbows back, palms flat, but the wheels aren't going anywhere. The pills! They haven't kicked in yet, or else they have kicked in too much.

Maybe I'm just too overcome. This vision isn't like my student-cum-chipmunk hallucination—this one, I know, is real. It *is* my mother. See how she walks, with her narrow hips constrained as if by a tight skirt, though in fact she is wearing jeans, very blue jeans high on her narrow waist, just like she always wore—the trends suit her, not the other way around. It's in the way she approaches me now too, like she always was: handsome and in control of everything, though silently, like small-town librarians or over-educated sheriffs or Franciscan priests.

"I thought you could use a hand," she says, and she kneels to pick up my copy of the *Times* that has fallen from my lap to the tight-weave carpet floor. The carpet is there to help designate the baggage claim's waiting area from the carousel's marbled baggage-grabbing zone. This simple concept seems enormously complicated suddenly, and when I look down at the paper now in my lap again, I see I have one of the crossword answers wrong: "willful" isn't "strong" but "stolid."

"Yes," I say. "It's good to see you."

"Come again?"

She is half-kneeling still, fingertips to the carpet like someone drawing up a football play—presumably, I won't be quarterback. Then she rises with her hands before her, where she is of course more comfortable. My mother always gets into restaurants, I used to joke in high school, because she always has reservations. It was one of the jokes that kept me up at night, those weeks after her crash—as in, "who's joking now?"

"Sorry," I say.

"I was thinking you'd like a push someplace."

"That's kind of you," I say. "You look great. A sight for sore eyes, and all that."

"Well, thanks," she laughs.

"Where are you headed?"

"Oh," she says, brushing the front of her jeans—her endless battle with lint, still unwon—"just a tourist thing."

"I didn't know you liked to travel."

She looks surprised by this. "Well, there are worlds you don't know about me."

"Sure," I said. After a moment I reach out and take her hand. She must think me confused and perhaps lecherous, starved for human contact—but this is more or less how I have always been, and who knows these dirty little secrets of ours, our stained underwear and abused bed sheets, better than our mothers? So, even uncomfortable, she doesn't pull away. She smiles that smile she would always show when I was off to do something as a kid—her love was a watchful one, an oversight role. Dad's was the active one, and how could it not have been, given his character? But Mom, she was the watcher, the nodder and smiler—I used to think that she was sitting there bursting with the desire to put her arms around me, to kiss my cheek and lavish me. And maybe that's how things would have gone, if I'd called her after our Greyhound bus station talk, or if I'd been a little more like Carlton. Or maybe if she had been allowed to grow older she would have become that way, grown into it—older people seem to understand that the only thing your lifelong economies get you is a nicer casket. But such bursting wasn't her, nor her way of loving; it was only what I wanted her to be. This, this smiling and knowing and simply *being there,* was how she loved. It was her, and who am I to say what's better or worse, me with my Emily Dickinson?

Her hands are soft and long. Her nails are unpainted and modestly kept, more practical for travel. She wears no rings. There are a few age spots, but otherwise she's a just-ripe banana, my mother, floating calmly on the surface of this world like a duck on the creek. How well she's aged! It's something I suddenly take pride in. Or maybe that's just what mama's boys think, for all the times they were patted on their heads and sent off with a squeeze of, if not love, tolerance.

And sure enough, she raises my hand and pushes its flesh with her own. "What is it you need?" she says.

Good question. Immediate needs, like getting help to the toilet, I am used to. But long-term needs or, dare I say, wants? I dunno. Tenure? Sanity for our mental health system? Some doctor to tell me what the hell is wrong with me and give me drugs that will fix it instead of turning students into chipmunks? To have my brother back and everything okay? To time travel? It's hard to say, harder to articulate. Nothing worth uttering comes to my head, to my lips. I am wanting not just of dexterity now, but—who'd have thought?—words. It makes her laugh a little, for she knows I have *never* been wanting for words, even in my timid youth in the shadow of Carlton, even during my divorce, and the long ambiguous aftermath. No, I always had words, even if I refrained from sharing them. I could think, as Dad used to say, with the best of them, and complain too. Always quick with a complaint, except now.

Oh Mom—I want of words! This is unprecedented, and it must mean, incredibly, that I don't have any complaints. I am happy!

Mom smiles like she has heard me think it. This changes everything.

"I'm a professor," I suddenly blurt, and this squinches her eyes a little. Maybe there is some pain for her, missing all of what she missed.

"I could have guessed. You look intelligent."

"It's just the suit. Even he'd look smart in one." With this I nod at Slack Jaw, who is now whistling and bobbing to his own whistle; as if on cue, he throws us a shy wave.

This makes her frown. She says, "High horses make dangerous riding."

"Some horse," I say, opening my hands to indicate my chariot, the wheelchair.

She softens. "I should mind my business," she says. "You've overcome a lot, probably."

I wave it off good-naturedly. "I'm doing all right, all things considered. It was rough there, but I've got a big brain, and I think I'm managing to come out sane."

She squeezes my hand and lets it go. It falls like a beanbag. I am suddenly thirsty. Over at Slack Jaw's wrinkled knees, the conveyor starts to move.

"I've missed you, Mom."

This is a mistake, I see very quickly. She rises to a height advantage that she probably never would have guessed she'd still have over me—her remaining son, now a shaky, vertiginous wreck. A happy wreck, but still, not her cup of tea. She gives that look of mild distaste, the pursing of the lips and the quick shaking of the head, which I come to realize suddenly I haven't inherited like I thought I would. Perhaps I inherited her good sense and this is why I am where I am. Perhaps I have inherited her sense of self-preservation, the will to be happy and yet dwell in dark places if need be. It is a strength to me, as potent as anything the drapes salesman passed on; it is also the very thing that is making my mother recoil now.

"I've got to get back," she says.

"Sure," I say. "But are you a protector now? Can I count on your prayers?"

She nods, though warily. A charity nod. It's unsettling to see it in her. She has other worries, as she always had. Dad, Carlton, the store, the past—she had worries up to the day she tried to make that left turn in her LeBaron. A worry was probably the last thing that went through her mind, before the windshield. Ha!

"Stay a minute," I say. "It's not your conveyor starting up." I nod at Slack Jaw, who's watching the bags and checking their tags. "It's mine. What, are you in a big hurry now?"

This she doesn't take to, but she wants to exit gracefully. Maybe it's the last time she'll get the chance. "Take care of yourself," she says.

It's funny how people who can walk can move so goddamn quickly when they want to. My chair goes fast, but when I'm smacked like this by my disability, healthy people are always outside my reach. I can only get to a select few, those who make themselves available, and also students, whom I can flunk. The others, the great hauling, frolicking mass of humanity, I can't touch. But really, I never could.

And now—again—this includes my mother, who is back to her carousel talking with someone, a man who has their luggage. I can see only her profile, and none of his, but clearly he's too young for her in his corduroy blazer and full head of hair and nice, thin build. A tall, handsome, athletic guy to be her companion in the later years—I wouldn't hold it against her. I'm not judgmental like that! If it's what she wants, then it's what she wants. She deserves better than loneliness. But I deserve better too—better than this quick, chaste, step-motherly hi-good-to-see-you-take-care-now. I want to tell her some things, namely that her Daniel Meyerson found love again and that she's okay, his new wife, but no Mom, and they live together still in a semi-retirement home and that he had a stroke but that there's hope for full recovery, or the possibility at least. There's possibility, I want to tell her, for lots of things, now that I've stopped grieving, or at least altered my grieving into something more productive—which seems to have happened just this weekend, imagine the coincidence! See—more possibility. I dwell in possibility now, as Emily said. It was the one of the few poems published in her lifetime. I think by possibility she meant pain, and also love, and immortality accordingly.

See Mom, how smart I am? I turned out smart after all. Even if I did kill my brother, I'm smart enough to suffer for it.

But she's heard all she needs to. Just like when we used to play gin rummy, I have played my cards too rashly. I am happy, and what more does a mother need to know? A mother like her—abandoned, then saved, converted, surrounded by boys, and taken from us too soon—it's all she cares to bear. And besides, this guy she's talking to—for his benefit she nods in my direction with a flick of her short bangs, though not looking my way, and her lipstick is cracking and creasing and slightly off at the corner of her mouth (I can see that much, amazingly, though I am only inching closer in my chair, which seems to be rolling in mud)—this guy turns to look at me, and then I stop my chair because I understand everything. It's Carlton, and they are both dead.

The dead, taking trips! So much for the finality of it all, the great last trip we living people think death to be. It's a series of voyages, a never-ending thing. What a revelation! The very thought makes me exhausted, and I don't need to get any closer. They are slinging bags over their shoulders—they have black and beige ones, like mine, no fussing with fun or vanity—and are about to head out the incredibly bright revolving doors. Do they drive? Is there a taxi-hearse waiting for them? Why don't they come to visit, being so close? I should be offended, that they are in Montana and didn't bother to call. I have a cell and everything. And where's God? And what the fuck about me?

Oh the crazy dead. I don't even want to think about it anymore. It's not our place to anyway, we the living. We think about carpools and meals and household dangers and rates of return and the humming of something wonderful beneath it all that we don't know for certain but really really really hope is there.

And besides, my brother has always exhausted me. He looks at me, smiles that smile of his that is more a head shake than a smile, and raises his eyebrows slightly. "You think you *killed* me?" he might be saying. "Fucking nancy." My left bicep begins to twitch, some tic I get once in a while, and I know I need to rest. The dead never need to rest, not even Carlton, whose last breath was river.

But he's not crazy anymore—except for that awful corduroy jacket, he's okay, and his eyes are the clear blue he had when we were kids. Once we went to play baseball at a diamond not far from the junior high, though I was still in elementary school. He'd organized the game, it was a nice summer afternoon with the smells of mowed grass and a roof being tarred someplace, and I had been allowed to come because they needed a catcher and none of his friends wanted to play catcher because, though it's a tough-guy position in the majors, for kids it kind of sucks. First batter, third pitch: foul-tipped hard, right into my throat. I had a mask and chest pad, but no throat guard. I took it right in the Adam's apple and fell over, clutching and writhing. I thought I might die; it was tough to get air, and though I was suddenly bellowing with tears, no one cat-called about fatty this or pussy that, Chubby Wubbenstein down for the count chocolate, because they had seen it, and they knew it hurt, and none of them had volunteered to play catcher anyway. These facts stood around me like a ring of wounded righteousness, there on home plate, as I wallowed in the pure, heavy power of it. I had it in me and wasn't about to let it go, wailing and coughing, until my brother came up to me—he was playing shortstop—and didn't kick me as I thought he might but simply sat down and massaged my shoulders. He sat cross-legged, like he was going to stay for however long it took, and I could have lain there for years with him like that, my face blotchy and a blur but able to see his eyes, which were pure with concern but also confident that I'd be okay. Confident, worldly, and sane— he willed the pain to stop, the panic to ebb. I jackknifed to my feet, and I even got to go play right field. I even caught a fly ball for the third out of the next inning, my brother trotting off the infield not even bothering to watch me make the play, just confident I would.

He never again looked at me like he had that day until now, way after his death, with the strap of a heavy bag denting his shoulder and my mother leading him out of the Great Falls airport into the bright Montana day.

Where had he learned this way to love? Why has it eluded me?

I am heated now. My pits are frothing with the organic underarm stuff I use because I am ultimately unsure what has caused my waxy-waney physical suffering so maybe it's commercially produced underarm stuff, which they still make plenty of in factories all over the world. Something about this distance, this time within time, possibility within possibility, gives me a new urgency. Wait, you guys! Why not stay? Why not stay and hear how happy I am some more? How smart I've become, how respected? Did I mention I gave a paper in New York City and they applauded? Oh it's crazy, both of you in Montana and leaving me again. I don't understand leaving. I'm too sane, too alive. I don't get it. I know for sure now that genius is a form of insanity, and that I qualify for neither. I have a lot to learn, and I'll get off my high horse if you'll stay and teach me.

Stay! Oh please stay, you crazy, awful, selfish, stubborn dead people!

But they are gone. Slack Jaw finds me, a weeping mess of a man, my *Times* on the floor a few feet behind me, my wheelchair facing the revolving door, which now is empty as a discarded candy wrapper and dark as a heart.

"Where were you going?" he says. "I left your brakes on, for safety."

He tries to lift me up in the chair, as I have slouched quite a bit, but I push his hand away.

He lowers my bag gently, too afraid to say anything. He stands there, slack of jaw, so true to his nature, wondering no doubt if I will be filing a complaint. I fumble at my eyes, succeeding only in wetting my face more, and tell him I want a Kit Kat and could he please go get me one from the vending machines and that I will pay him back and that I will be okay here by myself with the bag until he returns.

And life has small miracles and rarely gives you second chances, and I know how lucky I am to have one, how lucky I am to have not abandoned or been abandoned, to hold the pain and the joy in me such that one bubbles out at crazy-ass places like the Great Falls Airport just in time for the other one to take its place like a wave or an airplane at the terminal gate. How lucky I am, in other words, to be facing the doorway when June walks in, breezy and sunny and wholly alive, and sees me and knows what is on my face. She has brought flowers for me—they have made the trip on the truck seat beside her, no doubt, and are now bent toward her like the ones in our field outside the barn, following the sun as it moves overhead, and also their own inclinations. Flowers for me—I had of course called her to tell her of my lecture and my flight number, etc. But these flowers aren't because of that— they are because she has not yet succumbed to the drone of our everyday, hasn't yet circumscribed me inside it. I wouldn't blame her if she would, given the way I can be about time, time in my face and draping all around me, but maybe with what we've been through we have an extra kick or something. Or maybe this is what happy couples do all their lives. Who knows? You can't know these things.

Daisies and black-eyed Susans, a late-spring mix from the field. They go on my lap, where I am happy to have something fragrant and where June herself will probably be in a matter of hours because *that* still works just fine, thank God: I merely slobber on her a little more than I used to. "Baby," I say, and then I am in her arms.

She has to kneel to hold me, and this used to get me, but I'm over it now. The flowers are going to get mashed. "The flowers," I say.

She pulls back and smiles, happy to see me. Even though being in Montana is often lonely and sometimes a pain in the ass, especially in winter when I have to have help getting around, it makes us both happy.

"Aw, fuck 'em," I say, and she hugs me again.

Her arms. Her arms are so beautiful, and I'm not even looking at them. Why would I let go?

"What's up with your new look?"

"My hair? It's called the slack-back."

She laughs at my obtuse humor, but she's seen what's in my face and wipes my eyes. I won't tell her who was just here, or at least not till later. Some intimacies are best kept private. And we are still finding our footing, in terms of our inter-related suffering and guilt. It almost broke us, and certainly still swoons us—and it's a hung jury as to whether or not being together has made it easier, harder, or some macabre third option. We used to talk about it incessantly. Oh, the yodeling nightmares of self-judgment when your loved one knows the crime intimately.

"Tom and Jerry are making dinner," she says, "to celebrate your performance." She has the good sense to put things the right way.

"You have to sign for me," I say.

"No I don't," she says, one of the small miracles she manages to perform, still, after all.

The pills have finally stabilized me enough so I can lift up and go where my wife leads me. Life seems slow and murky and rather contemptuous of us, but I suppose that's intentional. It must, as Emily said, dazzle us gradually, lest we go blind. But sometimes you hit all the green lights and you smile and the person next to you smiles too. Sometimes you're that guy. Just like sometimes, too, you're the poor son of a bitch holding a Kit Kat in the glimmering new Great Falls Airport, worried about paperwork, looking at mysterious yellow petals on the empty airline wheelchair, and wondering why everything crappy happens to him.

Acknowledgements

No one writes a novel alone, and mine certainly benefited from the following people's support, insight, and love:

Early readers Valerie Miner, Julie Schumacher, Haddayr Coppley-Woods, Stacy Thieszen, Mark Anderson, Neil Sexton, Jill Rackiwiecz, Anne Shattenberg, Gail Mollner, and Margaret Kinney.

Everyone with the wonderful Parthenon Prize, especially founder John Spence and director Kelly Falzone, plus readers Barbara Santoro and Brittney Pugh, and of course judge Tony Earley. Also deep gratitude to Peter Honsberger at Hooded Friar and my sharp, loving, tireless editors, Sheri Swanson and Rachel Fichter.

Additional thanks to Scott Edelstein, Heller Landecker, and particularly my parents, Alan and Linda Muskin.

Finally, a special thank you to my wife, Andrea Bidelman, for her love, insight, and belief in me, all of which are unending.

Additional grateful acknowledgement goes to the arts colonies where I began intensive work on this book in fall of 2003: Ucross Foundation and Millay Colony for the Arts, whose complete and fully funded refuge was both heavenly and invaluable; also the Montana Artists

Refuge and New York Mills Arts Retreat for the opportunity to live and work in their wonderful environments at substantially subsidized cost.

About the Parthenon Prize

Established in 2007 by Nashville entrepreneur John Spence, the Parthenon Prize's mission is to give excellent, unknown authors a chance to place their works in circulation. In 2007 the competition received over 350 highly qualified submissions from throughout the country. The winner was awarded an $8000 cash prize and an offer of a full traditional, standard book contract. The final judge was Tony Earley, author of *Jim the Boy*, *Here We Are in Paradise*, *Somehow Form a Family*, and *The Blue Star*. In 2008 the prize was increased to $15,000, with the final judge being Alice Randall, author of *Pushkin and the Queen of Spades* and *The Wind Done Gone*. This year's winner, out of over 300 entries was Geoffrey Becker for his novel, *Hot Springs*. The competition is hosted annually.

For more information please visit the Web site:
www.parthenonprize.com